The Corsair's Shadow

J.T. Southwell

Wayfinder Press

To my grandfather, Robert "Pops" Spake —
your stories, your laughter, and your unshakable faith in hard work and
good character still steer every course I take.

Prologue

March 12, 1718 — Caribbean Sea

Captain Diego Navarro paced the quarterdeck of the Spanish galleon *La Fortuna*, boots clicking against damp planks. Hours ago the ship had been moored in Cartagena, her hold filling with silver, gold, and emeralds for the treasure fleet bound for Havana. Now she cut through black water alone, torn from the safety of convoy and daylight.

Orders had come at dusk—royal, urgent, impossible to question. *La Fortuna* was to break from the fleet and deliver a sealed chest "of utmost importance" directly to the King of Spain.

Breaking from the fleet was madness. Yet here they were.

"They could not have chosen a darker night," Navarro muttered. Low clouds smothered the stars; the horizon dissolved into the void. No moon. No allies. Only the creak of timbers and the smell of pitch and saltwater.

He gripped the hilt of his rapier, the cold metal steadying him. His other hand brushed the crucifix at his throat—an unconscious motion repeated too many times to count. "Keep the lanterns low," he ordered. "We'll not light the way for pirates."

The command spread across the deck like a chill. Sailors moved quietly, eyes darting toward the hold. They all knew the tavern tales—ships that vanished without a cry, their crews cut down by a shadow with black sails. *El Corsario*, the whisper always ended.

"Captain," said Lieutenant Ríos, voice tight. "The men are uneasy. They say the voyage is cursed."

Navarro forced calm. "Tell them to man their stations or they'll answer to my whip."

Ríos hesitated. "It's the cargo, sir. The hold grows colder by the hour. Some swear they hear—whispers."

"Superstitious nonsense," Navarro snapped, though the words came too quickly. "Whatever lies in that chest is the King's concern, not ours. Now to your post."

When Ríos left, the captain's gaze lingered on the hatch. The memory of that chill gnawed at him—the air below thin and cold as a crypt. He crossed himself once more and turned to the wind.

Unseen beyond the darkness, *La Fortuna* was already being hunted.

Less than a mile away, *The Specter* slid from the gloom—a sleek brigantine with sails blacker than the night sea. She moved soundlessly, her hull low and lean, built for speed and stealth.

At her prow stood Elias Grey. The wind tugged at his coat, salt spray stippling the leather. His eyes fixed on the faint lantern glow of the Spanish galleon.

"She's riding low," murmured Silas Morgan, his first mate. "Heavy with treasure."

"Slow, then," Grey replied, a half-smile ghosting his lips. "Ripe for the taking. But gently—we want what's inside intact. We are corsairs, not butchers."

Orders whispered through the crew. Steel rasped against whetstone, ropes tightened, dark sails trimmed. *The Specter* crept closer, her figurehead cutting the water like a blade.

"Hold steady," Grey murmured. "The prize is within reach."

When the Spanish voices carried across the water, Grey raised his hand. "Fire."

Ten cannons spoke at once. Orange fire split the night, the roar rolling across the waves. *La Fortuna's* stern shattered; splinters rained into the sea.

"¡El Corsario! ¡El Espectro!" someone screamed from the galleon's deck.

Grappling hooks hissed through the dark, biting into rail and rigging. Corsairs poured over the lines like shadows with swords.

Grey was first across. His cutlass flashed, precise and economical. Around him his men fought in disciplined bursts—no wasted motion, no wild shouting, only the clash of steel and the wet thud of victory.

"Protect the hold!" Navarro bellowed, drawing his rapier. He met Grey mid-deck, the blades sparking under lantern-fire.

"You'll not take this ship, Corsair!" he roared.

Grey parried smoothly, calm as a tide. "Keep your ship," he said. "I came for what's in your hold."

Navarro lunged; Grey sidestepped, turned the blade, and disarmed him in one fluid motion. The captain fell to his knees, clutching a bleeding arm.

"Order your men to stand down," Grey said. "No more blood tonight."

Navarro's jaw worked, then the fight drained from him. He nodded once.

"Secure the ship," Grey ordered. "Cut their wheel ropes, leave them boats. Balance, not butchery."

The battle faded into the groan of wounded timber. Smoke curled skyward; the serpent-and-anchor flag of *The Specter* fluttered black against it.

Silas joined him, blade red, eyes uneasy. "They whisper about the cargo. Say it's cursed."

Grey frowned. "Cursed?"

"They guarded it more than the gold."

Grey's expression hardened. "Bring me their officers."

Minutes later, three Spaniards knelt before him, faces pale beneath grime. Grey crouched, resting his cutlass across his knee.

"What's in the hold?" he asked. "Tell me, and you won't take a late night swim."

The eldest rasped, "Not treasure. Something sealed by the native priests. It chills the air... it whispers."

Another muttered, "It never should have left the Spanish Main."

Grey's gaze sharpened. "Take it aboard *The Specter*," he told Silas. "If your King treasures it more than gold, I'll see why."

Moments later, as the corsairs worked, Silas burst back into the cabin. "Spanish frigate off the port bow!"

Grey strode to the porthole. Sails loomed out of the black.

"Get the men aboard. Cut the lines!"

The corsairs moved with drilled speed. Ropes slashed, cargo hauled, sails unfurled. *The Specter* slipped free just as the frigate's first shot roared and fell wide.

Grey took the helm himself, steering by instinct. "We'll lose them in the darkness."

They vanished, the enemy's guns flashing futilely behind. When the thunder faded, only the hiss of foam remained.

"Silas," Grey said quietly relinquishing the helm, "have it brought to my cabin."

Candlelight flickered over the chest. Inside, nestled in crimson silk, lay an orb of obsidian—perfect, cold, and smooth, its surface veined with gold spirals and pinpoints of emerald that glimmered like trapped stars.

The air seemed to draw toward it. Shadows bent around it. A low vibration trembled in Grey's bones, too deep to be sound. The spirals appeared to ripple; the emeralds pulsed like a heartbeat.

He reached out—then a knock shattered the spell.

Grey blinked. The hum was gone, the chill fading to memory.

Silas entered, closing the door behind him. "So that's it?"

Grey nodded slowly. "The Spaniards called it cursed. Never meant to leave the shores of the Spanish Main."

Silas studied the orb from a safe distance. "If the King risked a galleon for it, it's worth keeping—or denying him."

Grey's gaze stayed on the sphere. "Gold I understand. This... this is something else. The Crown feared to lose it. That makes it ours."

Silas frowned. "And when their fleet comes for it?"

"Then we run faster."

Silas hesitated. "The crew's uneasy."

"Remind them we've stared down worse," Grey said.

He paused, the candlelight throwing sharp angles across his face. "Silas... if my gut is right, then we've stumbled onto something far greater than treasure. This is our responsibility now."

Silas held his gaze, then inclined his head. "Aye, Captain."

When he was gone, Grey sat before the orb. Its surface caught the candlelight, warping his reflection into strange, endless shapes.

He whispered, "What are you?"

The air seemed to tremble in answer—a faint, electric thrum, like the sea beginning to boil.

For the first time in his life, Elias Grey felt doubt—and understood that not all treasure was meant to be found.

CHAPTER ONE

Beneath the Waves

T he world above felt distant as Jake Morgan glided through the warm, clear waters of the Florida Keys. Sunlight streamed down in shifting ribbons, rippling across the sea floor in shimmering patterns. A coral reef teemed with life nearby, its colors swaying gently in the current. Schools of yellowtail snapper darted between rocks — the serenity of the scene at odds with the knot of worries dragging at Jake: overdue bills, lowball clients, a salvage job that would barely keep him afloat.

The steady rhythm of his breath echoed through the regulator, a constant companion as he kicked deeper. Each exhale sent a spiral of bubbles drifting upward. Behind the tempered glass of his mask, his green eyes stayed sharp and focused. There was ease in his movements — the product of years underwater — but the tightness in his jaw betrayed the weight he carried.

His gear was practical, not flashy. The neoprene of his dive suit clung to an athletic frame, worn thin in places from countless dives. The fins had frayed straps, and the scratches on his dive knife spoke of hard use. Beneath the hood, sandy-blonde hair curled at his temples, untamed even underwater. His sun-bronzed skin told of endless days under the Florida sun — the kind of life where function mattered more than form.

Ahead, the problem came into view: a sixty-five-pound plow anchor wedged deep into a coral outcropping, its chain arched lazily toward the surface, marked by a buoy left behind when the charter boat cut free. Another captain too stubborn — or too broke — to lose a couple grand's worth of tackle and just buy new gear.

Jake swam closer, brushing aside strands of seaweed as his gloves scraped against the rough coral. The work was routine — freeing stuck hardware for hire, jobs that rarely earned thanks and often sparked arguments over payment. Necessary, yes, but far from thrilling.

He wedged a pry bar beneath the plow blade and leaned into it, muscles straining as the anchor refused to budge. With a grunt muffled by his regulator, he shifted position and drove harder, but the steel held fast.

Unclipping a lift bag from his harness, he secured it to the shank. Taking a deep breath, he pressed his regulator beneath the bag and gave two quick bursts of air. The orange fabric ballooned, tugging with slow, steady force. Jake added more air, pressure mounting until the metal groaned, resisted — then tore free with a grinding scrape. Silt and broken coral clouded the water as the anchor lurched upward, straining against the lift bag while he guided it clear of the reef.

As the plume settled, something caught his eye. Half-buried in the sand where the anchor had been wedged lay a slender, dark shape. Jake brushed away the silt, gloved fingers tracing the outline of a corroded blade. The edge was jagged and broken, the steel nearly eaten through, but the hilt remained intact — a stub of cross guard jutting from the grip, a rounded brass pommel glinting faintly through a crust of green corrosion. The corrosion curled along the guard in a pattern almost serpentine, as if some forgotten emblem had once coiled there.

A knife. Old — older than anything that should've been here.

Jake turned it over in his hand, bubbles hissing from his regulator. It wasn't treasure, not really — just a relic, too far gone to be worth much more than curiosity. Still, the sight of it stirred something in his chest. Proof that the stories his grandfather told weren't only myths. History was out here, scattered across the seabed, waiting for someone stubborn enough to dig it out.

For a moment, he thought of Pops' voice — warm and amused — whispering through memory: *Every find has a story, boy.* The echo almost made him smile.

He slipped the knife into the mesh pouch on his dive bag. Maybe he could clean it up back at the shop, see if it was worth showing at the auction house tomorrow night. Another routine job might not pay much, but sometimes the sea left small bonuses for those who looked closely.

Jake kicked upward after the rising anchor, bubbles spiraling past his mask. At fifteen feet he hovered, checking his gauge out of habit, the knife tugging faintly at the pouch on his side. Three minutes of stillness — standard safety stop — then he angled toward the surface, where sunlight danced on the waves above and the shadow of his faithful vessel swayed, waiting.

He broke the surface and tilted his head back, pulling his mask down around his neck as sunlight flooded his vision. The air was thick with the familiar scent of saltwater and seaweed. A few strokes carried him toward his boat, *The Wayfinder*, rocking gently nearby.

She wasn't a beauty, but she was dependable — thirty-odd feet of weathered fiberglass, her once-white hull streaked with rust and salt. The aft deck was cluttered with coils of rope, dive tanks, and a stubborn winch that rattled with every swell. A small davit crane jutted from the stern, its arm scarred with use. Forward, the low wheelhouse squatted under a salt-crusted windshield, the lone wiper frozen halfway through its sweep. She wasn't fast or pretty, but she was solid — and she was his.

Jake clipped the davit's hook onto the chain and thumbed the switch. The crane groaned to life, its rust-streaked arm swinging outboard as the chain rose from the water. Slowly, the anchor broke the surface, seawater streaming from the plow blade. He steadied it with a boat hook, swung it over the rail, and dropped it onto the deck with a dull metallic thud.

He dumped the lift bag, watched it sag flat, and tossed it aside with the rest of his gear. Another job finished. Another paycheck earned. Except this time, he had something more — the knife resting in his dive bag, waiting to be cleaned, and maybe, worth a story.

Later that afternoon, *The Wayfinder* glided into Boot Key Harbor, its diesel engine rumbling steadily as Jake eased it toward his usual slip. The late sun painted the harbor in gold. Fishermen hauled crates of their day's catch onto the pier, the air thick with the scent of diesel and scales. A few slips over, tourists clinked drinks and laughed as they boarded sleek catamarans for sunset cruises. From the boardwalk beyond, the faint strum of a guitar drifted across the water, mingling with gull cries and the slap of waves against pilings.

As Jake throttled back, a skinny teenager in a faded marina shirt jogged down the dock, coiling a line over one shoulder.

"Got you, Mr. Morgan," the boy called, catching the bow line as *The*

Wayfinder drifted in.

Jake smiled faintly. "Appreciate it, Eli."

The kid looped the line neatly around the cleat, glancing at the weathered hull. "You heading out again tomorrow?"

"Maybe," Jake said, stepping onto the dock. "Got a few things to clean first."

Eli grinned. "Bet you found something good this time."

Jake just shrugged, amusement tugging at his mouth. "We'll see." He tossed the stern line to the boy. "Keep her steady, yeah?"

"Always."

Jake secured the rest of his gear, the easy exchange leaving behind a flicker of warmth — the kind of simple, wordless respect that used to pass between him and Pops.

The salvaged anchor and chain lay in a dripping heap on deck, still shedding seawater. With a grunt, Jake swung the anchor onto a dolly and began feeding the chain on top, the steel clattering against the wood. He wheeled it down the dock toward a faded pickup where the charter captain waited, arms crossed, sunglasses hiding his eyes.

The man was thickset, his skin ruddy from years in the sun. A salt-stained shirt clung to him, and a ballcap shadowed his face as he eyed the gear.

"Chain's all scraped up," the captain muttered, nudging it with his boot. "And one of the flukes looks bent. Don't know if it'll set right now."

Jake resisted the urge to roll his eyes. "It was wedged tight in a reef. You got it back in one piece, just like I promised."

The captain grumbled, searching for leverage. "Still think the fee's steep for what you pulled out."

Jake crossed his arms, meeting his gaze. "You'd have paid twice as much for a new setup. The agreement stands."

For a moment, the captain looked ready to argue. But with a reluctant grunt, he peeled a wad of damp bills from his pocket and shoved them into Jake's hand before climbing into his truck.

Jake tucked the cash into his pocket, watching the truck roll away before letting out a slow breath. It wasn't much, but it would cover the bills for another week or two.

He nodded to Eli on the dock before heading toward his workshop at the edge of the slips, the knife wrapped in a rag and tucked under his arm. The small building, once a boathouse, had become his domain — compact, practical, and crammed with the tools of his trade.

Inside, a single overhead bulb cast a weak glow, joined by the last streaks of evening sunlight filtering through dusty panes. Diving gear hung in neat rows along one wall; shelves sagged with tools, spare parts, and coils of rope. Above a battered wooden desk, curling nautical charts were pinned in a haphazard patchwork, their corners dog-eared from years of handling. And above the workbench hung a faded black flag with a serpent coiled around an anchor in the center, its edges frayed — the same flag his grandfather had flown on his own boat decades ago. Jake kept it there as both emblem and reminder: legacy, consequence, and the pull of the sea.

Jake set the knife on the desk, brushing aside scattered notes and a chipped coffee mug. He lingered, running a thumb along the corroded hilt. For a moment, he could almost feel the weight of years pressed into the steel — the stories it might have carried through salt and blood.

His gaze drifted to a nearby shelf where a framed black-and-white photo sat: his grandfather grinning broadly, a salvaged artifact clutched triumphantly in his hands. The photo was faded at the edges, the frame nicked and worn, but the joy in Pops' face was undimmed. Hanging from one corner of the frame was an old brass key on a strip of leather. The barrel was worn smooth, its notched bit dulled to a soft patina, the remnants of a design etched into the barrel long worn away — a keepsake Pops had given him years ago.

Jake reached for it almost without thinking, feeling the familiar weight in his palm. Most days he left it hanging there as a reminder, but tonight he slipped the cord over his head. The cool metal settled against his chest, bringing with it the faint comfort of Pops' presence.

Pops would have been thrilled with the find — a corroded knife with a story buried in its steel. His boundless curiosity had always pushed Jake to chase the unknown. He could almost hear the old man's voice now, brimming with excitement and mischief, spinning some wild account of the pirate who might've once gripped it. For a fleeting moment, the workshop felt warmer, as if Pops still stood at his shoulder.

Jake filled a battered bucket with fresh water and dropped the knife in. Saltwater relics needed rinsing, or they rotted to dust the moment they dried. Later, he'd scrub at it with a stiff brush, maybe chip away the thickest crust with a pick. If it looked promising, he could rig his old electrolysis setup in the corner — nothing fancy, just a car battery charger, washing soda, and a steel plate.

He glanced at the bucket where the knife lay ghosted beneath the surface. Pops would've seen it as a prize — a story waiting to be told. That was the difference. Pops had been content with the life they lived, proud of it. Jake, though, felt the weight pressing down. Salvage jobs and bills weren't enough. Not for him.

He ran a hand through his still-damp hair, staring at the knife until his reflection rippled across the bucket's surface. Maybe it was nothing. Maybe it was just another piece of junk destined to sit on a shelf with the other odds and ends he'd dragged up over the years. But deep down, he wanted it to be more. Needed it to be.

Jake let out a long breath and closed his fist around the key at his chest. *Every find has a story,* Pops had said — *it's just waiting for someone to listen.*

Outside, the marina had quieted. Charter boats eased back into their slips, laughter and music fading into the glow of dockside bars. In the pause that followed came the chorus of frogs and insects, filling the night with a steady hum. Jake gave *The Wayfinder* one last glance, her silhouette bobbing in the slip, then headed for the parking lot.

His old Toyota Land Cruiser waited beneath the swaying palms. Its sun-faded paint and salt-rusted bumper gave it more character than shine — but like *The Wayfinder*, it was dependable in its own stubborn way.

A ten-minute drive brought him to the edge of the island, where a weathered cottage sat tucked behind a line of palms. It wasn't much — a single bedroom, a sagging porch, and walls that carried the scent of seaweed no matter how often he scrubbed. But it was close to the water, cheap enough to keep him afloat, and quiet enough that no one bothered him.

Inside, the place bore the mark of a man who lived light and worked hard. Nautical charts curled along one wall above a chipped dining table stacked with unopened mail. The shelves held a few battered paperbacks and a scattering of relics too small or worthless to sell — a rusted pulley, a shard of pottery, a brass spike green with corrosion.

Jake dropped his keys on the counter and sank into the couch, the hum of the ceiling fan filling the silence. Tomorrow he'd finish cleaning the knife and bring it to the auction house. With luck, the sales might cover the bills for another week.

His eyes lingered on the cluttered shelf of relics. That old tug stirred in his chest — the same pull that had driven Pops, the same hunger that kept him diving. For all the rust and routine, some part of him still believed there was more waiting out there, hidden beneath the waves.

CHAPTER TWO

The Auction Encounter

The late-afternoon sun bathed Key West in gold. Palm fronds swayed, their rustle threading through live music drifting from nearby bars on Duval Street. Laughter and clinking glassware mingled with the crow of roosters strutting along the sidewalks.

Jake parked the Land Cruiser a block from the auction house. The door creaked as he climbed out, slinging a faded leather satchel over one shoulder. He studied the building at the end of the street—an old Key West landmark with stucco walls sun-bleached to bone, bright blue shutters framing tall windows, bougainvillea spilling across the façade in a riot of magenta. Nestled near the waterfront, it exuded a weathered charm: a place where history felt alive—and for sale.

He glanced down at himself: linen shirt with sleeves rolled, khakis thinned at the knees, boat shoes more salt than polish. Not exactly auction attire. The key on its leather cord rested cool against his chest—the closest thing he owned to jewelry.

The air carried the scent of saltwater and a whiff of cigar smoke from a shop down the street. At the valet station, a sleek coupe idled, chrome catching lantern light. Jake felt the familiar sting of being out of place. His sun-faded shirt and worn khakis stood in sharp contrast to the linen suits and cocktail dresses drifting toward the entrance.

He drew a breath, pushed open the weathered doors, and stepped inside.

The auction house fused old-world beams with modern polish. Vaulted ceilings rested on dark wood; walls lined with maritime relics—wheels, weathered charts, antique lanterns, storm-tossed paintings. Spotlights gleamed on glass cases awaiting their turn under the hammer.

The room hummed. Collectors in tailored suits sipped cocktails, laughter clipping above the murmur of negotiations. Salvagers lingered closer to the cases, calloused hands and sun-browned faces setting them apart from the polished crowd—the divide as clear as the glass between them and the treasures on display.

Jake drifted along the edges, eyes flicking between cases and people. Collectors moved with unhurried grace, curiosity detached, delight sharpened more by price than story. To them: trophies. To him: decompression stops and debt.

In one corner, his modest case waited. No showstoppers, just what the ocean gave back when asked right: a tarnished brass compass with clouded glass and faded scrollwork; a pair of small gold hoops dulled by time; a weathered fragment of a ship's wheel, its rim scarred where hands once fought storms.

The placards were short on specifics, long on mystique. He caught a few glances from well-heeled bidders and felt a pang of doubt. His hand brushed the satchel. The knife inside, wrapped in cloth, was more curiosity than prize—but it whispered of stories.

Snippets of clipped conversation floated past—origin, value, resale. His jaw tightened. To them, indulgences. To him, sweat and time.

Then a different voice carried across the room: clear, confident, warm enough to draw the ear closer.

"...and if you look closely, you can see the maker's mark here."

Jake turned.

She stood near a display, surrounded by onlookers. A crisp white blouse tucked into olive-green pants gave her a professional air; a leather-bound binder in hand hinted at purpose. Dark hair pulled into a loose ponytail, a few wisps framing her face; her skin glowed under the lights. Small gold leaf-shaped earrings glinted as she moved. But it was her eyes—dark, intent, alive—that held him. Commanding yet inviting.

She traced details on the map with precise ease, making the past feel present. Even seasoned collectors leaned closer. She didn't recite; she re-enacted. Her smile warmed at favorite points, a spark lit her eyes, her head tilted slightly when answering. She cared—really cared.

What struck Jake wasn't just her passion but the respect she commanded. In a room where deference was rare, people listened.

Her sweep of the room caught on his corner. She slowed, then stopped at his case. She studied the compass, the hoops, the wheel fragment, her hand hovering as if tracing invisible threads.

Jake stiffened, pride and unease colliding. The way she looked at the pieces felt like she was reading him.

She glanced up, eyes meeting his with a spark that caught him off guard. "These are fascinating," she said. "Did you recover them?"

"Yeah," he said. "They're mine."

Her smile deepened as she leaned to the glass. "The compass—late eighteenth, I'd guess. Intricate etching. Intact when you found it?"

"Mostly. Cleaned it up some."

She nodded, gaze sliding to the earrings. "Spanish work. Likely Keys trade routes."

"You know your stuff," Jake said, the words carrying more respect than his tone allowed.

"I try." Her smile teased. "I'm guessing you're not the meticulous-records type."

"Hard to do paperwork underwater."

Her laugh was light, genuine. When her gaze returned, warmth lingered. "Fair point."

For a moment the room's polish fell away. Sharp intellect and approachability, passion and humor—she blended them effortlessly. Jake realized he was enjoying this more than he'd admit.

She hesitated, then pulled a card from her binder and offered it. "Isabelle Alvarez. Historical Consultant."

He took it, fingers brushing hers, a nick along one knuckle catching the light—evidence of work, not polish.

"Jake Morgan. Salvage diver."

Her smile widened, a flicker of mischief in her eyes. "Nice to meet you, Jake Morgan. If you ever come across something unusual, let me know."

"I'll keep that in mind."

She lingered a beat, then turned away. He watched her go, her confidence and warmth lingering long after she disappeared into the crowd. For the first time that evening, something stirred beyond the usual transactions—an unexpected connection, intriguing and unsettling in equal measure.

Victor Serrano stood at the bar, a glass of Rioja poised lightly in his hand. Around him rose the muted symphony of clinking glasses, hushed negotiations, the occasional laugh—a polite cacophony he had long since learned to ignore. These gatherings were never about the people. They were about the opportunities they carried, often without knowing it.

His navy suit was immaculately tailored, sharp lines softened only by the silver gleam of understated cufflinks. He cut a figure of effortless refinement, though his dark eyes told a different story. They moved deliberately across the room, cataloging faces and cases with the precision of a predator circling shoals.

He lifted the glass for a slow sip, using the stem to steady the tremor in his left hand. It had worsened as of late—longer spells, arriving uninvited at odd hours. A nuisance. An insult. Control was everything, and each reminder of its erosion fed a quiet fury. He shifted the glass to his right, the hand that still obeyed.

His gaze settled on a modest display tucked into a corner, a stark foil to the opulent cases scattered through the room. Inside, a pair of delicate gold earrings rested beside a tarnished brass compass and a weathered fragment of a ship's wheel. The earrings caught him first—hammered gold hoops in the unmistakable style of the Spanish colonies.

Victor crossed the floor with measured steps, polished shoes whispering against the wood. These weren't pieces that would spark a bidding war, but he never measured value in dollars. Even the smallest relic could be a key—if you knew how to read it.

Nearby, a man leaned against the case with the unmistakable air of someone slightly out of place. Sun-faded shirt, worn khakis, a weathered look that spoke of long days at sea. A salvage diver, Victor surmised. He had met enough to recognize the type—men who stumbled onto treasures they barely understood. Men who were either useful—or expendable. Sometimes both.

"Interesting collection," Victor said smoothly, more statement than compliment.

The man's posture stayed loose, but his eyes were sharp as he glanced up. "Yeah. Thanks," he said curtly, Florida drawl edging the words.

Victor's faint smile didn't falter. "The earrings—exquisite. Spanish, late eighteenth century?" He gestured toward the case with a flick of his fingers. "They must have a story."

The man straightened, guarded. "Wouldn't know. Probably," he said with a shrug.

Victor inclined his head, feigning casual interest as his gaze slid to the compass. "From a wreck near here, I assume? These waters are rich with history... though not everyone can read what they bring up."

"Just off the Keys. Bits and pieces," the man replied, jaw tightening.

Victor let the silence breathe, then said lightly, "Sometimes it's the fragments that matter most. You never know where one clue might lead."

The diver didn't answer right away. Finally, he muttered, "Suppose so."

Victor savored the hesitation. A glint of brass at the man's chest caught his eye—an old key on a leather cord.

A grin curved his lips, more predator than polite. "You keep the interesting pieces close."

The man's hand twitched toward the key, then stilled. "Just a keepsake."

Victor lifted his glass in a silent toast. "As good a reason as any." With unhurried precision, he drew a sleek black business card from his jacket and offered it between two fingers.

Black Tide Global
Victor Serrano
Owner & CEO

"If you come across anything particularly Spanish," he said smoothly, "call me. Might save you the trouble of nights like this."

The man hesitated, then accepted it. The card was heavy, the lettering pressed deep.

Victor turned away with the measured grace of a man who always left on his terms. The Rioja caught the light as he crossed back to the bar, his expression composed. But his mind lingered on the exchange—the clipped answers, the twitch toward the key. Not the carelessness of a man with nothing to hide. Instinct. Guarding something worth guarding.

He allowed himself the faintest smile. Patience, he reminded himself, was a blade he had learned to wield. Persistence gave it weight. Tonight would be no different.

Polite applause rippled as the auctioneer took the stage. "Ladies and gentlemen, welcome to tonight's auction," he declared. "Every artifact here carries a story—some well-known, others still waiting to be discovered. Shall we begin?"

Collectors leaned forward, eyes gleaming, while sunburned salvagers stood along the edges, arms crossed. Jake stayed among them at the back, expression guarded.

"Lot number eight," the auctioneer announced, gesturing to an ornate brass sextant. "Late eighteenth century, faint Seville mark. A tool that guided countless journeys across the Atlantic."

Isabelle stepped forward, her calm voice drawing attention as surely as the spotlight. "This design was favored by Spanish naval officers," she said, gesturing with practiced grace. "The patina shows frequent use—likely a ship that saw action, not a display piece."

Collectors murmured appreciatively. Even the salvagers along the wall exchanged quiet nods. Isabelle had a way of making history feel immediate, alive.

Jake leaned against the wall, arms folded, letting the cadence wash over him. He wasn't here for spectacle. He was here for coin in his pocket and—maybe—for sharper eyes on the knife in his satchel.

Then Isabelle's voice cut through.

"That's incorrect."

Crisp certainty stilled the room. Heads turned as she stepped toward the glass case where an ornate dagger gleamed. The auctioneer froze mid-sentence.

She gestured to the hilt, hand hovering above the glass. "You're attributing this to a seventeenth-century Spanish naval officer, but the design is Moorish-influenced. That places it at least fifty years earlier." She flipped open her catalog without looking up. "Who authenticated this?"

The auctioneer cleared his throat. "We had it examined by—"

"I'd like to see the notes," she said, courteous but firm. "If the chain of custody is thinner than the brass, we're telling the wrong story."

Murmurs rippled. The auctioneer faltered, caught between authority and the sting of public correction. Isabelle's smile was faint but sure, her eyes bright with the thrill of setting the record straight.

From the back, Jake leaned in. She wasn't just rattling off details—she cared. She fought for the truth as if it mattered as much as the price tag. And from the look on her face, she was enjoying it.

Jake smirked. He hadn't expected that. Most people here were pretenders or opportunists. Isabelle Alvarez? She knew her craft and wasn't afraid to say so. And damn if that wasn't impressive.

When the auctioneer reached one of Jake's items—a tarnished brass compass—Jake's pulse quickened.

"Lot number sixteen," the man announced. "Recovered from a wreck off Florida's coast, this compass features intricate etching and a remarkably preserved casing. Submitted by local salvage diver... Jake Morgan."

Jake straightened as the spotlight lingered. A few heads turned. Across the room, Isabelle's gaze found him; she offered the faintest smile, warm and genuine. For a moment the noise fell away.

Then Jake caught Victor Serrano near the bar. The man's expression hardly shifted, but his gaze lingered too long. Heavy. Jake looked away, reminding himself: just another collector. Still, the look clung.

Bidding began modestly. Paddles rose without urgency. The cadence rolled on, the room's energy dulled compared to earlier lots. Jake kept still. Most finds weren't crowd-pleasers.

The hammer fell just above reserve. He exhaled, shoulders easing though his jaw stayed tight. Enough to cover a bill or two. Pops would've called it a win. To Jake, it felt like treading water.

Victor Serrano, meanwhile, was making himself known. Now seated near the center, he raised his paddle with surgical precision, cutting off rivals before they gathered steam. Spanish relics drew his most decisive strikes.

The crowd noticed. Murmurs followed each win, growing sharper when he claimed a seventeenth-century silver coin well above estimate.

Near the front, Isabelle's brow furrowed. She glanced back, catching Jake's eye. *What's his deal?* her look seemed to ask.

Jake gave the faintest shrug. Unease coiled.

Then the auctioneer lifted a pair of small gold hoops—Jake's find.

"Lot number twenty-four. Spanish in origin, late eighteenth century. A delicate example of maritime trade and craft."

The opening bid was modest. Jake barely listened—until Serrano's paddle rose. Another bidder countered. Serrano answered at once. Back and forth the numbers climbed, far past the earrings' worth. Murmurs swept the hall until the rival faltered.

The hammer fell. Victor didn't blink. Two months of slip fees—gone with a flick of his wrist.

Jake's eyes narrowed. Serrano wasn't collecting. He was hunting.

"Submitted by local salvage diver... Jake Morgan," the auctioneer announced.

Morgan.

The name snagged Victor's attention like a hook. He had read it before—again and again in brittle records—but hadn't expected to hear it spoken here, tonight.

His gaze followed the auctioneer's toward the man at the back. The same salvage diver from earlier: stubborn posture, sunburned skin, eyes that measured more than they revealed. Now the name tied to him. Enough to make Victor take notice.

He swirled his wine, masking the faint tremor in his hand as though nothing had changed. But everything had. Names carried weight. And *Morgan* was not one to ignore in this setting. Whether coincidence or something more, he would find out.

Patience and persistence had always served him well in deeper waters. Now he had a new line in the water.

As the auction neared its midpoint, one of the night's prized pieces was unveiled—a weathered but intact Spanish naval medallion.

"This medallion," the auctioneer proclaimed, "is tied to a famous seventeenth-century galleon. Its intricate design and remarkable preservation make it a truly unique find."

Victor's gaze locked on the medallion glinting under glass. He had seen its likeness before—not in a museum, but in a battered shoebox his grandfather kept tucked away, a relic of another life. He remembered its dull weight in his boyhood palm, the tang of tarnish on his skin as his grandfather pressed it into his hand and whispered: *This is what they took from us.*

The auctioneer's polished words kept rolling—provenance, estimates—but Victor dismissed them as noise. This was no mere relic. It was a fragment of an empire his ancestors had built—and lost. A reminder of what had been stripped away.

And a promise of what could be reclaimed.

Victor raised his paddle, cutting off the competition without pause. The bid was sharp, higher than necessary—but restraint was for men who measured worth in coin.

Money could be replaced.

Legacy could not.

Isabelle drifted toward Jake as the auction paused for a break, her pace casual but deliberate. She stopped within arm's reach, gaze flicking briefly toward Victor. He sat near the center with the calm composure of a man who rarely needed to exert effort to keep control. Overhead lights caught the hard angles of his face, his paddle idling in his hand like a weapon waiting to be drawn.

"Congratulations on selling the earrings. I told you—you've got an eye for the good stuff," Isabelle said with a warm smile.

Jake shrugged. "Thanks, but I think he overpaid," he said, nodding toward Victor.

"He seems especially fixated on anything Spanish," she murmured, curiosity flickering.

Jake's mouth curved in a wry line. "Lucky me, I guess."

Her brow arched. "Have you seen him here before?"

Jake shook his head. "No. Met him earlier, though. Hard to miss." He shifted the focus back. "When did they bring you on?"

"A couple of weeks ago," Isabelle said. "Consulting for the auction house. I also curate relics at the Maritime History Center—and I teach a few classes up at FIU."

Jake raised an eyebrow. "Do you ever sleep?"

Her smile warmed, playful. "Who needs sleep when you love what you do?"

They stood a moment in companionable quiet, the hum of the crowd filling the space. Isabelle broke it first, thoughtful.

"At the History Center, I work with local divers and salvage crews all the time—cataloging finds, tracing origins. It's like piecing together a giant puzzle." She shook her head, smiling. "But I leave the actual dives to people like you. We've probably crossed paths without knowing it. What's the most interesting thing you've brought up?"

Jake thought, then smirked. "Most interesting? A shipping container full of beer cans. Half burst on the way down. When I cracked it open, the water smelled like a frat party." He shook his head. "That's about as exciting as it gets—lost cargo, busted fishing boats, jobs people don't want reported."

Isabelle's lips curved, though her eyes stayed sharp. "Funny, because what you brought tonight says otherwise." She nodded toward his case. "That compass, those earrings—they're not ordinary. Maybe you don't give yourself enough credit."

For the first time that evening, his mouth tugged into something like a real smile. "Maybe," he admitted before he could catch it.

The auctioneer returned to the podium. "Looks like we're starting again," she said, then turned back with a small smile. "I should get up there."

Jake followed her gaze, then offered a faint, teasing grin. "Yeah... it was nice chatting with you. Go enlighten the rich crowd."

Her eyes brightened. "I'll do my best," she said, light but sincere. She glanced back once as she walked away. The ease between them lingered, and for the first time in a long while, he felt his guard slip—just a little.

The auction wound down to its final items, the room thinning as conversations spilled into the night. Laughter and voices mingled with the wash of waves against the dock. Jake lingered near the back wall, arms crossed, eyes on the stage but mind elsewhere.

The knife in his satchel tugged at him—not valuable, maybe not even salvageable, but different enough to gnaw at his thoughts. Still, it wasn't the blade that held him. It was Isabelle Alvarez. A wildcard in a world he'd come to expect as transactional and predictable. Her passion for history, her sharp eye, her ability to connect—she stood apart.

Across the room, Isabelle finished a polite conversation and caught Jake watching her. She tilted her head, curiosity flickering.

Jake hesitated. Approaching her meant offering more of himself than he was used to. But something in her sincerity, her clear expertise, made her the first person he'd consider trusting with the knife.

He adjusted the satchel strap and stepped forward. She noticed and smiled faintly—warm, inviting, with that spark in her eyes that said she welcomed the question.

"Hey," Jake said, voice low, almost tentative. "I found something on a dive yesterday. Not sure what to make of it." He patted the satchel. "You mind taking a look? Off the record."

Her brows lifted, eyes brightening. "You're trusting me with a mystery already?" Her smile carried surprise and genuine delight. "I'd love to see it."

He unbuckled the flap and drew the knife wrapped in cloth. He laid it across his hand and offered it out. The corroded blade caught the light in dull, jagged angles, but the hilt still bore the faint curve of a cross guard and a brass pommel stained green with age.

Isabelle leaned in, eyes alight. "This is... incredible." Excitement edged her restraint. She angled it toward the light, fingers hovering above the hilt. "The blade's too far gone to read much, but the hilt tells a story. Brass pommel, traces of leather wrapping—seventeenth to early eighteenth century. Short, functional. More a sailor's knife than ceremonial."

She looked up, bright. "Even in this condition, it's fascinating. Not the kind of thing that surfaces every day. Definitely worth keeping. Where did you find it?"

Jake hesitated, then shrugged. "Wedged under an anchor. I figured it wasn't worth much, but... it felt different."

Her gaze returned to the knife, tone softening. "Maybe not in dollars," she said gently. "But value isn't always about money. Pieces like this carry stories—the people who held them, the lives they touched. That's worth holding onto."

He studied her a moment, the corners of his mouth lifting. He slipped the knife back into his satchel. "Thanks for taking a look."

"My pleasure." Isabelle's smile was easy, sincere. "And like I said before, if you come across anything else interesting, don't hesitate to reach out."

Jake gave a small nod and headed for the doors. Warm night air met him, dockside sounds spilling into the quiet he carried. For all his doubts, he found himself holding onto her words as much as the knife.

Victor watched from the shadows near the bar, his second glass of Rioja untouched. He had already noted the name, but seeing the man up close was different. There was a guardedness in Morgan, a reluctance hinting at something beneath the surface. And Alvarez—the ease between them—hadn't escaped his eye.

He didn't need to move tonight. Not force. Not yet. First, pressure points.

He drew his phone and tapped out a brief message: *Luca. I have a job for you. Call tonight.*

Sliding the phone back into his pocket, Victor lifted his glass at last. *Now to see what surfaces.*

CHAPTER THREE

Currents of Home

The first light of morning slid through the blinds of Isabelle Alvarez's apartment, banding the narrow kitchen in gold. Outside, palms rustled and gulls argued above the hush of an outboard on the canals that braid into Largo Sound. Key Largo woke slowly, reluctant to surrender the night.

Isabelle padded across cool tile, hair in a loose braid. She filled the kettle, scooped dark Colombian grounds, set the coffee to brew. On the counter, a half-wrapped arepa waited under a dish towel.

Her apartment wore two lives without a fight. One wall: maps, logbooks, a corkboard freckled with sketches and tight notes—the working world of a historian and marine archaeologist. Opposite: traces of home—a woven textile her grandmother made; a carved mask from Cartagena; her mother's necklace, beads catching the window light like a small flame, brilla para servir, her mother's rule.

On the shelf by the corkboard sat her father's compass, brass dulled to honey. He'd given it to her after her mother died: even when you lose your bearings, you can still move forward. Sometimes the needle stuck before finding north. She never minded; it felt honest.

She carried her mug to the table. A photograph of Cartagena's harbor tugged her eye—the old walls rising above the sea, sun flaring off stone that had stood its ground for centuries. She heard her grandfather: corsairs and galleons, treasure lost to reefs—the past waiting for the right listener.

Her father gave the past weight and measure; her mother taught her to read meaning in metal—the Muisca lines, Tairona motifs, colors carrying memory older than empire. Between them, Isabelle learned a reverence belonging to both head and heart.

The kettle clicked. She poured, pressed, stood at the window. The necklace glowed; with it rose a tug: artifacts still out there, stories not yet told. Not everything belonged to Spain and its hunger. Older voices—her people's voices—had been scattered or sold by the handful.

By noon she'd be at Florida International University, Biscayne Bay framed in the windows. Classes full, if not always with believers. She'd coax curiosity from the back row, argue that sea routes and ship timbers mattered because people had mattered first. After that: museum emails, collectors' inquiries, a stack of reports at the Maritime History Center. Some days felt like three jobs braided into one.

She sat, letting the room be quiet. The child she'd been—small hand in her grandfather's—was never far from the woman she'd become. That child believed the past was alive. The woman believed it was her work to prove it.

The coffee cooled while she flipped through notes: office hours, lecture outline, a reminder about the conservation queue. The sun climbed; beads in the window brightened to ember.

Isabelle touched the necklace. A tether. A promise. She would teach and grade and catalog. Beneath it, another rhythm beat—the pull toward older stories and the hope she'd bring one home intact.

She rinsed the press, packed the satchel—notes, pencils, a rolled chart she loved for its patient inked coastline. Keys in the bowl, one last look at the corkboard's patchwork of maps and questions.

Outside, noon light. A warm breeze off Largo Sound smelling of mangrove and salt. She locked up and headed down the stairs—the life she'd built waiting: lecture first, then the Center. The past wasn't gone. It was waiting to be heard.

By quarter to noon, Isabelle took the long curve of the causeway with the window cracked, letting salt air push through the car. Miami's skyline thinned in the rearview as Biscayne Bay opened into flat sheets of light. Ahead, the Biscayne Bay Campus rose from the mangroves—low buildings, bright stucco, palms moving in the onshore breeze. Not a fortress of academia; a place built to listen to water.

She parked beneath a palm. Heat carried mangrove green and a faint diesel tang from the research dock. Gulls circled; a winch clanked; students crossed with clipboards and buckets. A small vessel bobbed at the fenders—*Pelagia*—while two undergrads coiled lines, serious-faced and sunburned.

Inside the humanities building, cool air gathered against her skin. Five minutes to the hour. Laptops open; a student asleep on a backpack; three friends copying problem sets. Beyond them, tall windows framed a slice of water where sunlight slid in clean bands across the floor.

She set her satchel down. The room quieted.

"Good afternoon. Settle in. Today we're going inland."

Brows rose. "Close your eyes. Humor me."

Screens dimmed.

"Picture a lake in the Colombian highlands," Isabelle said. "Thin, cold air. Morning mist. A dark mirror. People gather with baskets of gold and emeralds—work by hands that learned from those before them. At the center, a raft waits. On it stands a leader dusted in powdered gold until he gleams like morning."

She let the image breathe.

"The raft is paddled out. Music climbs. Offerings arc into the water: gold not to hoard but to surrender; emeralds not to flaunt but to give. A covenant with the divine."

"Open your eyes."

A marina-cap student leaned forward. The sleeper sat straighter.

"To the Muisca," she said, "this was devotion. Wealth measured by what you released. When the Spanish heard it, they didn't hear devotion. They heard a kingdom of gold."

She clicked to an engraving—crude awe in ink.

"A ritual became a legend—El Dorado. From legend came expeditions. From expeditions came fleets. To ferry imagined wealth, Spain built a maritime machine—convoys of galleons, guarded routes, predictable seasons. Which means," she gestured toward the bay glittering outside, "to understand why so many ships sailed past places like this, you begin up there—at a mountain lake where people learned to give away what they valued most."

A hand went up. "Professor... was El Dorado real?"

"The ritual was real. The generosity was real," Isabelle said. "What wasn't real was the Spanish assumption of a city of gold to be taken. Misunderstanding—sometimes deliberate—makes conquest easier. Flatten a people into a story that fits your hunger, and the rest follows."

She moved to the windowsill, fingertips on cool metal.

"Maritime archaeology inherits the aftershocks of that hunger. Fleets carried metals pulled from colonized lands, maps dressed in myth. Some ships made it home. Many didn't. Storms, reefs, greed, war."

A small smile. "The sea remembers more honestly than the paperwork."

Routes arced from Cartagena and Portobelo to Havana, then Seville. "Escorts here. Hurricane season there. Choke points—reefs like knives, currents like hands. We don't only catalog timber and ballast. We listen for a chain that starts at dawn on a lake."

"La memoria no es sólo fechas. Es el hilo humano que no se corta." Heads lifted.

"Memory isn't only dates. It's the human thread that refuses to break."

A student in a sea-green hoodie raised a hand. "How do we avoid repeating that distortion? We're still outsiders most of the time."

"By refusing to treat people as footnotes to ships," Isabelle said. "Build teams with descendant communities. Ask who benefits from the story. Remember objects aren't just evidence—they're someone's prayer, labor, grief."

Silence—the good kind. The clock edged past the hour.

"Read the Serranilla Bank case study," she said, closing her laptop. "Consider currents not just as water, but as history—forces pushing objects and people along paths they didn't choose."

Chairs scraped. The marina-cap student lingered. "If I want to do this, do I have to love paperwork as much as shipwrecks?"

"More," Isabelle said.

He winced, laughed, left. The sea-green hoodie stayed. "First-gen, no dive cert yet," she said—half apology, half challenge. "Do I have a place in this?"

"Yes. Start with swimming. Then diving. Then field schools. Most of the job is patience. The rest is listening."

"Gracias, profe."

"De nada."

The room emptied. Isabelle squared her notes—corners true, a habit from her father—and flicked off the projector. Outside, the bay wore a pelt of white light; wind roughened the surface into small bright scales. She pictured gold dust falling into a dark lake, arcs widening, then fading.

If she drove now, she'd beat the worst of US-1. The Center would be quiet by mid-afternoon. She adjusted her satchel, took one last look at Biscayne Bay.

"The past isn't gone," she murmured. "It's persistent."

She stepped into the hall and let the door ease shut.

Key Largo's afternoon went soft as Isabelle pulled into the gravel lot beside the Maritime History Center. Sun-bleached stucco; beyond the mangroves, Blackwater Sound flat as a coin. Inside, cool air and the hum of fluorescents. A dehumidifier ticked like a metronome.

"Afternoon, Professor," Aida called—cat-eye glasses, wry smile. "Two crates from Marathon. Fisherman wants a tax letter and his name in the newsletter."

"Done," Isabelle said, signing the log. "Location?"

"'East of the shoal, south of where the water goes wicked teal.' He drew an X. Very legal."

In back, Isabelle tugged on nitrile gloves and tightened her braid. Steel shelving labeled by century and material; archival boxes in rows; a rolling photo table with a color card taped to the edge. The whiteboard triage: *Desalination—iron fasteners; Catalog—hinge (concreted); Electrolysis—check leads*. A tub of freshwater held a snarl of iron pieces leaching salt.

She cut tape. Foam. Tyvek. A length of timber three feet long, nail scars pocking one face. Waterlogged grain yielded under her gloves. A scrap of copper sheathing clung green to one edge.

"Hello," she said.

She photographed with the color card, chalked an accession on a slate, measured: length, width, thickness, nail spacing. *Bevel on one edge; carpenter's mark ghosted; copper flared around a knot. Condition: stable when supported; do not dry; move to PEG queue if accepted.*

Next: an iron hinge the length of her forearm, so thick with coral and shell it looked like a reef. She weighed it, winced, set it beside the electrolysis tank, and checked the battered but reliable rig—two grants, one generous electrician, miles of paperwork. Card: *Hinge, leaf-and-strap, concreted; 18th–19th c.; source: Marathon fisherman.*

The second crate held smalls: a brass sheave from a block, bright where something had rubbed it clean; a short run of lead scupper pipe; shards of salt-white and blue ceramic. Photo, measure, note, condition. "Relic," she wrote once, and let the word sit—not for saints, but for people who worked and bled.

"School group at four," Aida said in the doorway. "Want the anchor talk, or should I?"

"I'll take them," Isabelle said, stripping off her gloves. "Could use a stretch."

In the small gallery: a bronze cannon behind glass; green-glass net floats; ballast stones labeled Basalt (Azores) and Flint (England). A wall chart traced the Florida Straits, the Gulf Stream a blue vein.

The kids blew in sunburned and loud.

"Welcome," Isabelle said, smiling them into a semicircle. "Help me decide which relic has the best story."

The cannon won by size; she indulged it, then steered them to the brass sheave.

"What did this do?"

"Decoration?" a boy said.

"It worked," she said. "All day. Rope ran over it while sailors hauled with hands like sandpaper. If it jammed, the line could part and whip back. If it ran true, the ship lived. When we clean it and store it in a dark, dry box, we're not hiding it. We're letting it rest after a few centuries of shift work."

A girl pointed at copper sheathing. "Why put metal on wood?"

"Because the sea eats," Isabelle said. "Tiny creatures drill into timber. Copper makes the hull taste bad. An old way of saying: not today."

Questions, laughter. Yes to pirates, yes to treasure; maybe to provenance; we're working on it to names. Eyes caught on ballast stones—how a dull rock could say a hull once touched England.

After, she washed her hands and returned to the hinge. Leads clipped; bubbles feathered up as current passed. She checked the sacrificial anode and logged salinity; low amps tonight—steady is kinder than fast. Iron began surrendering salt. She logged time and voltage, checked the dehumidifier—51% RH. Acceptable. Barely.

A buzz: two photos from her sister on a Peruvian mountainside—*no phone for a week; don't worry; love you*. Isabelle sent back a heart and a shot of the brass sheave: *not El Dorado, but it worked just as hard*.

By six, the light went mango-soft. She finished measurements, slid the timber into a labeled tray, padded it with damp towels so it wouldn't warp while it waited for PEG. She wiped the table, added a neat line to the ledger, then let the day settle through her bones.

On her way out, she paused in the gallery. The cannon took the last of the light like a black river stone. The brass sheave glowed brighter for being small.

"Rest," she said softly—in Spanish, her mother's word when a piece finally caught the light just so. She killed the lights one bank at a time.

Outside, Blackwater Sound wore early evening like brushed silk. She locked the door and watched a lone skiff draw a white seam. The day had been full of overlooked things—the kind of labor no one wrote songs about. It suited her. It also left a bright, restless place lectures couldn't soothe.

Dinner. Emails. A few more notes. Beneath the steady rhythm, the older one—beating toward a mountain lake and family stories kept like coals. Somewhere between those pulses, something waited. Not yet. Soon.

Dusk layered itself over Key Largo. Isabelle paused in the doorway, listening to the same small sounds that had opened her morning—the clock, the vent, the palms—but heavier now, settled. Keys in the dish, shoes off. The room held its familiar peace.

Dinner was simple—onions and garlic softening, tomatoes added, an arepa crisping. She cued her brother's playlist: gaita, then the cumbia that always set one of her mother's feet tapping. The music stitched the quiet to home.

While the sauce simmered, Isabelle opened the laptop. FIU first: two Serranilla questions; a thank-you from the student in the sea-green hoodie—*called my abuela for her stories*. Isabelle typed back: *Keep asking. Oral history is a library with no walls.*

Next window: *Displaced Colombian Relics*, her private spreadsheet—date, source, object, last-seen, chain-of-custody. A gray half-entry: *Muisca tunjo? — private preview, Coral Gables — registrar rumor.* Rumor felt like a tug on a sleeve.

She ate by the open window, breeze lifting the curtains. Cartagena rose with the gaita line—her abuelo turning streets into history. She rinsed the bowl and pulled the laptop close again.

Two emails, clean and careful.

To Marta at the Museo del Oro: subject Inquiry—possible Muisca tunjo (private preview, Miami). Label incomplete, provenance unclear (possible "Connaught"). If I secure a viewing, advise on typology and red flags? Photos/measurements and any docs allowed. If genuine and compromised, I want the right people in the room. P.S. Does "Connaught" ring a bell (dealer/family, mid-century)?

Send.

To L., the registrar with keys to quiet rooms: subject Discreet viewing request—South American goldwork. If the preview includes a Muisca tunjo/pendant, could we arrange an off-hours look for authentication notes? No fee, no letterhead. Docs appreciated if permitted. Priorities: correct ID and clear chain-of-custody. — I. Alvarez

She set the laptop aside. She printed a sticky—*Tunjo — Coral Gables?*—and added chain, Marta, typology photos. She placed it on the corkboard beside a map tracing currents north from Colombia.

She should have stopped. Instead, her gaze slid to the empty chair across the table. The auction had been what—two nights ago? Bright room, quick talk. The salvage diver built by salt and habit had listened as if words were charts. Most people left no wake.

Jake Morgan had left a small one. Not for anything he'd said—he hadn't said much—but for how he leaned toward information, not shine. She pictured the nick on his knuckle, the way questions set his eyes. She'd dismissed him on principle, then spent five minutes wondering why.

"Stop it," she told the chair, smiling.

She crossed to the window. Up close, the necklace's beads were tiny worlds—seed-red, sun-yellow, a hammered charm that held a thread of light. She touched it. "Que vuelva a casa," she whispered. Let it come home. Let what was taken find its way back, unbroken.

Her phone buzzed—her brother, signal from the mountains: a half-repaired pendant on their mother's bench—*had to dig out her tools—felt like she was here.* Isabelle sent back a shot of the corkboard with the new sticky. *Working on something small that might matter. Call tomorrow.*

She opened her paper journal—the linen one with faint grid that kept her handwriting honest—and dated the page. Three headings, promises more than labels:

Que sé — Private preview; Coral Gables; rumor via registrar. Label sug-

gests Muisca. "Connaught" uncertain.

Qué sospecho — Label misread possible; 1960s export loopholes likely; "Connaught" more dealer than lineage.

Qué haré — Secure viewing (off-hours). Full photo/measurements; color card; scale. Ask for docs; scan alloy if allowed. Loop Marta same day. If genuine + compromised: start quiet repatriation path. Don't let story outrun facts.

She rinsed the pan, left the corkboard lamp on like a harbor light, and stood at the window, letting the dark touch her face. A skiff moved along a canal—the hiss of wake on concrete. She thought of Biscayne Bay at noon, of Largo Sound holding the night, of a lake haunted by devotion—and, because it was honest, wondered what Jake Morgan was doing now.

The apartment felt too still. She slipped into sandals, took her keys and a light jacket, and stepped into warm salt air, letting the footpath draw her toward the canal.

The stairwell smelled of old paint and saltwater. Two flights down, the door gave onto the night. Porch lights and marina bulbs stitched small constellations along the canal. A breeze slid in from the flats.

She followed the path of crushed shell and sand. On the right, pastel balconies stacked like decks; on the left, mangroves rooted in black water. Somewhere down-current a skiff idled, coughed, settled.

Walking peeled back the day until she could hear smaller sounds: wind in fronds, the hollow clack of a halyard, a mullet breaking the surface and vanishing. She paused on a footbridge, leaned on the rail. Moonlight made a thin skin on the canal.

Her phone buzzed. Papá.

"Hola, mi niña."

"I'm walking," she said. "The good kind."

They traded notes—Marta's exclamation points, the thin "Connaught" trail, London in the seventies.

"Thin is honest," Isabelle said.

"How was class?"

"Good," she said. "Heavy. Guatavita first. Walking a room from gold as hunger to gold as offering takes time."

"Y así es la vida," he said. "Do you remember your mother's phrase when a piece finally took the right shine?"

"Brilla para servir," Isabelle said. Shine to serve.

"Eso. Gold is responsibility, not a prize."

"If this figurine is real—and wrong—I'll put the right people in the room. Quietly. No headlines."

"I know. If you need the boring professor, I can cite laws until the air goes out of the room."

"I might," she said, smiling.

They said goodnight. The line clicked; the night reassembled. *Brilla para servir.* Not a bad compass.

She walked on. Kayaks lay chained to a rack like bright animals waiting for morning. A fisherman at the dock's end threw a cast net—silver quarter-moons. Under a streetlamp she typed one note: *Connaught — London boutique dealer? 1970s auctions? Ask L. for clipping.*

The canal widened toward the sound. Mangroves broke to make a room for more sky. A late motor stitched a faint diesel thread into the air.

Jake drifted across her thoughts like a boat crossing her bow and leaving only the nudge of wake. Salvage divers split neatly: those who spent stories, and those who knew stories were expensive to hold. She'd filed him, tentatively, in the second column—and tucked the file where she wouldn't have to admit she'd made space.

At a low bridge she rested a palm on the worn rail. A dried mangrove leaf had blown against her sandal. She let it fall, a patient oval riding the small tide toward Largo Sound.

"Escuchar. Verificar. Devolver," she said. Listen. Verify. Return.

Her phone vibrated again—an email ping. *Re: Private preview—yes, off-hours is fine.* She didn't open it; she let the knowledge sit like a tool that fit the hand.

On the walk back, a gecko skittered up a wall. A cat watched from a stoop. The fisherman freed his net—the relieved whoomp drew a private cheer from her for small victories in the dark.

Up the stairs, a warm coin of light burned in her window. Inside, that circle would hold steady over maps and stickies. For a beat she pictured the board as coastline and the new sticky as a harbor light.

At the desk she broke her rule and opened the registrar's email. *Off-hours. Bring camera and calipers. Discretion.* An address in Coral Gables. *No document copies without approval.*

She replied: *Thank you. Confirmed. I'll come alone.* Then powered the phone off. Resolve needs a full stop.

She stood where she'd stood a hundred times: between the necklace catching the last frail light and the map of currents running north. From here the canal was only an idea, the ocean a pressure you felt in your ribs. She let the quiet come up—not to end the day, but to keep it from spilling.

"Tomorrow," she said to the room. Not a promise. A plan—off-hours, Coral Gables—quiet eyes on a figurine that might not legally belong in that room.

The night held. The relics rested. And the direction tugging at her didn't ask her to leave herself behind to follow it.

CHAPTER FOUR

The Weight of Legacy

T he glass stretched from floor to ceiling, a seamless wall of light overlooking the Port of Algeciras. Below, cranes moved with the precision of colossal metronomes, lifting and lowering containers through misted dawn. Trucks crawled in luminous rows, taillights blinking through haze. Beyond the bay, the Rock of Gibraltar loomed against the paling sky—a jagged monument that had watched the rise and fall of empires.

Victor Serrano stood with his hands loosely clasped behind his back, a dark silhouette framed against the panorama. From this height the port seemed ordered, tamed—a miniature world that obeyed his command. To others it was trade, tonnage, and logistics. To Victor, it was power made visible.

Behind him, the office hummed with restrained energy: the whisper of ventilation, the pulse of data on glass displays. Figures streamed across a curved wall—freight rates, customs clearances, manifests from Shanghai and Veracruz. The scent of wax polish rose from the long mahogany table, a quiet reminder that control could be fragrant as well as cold.

Victor adjusted a cufflink and touched the console. Shipping lanes flared into light—arteries of commerce encircling the world. At their center pulsed Algeciras. He had chosen this city precisely because of its position at the strait: every ship between the Atlantic and the Mediterranean passed beneath its cranes. It was a gate, and Victor Serrano was the gatekeeper.

A tremor flickered across his right hand. He stilled it against his thigh and, without looking, shifted the display. Modern routes dissolved into older images—digitized charts, brittle manuscripts, sketches of coastlines inked in the hand of Spanish officers. Fragments of history filled the screen: faded seals, archaic script, the lingering shadow of Elias Grey.

He studied the collage for a long moment, then turned toward the glass door. Storm clouds were gathering beyond the horizon—dark, patient, and inevitable. They suited him.

The boardroom ran the length of the floor, a blade of light suspended above the harbor. On one side, Algeciras unfolded in restless geometry; on the other, a row of world clocks ticked in calm agreement. Twelve leather chairs ringed the polished table. The head seat waited.

Victor entered without announcement. Conversation stopped mid-sentence; pens and tablets froze.

"Buenos días," he said, taking his chair.

"Buenos días," the board echoed.

Reports began.

"Throughput up three-point-two percent year-on-year," said the COO, Marcos Ibarra—a compact man with a sailor's squint. "Minimal rollover from the Eastern Med diversions. Dwell time down. On-time departures ninety-six percent."

Victor nodded once. Reliable, expected. Black Tide prided itself on precision; lateness was weakness.

Port Operations added, "Tanger-Med granted two new night slots. That moves West Africa arrivals forward by twelve hours."

"Good," Victor said. "Twelve hours is a lifetime when others sleep."

Finance followed: hedges within band, margins expanding, cold-chain demand climbing.

"Approved," Victor said. "Stagger expansion—Barcelona, Lisbon, Veracruz. No monuments."

He leaned back as dashboards bloomed across the wall: lane performance, customs times, warehouse utilization. Clean, public data—the visible skin of the machine. Only a few in the room knew there was another layer beneath.

"Security," he said.

The head of corporate risk cleared his throat. "Two intrusions at the Valencia yard. Opportunistic. Intercepted."

"And the quiet lanes?" Victor asked.

A hesitation—fractional, telling. "Stable."

Victor let silence do the work, then turned his gaze to Marcos.

"Stable," the COO confirmed, his tone carrying subtext. "Sensitive consignments through Seixal and Gioia Tauro. No flags, no inspections. Valencia not recommended—too many new eyes."

Victor inclined his head. The board heard only that operations ran smoothly. He heard confirmation that his shadow routes—fast, invisible corridors through customs—remained intact.

"Compliance?" he asked.

"Exemplary," legal counsel said quickly. "We hosted an inspector workshop last week. They left impressed. The head of the Algeciras unit complimented our transparency."

Victor allowed himself the faintest smile. "Good. Admiration is a convenient blindfold."

A ripple of cautious laughter moved around the table.

They progressed: labor unrest in Santos—add relief crews before strikes; weather system over the Bay of Biscay—pre-stage tugs, advance pilotage; insurance clauses—replace *acts of God* with *acts of weather*. Language was leverage.

The communications director, perfectly pressed, ventured, "A journalist from *El Diario* is profiling 'The New Captains of Trade.' They've requested an interview. Favorable exposure."

Victor weighed the word *captains* as though it were poison. "Decline. Send them to Marcos. Let the story be the machine, not the man."

He rose and faced the window. The Rock stood pale and immovable. "We don't grow like others," he said quietly. "We connect arteries. We put our hands where the blood must pass. Think in straits, not rectangles. The world is still geography, no matter how many spreadsheets we drape across it."

When the meeting ended, chairs slid back in careful silence. Executives murmured as they left, relief whispering in their wake.

"Marcos," Victor said.

The COO remained.

"The quiet lanes," Victor repeated.

"Clean," Marcos said. "Collectors are restless. Rumor of a piece moving through Tangier. Nothing confirmed."

"Chatter is weather," Victor replied. "Signal is current. Keep me in the current."

Marcos nodded. "Of course."

"You did well," Victor said, and that single phrase was worth more than any bonus.

When he was alone, Victor stood by the window again. The harbor pulsed beneath him; the Rock kept its vigil. He pressed his palm to a seamless section of wood paneling. A hidden door clicked open, soundless against the hum of the world beyond.

He stepped through into darkness.

The hidden room was a sanctuary of silence. The noise of the port vanished, replaced by the soft hiss of conditioned air and the dry scent of parchment. Spotlights hung low over oak panels and long worktables strewn with charts, letters, and relics.

Here, Victor Serrano was not CEO but heir—the custodian of a tarnished legacy.

He moved to the central table. Maps lay open in layers of centuries: Caribbean coastlines inked in archaic Spanish, edges browned and curling. One letter drew his eye, the script trembling with haste: *He has vanished again, perhaps to that cursed island where reefs rise like teeth and shadows conceal its shore. Yet he carries the treasure still, and His Majesty demands its return.*

Victor had read the words a hundred times. Grey's gift had been disappearance. The island had no name; sailors who reached it once never found it again.

He let his fingers rest on the page, then turned to the shelves. Artifacts stood in careful ranks: a corroded sextant, a shard of painted pottery, a serpent carved from obsidian, a jade pendant spiraled with lines, a gold disc rippled like water. To scholars these were curiosities. To Victor they were coordinates.

He had seen the same shapes recur across cultures—serpent, spiral, circle—symbols of time and renewal. The Spaniards had called such things cursed because they did not understand them. Curses were merely fear disguised as faith.

He opened a lacquered case and lifted a burned naval logbook, its cover brittle as ash. One surviving line had driven him for decades: *The treasure is no ordinary gold nor silver. It burdens the men, even in thought.*

His ancestor Don Rodrigo Serrano had been disgraced for failing to return that treasure to Spain. Officially it was lost to pirates. Privately, Victor believed Grey had hidden something far greater than plunder—something that had once been sought by kings not for wealth, but for salvation.

He felt the faint tremor return. Doctors had called it the inevitable march of Huntington's disease—progressive, untreatable, relentless. They could manage symptoms, never arrest them. But centuries ago, a dying monarch had commanded fleets to chase an object across oceans. Whatever Grey had taken was worth an empire's desperation. Worth his own.

He steadied his hand on the table and whispered to the empty room, "Patience is a weapon."

It had always been his sharpest blade.

He activated the recessed screen beside the maps. Digital overlays flared: Spanish fleet routes, Grey's suspected path, sailor tales of storms that erased entire squadrons. Lines converged toward Brazil, then scattered into nothing. An island without a name.

"Every shadow has a shape," he murmured.

A slim folder waited on the table: Luca Moretti's latest report.

Subject: Morgan, Jacob Thomas — 34, U.S. citizen. Residence: Marathon, Florida. Occupation: commercial diver and small-vessel owner (The Wayfinder). Prior record: juvenile arrest, Monroe County, 2006 — breaking and entering, attempted theft of marine property (an abandoned salvage vessel). Charges dropped after restitution. No further offenses.

Profile: Irregular income from recovery work. Keeps to routine between the marina and local workshop. Social circle limited to dockside contacts. Mechanical aptitude noted.

Historical linkage: Preliminary genealogical overlap identified with Morgan, Silas (b. 1682, England — first mate to Captain Elias Grey, La Fortuna). Family records from Nassau and early Marathon show a Morgan line descending from a "Thomas Silas Morgan," born c. 1730. Verification in progress.

Below, another page:

Subject: Alvarez, Isabelle — 32, Colombian heritage. Maritime historian, Florida International University. Current research: pre-Columbian civilizations of northern South America, with emphasis on Muisca cosmol-

ogy and artifact symbology—serpent and solar motifs recurring in colonial records. No familial or professional link to Morgan established.

Assessment: Alvarez's academic focus overlaps thematically with Muisca references appearing in recovered Serrano-era dispatches. Morgan's bloodline suggests potential continuity to the Grey–La Fortuna file. Neither subject aware of surveillance. No contact with each other since the Auction in Key West. Recommend continued low-profile observation until corroboration.

Victor read in silence. A diver whose ancestry ran red with legend; a historian chasing myths the Spaniards had feared to name. Coincidence—or convergence beginning to take shape.

He paused on the note about the juvenile arrest. A boy breaking into a salvage yard to steal a rusted boat. Foolish, yes—but hunger left its own kind of lineage. Some obsessions were inherited long before they were understood.

He closed the folder and set it precisely atop the burned logbook. Two ordinary lives aligned by tide and blood.

"Blood remembers," he murmured. "It always does."

The folder lay still beneath his hand, a patient promise. Beyond the narrow window, Gibraltar glowed pale against gathering storm.

The clinic occupied the top floor of an unmarked glass-and-stone building on Algeciras's north side—anonymous, discreet, designed to be overlooked. From the street, it could have housed accountants. Privacy was its true currency.

Victor arrived without escort. No insignia, no aides. Inside, staff lowered their eyes and vanished through silent doors.

Dr. Ignacio Herrera waited in a windowed examination room, a folder already open before him. "Señor Serrano," he said with a small bow. "Thank you for coming."

Victor unbuttoned his jacket and sat. "Let's make it brief."

The doctor adjusted his glasses. "Tell me how you've been feeling."

Victor's gaze drifted to the window, to the glint of the strait beyond. "The tremors are worse," he said. "More frequent. My grip—less certain than last month."

Herrera nodded slowly. "And speech? Coordination?"

"Still manageable."

The doctor hesitated before speaking again. "I can increase your regimen. The medication won't slow the progression, but it may lessen the spasms and help you rest."

"I don't need rest," Victor said evenly. "I need control."

"You know that's temporary," Herrera replied, his tone gentle but firm. "Huntington's remains progressive. There is no cure. The stronger medication will buy comfort, nothing more."

Victor looked at him for a long moment, eyes unreadable. "Then prescribe it. I'll decide when to use it."

The doctor nodded, writing quickly. "You'll likely feel drowsiness. Avoid alcohol if—"

"I don't avoid anything," Victor said. The edge in his voice was quiet, final.

Herrera folded his hands over the folder. "Forgive me. My duty is to prepare you."

"And mine," Victor said, rising, "is to endure."

He buttoned his jacket with measured precision and turned to leave. At the doorway, Herrera's voice followed softly: "You don't have to face it alone, Señor Serrano."

Victor paused without turning. "Everyone faces it alone, doctor. Some of us simply refuse to call it that."

He stepped into the corridor. His reflection slid along the polished doors as he walked. The tremor caught his hand again—brief, sharp—and he gripped the railing until it passed. When it did, he opened his fist, studying the family ring: twin towers, rampant lion, *Fidem servabo. I will keep the faith.*

Don Rodrigo had failed the crown. Victor would not fail himself. Even if his body betrayed him, he would not surrender his name.

He rode the private elevator down in silence, the port rising into view through the glass. All his empire below, all his power—and still, the quiet ruin inside his own flesh.

But there was something that could defy it.

If a dying king had sent fleets across oceans to retrieve a single object, then the legend could not be madness. Don Rodrigo's failure had stained the family for centuries. Victor would not repeat it.

He clenched his hand, the tremor stilled by will alone. "No," he whispered. "Not yet."

The doors opened to the underground garage, where his car waited gleaming in the dim light. He entered without help, settling into silence. As the driver guided them up the ramp toward daylight, Victor looked out over the cranes and the Rock of Gibraltar beyond—the sentinel that judged without pity.

For him, this was no longer ambition. It was survival.

The Serrano estate clung to the cliffs west of Algeciras, terraces stepping down toward the restless sea. From the road, the house was nothing but white stone and silence, hidden among olive trees. From within, the view was endless—the strait spread wide and dark, ships crawling through the channel like slow sparks of light.

Victor entered through a side door after nightfall, dismissing his driver with a gesture. The house obeyed him in silence—lights blooming one by one, the faint hiss of sealed doors.

Dinner waited untouched on the table. He took a single bite, then pushed the plate aside and reached for the Rioja instead. The wine steadied his hand.

Later, he crossed to the exercise room where glass walls overlooked the black water below. He stripped to a training shirt and drew a rapier from the rack. The first movements came easily—thrust, parry, riposte—rhythmic, precise, cleansing. Then the tremor found him again. The point wavered; the blade slipped off line.

A snarl broke from his throat before he could stop it. He hurled the weapon across the room. It struck the far wall with a metallic crack and fell, spinning against the marble floor.

For a moment the only sound was his breathing. Then he walked over, picked up the sword, and returned it carefully to its stand. Control reclaimed, layer by layer. He pressed his hand to the mirror, palm trembling against glass. The reflection stared back—eyes hard, body betraying.

"Not yet," he whispered.

He showered, changed into dark slacks and a pressed shirt, and poured another measure of Rioja. Out on the terrace, the night wind rolled in heavy carrying the scent of saltwater. The sea below whispered against the rocks; the Rock of Gibraltar glimmered pale in starlight.

He thought of two names: Isabelle Alvarez and Jake Morgan. A historian drawn to the myths of the Muisca. A diver whose blood traced back to Grey's lost crew. Two small figures, both standing on the edges of the map that had consumed him.

He turned the glass in his hand. The surface rippled once, steadied.

"They don't know it yet," he murmured, voice low and certain. "But the tide's already turning."

He lifted the glass toward Gibraltar, its pale mass unwavering against the dark. "And when it brings them to me—" a thin smile touched his mouth—"I'll be waiting."

The wind carried the words out across the strait. Below, the ships moved on, their lights scattered across the water like constellations in motion. Above, the stars wheeled cold and indifferent.

Victor Serrano stood on the terrace, patient as stone, certain as tide.

CHAPTER FIVE

Low Air

The call came early, before the sun burned the haze off the water. Jake was in his cottage kitchen nursing a coffee, the chipped dining table still stacked with unopened mail. His phone buzzed across the counter, rattling beside the mug.

The number wasn't saved, but the voice was—Ramos, a fisherman known for short tempers and long grudges.

"Boat went under in the squall last night," Ramos said without preamble. "Thirty-footer, just me onboard. I made it in, but she's on the bottom. Nets, engine, electronics... I need proof for insurance, and if you can bring anything up, all the better."

Jake rubbed a hand over his jaw, still rough with sleep. Jobs like this weren't glamorous, but they kept fuel in *The Wayfinder* and the lights on in the workshop and cottage.

"You got a fix on where she went down?"

"GPS was still running when I jumped. I marked it." Ramos rattled off a string of numbers. "She won't be far. I'll pay cash."

That last part mattered. Jake scribbled the coordinates on a notepad beside the clutter, settled on a rate that made Ramos grumble, then ended the call.

He stood a moment, leaning against the counter, listening to the faint hiss of tide pulling at the flats behind the house. Early light crept through salt-clouded windows, striping the floor in gray-gold. He carried his mug onto the sagging porch. From there, the view spread wide: mangroves bristling at the water's edge, shallows flashing silver where baitfish dimpled the surface, a heron lifting slow and deliberate into the sky.

It wasn't much—the cottage, the porch, the stubborn smell of salt baked into the walls—but mornings like this made it hard to hate. He sipped, let the briny air settle in his chest, then set the mug on the rail. Another day, another salvage.

He grabbed his duffel and headed out. The old Land Cruiser coughed to life, then settled into a growl. Ten minutes later he pulled into the lot beside **Boot Key Harbor**.

The marina was waking. Charter captains barked orders while loading bait coolers; dive crews clattered tanks down wooden docks; an old trawler wheezed against its lines. Pelicans loitered on pilings, fat and patient, while the bridge to Vaca Key carried a trickle of southbound traffic.

Eli was already on the dock, coil of line over one shoulder, salt still crusted in his hair.

"Morning, Jake."

"Morning," Jake said, stepping aboard. "You're in early."

"Cap'n Vega's charter's running a sunrise trip. Figured I'd beat the rush."

Jake nodded, checking his lines. "Smart move."

Eli's gaze lingered on the tanks and lift bags stacked by the gunwale. "Salvage job?"

"Boat went down in the storm last night," Jake said, tightening a cleat hitch. "Owner needs proof for insurance—and whatever I can haul up."

Eli gave a low whistle. "Rough luck."

"Yeah. Storm chewed her up pretty good, from what I heard."

Eli nodded, eyes thoughtful, then straightened the coil on his shoulder. "You'll find her."

Jake's mouth tugged faintly. "Keep the slip clear for me."

"Always do."

Jake stepped aboard *The Wayfinder* and dropped his duffel on deck. He ran his checks—fuel, lines, air, gear. The diesel turned over with a throaty growl, steady underfoot. He cast off, eased her clear, and brought the bow around toward the channel.

Jake fed in throttle. The bow lifted, spray feathering off the rails. The engine drummed through the deck, steady and sure. Swell rolled under her, lifting and dropping him as if the sea were testing his balance.

Gulls wheeled overhead, their cries cutting through the motor's drone.

Out here the air sharpened—cleaner, harsher—diesel and salt biting the back of his throat. Land shrank behind into a low smear of mangroves and roofs against the pale horizon. Ahead, only water.

The GPS blinked Ramos's coordinates, a lonely set of numbers in the blue. As he neared them, Jake throttled back and flipped on the side-scan sonar. It wasn't state-of-the-art—just a used rig from a charter captain who'd upgraded—but Jake knew how to coax meaning from grainy shadows. Years of salvage had trained his eye to see more than noise.

The first passes showed only sand ripples and coral heads. He steered a methodical grid, the transducer's hum filling the cabin like a heartbeat.

On the third sweep, something unexpected bled onto the screen—not a neat fishing-boat silhouette, but a scatter of long, narrow shapes, irregular and half-buried. Timbers. The shadows looked warped, old. Not modern wreckage. Jake leaned closer, pulse quickening, and dropped a digital marker.

"I'll be back for you," he muttered. But not what he'd been hired for.

Another pass to the east, and there it was—the fisherman's boat, lying on her side, bow angled into the sand. Clear as day.

He exhaled slowly, a flicker of satisfaction in his chest. Found. The rest was sweat and air.

Still, his gaze snagged on the earlier marker blinking a few hundred yards off. The odd scatter of timbers tugged at him, patient as a hooked fish. He shook his head, throttled back, and began to rig his dive gear.

Work first. Curiosity later.

He always told himself that.

Jake moved through his pre-dive routine with the steady rhythm of a hundred dives. He checked wind and current, then adjusted *The Wayfinder's* throttle until she hovered steady above the wreck pinned on the sonar. Depth read about fifty feet—shallow enough, but unforgiving if things went wrong.

He throttled back and killed the diesel. Quiet rushed in—water pattering against the hull, the davit sheave ticking as the crane settled, gear shifting faintly below deck. He went forward and dropped the anchor, paying out chain until it bit and set. *The Wayfinder* swung gently in the current, holding steady.

At the stern, he hauled out a weighted shot line, clipped a buoy to the top, and tossed the weight overboard. Rope hissed through his hands until it hit bottom and went taut. A clean marker, his way home.

Only then did he gear up. Harness over shoulders, tank straps cinched. Regulator checked, mask rinsed, fins clipped to his wrist. No wasted motion—habit making the ritual as natural as breathing.

He sat on the gunwale, mask fogging at the edges, regulator in place. The water below shifted from slate to cobalt. With a final gauge check, he rolled backward into the sea.

The world changed at once. Wave slap and anchor groan dulled to nothing, replaced by the hiss and bubble of his breath. Sunlight fractured into ribbons as he descended along the line. Pressure squeezed his ears; he equalized with practiced swallows.

The fishing boat rose out of haze like a carcass on sand. She lay on her side, hull split by the storm, bow angled into current. Nets trailed from the stern like torn shrouds, snagged on the prop. Bait buckets skittered in the surge.

Jake hovered, then unclipped the waterproof camera. He circled slow, snapping frames: cracked hull, bent rails, broken fittings—proof of loss. The flash lit gouges where the storm had slammed her down; the nameplate hung by a single bolt. She wasn't coming back.

He clipped the camera away and turned to the nets. A sodden tangle wound tight around the prop shaft. He drew his knife and began slicing. Each cut freed a section, rope drifting upward in lazy curls. Slow work that chewed air and burned shoulders.

When the nets were clear, he turned to the engine. The outboard sat stubborn, heavy but salvageable. He wormed a strap beneath the casing, fingers searching through silt until it cinched. From his belt he unclipped a yellow lift bag, flattened by pressure, and clipped its D-rings to the rig.

Satisfied, he pulled a wrench from his pouch and went to work. Bolts gave one by one, bubbles streaming past his mask with every twist. When the last loosened, he thumbed the inflator. The bag bloomed, jerking upright and yanking against the strap. The outboard tore free with a groan he felt more than heard. Silt boiled upward as the bag strained for the surface. Jake steadied the load, guiding its rise until it cleared the wreck.

His gauge was dropping—too much knife work, too much fiddling. He finned for the anchor line and began a careful ascent.

He broke the surface in a burst of bubbles, regulator clenched in his teeth. The lift bag bobbed beside the stern, tugging the outboard like a stubborn buoy. He spat the mouthpiece, hauled a breath, and kicked for the ladder. The rungs rattled under his grip as he climbed aboard, water streaming from his gear.

He shrugged out of the harness and clipped the davit's cable to the engine. A flick of the switch set the winch whining, the motor rising slow and dripping from the sea. He swung a fender under the casing and guided it in; the outboard settled with a clang that shuddered through the hull.

Jake steadied it, then hauled the nets aboard: foul, dripping, a heap that stank of salt, rot, and fish. He leaned on the gunwale, chest heaving, deck cluttered with the spoils of someone else's misfortune. For Ramos, it meant insurance and maybe salvage value. For Jake, another job done.

He pushed his mask up, letting the breeze dry his face. At the helm, the GPS glowed steady in the console's shade. The fisherman's coordinates were logged and satisfied. Just below, another waypoint blinked back—the odd scatter of timbers.

His eyes lingered. Old wood where fiberglass should be. It tugged at him. He checked his gauge: borderline stupid, but enough for a quick recon if he stayed disciplined. By the book, he should swap tanks and take a surface interval.

He rubbed a salty hand over his face, but curiosity was already pulling. He reset the mask, bit down on the regulator, and rolled backward into the blue.

He dropped fast, equalizing every few feet as pressure squeezed around his skull. The water here was murkier, the storm having kicked up silt that still hung in the current. His light cut a narrow tunnel through green-blue haze.

The waypoint pulsed on the handheld clipped to his harness. He kicked harder until shapes resolved out of blur.

Timbers.

They jutted from the sand like bones—long, warped, blackened by centuries of salt. Some collapsed in heaps, others angled upward as if clawing for the surface. Barnacles crusted every edge; fish darted through gaps. Not the neat outline of a modern hull—older, heavier—the wreckage of something that went down hard and never came up.

Jake hovered, scanning. His beam slid across broken planks, a corroded iron spike, the shattered rim of a barrel. He finned slowly, running a gloved hand along a timber that splintered to powder under his touch. His pulse thudded louder than the regulator's hiss.

Nothing yet. Just graveyard quiet. A school of jacks burst past in a silver flash and vanished, and for an instant he felt like an intruder on a place forgotten for a reason.

He swept wider. A mound of debris loomed, half-buried in silt. He probed, shifting fragments—a length of chain fused with rust, a lump of unidentifiable iron.

His gauge ticked lower.

Then the light caught something different. Not wood. Not stone. A shape half-hidden beneath two collapsed beams, edges smoother than the wreck around it.

He angled closer, heart hammering. A cylinder, forearm-long, green with corrosion but intact. Brass or copper. Beneath the encrustation, faint as a ghost, the impression of a crown.

A dispatch tube.

He wedged his pry bar into the gap, testing the beams. The timber groaned but held. He jammed deeper and heaved. The cylinder shifted but wouldn't budge. Silt swirled, choking visibility.

His gauge slid into the red.

One last surge. The tube wrenched free—triumph flared—then something slammed his shoulder, driving him sideways into the wreck. Pain fired down his arm; the regulator nearly tore from his mouth. Bubbles and silt exploded, blinding. Weight pinned him against splintered wood. He clutched the tube, but his right arm was trapped beneath it. For a heartbeat he didn't know what had struck—only that he couldn't move.

He shoved. Nothing. The wreck groaned, timbers shifting above. He thrashed again, bubbles roaring past his mask, vision starting to tunnel.

Stop. Breathe. Think.

He forced air slow through the regulator, fought to calm the pounding in his chest. His free hand groped along his belt until it closed on the pry bar. He levered beneath the weight. Metal screeched on wood. He heaved. Nothing.

Again.

Muscles shook. He sucked hard—nothing. The hiss was gone. The needle sat buried in the red.

Darkness pressed in. He jammed the bar deeper and shoved with everything left. The timber shifted—an inch. Enough.

He wrenched his shoulder free—skin tearing on splinters—and kicked hard off the wreck. The timber settled with a dull thud where he'd been, but he didn't look back.

He drove upward, legs burning, air gone. Lungs screamed, body begging to rip out the regulator and drink seawater just to fill them. Black crept at the edges.

He kept the reg in and bled a steady stream of bubbles, forcing the ascent to stay controlled even as panic clawed.

Pressure eased with every foot. Water brightened from blue to silver. The need to breathe clawed harder. His chest convulsed, diaphragm spasming. He bit the mouthpiece and kept rising, vision narrowed to a tunnel of light.

Surface. He burst through in a spray, tearing the regulator free. The gasp he dragged in was ragged and raw, but it filled his lungs. He floated, sky blinding, waves slapping his mask. For a long moment he lay still, limbs trembling, listening to the world return—gulls calling, water hissing against the hull, the simple fact of being alive.

The tube was still clutched to his chest, heavy and cold. He hooked an arm over the gunwale, hauled himself half out of the water, and heaved it onto *The Wayfinder's* deck. Then he dragged himself aboard and sprawled beside it. He lay there a minute, chest heaving, staring up at bright, cloudless sky while the boat rocked beneath him. His hands trembled—not from cold but from the fight for air, and from the weight of what he'd dragged out of the deep.

At last he sat up, water running in rivulets across the deck. The cylinder rolled in his palms, green with corrosion, brass blistered by centuries of salt. His thumb traced a faint crown pressed into the metal. Spanish—it had to be. Dispatch tubes carried orders, reports—things men guarded with their lives.

He turned it in his hands, listening to the faint slosh against the hull. His pulse still hammered, but curiosity pressed harder. Something was inside—sealed tight enough to last centuries.

A sting along his shoulder pulled him back. His wetsuit was torn, threads hanging loose, blood seeping from fresh cuts where timber had raked him. Raw skin streaked red down his arm. He flexed, winced; nothing felt broken. A reminder of how close he'd come.

He leaned against the gunwale, the tube balanced across his knees. Pops would've lit up like a kid on Christmas if he could see this. *That's history, boy,* he'd say, eyes shining with the old stories. The thought almost made Jake smile, but it twisted inside him. Pops was gone—and the salvage yard Jake had walked away from went with him. There was no one to share it with.

The tube gave a faint rattle when he shifted it—something moving inside. Jake's pulse kicked. This wasn't salvage. This was different.

He stood unsteadily and stowed the tube in a dry locker beneath the helm, tucking it away as if it were alive. The lock clicked. He stood a moment longer in the salty wind, steadying the tremor running through his muscles.

The wreck had nearly kept its secret—and him. But not quite.

Afternoon light slanted low as *The Wayfinder* nosed into Boot Key Harbor. Jake throttled down, guiding her between the jumble of slips, hulls clapping softly against fenders. His shoulder ached with each turn of the wheel; the wetsuit had dried stiff with salt and blood. On the dock, he spotted Ramos waiting.

The fisherman stood arms crossed, wearing the permanent scowl of a man who expected disappointment. Jake tossed a line, cinched it, and hefted the recovered nets onto the dock. They landed in a foul, dripping heap.

"Got some of your gear," Jake said. His voice was hoarse, throat still raw from the desperate gasp that pulled him back.

Ramos's eyes narrowed, flicking to Jake's shoulder. "You're bleeding," he said, chin tipping toward the torn neoprene and dark streak down Jake's arm.

Jake glanced, shrugged. "Wreck was messy. Nothing serious."

Ramos grunted, unconvinced but unwilling to press. His gaze shifted to the outboard strapped down on deck. He stepped forward and ran a hand along the casing, still slick with seawater. "Didn't think you'd get this back."

Jake rolled his sore shoulder, winced. "Told you I'd try."

He pulled the waterproof camera from his duffel, popped the memory card, and pressed it into Ramos's hand. The images would tell the story:

cracked hull, storm gouges, proof no adjuster could argue with. Ramos gave a grunt—thanks or relief. He peeled off a roll of bills, thumbed through, and shoved the stack into Jake's palm.

Jake pocketed the cash without counting. His gaze drifted—just for a second—toward the helm, to the dry locker where the dispatch tube lay hidden.

"Anything else down there worth the trouble?" Ramos asked, squinting.

Jake shook his head. "Nothing you'd want."

That was enough. Ramos hitched the nets higher, muttered something, and shuffled down the dock, already calculating what could be salvaged and what would be written off.

A voice came from behind. "Rough one?"

Jake turned. Eli stood on the dock, wiping his hands on a rag, eyes on the torn wetsuit.

"Pushed my luck a little too far," Jake said. "Owner'll get his insurance, though."

Eli nodded slowly. "You bring anything back?"

"Engine. Nets. Enough to make the guy believe in luck again."

Eli smiled—a quiet mix of admiration and awe. "You always make it look easy."

Jake shook his head. "Not today."

Eli's gaze flicked to the blood drying on Jake's sleeve. "Need me to hose her down or refuel?"

"Tomorrow," Jake said. "She earned the night off."

The kid nodded once, that easy, unspoken understanding of dockhands everywhere, and moved on.

Silence settled again. Jake leaned against the gunwale, letting the day's weight sink in. His shoulder throbbed, blood tacky under torn neoprene. The near miss replayed in jagged flashes—the timber's slam, the suffocating squeeze, the frantic crawl to daylight. He exhaled slowly, a tremor still in it.

Then he reached for the locker. The tube rolled into his hands, colder than it should be, heavier than steel. Corrosion crusted its seams; the faint crown still etched in the brass like a whisper from another century. Whatever was sealed inside had been meant to survive. He traced the crest and, for the first time in a long while, felt something stir that wasn't fatigue or bitterness.

Not salvage. A story.

He glanced toward the road back to his cottage. A shower and bed tempted—a beer even more, but curiosity was louder. His boots carried him to his workshop, its tin roof catching the last orange light.

The padlock clicked under his key; the door groaned wide. Familiar air met him—salt, oil, old wood—the scent of years lived on the water.

Jake shut the door and set the tube on the bench. Brass, green with corrosion, seams caked thick. He flicked on the lamp. Its yellow cone flared across the metal, making it look ancient, pulled from another world.

He stood with palms on the bench, chest rising heavy. The ticking wall clock and the slap of tide filled the silence. The tremor in his muscles lingered—the memory of timber pinning him, lungs burning.

Finally he sat and took the tube in both hands. Cold. Heavier than it looked. He traced the faint crown, edges eaten soft by centuries. Definitely Spanish. He turned it, eyeing the endcaps: one fused shut by saltwater, the other scarred where a latch once was, now useless under crust.

He rinsed a rag and wiped the seams. Green flakes streaked away. He tried a wrench—careful first, then harder. Nothing. A hiss of WD-40 across the threads. Still nothing.

He set the wrench down and rubbed his eyes. Forcing it could ruin whatever survived inside. Paper, parchment—one rough breath and it would crumble. Pops's voice rose from memory: *Some things are worth waiting for, boy. History doesn't give up her secrets easy.*

He leaned back. The stool creaked; his shoulder burned under the torn neoprene. He dug out a first-aid kit and, one-handed, cleaned and taped the wound. The sting hissed between his teeth. His eyes never strayed far from the tube.

What might it hold? Orders? A map? A report bound for Madrid, lost to storms and centuries? Whatever it was, men sealed it certain it must survive—and now it sat in his hands.

He flexed sore fingers, weighing options. He could hammer the cap—brute force—and hate himself if he destroyed the contents. No. This needed someone who understood how to unlock the past without breaking it.

One name surfaced: *Isabelle Alvarez.*

He blew out a long breath. He hadn't seen her since Key West, since the auction where she'd called him reckless. She'd probably say the same again.

But if anyone could open this right, it was her.

Night crept in—halyards clinking outside, a trawler's generator humming two slips down. Jake rested his elbows on his knees, the tube balanced across them, its weight tugging at him like gravity.

He pictured Pops on the porch in Marathon, cigar smoke curling, eyes alive with old family tales. *Treasure isn't always gold, Jake. Sometimes it's the story.* His hand found the small brass key at his neck, squeezing it tight.

He tightened the bandage, shoved the kit aside, and brushed his thumb over the crown. Possibility stirred in his chest—and with it, an unease he couldn't name.

He set the tube down gently, as if it might break, and killed the lamp. Shadows swallowed the room, but he could still feel the weight of it there.

The marina was quiet when he stepped out. Night pressed close, warm and heavy, water slapping pilings in a patient rhythm. Masts rocked in their slips, anchor lights glowing like scattered stars.

He slung his duffel over one shoulder, the dispatch tube wrapped inside and heavier than it had any right to be. He paused, listening to laughter drifting from a bar down the street, cicadas buzzing in the mangroves. The world sounded the same, but he knew it wasn't. A cold beer and easy company tempted. His body ached; his shoulder throbbed. What he needed was a shower, rest, and space to think.

Every scrape burned, each step a reminder of the wreck pressing down and how close he'd come to not coming back this time. He exhaled through his teeth, pushed the thought aside, and kept moving.

The Land Cruiser groaned awake. Headlights cut a pale tunnel through the dark. He sat a beat before shifting into gear, the duffel resting silent on the passenger seat, the tube hidden inside. He thumbed his phone, hesitated, then typed:

Found something you might want to see.

After a pause, he snapped a picture of the tube and attached it. *That "next interesting thing" you were asking about.*

The reply came quicker than expected. Isabelle: *You're kidding. That's incredible. Meet me at the history center tomorrow morning. We need to see this properly.*

Despite the ache in his bones, the corner of his mouth lifted. He dropped the phone in the console, eased into gear, and rolled out onto the road south.

Water pressed in on both sides—black and endless, moonlight skimming the shallows, broken by bridge spans and distant markers. Night wrapped close around his headlights, asphalt unspooling beneath the tires. The duffel sat silent beside him, its weight pulling at him more with every mile.

Tomorrow, he thought. *Tomorrow it begins.*

CHAPTER SIX

Patience and Hunger

The Land Cruiser rattled north, the Overseas Highway a gray ribbon strung over water. Jake kept one hand steady on the wheel, the other braced low against his side. The tape he'd slapped over his shoulder tugged with every bump, the ache flaring when he shifted. Beyond the guardrails, the Atlantic flashed silver on his right, the Gulf stretched darker on his left. Bridges carried him from island to island until the sun-bleached shape of the history center came into view.

The building looked more like a utility shed than a museum: a stucco rectangle tucked beside mangroves, a half-empty gravel lot, a modest wooden sign stenciled in navy—Maritime History Center. Behind it, Blackwater Sound spread flat, morning haze still hanging low over the water.

Isabelle was already outside, waiting by the glass doors. She looked like she belonged here—pale blouse with sleeves rolled, dark trousers, flats that had seen more labs than lecture halls. A satchel cut across her shoulder; a lanyard clipped at her collar. Humidity had teased a few strands loose from her bun, curling them against her cheek. A scuffed brass compass—her father's—knocked lightly against her collarbone as she waved him in.

Jake climbed down stiffly, duffel slung in his left hand. The motion pulled at his bad shoulder; pain lit across his chest. He clenched his jaw, trying to hide it, but Isabelle saw anyway. When he shut the truck door, his T-shirt rode up just enough to show the edge of athletic tape under his arm.

"You didn't just sleep on that funny," she said. "That looks bad."

He tried a grin that came out more like a grimace. Wind-tossed hair, jaw rough with stubble. "Morning to you, too."

"I'm guessing you haven't seen a doctor about that."

"It's fine." He rotated the arm half an inch as proof and regretted it instantly. "Occupational hazard."

"That's not a diagnosis." She pushed the door open with her hip. "Come on. Before you prove my point by passing out."

Inside was cool and faintly metallic—paper, nitrile gloves, the tang of wet iron leaching in tubs. The low rush of the vents blended with the muffled slap of water through the mangroves. Somewhere down a side hall, a pencil scraped across a log. Jake paused past the threshold.

Glass cases glowed under muted light—coins, ballast stones, sextants laid out for tourists and school groups. Ship models perched under spotlights, sails frozen mid-billow. No flashier than a dockside museum—quieter. Reverent. Like the past had been sealed in boxes and left to breathe on a timer.

He shifted the duffel on his left side. This wasn't his world. On a wreck, finds came up slick with silt, stinking of rot, tossed into buckets beside knives and spare O-rings. Here, every piece had a placard. Every object meant something beyond itself. It made him feel like he was carrying contraband.

Isabelle didn't slow. She swiped her badge at a coded door; the light clicked green. He caught glimpses of workspaces: corkboards pinned with sketches and notes, a laptop among rolled charts, folders spilling across a desk. A coffee maker waited in the corner, the faint aroma drifting.

She moved differently here than at the auction—no need to spar. The center seemed built around her stride.

"Here," she said, pushing into the conservation lab.

Cooler. Cleaner. Archival boxes stood in ranks, labeled by century and material. A rolling photo table waited with a taped color card; whiteboard notes crawled across one wall. Tubs of fresh water held iron pieces soaking along the far side. The air was sharper here, tinged with rust.

It felt like the reverse of a wreck dive: instead of the sea trying to strip things apart, this was where the sea's damage was undone an inch at a time. Pops would've loved it—would've walked the aisles with his hands behind his back, nodding solemn approval. His fingers, almost without thinking, found the worn barrel of the brass key hanging on its leather cord at his chest.

"You brought it?" Isabelle asked, voice shifting into work mode.

Jake set the duffel on a long table. "As promised."

Her eyes lingered on him a fraction longer than the bag. Under the fluorescents, a bruise shadowed faintly through the thin cotton of his T-shirt. Her jaw tightened. "And you," she said, "are going to sit."

"I'm good," he said automatically.

Her look said otherwise.

He sighed into the chair. The tape tugged as he sat; the ache spread sharp across his shoulder.

"Thank you," she said, tugging on nitrile gloves. "Now—let's see what you nearly broke yourself for."

He eased the dispatch tube into the light. Corroded brass looked older here—green ridges catching shadow, seams crusted like scar tissue. The faint crown pressed into the cap gleamed under the lamp.

Isabelle pulled a small scale and calipers closer, snapped two quick photos with a gray card in frame, and jotted measurements in a log. She leaned in with that measured, intent expression, like she could read the object without opening it. "Spanish," she murmured. "Eighteenth century, by the alloy. Definitely navy issue."

"Pulled it out from under timbers," Jake said. "Nearly stayed there with it."

Her head snapped toward him. "You didn't mention that in your text."

"Didn't seem like the kind of thing to put in writing."

Irritation, laced with something like fear, crossed her face; she shook it off and laid out a strap wrench and cloth with precise, economical motions.

"You're lucky," she said quietly.

"Luck's overrated."

"No." She met his gaze briefly, then looked back at the tube. "Luck got you in the door. Discipline keeps you there."

He leaned back, letting the chair take his weight. The lab felt too ordered, too careful. He wanted to joke, but the words caught. His knee bounced nervously. The truth was that the tube didn't feel like it belonged to him. It belonged to time, and time wanted it back.

"Sit still," Isabelle said, adjusting the lamp. "Don't vibrate a hole in my floor while I get this open."

His knee bounced once before he caught it. "Sorry. Just excited."

"I know. Me too."

"Tell your face that."

Her eyes flicked up—exasperation tugging at the edge of a smile. "Shut up."

The grin lingered, softer now. "My grandfather used to say some things are worth waiting for."

"He was right."

The vent's hush and the faint, distant slap of a wave against the mangroves filled the pause.

The lamp's circle of light caught the tube full on, shadows deepening in the green crust. Isabelle ran a fingertip along the seam.

"Threaded seal. Built to survive storms—maybe even a sinking."

Jake hunched forward, resisting the urge to reach out. The motion tugged his shoulder; he hid the wince with a crooked grin. "Looks like it worked. Thing's been napping on the bottom for a couple hundred years."

"Let's hope the contents are intact." She reached for the strap wrench.

"I could've cracked it open last night."

"You would have cracked it for sure." Clipped, but warm underneath. "Which is why you're over there and I'm here."

"You take all the fun out of this."

"This isn't fun." She tightened a pipe wrench around the cap. Metal groaned. "It's preservation."

"It's a little fun."

A twitch at the corner of her mouth. "Yeah. It's a little fun."

The wrench slipped, skittering on corroded brass. She reset, lips pressed thin.

"Stubborn," she muttered.

"Want me to give it a shot?"

"You'll force it. Forcing ruins things."

He raised his good hand in surrender. "Hey, I left it intact."

She dabbed distilled water into the crusted seam, waited, then tried again—gentle pressure, then firmer. The cap held. She set the tube down and took up a thin wooden pick. Tick, whisper, rasp—careful strokes lifting flakes of corrosion, brushing threads clean.

Jake watched. Not his way—his world was pry bars, hammers, lift bags—but her patience had a deliberate rhythm he admired.

She tried the wrench again. Protest in the metal; then the slightest give, a hairline of clean brass winking through.

Jake held his breath.

"Almost," she whispered. She worked it back and forth, loosening grain by grain until, at last, with a dry pop, the cap gave.

They didn't move. The sound wasn't loud, but it jolted them both. Isabelle exhaled for the first time in a minute. "There." She touched a little microcrystalline wax along the freed threads to keep them from flashing green.

"Admit it—you thought it was welded shut."

"Not for a second." The tremor in her hands said otherwise.

Isabelle picked up a pair of long tweezers and a roll of parchment slid free—brittle as bone, edges salt-stiff, but whole. She slid it onto a silicone release sheet, logged a quick accession note, and set aside a clear tray. "Humidification tent later," she murmured, mostly to herself.

"Still intact," Jake said softly.

"Barely."

The parchment lay under the lamp, edges curled but whole. Isabelle leaned close, gloved hands braced on either side of the page. The Spanish hand was elegant, precise—curling letters marching between clusters of strange symbols, entire words swallowed by a cipher.

"Naval report," she murmured. "Part ciphered, part plain."

Jake frowned. "So, what can you actually read?"

She adjusted the lamp and began, her tone slow and careful.

"Dated the third day of May, 1718, off Havana, en route to Cádiz. *To the Honorable Commanders of His Majesty's Fleet, Cartagena Station, I submit this report regarding the loss of the treasure borne aboard La Fortuna, taken by the corsair known as El Corsario, master of the vessel El Espectro.*"

Jake's shoulder brushed her sleeve as he leaned closer. "Corsair. Treasure. The Specter," he said, low. "Elias Grey."

Her head snapped toward him. "You know that name?"

He rubbed the table's edge with his thumb, then the worn key at his chest. "My grandfather, Pops, told stories of Grey and his crew. He swore Grey's first mate—Silas Morgan—was... our ancestor."

"You're saying you're a descendant of Silas Morgan?" Not skeptical—sharp with curiosity, like a lens snapping into focus.

"That's how Pops told it." A half-shrug, half-smile. "Maybe it was a bedtime story. But..." He tapped the table next to the letter. "Seeing this makes you wonder."

Astonishment flickered in her eyes. "If that's true... that's extraordinary." Then she continued to read.

"On her voyage from Cartagena to Havana, the galleon was intercepted and plundered. As you know, the corsair's men seized a score of chests filled with silver coin, several bars of worked gold, and no fewer than three coffers of emeralds drawn from the Muzo mines—yet these, though grave enough, were not the greatest loss. Survivors spoke of un objeto de suma estima, por algunos condenado por idolatría. It is this object, more than the silver and emeralds, that compels the Crown to see the corsair hunted without rest."

Her eyes lingered on *idolatría*. She drew in a breath. "Siecaza," she whispered. Her fingers brushed the outline of her father's old compass in her pocket, a reflex born of memory more than thought.

Jake looked up sharply. "What's Siecaza?"

"It must be," she said softly. "Cartagena. The Spanish navy. Idolatría. The timing. My abuelo told me stories about the Spanish and the Muisca people. Said they took something sacred, not just gold. Something meant for the gods. And he said it never reached Spain."

Jake studied her face—the professional mask slipping into something fiercer, personal. "So this isn't just a job for you. Is it?"

"Not anymore. If that treasure was Muisca and it never reached Spain—maybe there's a chance to bring it home."

The word home hung heavily in the air.

Jake leaned forward, the ache in his shoulder forgotten. "If Grey's name and El Espectro are here, then the rest..." His hand hovered over the encrypted words. "It's got to say where he went."

She scanned further. "Listen to this."

"The last confirmed sighting of El Espectro places it near ⟨◊□◊⟩, a treacherous and remote chain of islands. This region, marked by perilous reefs and heavy fog, has long been shrouded in rumor. Navigational records describe a route from ⟨◆□◆⟩, westward past ⟨△□⟩, and continuing along a bearing of ⟨□◊⟩. The islands lie just beyond these landmarks, obscured by natural hazards that have deterred exploration."

She glanced at Jake, the lamp's glow sharpening the line of her jaw. "Those symbols are encryption. Names, bearings, distances—exactly what we'd need to follow him."

Jake exhaled through his nose. "So the Spaniards knew where Grey was headed, but locked it up in code."

"Exactly."

She went back to the text.

"Despite the deployment of frigates to intercept, the corsair escaped into these waters. It is my conviction that he sails still with the object in his possession. To pursue him further will require reinforcement, and perhaps a push into waters beyond the customary lanes. I therefore request additional ships and provisions to carry out this mission, for without them the pursuit cannot succeed. Should this treasure remain in the hands of the corsair, the consequence to the dominion of Spain will be grave.

For the honor of His Majesty, and to restore what has been taken, I stand ready to devote my command until the corsair is captured and the treasure returned.

In loyalty and service,

Don Rodrigo Serrano

Captain of His Majesty's frigate Santa Teresa, Cartagena Station."

Jake repeated the name, brow furrowed. "Serrano..." He shook his head. "Feels familiar. Can't place it though."

Silence lingered, broken only by the vent's hush and a distant gull.

"These portions—the ones that matter—they'll take time to solve," Isabelle said, her voice tight with discipline.

Jake's jaw clenched. "So we've got Grey. We've got the ship. We've got the treasure. But not the trail."

"Not yet—but we will. And if Siecaza exists, we don't 'finders-keepers' it. We shepherd it back."

"We have to crack the rest," Jake pressed. "If the Spanish thought they knew where Grey was heading, that's where we need to go."

Her eyes lifted, bright, urgency matching his. "Easy, sailor. I want to know just as badly—more than you realize. But if we rush and misread one mark, we could lose the chance to prove any of this. Lose the chance to bring it home."

He blew out a breath. "We could also lose it to someone else if we take too long. I'm sick of scraping by, Isabelle. This kind of money—it could change everything."

"Who else would even be looking for this?" Her brow arched, but her tone carried challenge more than doubt.

Jake shrugged. "Doesn't matter. I just know I can't let something this incredible slip through my fingers. Not again."

Her gaze sharpened. "Again?"

His jaw worked. He met her eyes for a beat before looking away, the sigh leaving him slow and heavy. The muscles along his taped shoulder twitched; pain flared and he hissed through his teeth, hand instinctively pressing the wound.

"Jake..." Her sharpness softened. She was already pulling the first-aid kit from a cabinet. "Shirt off."

He managed a lopsided grin, grateful for the break in tension even if the ache lingered. "Pretty forward of you."

"Don't make me say it twice."

He tugged the shirt over his head one-handed. The bandage beneath was soaked, edges curled with sweat and blood. The skin was raw, streaked red where timbers had raked him. Isabelle's lips parted; she said nothing—just reached for antiseptic.

"This is going to sting."

"Go ahead."

Cold swab on hot skin. Jake hissed, teeth clenched, but didn't pull away. Isabelle's hands stayed steady; her eyes flicked up once—measuring his silence, maybe his stubbornness—then back to work.

"So, what did you mean by 'not again'?" she asked, tone soft but insistent. Offering a distraction from the sting, but also a genuine question.

Jake stared at the floor for a moment. "Couple years ago, a friend and I were chasing down a lead off the coast of the Dominican Republic." He paused, the memory souring his voice. "It didn't end well. It's the reason I'm back here, salvaging."

"I'm sorry to hear that," Isabelle murmured, not pressing, but not looking away either.

She uncapped a tube of skin glue and ran a thin line along the worst cut. Jake drew in a sharp breath at the burn but held still. She pressed the edges together with careful fingers, then smoothed fresh tape over it—firm but gentle.

He flexed his shoulder carefully, testing her work. His grin was thin but stubborn. "Thanks, doc."

"Just try not to bring down any more wrecks on top of yourself," Isabelle said with a smirk.

Jake chuckled, the sound low, then sobered as his gaze drifted back to the parchment. "So... now what?"

"We proceed carefully," she said—no heat, just resolve.

"Your lab, your rules," he added, catching himself. "Partners, then?"

A small curve touched her lips. "Partners. But I set the pace."

"Thought you might say that."

The parchment went into a sleeve, then an archival box; Isabelle turned to the safe. She locked the archival box anyway and double-checked the hasp. Jake tugged his shirt back on, careful of the tape, face pale under fluorescents.

"You need food," she said.

"I'll live."

"That's not the same thing." She slung her satchel. The compass tapped once at her collarbone. "Come on. There's a place down the road. Outside seating."

His stomach growled. Isabelle arched a brow. He sighed. "Fine. But only so you won't think I'll keel over."

She let the corner of her mouth lift and pushed through the door ahead of him.

The restaurant was a squat building with peeling blue paint and a row of faded umbrellas along the dockside deck. Locals leaned on railings with plastic cups of beer; tourists in fishing shirts crowded around baskets of fried grouper. The air smelled of fryer oil, a sharp change from the metallic tang of the conservation lab.

Isabelle picked a table at the deck's edge where the mangroves thinned and Blackwater Sound spread wide as glass. Boats moved slow in the channel, wakes shimmering into nothing.

Jake took the chair opposite, shoulder stiff. He kept his back to the rail, scanning the deck, the lot, the water. Habit.

The waitress arrived with a pad and a tired smile. "How 'bout I start y'all with something to drink?" she asked, Keys-casual.

"Couple of beers?" Jake asked, glancing at Isabelle with a grin. "Feels like we earned it."

Isabelle's smile was quick but real. "Beer sounds perfect right now."

"I'll grab those and be right back to get your order," the waitress said, already moving.

A few minutes later she returned, setting two frosty bottles on the table, each with a wedge of lime tucked into the neck. Jake thumbed his wedge into the bottle; a fizz of citrus lifted.

"Now, what can I get y'all to eat?"

"Grilled yellowtail snapper," Isabelle said without hesitation.

Jake surprised her by nodding. "Same for me."

"Great choice. I'll have that out in a jiffy," she said before retreating to the kitchen.

"Didn't peg you as the grilled type," Isabelle said once the waitress left.

"Trying to be respectable," he smirked. "And I'm watching my figure."

Her laugh was quick, softer than she meant it to be. "Respectable isn't how I'd describe prying a Spanish wreck apart with one good arm."

He shifted; the grin slipped into a wince. "Fair point."

Silence stretched comfortably without snapping.

"I keep thinking about those words," Isabelle finally said. "Corsario. Tesoro. Espectro. Cartagena. And then the ciphered clusters—names, bearings, routes. If we can solve those, we'll know exactly where Grey went."

Jake leaned in on his good arm, eyes steady. "Are you ready for an adventure, Miss Alvarez?"

"Ay, Dios mío," Isabelle said with a small laugh. "An adventure with you? Not sure that would be good for my health."

Jake grinned at the jab, but it softened quickly, leaving something earnest in its place. "Maybe not. But it'll be worth the risk."

Her eyes flicked to him, searching. "Your shoulder—will it hold up if this leads somewhere?"

"Give me a few days and I'll be good as new," he said lightly, though his mouth was tight. "You patch me up, I bounce."

"You think pain is optional."

"Comes with the job."

"Jobs don't usually involve suffocating under a Spanish shipwreck."

Jake shrugged.

This time she didn't smile. "You're reckless."

"Maybe," he said. "I prefer motivated."

The plates arrived—snapper seared and flaking, rice and beans. Isabelle squeezed lemon over her fish, buying a moment.

"You weren't wrong before," she admitted. "Part of me wants to drop everything and run after the treasure, cipher and preservation be damned.

But that's the part that grew up on stories. The trained part knows better."

"So which part's winning?"

"Ask me after we finish eating."

He half-grinned. "I'll take that as progress."

They ate in the hum of conversation. After a minute, Isabelle set her fork down.

"You keep talking about your Pops," she said. "What about you?"

Jake hesitated, tipping his beer bottle toward his lips for a moment of reprieve. When he set it down, he spoke carefully.

"Not much to tell," he said. "Grew up in the Keys. Family ran a salvage outfit out of Marathon. Nothing fancy, just recovering lost cargo, sunken fishing boats, that kind of thing."

"Sounds like a childhood out of a storybook."

"The Jungle Book really. Only I had Pops and a leaky boat instead of wolves."

Her mouth curved. "That actually explains a lot."

He shrugged, but his grin softened. "My dad kept it alive as long as he could. Now it's just me, taking what jobs I can."

"And you still chose the water."

"Couldn't do anything else if I tried." Softer: "It's in the blood."

"That, I understand," Isabelle said, taking a sip of her beer. "Does your family still live on Marathon?"

"My mom and dad do, yeah," Jake replied. "But Pops died a few years back—before my dad lost the business."

Her expression softened. "I'm sorry to hear that. Sounds like he was a big part of your life."

Jake's eyes glazed, the weight of memory slipping through. "He was the best. I just... hate that I didn't spend more time with him while I had the chance."

Isabelle's hand toyed with the lemon wedge on her plate. "I know that feeling. My abuelo passed a few years ago too. He used to tell me stories—about the Muisca, about what the Spanish took from Colombia. I didn't always listen the way I should have." Her voice thinned slightly, but steadied. "Now I'd give anything to sit with him one more evening, hear those stories again."

"What was his name?" Jake asked.

"Abelardo," Isabelle said, gazing into her beer bottle, a grin tugging at her lips at the memory.

Jake raised his bottle in a quiet toast. "To Abelardo and Pops—may they never be forgotten."

Isabelle's smile softened as she lifted hers to meet his. The bottles clinked gently. "To Abelardo and Pops."

Once again, the comfortable silence stretched between them, broken only by the murmur of the deck and gulls wheeling overhead. For a moment, neither seemed eager to fill it. Finally, Jake cleared his throat and leaned in slightly.

"What about you? You're the careful one with gloves and tweezers—where's that from?"

Isabelle's expression softened, her gaze drifting briefly to the Sound. "It started with my dad. He's a professor of Latin American history—still teaches at the university. When I was a kid, he'd take me to museums and archaeological sites, explaining the stories behind everything we saw. To him, it wasn't just history—it was about understanding who we are and where we come from."

A faint smile curved her lips. "He always said I had a knack for puzzles—whether it was figuring out how old maps aligned or piecing together fragments no one else noticed. I guess that's why I love this work so much—it's like solving a story that's been waiting centuries to be told."

Jake listened, beer loose in his hand, the other resting on the table. "Sounds like he inspired you to dig deeper."

"He did," Isabelle said warmly. "He taught me to treat history with care, to respect the responsibility of uncovering the past. He'd always say, 'Preserving heritage isn't just about the objects—it's about the people who created them.' That stuck."

Jake nodded, impressed. "Makes sense. You definitely have a knack for it."

Isabelle tilted her head, a playful glint in her eyes. "Well, when your dad takes you to dig sites instead of amusement parks, you either fall in love with it... or swear it off forever. For me, it was an easy choice."

Across the deck, Luca Moretti sat at a table, his casual polo and khaki shorts blending with the bustling lunchtime crowd. A baseball cap shaded his angular face, its brim low enough to obscure the sharp intensity of his dark eyes. Clean-shaven, neat—an ordinary professional on a quick break. Unremarkable, if you didn't know where to look.

But the details told a different story. A contained stillness. The way his long fingers tapped once against his phone and then stopped. He typed a brief message—*to: Victor—They're talking. Four words mentioned: Corsario. Tesoro. Espectro. Cartagena.* He set the phone face down and picked up his drink. The friendliness he'd worn for the waitress earlier evaporated the moment she turned—like a blade sheathed and then unsheathed again. His gaze stayed fixed on Jake and Isabelle, cataloging every gesture he could lip-read across the noisy patio.

The waitress reappeared at his elbow. "Another?"

He turned with easy warmth, the mask sliding back into place. "That'd be great, thanks."

"Be right back, hon."

He nodded, letting a polite smile linger. When she moved away, the light in his eyes went cold again.

Jake pushed his plate aside, appetite dulled by fatigue. "So what's the next step?"

"Back to the lab," Isabelle said, dabbing at her mouth. "Stabilize the parchment. Build the cipher alphabet. It'll take time."

"Time we might not have."

"Better time than mistakes. You want treasure, Jake? Then you'll have to trust me on how we get there."

His grin came back, thin but real. "Guess I already do. And for the record—it's not all about the payday."

The honesty in his tone caught Isabelle off guard. She blinked once, then softened. "Good. I didn't think it really was."

Jake smiled, glad she didn't see him as just another diver looking to get rich quick. He watched her fuss with napkins. "You always this careful with lunch, too?"

"Somebody has to balance out your chaos."

"Chaos makes life interesting."

"Chaos gets you crushed under a galleon beam."

He chuckled, then shrugged with his good shoulder. "Fair. But you didn't walk away empty-handed either."

"True." Her lips curved. "Maybe we're both a little reckless in our own ways."

Jake tapped the table between them. "Then I guess that makes us even."

For a beat they held each other's gaze; the hum of the deck faded. Not a declaration—yet—but a promise of something building. Isabelle looked away first, the corners of her mouth softened.

Luca moved with practiced ease, slipping into the flow of foot traffic as if he were just another pedestrian on the bustling street. Key Largo's laid-back rhythm swallowed him whole, yet the sharp cadence of his steps betrayed a man accustomed to a deadlier pace.

He kept his distance, cap brim low, tracking Jake and Isabelle with patient economy. Every turn they took, every pause to glance around, met with his effortless invisibility. Years had taught him how to vanish in plain sight, to become scenery.

Snatches of their voices carried back—Isabelle's laugh, Jake's low reply—but he didn't need words. The way they leaned toward one another told him enough: trust was building. Dangerous for them. Useful for him.

As they neared the Maritime History Center, Luca slowed, folding into a knot of tourists snapping photos. He drew his phone from his pocket, thumbed out a brief message: *Still on them. They're heading into the center.* He slid the phone away and adjusted his cap. His face remained neutral. The knife in his pocket pressed a familiar weight against his palm as he lingered across the street, letting the pair disappear inside.

Patience wasn't his strength, but inevitability was. They would lead him where he needed to go. And when the time came, they would never see him until it was too late.

CHAPTER SEVEN

Shadows in the Cipher

T he history center was nearly empty when they returned. Afternoon heat pressed against the windows, sunlight slanting through the mangroves in thin bands. The front desk was unattended, the corridors hushed.

At the door hung a laminated placard: *CONSERVATION IN PROGRESS—LIMIT LIGHT EXPOSURE.* Under it, a typed policy: *NO PHOTOGRAPHY OF ORIGINALS IN ACTIVE TREATMENT.* Jake's jaw worked. His world measured speed and firsts; hers measured how long something could still speak after everyone was gone.

Isabelle swiped her badge, and the familiar tang of paper and wet iron met them as the lock clicked open. Inside, the room was cool and orderly, humming with the steady breath of the AC. She paused at the wall monitor, logged the room's humidity and temperature into a spiral-bound conservation log, then initialed with a tiny, practiced flourish. It wasn't ceremony—it was proof for the future that someone had cared enough to be exact. Jake watched the pen scratch and felt a pinch along his taped side—glue that pulled when he leaned—a reminder that his own work left different marks.

Jake's eyes went straight to the archival box on the far wall. The faint gleam of the mylar sleeve caught under the fluorescents, a reminder that the original parchment was sealed away.

Isabelle began laying out what she'd prepared: a copy-stand, angled lamps, a notebook, and crisp, high-resolution prints she'd captured earlier under the conservator's lights—controlled exposure, timed precisely—so the original could stay sealed. Each page caught the light, black script and symbols stark against white paper. She arranged them across the long table, reassembling the letter in duplicate, leaving the fragile original untouched in its sleeve.

Jake eased into a chair, watching her work. "So we're working from the knock-off now."

"That's the only safe way," she said, sliding on nitrile gloves out of habit. "The original's light-sensitive. Every hour it spends exposed shortens its life."

"Seems like a waste, hiding it away."

"Preserving it isn't hiding it," she said, adjusting the lamp. "It's making sure the truth lasts longer than we do."

He smirked. "Guess that was aimed at me."

"If the shoe fits."

She bent over one of the prints, already drawing a grid in her notebook. Her pencil moved in precise strokes, mapping letters against symbols. The page filled with neat rows: A–Z, each space waiting for a match.

On the photocopy, Isabelle circled clusters of geometric marks—diamonds, crosses, half-moons—threaded among elegant Spanish script. Some words were clear: *corsario, Cartagena, tesoro, idolatría*. Others broke into lines of symbols, place names and bearings locked away behind code. She pointed with her pencil. "Here. Look at this section again."

Jake leaned closer, his shadow falling across the page as she read aloud:

"*The last confirmed sighting of El Espectro places it near* ⟨◊□◊⟩, *a treacherous and remote chain of islands. This region, marked by perilous reefs and heavy fog, has long been shrouded in rumor. Navigational records describe a route from* ⟨◆□◆⟩, *westward past* ⟨△□⟩, *and continuing along a bearing of* ⟨□◊⟩. *The islands lie just beyond these landmarks, obscured by natural hazards that have deterred exploration.*"

Jake blew out a breath. "It's all right there—directions, names, the trail. Just locked up."

"Exactly." Isabelle tapped the symbols. "These clusters hide the critical information. A place name here, a landmark there, bearings and courses. That's how naval ciphers worked: leave the formal report legible, but bury the real orders where only someone with the key could read them."

Jake ran a hand through his hair, restless. "So how do you crack it without the key?"

Isabelle didn't look up immediately. She rested the tip of her pencil against the symbols, then drew a thin line down to the empty grid in her notebook.

"You don't crack it with a single trick," she said finally, voice steady. "You build the key out of small certainties and test them until the whole thing clicks. First: frequency. Symbols that repeat are rarely names—they're articles, prepositions, directions. In Spanish that gives you *de, la, el, a,* or words like *isla, norte, sotavento.* If a sign accounts for a big slice of the text, it's probably a vowel." She tapped the column of letters she'd penciled. "So you map repeats to likely common words and see what shapes the surrounding text makes."

She peeled a sheet of vellum from the pad and laid it over the print, then wrote tentative substitutions in pencil across the translucent layer. "Second: cribs. We already have plain words in the report—*corsario, Cartagena, tesoro, idolatría*—they're anchors. If a symbol cluster sits next to a known word, we can guess the grammar and narrow the options. Third: pattern matching. Look for double letters, suffixes—Spanish endings are predictable. And fourth: corroboration. Every substitution has to check against every other instance of that symbol. If one guess breaks eight other lines, it's wrong."

Her mouth thinned. "We act like a patient net—small loops, slow tightening. Tedious, exacting, but it works."

Her pencil traced the lines again, circling repeats. "See this? That diamond reappears four times. Too common for a unique name. More likely something like *isla.* And here—this triple cluster repeats in two separate bearings. Directional language, almost certainly."

Jake's jaw worked. The porch stories, Pops's smoke-drift tales of Elias Grey and *The Specter,* were no longer ghost stories. They were lines in a report, tethered to symbols waiting to be unlocked.

"You should be lying down," Isabelle said without looking at him.

"I'd rather be useful."

Her pencil scratched across the vellum. "Then how about some coffee? Strong. This might take a while."

Jake arched a brow. "So I'm your errand boy now?"

"Consider it field support," she said, still bent over the page. "I can't decipher centuries of naval code if you're sitting there breathing down my neck."

Isabelle's notebook filled line by line, then page by page. The grid stretched wider, neat rows of letters facing down clusters of symbols, empty spaces waiting to be matched. The pencil tapped in rhythm: circle, note, scratch out, write again. Each sound was steady, deliberate, like the ticking of a clock only she could hear.

Jake shifted in his chair for the fifth time. The AC hummed. Outside, somewhere beyond the mangroves, a gull screeched once, sharp and lonely. He rubbed at his shoulder, winced, then leaned forward again. "So how long before this starts making sense?"

"As long as it takes," she said, eyes never leaving the page. "Naval ciphers weren't made to be easy."

"Yeah, I'm getting that." He leaned back, legs stretched under the table, heel bouncing restlessly against the tile. "Ever think about running it through a computer?"

That earned him a sharp look. "If you want software guesses, you'll get noise. This is about patterns. Language. Discipline."

Jake smirked, unrepentant. "Just trying to move this along, that's all."

Her pencil ticked twice against the margin, then slid the page slightly toward him. "Here. Look at this cluster—diamond, cross, crescent. It repeats three times in one section. Too common to be a proper name. More likely *isla,* or *las.* That gives us a foothold."

Jake squinted, head cocked. "So it's the name of an island."

"Possibly," she said, jotting the letters lightly over the symbols on her vellum overlay. "But we test it against every instance. If it fits everywhere, we keep it. If not, it goes."

Jake scratched his chin. "Sounds like your version of salvage work. Test a line, see if it holds, then pull."

A corner of her mouth quirked, though she didn't look up. "Except the wreck doesn't fall on your head if you misread the angle."

She circled a longer string: triangle, crescent, two bars. "This feels geographic. A feature, maybe. Could be *boca*—a mouth of something."

Jake's brow lifted. "Dragon's mouth?"

Her pencil froze for a second before she jotted quickly in the margin. She didn't answer, but the rhythm of her work sharpened, faster now, more intent.

Jake grinned, leaning back like he'd scored. "Nailed it."

"Don't gloat. One potentially correct hunch doesn't make you a cryptographer."

Still, there was a light in her eyes now, a faint spark that hadn't been there before. She shifted to another section, tracing a jagged sequence of angular signs. "This one's longer. Could be a proper noun. A coastal feature—maybe cliffs, maybe stacks."

Jake tipped his chair back on two legs, smug tilt in his grin. "Just let me know when you're ready for the next answer."

Isabelle rolled her eyes, but the pencil never slowed. Scratch, circle, test. The grid was filling. Slowly, carefully, the cipher was loosening its grip.

The pencil paused mid-scratch. Isabelle leaned closer, eyes narrowing at the repeated diamond-cross cluster she'd been circling since they started. Her lips moved silently as she penciled in tentative letters above it: *las... islas.* The word grew across the page, each letter settling into place like it had been waiting.

"*Las Islas...*" she murmured. Her pencil pressed the final curve. "*...de Sombras.*"

Jake sat up straighter, the chair legs scraping the tile. The name dropped between them, heavy as an anchor. "Shadows," he said quietly. "The Islands of Shadows." His pulse thudded, quickened.

For a heartbeat Jake wasn't in the lab. He was on a back porch, the stickiness of summer on his skin, Pops tracing an imaginary coastline against the night. *Some places don't want to be found the same way twice,* Pops had said, smoke threading the air. *You have to learn how they hide before you can learn where they are.*

Isabelle's brow furrowed. "It fits the pattern too cleanly to be coincidence." Her voice was tight with certainty. "That's one landmark."

She slid her finger lower, to the jagged cluster where Jake's earlier guess had stuck in the margin. The letters she penciled in—*boca*—clicked neatly against the geometry. The rest unspooled around it, falling into place like tumblers in a lock.

"*La Boca del Dragón,*" she read aloud.

Jake leaned back with a lopsided grin, smug as a boy with a winning hand. "Told you."

Her pencil tapped faster, a betraying rhythm. She didn't look up. "Enjoy it while it lasts."

The third string—angular, stretched like a coastline itself—resisted. She muttered through endings, crossed them out, wrote again. Her eraser whispered across vellum. Jake watched her knuckles whiten where she gripped the pencil, her focus sharpening until finally the line stilled.

"*Los Farallones,*" she said.

"Cliffs," Jake echoed softly.

"Sea stacks, more precisely," Isabelle corrected, her tone clipped but charged. "Jagged rock spires. Dangerous. Sailors dreaded them."

Jake nodded slowly, letting the image build: a mouth of a dragon, a wall of rocks, and an island hidden in shadow beyond them. His grin thinned. "So Grey was steering past a dragon's mouth and a wall of jagged stone toward an island of shadows. That doesn't sound ominous at all."

A faint smile tugged at her mouth, but it didn't reach her eyes. She slid her pencil to the last short cluster near the margin—this one paired with numbers. Her movements slowed, deliberate. "This one's different. Not a name. A bearing."

She traced the figures, penciled in substitutions, then leaned back, her breath slipping out. "*Doscientos setenta y cinco grados.* Two hundred seventy-five—from the Boca."

Jake let out a low whistle. "A course. Almost due west."

The room seemed to contract around the moment. The symbols that had guarded their meaning for centuries now lay broken open in pencil and graphite. Isabelle sat up straighter, voice firmer now as she read the passage again, this time uninterrupted:

"*The last confirmed sighting of El Espectro places it near—Las Islas de Sombras—a treacherous and remote chain of islands. This region, marked by perilous reefs and heavy fog, has long been shrouded in rumor. Navigational records describe a route from—La Boca del Dragón—westward past—Los Farallones—and continuing along a bearing of two hundred seventy-five degrees from the Boca. The islands lie just beyond these landmarks, obscured by natural hazards that have deterred exploration.*"

For a long moment neither spoke. The words hung in the air—shadows, a dragon's mouth, stone cliffs, and a westward course. A trail as sharp and undeniable as a line on a chart.

Isabelle exhaled slowly. Her professional calm wavered, heat rising in her eyes. "They recorded exactly where he went."

Jake leaned closer, his voice rough, carried on equal parts triumph and unease. "And Grey wasn't just a story."

But Isabelle's eyes lingered not on the decoded landmarks, but on the word scrawled earlier in the plain text: *idolatría.*

"They weren't chasing treasure," she said quietly, almost to herself. "They were chasing something they feared."

Jake frowned. "Feared?"

She nodded, her finger hovering over the word. "The Spanish used *idolatría* for anything sacred they wanted to strip from the people they conquered—idols, relics, objects that carried power, even if they didn't understand it." Her voice thinned. "My *abuelo* used to tell me stories about Siecaza—the Dwelling of Sacred Stone. He said the Spanish stole it from the Muisca, and that it cursed anyone who tried to carry it away. Hearing it called *idolatría* here...it's like watching them take it all over again."

Jake studied her, seeing the careful maritime archaeologist give way to the Colombian woman beneath. "That must be tough."

She nodded once, but didn't answer, eyes still fixed on the page.

Jake shifted in his chair, the ache in his shoulder flaring. He covered it with his hand, jaw tight.

Isabelle caught the motion instantly. "You should stop before you tear that open again."

"I'm fine."

"You're not," she said, tone gentler now. "You've been wincing for the last hour."

He gave a short laugh, more self-deprecating than amused. "Old habit. Hide the pain, keep moving."

Her eyes softened, but she didn't look away. "You don't have to burn yourself down to prove something."

"Feels like I do," he muttered, then shook his head. "But maybe not to you."

For a beat, the hum of the AC filled the space between them. Isabelle reached for her notebook, but her hand lingered against the paper before she spoke.

"My *abuelo* used to say, *La memoria es un hilo humano que no se corta.* Memory is a human thread that doesn't break. Even when things are stolen or hidden, the truth finds a way to surface again.

That's why I do this. Not just for history, but for what was lost—and for who lost it."

Jake studied her, struck by the quiet fire in her voice. "That's a better reason than gold."

Her mouth curved, faint but real. "Maybe. But gold helps keep the lights on."

He chuckled, and for a moment the weight of the cipher lifted—leaving just the two of them, the parchment between them, and a trail that stretched west into shadow.

The photocopy lay between them, the once-impenetrable symbols now scrawled over with penciled words: *Islas de Sombras. Boca del Dragón. Farallones. 275°.*

Jake tapped the margin with his good hand. "Alright, we've got the trail. So where the hell are these places? *Sombras, Dragon's Mouth, Farallones*—none of those show up on any chart I've seen."

"They wouldn't," Isabelle said, tucking a loose strand of hair behind her ear. "Some are old names, colonial descriptions. Pilot books loved metaphors—dragon mouths, shadowed islands, *farallón* spires—while charts quietly renamed them. That's why we need references." She leaned back, stretching her hand across the notebook full of substitutions. "FIU—Florida International University—has an archive: colonial pilot books, old *cartas náuticas,* shipping ledgers. If these names appear anywhere, it'll be there."

Jake gave a dry laugh. "So, homework."

"Research," she corrected firmly. "If Grey's pursuers wrote this, then the Spanish Navy was mapping those waters. The archive will have the records."

He tilted his head, weighing it. "And if it doesn't?"

"Then we start cross-referencing accounts, logs, even missionary reports. There are threads everywhere—you just have to know where to pull."

Jake's gaze went back to the words on the page, his jaw tightening. "So we're chasing shadows with paperwork."

Her eyes softened, though her tone stayed steady. "Sometimes shadows are all that's left. But they can still lead you forward."

Isabelle rolled up the photocopy and slid it into her satchel. The original parchment remained sealed in its mylar sleeve, resting in the archival box like a casket. A second photocopy she handed across the table to Jake.

"Just in case you feel like some late-night studying," she said with a quick grin.

Jake tucked it into his duffel bag, shaking his head. "Don't hold your breath. But...thanks."

Her smile softened as she leaned back, her tone quieter now, steady with conviction. "The truth will come. But we can't force it. We'll take what we've found to Miami. The FIU archive will give us what the letter can't."

She leaned back, a grin slipping through. "I'm teaching my Advanced Maritime Archaeology class tomorrow afternoon. Why don't you meet me afterward? I can show you the archives, and we can dive back in—figuratively speaking, of course."

Jake smirked, catching her playful tone. "Figuratively, huh? Just making sure I'm not signing up to lug heavy artifacts around."

"Not unless you're volunteering," Isabelle quipped. Then her voice steadied, her passion unmistakable. "But seriously, the archives have maps, logs, old ship manifests. If there's any chance of pinpointing the route from this letter, it'll be there."

Jake nodded, determination kindling again. "Alright. I'll see you there."

Her expression softened. "Good. Just promise me one thing, Jake."

"What's that?"

"Don't underestimate what we're dealing with. This isn't just about artifacts or even treasure. It's about voices silenced for centuries, cultures erased by greed and conquest. Every piece we uncover is a thread to someone's truth. If we can bring even a fragment of that back...that's worth risking everything for."

Jake held her gaze, the weight of her words pressing on him. "I hear you," he said quietly. Then, with a faint smirk: "See you tomorrow, Professor Alvarez."

Her laugh was quick, genuine. "You better not be late, Morgan." The playfulness lingered only a moment before fading to sincerity. "And Jake...thanks. For trusting me."

He hesitated, his faint smile faltering. "Thanks for trusting me too." The quiet vulnerability in his tone betrayed the confidence he usually carried.

She offered a warm smile, tinged with understanding. "See you tomorrow."

Jake slung his duffel bag over his shoulder and paused at the doorway. His hand lingered on the frame before he looked back. "We'll figure this out. Together."

Her lips curved into a resolute smile. "Together."

For a fleeting moment, the air felt heavier, charged with the gravity of their shared path. Then Jake nodded and stepped out into the hallway toward the exit.

Outside, Jake climbed into the Land Cruiser, gripping the wheel as the engine rumbled to life. Trust wasn't just a risk—it was a weight he'd buried with mistakes he couldn't undo. Letting someone in again meant gambling on himself, and failure carried a cost he wasn't sure he could pay twice.

But Isabelle was different. She wasn't asking for blind faith—she was earning it, piece by piece. And for the first time in years, Jake felt the certainty that maybe, just maybe, he wasn't in this alone.

"Together," he muttered, testing the word as he pulled onto US-1. The fading light stretched long shadows across the road.

A squall rolled off the bay as Jake crossed the bridge onto Islamorada, the first fat drops ticking the windshield before the sky opened. Wipers beat a steady rhythm; the highway turned to a slick ribbon. Sodium lamps smeared the wet asphalt; spray ghosted off the median.

Two white eyes hung back in the rearview—unhurried, patient. Predators knew how to stay concealed.

As the Land Cruiser rolled down the highway, Luca eased back in the driver's seat of the black sedan, eyes fixed on the taillights ahead. A crumpled paper bag from a food truck sat on the passenger seat, the smell of fried empanadas mixing with leather and engine oil.

He unwrapped one, bit cleanly, and chewed without hurry. He pinched the crimped seam flat with neat, practiced pressure. His gaze never left the road. The wait was always the hardest part—the slow crawl of time while his targets moved, unaware of the net tightening around them.

The phone buzzed once on the console. Luca didn't check it. Serrano could wait. His focus stayed on the chase, on the rhythm of distance and speed, on the steady pulse of the tail.

A few crumbs fell across his lap. He brushed them away, the movement casual, almost careless. To anyone watching, he might look like just another man heading home from work, eating on the drive.

But Luca wasn't ordinary. The food was fuel, nothing more. His real appetite was fixed on the truck ahead.

As Jake turned onto a darker stretch of highway, Luca's lips curved in the faintest smile. "Let's see where this leads, Morgan," he murmured. The empty bag crumpled in his fist and hit the floorboard as his other hand tightened on the wheel. The next move was coming, and he'd be ready.

CHAPTER EIGHT

Tracing Forgotten Paths

J ake gripped the wheel of his Land Cruiser, jaw tight as he weaved through Miami's relentless traffic. The city's chaos was a far cry from the slow rhythm of the Keys, but there was no avoiding it today. He exhaled sharply and glanced at Isabelle's handwritten directions on the seat beside him. Her precise script stood out against the clutter of his dashboard—a clear guide in a place that felt anything but familiar.

Turning off US 1, the urban sprawl melted into the greener, quieter landscape of the Biscayne Bay Campus of Florida International University. Rows of trees framed the entrance, campus buildings peeking out among expanses of grass and clusters of palms, the water nearby catching the afternoon light.

Jake eased into a lot crowded with polished sedans and glossy SUVs, his Land Cruiser's battered frame sticking out like a relic from another life. Across the rows he spotted Isabelle's dark blue CR-V tucked neatly between two compacts, its paint catching the sun. He killed the engine, slung his satchel over one shoulder, and stepped into the current of purposeful students streaming past—heads down, strides brisk. Their easy momentum only sharpened his sense of being out of place.

"Academic Center 1, room 201," he muttered, scanning the signs and adjusting his stride to match the flow of the crowd.

Posters for archaeology lectures and cultural workshops lined the walkways, the campus alive with activity.

Jake paused at a flyer listing Isabelle's name for a lecture on trade routes, smirking. "Of course."

Finding the correct building, Jake climbed the stairs to the second floor. The hallway outside room 201 was quieter, lined with flyers and announcements fluttering faintly in the draft from an open window. Isabelle's voice carried through the door, clear and confident, rising above the hum of a projector and the quiet clatter of laptop keys.

Jake hesitated for a moment, then slipped inside quietly, leaning against the back wall. The faint scent of dry-erase markers and worn books filled the air, mingling with the muffled rustle of students shifting in their seats.

His eyes immediately found Isabelle at the front of the lecture hall. She wore a tailored green blouse that complemented her warm complexion, slim khaki chinos, and white flats. Her wavy hair was pulled back into a ponytail, though a few loose strands framed her face as she gestured toward the projector screen, its buzz barely audible over her words.

Jake couldn't help but admire the way she commanded the room. Her gestures were fluid, each movement deliberate yet natural, as if her enthusiasm guided every word. Students leaned forward, scribbling notes or nodding along, captivated by her passion. She wasn't just sharp—she was magnetic, completely in her element.

"...and this is why context is crucial in maritime archaeology," Isabelle was saying. Her voice carried a melodic rhythm that matched the quiet tapping of keys on laptops. "A single artifact pulled from a wreck doesn't just tell us what was on board. It tells us about trade routes, cultural exchanges, and even the personal lives of the people who sailed those ships. For example..." She gestured to a slide showing a worn clay jar. "This amphora, recovered from a wreck off the coast of Italy, contained traces of olive oil. But when we analyzed residue from its interior, we found something surprising—cardamom and turmeric."

She paused, scanning the room as students scribbled notes. "Now, think about that. Cardamom and turmeric aren't native to Europe—they're from South Asia. This single amphora is proof that spices from India were making their way into Mediterranean trade centuries earlier than previously documented. What does that tell us?"

A student near the front raised a hand. "That it was part of a trade route?"

"Exactly," Isabelle said, her face lighting up. "It's not just an artifact. It's a tangible connection between distant cultures. It shows how ideas and goods traveled, and how interconnected the ancient world truly was."

Jake leaned back, watching her with newfound appreciation. She wasn't just good at what she did—she was exceptional. The students hung on her every word, and Jake couldn't help but feel the same. There was something in the way she spoke about artifacts as if they were living things, each holding a story waiting to be uncovered. It reminded him of the sea—how every wreck he dove told its own tale of adventure, loss, or survival. Isabelle saw the past the way he saw the ocean: vast, mysterious, and worth chasing.

After a few more minutes, Isabelle glanced at the clock. "Alright, that's all for today. Don't forget to email me your proposals for the research project by Friday. And remember, context is everything!"

As the students packed up, Jake waited until the room had mostly emptied before making his way to the front.

Isabelle noticed him and smiled warmly.

"Hey," she greeted, slinging her bag over her shoulder. "You found it okay?"

Jake chuckled. "Let's just say I don't think I'm cut out for college life. But your class? That was something else."

Isabelle raised an eyebrow. "Something else? Is that a compliment or a critique?"

Jake smirked. "Definitely a compliment. You've got a way of making this stuff feel real—like it matters."

Isabelle's smile softened. "Because it does matter. History's not just about the past—it's about how we understand ourselves. I'm glad that came through."

Jake nodded, his respect for her deepening. "Ready to dive into some old maps and charts?"

Isabelle grinned, motioning for him to follow. "The archives are just across campus. Let's see if we can figure out where Grey was hiding."

"Alright, Professor," Jake said, a faint smirk playing on his lips. "Lead the way."

As they walked out into the Florida heat, Jake found his steps lighter than they'd been in weeks. Together, they were piecing together something big, and for the first time in a long while, Jake felt like he wasn't walking the trail alone.

Luca leaned against the hood of his black sedan, a cigarette balanced between his fingers. The Florida heat pressed down, making the asphalt shimmer, but he appeared unbothered. A pair of sunglasses and a worn baseball cap shaded his face, giving him an air of anonymity. He had dressed the part today—khaki shorts and a lightweight button-up shirt—a deliberate choice to blend into the casual campus atmosphere.

His gaze followed a pair of twenty-something students strolling past, their laughter carrying on the breeze. One glanced in his direction, her smile lingering before she turned to whisper to her friend. Luca returned the smile with ease, tilting his head just enough to sell the charm.

"Maybe next time, honey..." he murmured, voice laced with wry amusement. The cigarette burned low; with a flick of his fingers, he sent the butt skittering across the pavement.

His phone vibrated in his pocket, and he retrieved it with a fluid motion, glancing at the screen. A single message from Victor: *Report status.*

Luca smirked faintly, typing a quick reply: They're meeting at the archaeologist's school. Could take a while.

He slipped the phone back into his pocket, scanning the courtyard for signs of activity.

He had been waiting fifteen minutes now, patience wearing thin. Jake had entered the academic building, and while Luca had considered grabbing a coffee or another bite to eat, he stayed rooted near his car.

The rhythm of his waiting broke when he caught movement out of the corner of his eye. Across the grassy courtyard, Jake and Isabelle emerged from the building, walking side by side with a determined stride.

Time to move. Luca straightened, brushing a faint streak of ash off his shirt before adjusting the strap of a simple messenger bag he carried today. Without missing a beat, he began to follow, movements casual but deliberate. He slotted himself into the ebb and flow of campus life, just another person on a mission in the midday sun.

The archives of the Maritime Studies department at Florida International University were a haven for scholars but felt daunting to Jake. Shelves loomed high, stacked with leather-bound books, brittle maps, and ancient ship logs, all surrounded by an air of hushed reverence. Jake shifted in his seat at a large oak table, feeling more like an intruder than a researcher. He wouldn't have been surprised if someone had said, Hey, what are you doing here? he thought.

Isabelle unrolled a large, brittle map of 18th-century Spanish trade routes across the oak table. The parchment unfurled with a soft crackle, its edges frayed and yellowed from centuries of exposure. Faded ink bled into faint stains where water had once seeped into the fibers, leaving pale brown halos around long-forgotten smudges.

"Take a look at this," she said, smoothing the surface with delicate hands to avoid tearing the fragile material.

The faint scent of aged paper rose as she leaned closer, her focus sharpening. Jake stepped up beside her, his shoulder brushing hers as he peered down at the intricate details. A dull tug in his upper arm reminded him to shift his weight; he rolled his shoulder once, quietly, before leaning in again.

The map's inked lines, faded but still legible, snaked across the page, marking trade routes that once thrived under Spanish dominance. Thin annotations in an elegant, slanted hand—likely a navigator's—were scrawled beside symbols of reefs and islands. The ink shifted from black to rusty brown in places, evidence of the map's age. Tiny holes dotted the corners where pins had once anchored it to a ship's chart table.

"Primary Spanish trade routes came across the Atlantic from Spain," Isabelle began, tracing one of the boldest lines with her fingertip, careful not to press too hard. "They followed the northern coasts of the Dominican Republic and Cuba to Havana." Her finger paused at the southern edge of the map, where the lines branched into thinner, less-traveled routes. "But some came down here—just off the coast of Venezuela and Colombia. These routes were essential for bringing supplies from Spain to the colonies and, more importantly, for transporting gold and silver mined in this region back to Havana before the final journey to Spain."

Jake leaned in closer, studying the faint, looping routes etched onto the map. "Like the La Fortuna," he said, glancing at Isabelle for confirmation.

"Exactly." Isabelle's eyes lit as she pointed at him. "The La Fortuna was almost certainly part of one of these southern trade convoys, traveling from Cartagena to Havana. That was one of the main routes for transporting gold, silver, and other resources mined in South America."

"So, what else do we know?" Jake asked, his tone thoughtful as he traced the path with his finger.

Isabelle reached for a paperweight, her enthusiasm evident. "First, we know from historical accounts that Elias Grey attacked La Fortuna somewhere between Cartagena and Havana—roughly here," she said, placing the weight on the map about halfway along the route.

"Then we have La Boca del Dragón and Los Farallones from the letter," Jake said, brow furrowing. "But we don't know where they are."

"That's true," Isabelle replied, flipping through her notes. "But the Spanish Navy apparently did, so we'll need to search their logbooks or navigational charts for any references."

Jake leaned over the map, tracing a path with his finger. "Grey wouldn't waste time after hitting La Fortuna. He'd want to vanish fast, which means his destination had to be within a few days' sail."

Isabelle nodded, tone focused. "The Specter was a brigantine—faster than a galleon, averaging six to eight knots. He could've covered three hundred fifty to four hundred fifty nautical miles in good conditions."

Jake's finger paused near the Venezuelan coast. "That puts him around here," he said, frowning. "But this area's close to a major trade route."

"Too risky," Isabelle agreed, leaning closer. "He'd have steered clear of well-traveled waters. Captains would avoid places like La Boca del Dragón or Los Farallones—dangerous, remote, practically uncharted."

Jake nodded, gaze sharpening. "Perfect for someone who didn't want to be followed."

He leaned back slightly, mind working through the possibilities. "So we're looking for references to those names—or anything describing reefs, fog, or other hazards in this area."

"Exactly," Isabelle said with a small grin. "And with luck, the Spanish logs might give us just enough to pinpoint where Grey was heading."

Jake leaned over the map, finger tracing the southern trade route. "Alright, so we're looking for logs from the southern convoys. What's our best bet—Havana or Cartagena?"

"Cartagena, without a doubt," Isabelle replied, tapping the map near the Colombian coast. "Havana was the final stop for nearly every Spanish convoy before heading back to Spain. It's the obvious choice for the Navy's main records, but that also makes it an overwhelming pile to sift through."

Jake straightened, brow furrowed. "But wouldn't they also mark them on their charts?"

Isabelle tilted her head, considering. "Not necessarily. If these islands were remote or especially dangerous, they might not have been consistently recorded on maps, especially if they were only relevant to certain routes. That's why logs and personal accounts are so valuable. Captains often recorded hazards or landmarks that weren't common knowledge—or that they learned the hard way."

Jake smirked faintly. "So, we're chasing the captain's scribbles."

"Exactly," Isabelle said, grin widening. "And if we're lucky, those scribbles might give us exactly what we need."

"Sounds like we have a bit of reading ahead of us," Jake said with a wry grin, leaning back in his chair.

"Hope you're ready to brush up on your Spanish," Isabelle teased, eyes sparkling. "Most of these logs are written in eighteenth-century naval script—beautiful, but a nightmare to decipher."

Jake chuckled. "Great. Just what I needed—an extra layer of mystery."

Isabelle reached for a stack of logbooks, her expression growing more serious. "Mystery's part of the fun, Jake. And if these logs get us closer to Las Islas de Sombras, it'll be worth it."

Jake watched as she opened the first book, his admiration flickering at her determination. "Alright, Professor. Let's find some scribbles worth chasing."

Luca lingered in the shadow of the Marine Sciences building, movements unhurried but deliberate. The archive reading room sat at street level with a broad, slightly reflective window; he angled himself to one side, letting the shade and his polarized lenses kill the glare. He'd already scanned the perimeter twice, checking for cameras or curious onlookers. The campus was quiet—a stark contrast to the intensity of his task.

Through the glass, Luca spotted Jake and Isabelle poring over an old map. Their heads were close together, their focus absolute. Jake gestured to a particular section, finger tracing the route, while Isabelle nodded, flipping through a set of notes. Luca's pulse quickened. Whatever they were working on, it wasn't idle curiosity. This was a lead.

He pulled out his phone, tilting it to catch a clear angle on the table. A few quick snaps captured the map and the faint lines Jake had been pointing to. The curved coastlines and scattered annotations hinted at something significant—maybe a hidden route or uncharted location. He zoomed in for a clearer view, the lens locking on a cluster of jagged markings that could have been islands.

"Got you," he muttered, smirk returning.

As Luca reviewed the images, his phone buzzed again. Another message from Victor: *Secure intel. Report back ASAP.*

Luca sighed, slipping the phone into his pocket. He didn't like being rushed. This kind of work required finesse. Victor could wait—if Jake and Isabelle were onto something big, there'd be time to exploit it.

Just as he pocketed his phone, Jake leaned back in his chair and glanced toward the window. Their eyes locked.

Luca didn't flinch. He held Jake's gaze, expression calm and neutral. No tension, no panic. Just the faintest hint of disinterest, as though his mind were a thousand miles away. After three beats, Luca shifted his focus to the bay, lifting his phone as if capturing another scenic shot. No sudden movements. No tells.

When he looked back, Jake's attention had returned to Isabelle and the map. Luca allowed himself a small exhale. Time to move.

"Something wrong, Jake?" Isabelle asked, looking up from the logbook she'd been flipping through, concern edging her voice.

Jake's brow furrowed as he leaned back, gaze flicking toward the window. "I don't know... there's a guy sitting out there who was looking at me. He looks familiar."

Isabelle's eyes sharpened. "Do you think he's watching us?"

Jake's voice dropped, calm but deliberate. "Maybe. Don't turn around. Come around here and act like you're checking something over my shoulder."

Isabelle rose slowly, movements measured. She circled the table, steps casual, before leaning over Jake's shoulder. Her hair brushed his neck, a soft floral scent enveloping him, and he felt the faint warmth of her presence as she leaned close.

"Right here?" she asked, pretending to focus on the logbook in front of him.

For a moment, he didn't answer—distracted by her. "Uh... yeah," Jake murmured. "Just glance out the window."

Isabelle's eyes flicked toward the bench outside, her gaze darting to the man for only a heartbeat before returning to the page. Her voice stayed low. "He looks familiar to me too, but I can't place him. Maybe he just has one of those faces?"

Jake wasn't convinced. His jaw tightened as he met Isabelle's gaze. "Or maybe he's following us."

Isabelle's brow knit, unease tightening her expression. "You really think so?"

Jake hesitated, instincts nagging. "I don't know yet. I'll be right back."

Before Isabelle could protest, Jake pushed his chair back, his boots clopping softly against the polished floor as he crossed the hall. A pinch in his shoulder made him adjust his swing as he reached the door; he pressed it open and stepped into the muggy heat of the afternoon.

His gaze locked on the bench where the man had been sitting—but it was empty.

Jake's chest tightened. His eyes swept the courtyard, scanning every potential hiding spot—the clusters of palms, the shaded alcoves by the entrances, even the distant cars in the lot. Nothing. The gentle rustle of fronds and the faint hum of passing students did little to mask the rise of tension in his chest.

He strode toward the bench, jaw tight, searching for any sign of where the man had gone. A cigarette butt lay smoldering on the concrete nearby, a faint tendril of smoke curling upward—fresh enough to confirm Jake wasn't imagining things. His eyes darted toward the main walkway, but the crowds offered too many possibilities.

"Damn it," Jake muttered, frustration bubbling over as he raked a hand through his hair. Whoever the guy was, he hadn't just wandered off. He'd slipped away, deliberately and with purpose.

Luca sank back into the shadows of his car, the tinted windows cloaking him from the bustle of campus life. His sharp eyes followed Jake's every movement, noting how his gaze lingered on the empty bench. A slow, predatory smirk curled at Luca's lips. He was a hunter, and Jake was unwittingly leaving him a trail.

His fingers tapped idly on the steering wheel, the rhythmic beat matching the thrum of his pulse. The engine was off, the interior silent except for the faint creak of leather as he shifted. Outside, the world moved on, oblivious. A group of students strolled past on the sidewalk, their laughter carrying faintly through the glass. Luca didn't spare them a glance. His focus remained locked on Jake.

A smirk spread as he watched Jake scratch his head and glance around one last time before turning back inside.

Luca retrieved his phone and scrolled through the photos he'd taken. The jagged lines of the map became clearer with every glance—a cluster of islands marked with faded script. He zoomed in, scrutinizing the details, a smirk tugging at his lips. This wasn't just a vague clue—they were narrowing in on something big. He tapped the phone lightly against his palm, weighing his next move. Should he let Serrano call the shots, or was this an opportunity to seize the advantage for himself? Either way, this information had power, and Luca knew exactly how to leverage it. Timing, as always, would be everything.

He connected his phone to the car's Bluetooth and dialed. The line clicked, and a low, authoritative voice answered: "Report."

"They've got something," Luca said evenly, voice calm but charged with purpose. "A map, old trade routes—potentially a location in the southern Caribbean."

A weighted silence hung over the line before Victor Serrano's unmistakable growl cut through. "And you're certain it's worth my time?"

Luca's smirk flickered. "You don't pay me to make that call, Serrano. You pay me to find the pieces. If you want my opinion, whatever they're chasing, it's not a wild goose."

Victor's tone sharpened, steel beneath controlled anger. "Opinion noted. Stay on them. I want specifics—coordinates, dates, anything that gets us ahead."

"Understood." Luca's response was clipped, professional. "I'll have something for you soon."

The call ended abruptly, the line going dead with a finality that left no room for missteps. Luca leaned back, the smirk sliding from his lips as his gaze shifted to the reflective glass of the archives building. The stakes were rising. He could feel it, a taut string pulling tighter with every passing moment.

That was how he liked it. A hunt without pressure wasn't worth chasing.

When Jake returned to the archives, Isabelle was waiting near the table, arms crossed, her face etched with a mix of worry and curiosity. "Well?" she asked as soon as he stepped inside.

"He's gone," Jake said, voice clipped and tense as he leaned against the edge of the table. His eyes narrowed, tone sharpening. "But that wasn't just some guy taking a stroll. Whoever he is, he knew what he was doing."

Isabelle's brows knit as she processed his words. "What should we do?" she asked, concern edging toward fear.

Jake met her eyes, voice softening as he tried to reassure her. "I'm not sure yet, but let's be careful. Keep an eye out, and if we see his face again, we'll deal with it then." He offered a small, lopsided smile, trying to defuse the tension. "So, found anything yet?"

Isabelle exhaled, shoulders relaxing as she pulled the open logbook closer. "Actually, yes," she said, tone regaining focus. "Listen to this."

She flipped to a marked page, finger tracing the neat, slanted script of an 18th-century Spanish captain. Clearing her throat, she read aloud:

"Día 14 del mes de marzo del año de Nuestro Señor 1716. Today we passed near La Boca del Dragón, a treacherous channel infamous among our fleet. The waters churn with unpredictable currents, and a dense fog lingers, swallowing the horizon even under the midday sun. It is said that beneath its surface, sharp rocks rise like the teeth of a beast, waiting to rend the hulls of unwary ships. My men whisper of curses and specters, but I believe it is the unpredictable nature of these waters that has earned its dark reputation. We adjusted our course to avoid the worst of it."

Jake leaned closer, interest piqued. "Sounds charming."

Isabelle nodded, flipping the page to continue.

"We then passed Los Farallones, a jagged cluster of islets rising abruptly from the sea. Barely more than bare rock, their presence is as much a warning as a landmark. Many a ship has met its fate on those cliffs, their remains

claimed by the relentless waves. Few dare to linger here, for the winds howl with such ferocity that they can strip sails and shatter masts. This is no place for salvation, only survival."

Isabelle paused, voice trailing off. She glanced at Jake. "If Grey wanted to vanish, he couldn't have picked a better place. Between the fog, the currents, and the reefs, no one would come looking unless they absolutely had to."

Jake rubbed his chin thoughtfully. "Does he give any other reference to his position? Something we can use to place him on modern maps?"

Isabelle flipped back to an earlier section of the log, eyes scanning quickly. "Wait," she said, finger tracing a line. "He mentions passing Barbados. Listen to this."

She cleared her throat and read aloud:

"Día 12 del mes de marzo del año de Nuestro Señor 1716. As the first light of dawn broke over the horizon, the island of Barbados emerged from the mist, its rugged cliffs lit by the morning sun. The sight brought a momentary reprieve to the weary crew, their spirits lifted by the familiarity of its shores. Yet, the joy was fleeting; whispers of the perilous waters ahead tempered their relief. By mid-afternoon, we skirted the northern reefs, the sea churning against hidden shoals that could splinter a hull in moments. Adjusting our course westward, we sailed toward La Boca del Dragón, a place the men regard with hushed dread, for its reputation is as dark as the depths themselves."

Jake straightened, leaning over the table. "So, if they passed Barbados on March 12 and reached La Boca del Dragón two days later..."

"They would've been sailing southwest, following the trade route," Isabelle interjected, grabbing a modern map. "At a speed of four to six knots, they could've traveled roughly..."

"Two hundred forty nautical miles," Jake answered as Isabelle set the map in front of them and hovered over it.

"It would put them here, near these waters." Isabelle's finger hovered over the straits between Venezuela and Trinidad and Tobago. Her eyes lit. "It makes sense. The currents there are notorious, and the fog would've made it nearly impossible to navigate without intimate knowledge of the waters."

Jake leaned in, tapping another point on the map. "Right, and if they passed Los Farallones on the same day, it has to be close—maybe another fifty nautical miles west at most." His finger slid off the Venezuelan coast, tracing with precision. "Here," he said, hovering over a small rocky island. "Now we just need to plot our course, Captain," he added, flashing a jovial grin at Isabelle.

Glowing with the moment, Isabelle leaned over the map with a protractor and a ruler in hand. "I assume you know how to use these since you're such a seasoned man of the sea," she teased, playful skepticism in her voice.

Jake feigned insult, clutching his chest theatrically. "I'm wounded, Professor. Of course I know how to use them." He took the tools with a mock flourish, grin widening. "Now, let's see. A bearing of two hundred seventy-five degrees..."

He aligned the ruler with the angle on the protractor, movements smooth and practiced. Isabelle watched him work, a small smile tugging at her lips. "Looks like someone paid attention in navigation class."

"More like trial and error. Mostly error," Jake said, drawing a straight line across the map, his pencil stopping as it intersected a cluster of small islands. For a moment, he stared at the spot, the faint shadow of a smile fading as the weight of it settled.

"Las Islas de Sombras," he said quietly, circling the area with deliberate care. His voice carried no bravado now, only the reverence of someone stepping closer to stories he'd grown up chasing. His thoughts tugged back to nights on the dock with Pops, listening to tales of Elias Grey and Silas Morgan.

"Jake?" Isabelle's voice cut through, soft but curious.

Jake leaned back, exhaling slowly. "I've heard tales about Grey so many times, like they were some kind of myth. I can't believe it was all true." He glanced at her, eyes bright but thoughtful. "Guess I never really believed it until now."

Isabelle smiled, excitement tempered by his introspection. "It's not just a story anymore. This map, the letter... it's proof."

She leaned over the table, fingers lightly tracing the path Jake had marked. Her enthusiasm returned, now carrying a deeper sense of fulfillment. "This is why I do this. History isn't just a collection of stories—it's out there, waiting to be uncovered. And right now, we're standing at the edge of something incredible, and the possibility of returning one of the Muisca's most sacred idols."

Jake watched her, a faint smile tugging at his lips as her words resonated.

"You really have a way of making this all come alive."

Her laughter was soft, eyes bright with excitement. "I'm glad you decided to share this with me."

"Me too," Jake said, voice quieter, his smile warm as it met hers.

For a moment, the room seemed to hold its breath. The weight of their discovery settled between them, unspoken but deeply felt. For Jake, it was purpose and a tangible connection to his past—a bridge between legends he'd chased and the reality unfolding. For Isabelle, it was validation—a chance to right a wrong for her people, to rewrite a forgotten chapter of history and bring it into the light.

Jake's gaze lingered on the map, confidence evident. "First step's done. Now comes the fun part."

"By fun, do you mean drafting a proposal, securing funding, and submitting applications for permits?" Isabelle asked, raising an eyebrow with a faint, knowing smile.

Jake's exhilaration deflated almost instantly. "A proposal? Permits?" He stared at her, incredulous. "How long is that going to take? Six months? A year?" His voice rose with frustration as he pushed his chair back and began pacing. "If that guy really is following us, it'll be gone long before then."

Isabelle straightened, her smile fading. "I thought we agreed we'd do this the right way," she said, tone measured but firm.

"I thought you meant documenting everything. Not putting out a damn press release!" His voice was sharp but wavered with the weight of his own fear. "If someone else isn't already on this, they will be as soon as we go public."

"This isn't about publicity, Jake. It's about accountability," Isabelle countered, voice tightening. "You don't bulldoze your way through history because you're in a hurry. We do this the wrong way and we could jeopardize everything we've worked for."

"And if we wait, we risk losing it anyway! You saw that guy—he wasn't just some passerby. Someone else is already watching us."

Isabelle's jaw set. "Then don't make me clean up your mistakes later."

Jake froze, chest heaving, the line landing with quiet force. For a heartbeat it looked like he might relent. Then he slung his satchel over his shoulder, his movements abrupt and final. "I appreciate everything you've done, Isabelle," he said, voice cold and clipped. "But I can't afford to wait.

I'm sorry."

"Jake, wait—" Her voice caught, but the door had already swung shut behind him. The echo of his footsteps faded, leaving her in the heavy silence of the room.

For a long moment, she didn't move, the quiet settling heavily around her. She stared at the scattered maps and notes, her chest tight with frustration and something deeper—an ache she couldn't quite name.

"This isn't just your fight, Jake," she whispered to the empty room, her voice trembling slightly. "It's ours."

She sank into her chair, hands gripping the edge of the table as her mind raced.

She replayed the argument, searching for the words she could've said differently, the moment she could've reached him before he shut her out. But the harder she searched, the hollower it felt.

Her gaze drifted to the map Jake had circled. Las Islas de Sombras. It wasn't just a name anymore—it was a destination; a piece of her culture thought lost to the sea she might be able to return. And she wasn't about to let it slip away.

With a deep breath, Isabelle straightened, determination hardening her expression. "I'll figure this out. With or without you, Jake."

Jake yanked open the door to his Land Cruiser, his movements sharp and deliberate. He tossed his satchel onto the passenger seat, the thud echoing in the stillness. Sliding into the driver's seat, he slammed the door, gripping the wheel so tightly his knuckles turned white. "Way to go, Jake," he muttered bitterly, voice low and full of self-loathing.

Leaning back, he stared at the headliner, exhaling a shaky breath. "One look at a smart, beautiful woman, and you almost throw this whole damn thing away." The words lingered, hollow and sharp in the quiet cab.

Jake's gaze drifted to the satchel, its frayed edges a reflection of his own fraying resolve. "I can't lose this opportunity," he murmured, heavy with desperation. "It's my only chance to make things right." Memories of his father's quiet disappointment crept in—of the business he'd left behind, of broken promises and unspoken regret.

He'd failed too many times before. He couldn't afford to fail again. "Grey's trail isn't going to wait for permits and paperwork," Jake growled, shoving the key into the ignition. The engine sputtered to life, its familiar rumble grounding him, if only for a moment.

He leaned forward, resting his forehead against the wheel as the weight of his decision pressed down on him. "I'm sorry, Isabelle," he muttered. "But I've got to do this my way."

Straightening, Jake gripped the wheel with renewed determination. The truck lurched into motion, pulling out of the parking lot and onto the darkening road. His jaw was set, the map's coordinates etched into his mind like a lifeline.

The past wasn't going to fix itself, and neither was his future. But as the headlights cut through the night, Jake couldn't shake the gnawing sense that he'd just left behind something—or someone—he might need more than he realized.

CHAPTER NINE

Calculated Risks

L uca sipped his coffee as he trailed Jake's Toyota south along the Overseas Highway, the faint hum of his engine the only sound in the night. The road cut a thin silver slash over dark water, guardrails winking in his headlights. Beyond lay endless black ocean, broken only by the blink of a buoy or the ghost of a mangrove clump.

The steady pace left too much room to think. Whatever Jake and Isabelle were chasing, it wasn't trivial. They'd met at the auction, circled back at the history center, then buried themselves in maps of the southern Caribbean. That gave Luca direction—but not proof. He needed something solid to hand Victor, something more than theory.

He drummed his fingers on the wheel, eyes fixed on the glow of Jake's taillights. His thoughts drifted to the worn satchel Jake carried everywhere, slung like a limb. Men like him didn't cling to baggage without reason. If it held anything useful, Luca meant to find it.

Brake lights flared ahead. The Toyota slowed, turning off into a gas station whose flickering neon sign washed the lot in sickly green. Only a pair of trucks sat under the harsh lights. Luca eased off the accelerator and glided past. Cicadas buzzed in the humid dark as salt air drifted through his open window.

He took the next turn into the shadowed lot of a closed sushi bar, headlights off. The darkness swallowed him. He killed the engine, adjusted the mirror, and kept Jake in view.

The Land Cruiser door slammed, the sound sharp across the quiet. Jake strode to the pump, shoulders tight, agitation plain even at a distance. Luca's mouth curved. *Trouble in paradise.*

Jake worked the pump with quick, clipped movements, venting frustration through efficiency. When he finally capped the tank, he turned abruptly and headed inside the station.

Perfect.

Luca slid from his car, boots silent on the asphalt. He moved with the loose confidence of a man who belonged there, eyes focused and steady. Circling the truck's driver's side, he stayed clear of the windows. Through the glass, Jake's shape moved among the coolers.

His hand hovered on the latch for only a breath before he pressed it. The mechanism clicked softly; he caught the plunger switch so the dome light stayed dark. The smell of worn leather filled the cab.

There it was—the satchel, resting against the bench seat.

His pulse ticked higher. *There you are.*

He slipped a hand inside. Fingers met canvas, then paper. The satchel sighed softly; the sound felt enormous. A manila sleeve slid free just far enough to show faint ink and loops of script—symbols, slashes, geometric marks, Spanish lines woven between.

He flipped his phone, screen glow cutting a pale stripe across his face, angled it, pressed the shutter.

The door chime bit through the night.

Luca froze, heart stuttering once before control snapped back. Through the glass, Jake emerged, patting his shorts with a scowl.

Damn it, Morgan.

A second photo—quick, deliberate. He slid the parchment back, the sleeve into the satchel, clasp fastened. Jake was halfway across the lot.

Luca eased the door shut; the latch thudded softer than it should. He ducked behind the pump island as Jake reached the truck.

Jake leaned inside. "Idiot," he muttered, grabbing his wallet, then slammed and locked the door before heading back toward the store.

Only when the chime rang again did Luca breathe. A grin edged across his face as he straightened, calm returning like muscle memory.

Back in his sedan, he scrolled through the photos. Faded ink. Strange sigils. Spanish words clear as day—*Corsario. Tesoro.*

His grin sharpened. A hunt for pirate treasure. Victor would pay handsomely for this.

He watched Jake reappear with a six-pack, climb in, and drive off, none the wiser. Luca lingered a moment, then followed, satisfaction settling deep. He'd found what he needed—something Victor could build an empire on.

Now, he decided, he needed a drink.

Jake Morgan stirred as the buzz of his phone split the quiet. He groaned, reaching across the nightstand, knocking an empty bottle to the floor. "Shit." The glow lit the small cottage in cold blue, shadows stretching across worn furniture and scattered nautical relics—a cracked compass, brass dividers, a framed photo of his parents on the water.

The screen read: *Isabelle Alvarez.*

Jake sighed. "Do you know what time it is, Professor?" His voice was rough, sleep-heavy.

"Yeah." Isabelle's tone was soft but steady, threaded with hesitation. "Sorry. I wouldn't have called unless it mattered."

He sat up, rubbing his eyes as the ceiling fan clicked overhead. "Alright. What's on your mind?"

Silence. Then, quieter: "I couldn't sleep, Jake. This whole thing's been turning in my head since you walked out."

He leaned back, one arm behind his head. "You're not the only one losing sleep. Guess that makes us partners in insomnia."

"Lucky me," she said, dryness touched with warmth. "I've been thinking about what you said—about the risks, about the man watching us. You're right. If we wait too long, we could lose everything. I could lose *Siecaza.*"

That caught him. "Not what I expected you to say."

"I'm not saying I'm fine breaking every rule," she added quickly, frustration flickering through. "But I get it now. This is bigger than the system we're used to. If we don't act, someone else will—and they won't care about doing it right."

Jake stayed quiet, surprised by the mix of fear and conviction in her voice.

"But if we're doing this," she continued, firm again, "we document everything—photos, notes, every step. No permits doesn't mean no ethics. This isn't just about treasure."

He exhaled, gaze drifting to the satchel slumped on the chair, leather edges worn from years of salt and sun. The letter inside had once felt like salvation; now it felt heavier—like responsibility.

"You really believe in this," he said.

"I do," she answered. "And I think you do too. You wouldn't chase Grey's trail if it was only about gold."

He chuckled quietly. "Gold wouldn't hurt."

"Of course not," she said, smiling through the line. "But that's not all you're after, is it?"

His eyes lingered on the photo of his parents—his mother's easy smile, his father's hands on the tiller. He heard Pop's old stories of Silas Morgan standing with Elias Grey to the end. Jake swallowed. "You're not wrong. Alright, Professor. I'll document everything. But that doesn't mean you're in charge."

"I wouldn't dream of it," Isabelle said, lighter now but sincere. "Thank you, Jake. Really."

For a moment neither spoke. Only the faint lap of waves outside filled the silence.

"Guess we'll see where this takes us," he said.

"We will. Get some rest, Jake. Tomorrow's a new day."

"Yeah. Night, Isabelle."

"Goodnight, Jake."

The call ended with a hollow click. Jake let the phone rest in his lap, gaze drifting toward the ceiling. Isabelle's conviction had awakened something nameless in him, something he hadn't felt in a long time. It felt good to be on the same side again.

His gaze returned to the satchel, its leather catching the dim light. More than paper and ink—it was a crossroads, a reminder of how far he'd come and how far he still had to go. He closed his eyes, letting the waves fill the silence she'd left behind.

Morning bled through cheap motel curtains, slicing the stale air into bars of gold. The carpet was burned, the dresser chipped, the air unit droning its tired rhythm.

Luca Moretti stirred. Sheets twisted around his legs, damp with heat. Beside him, a blonde woman slept, hair fanned across the pillow, breathing slow. He studied her with the distant interest of a man observing a painting he hadn't chosen. Pretty enough. Forgettable.

He slipped from bed without a sound. In the bathroom, the fluorescent light flared against cracked glass. His reflection stared back—lean frame, shadowed jaw, hair tousled into careless disorder. Scars mapped his skin: thin white lines on his forearms, a curved one along his ribs from a knife in Naples. Over them, ink—coiled serpent on his bicep, *Fortes fortuna adiuvat* across his chest.

"An autobiography," he muttered, voice gravel-rough.

He turned the faucet; pipes coughed up a weak stream. Steam rose as he stepped under the water. It ran down his ribs, tracing the old wound. Naples. Rain, diesel, a blade flashing. The other man had been fast. Luca had been faster.

He tilted his head back, letting the memory fade like smoke.

When he stepped out, he toweled off quickly—shirt, jeans, watch, knife. Duffle open, he packed with methodical precision.

The woman hadn't moved. He didn't leave notes. Attachment was liability.

Outside, the Florida sun already pressed down in damp waves. Sunglasses on, he crossed the lot to his black sedan—clean, unremarkable, exactly as it should be.

At the front desk, the clerk looked up as he dropped the key.

"Checking out?"

"Yeah." The word rolled off his Italian lilt. A brief smile. "Room's all yours. Might have to wake the guest I left."

The clerk's brow arched, amused. He was already gone.

Sliding behind the wheel, he tossed the duffle on the seat and opened his phone. A quick text:

On my way. ETA five minutes.

Send.

The engine purred to life. Key West stirred around him—tourists with coffee cups, fishermen loading coolers, a jogger cutting across the light. None of it touched him.

His focus sharpened as he drove toward Victor. The photos were safe—proof, leverage, currency. He thought of the old letter, of the names scrawled across it, and smiled, thin and predatory. The game was shifting. And Luca Moretti had always known how to play.

The muted hum of the air conditioner mingled with the faint tang of salt drifting in through the half-open balcony doors. Morning sunlight filtered through gauzy curtains, painting the polished marble floor in pale gold. Outside, turquoise water lapped against the docks, its rhythmic slap muffled by thick panes of glass.

Victor Serrano sat in a high-backed armchair angled toward the balcony, the phone resting on the table beside an untouched café con leche. Even in these moments of quiet, his mind churned. Beyond the glass, the water shimmered like a sheet of hammered silver. It reminded him of Spain's coastline, of summers in Cádiz spent running the family villa's stone corridors as a boy—before the ache in his bones, before the tremors.

His left leg stiffened again, a slow, stubborn cramp winding its way up from the calf. He pinched the muscle, kneading it with steady pressure, his expression unchanging. He had trained himself long ago never to betray weakness outwardly. Even here, alone, he masked the effort as an idle gesture.

Still, the body betrayed him in ways he could not always control. The tremors came now with more frequency, subtle flutters in his hand that he hid beneath deliberate movements. When his jaw tightened, it was less from pain than from fury—fury that his own flesh dared to disobey him.

Not yet, he told himself. *Not while I am this close.*

A knock at the suite door drew him back. "Enter," he called, voice calm but carrying command.

Luca Moretti stepped inside, aviator sunglasses hooked at his collar, dressed in dark jeans and a fitted polo that gave him the casual confidence of a man unconcerned with appearances. His smirk was familiar—half irreverence, half challenge.

"Nice digs," Luca said, eyes sweeping the opulent room. "Resort life suits—"

Victor raised one finger without looking up from his phone. The silence stretched, filled only by the soft tapping of his thumbs as he finished composing a message. A slight tremor ghosted through his hand, hidden by the deliberate precision of each keystroke. He paused long enough to fish a small vial from his pocket, dry-swallowing two pills before continuing the message. The bitter taste clung to his tongue, a reminder that control came in measured doses.

Luca clocked the movement—the subtle shake, the pills, the forced composure.

A flicker of insight crossed his expression: *weakness*. The old man was fighting his own body. Luca filed it away behind his smirk like a knife slipped into a sleeve.

When Victor finally set the phone down, his gaze lifted. His eyes, sharp and unwavering, pinned Luca with the weight of command. "Have a seat, Moretti."

Luca sauntered farther inside, tossing his phone on the coffee table before dropping onto the sofa opposite. He sprawled there, an arm draped casually over the backrest, smirk intact. "You know, if I didn't know better, I'd say you're avoiding Algeciras. Must be easier to count your enemies from paradise, huh?"

Victor's lips twitched, though the smile never reached his eyes. "The fewer distractions, the better." He extended his hand. "Now, what do you have for me?"

Luca slid his phone across the glass surface. "Take a look."

Victor picked it up, adjusting his grip against another faint tremor, and brought the screen closer. He studied the image—the faded script and intricate seal, the strange symbols scrawled across parchment. Words leapt from the page: *Corsario. Tesoro. Espectro.*

His jaw tightened, though his expression stayed composed. "Where did you get this?"

"Your boy Morgan's been carrying it around," Luca replied, settling deeper into the sofa. "Like it was the crown jewels. Didn't take much to get a peek though."

Victor's grip on the phone hardened. He remembered a time when his strength had been absolute—on the fencing floor in Seville, the saber flashing, muscles honed to quick precision. Now, holding a simple phone, his fingers threatened to quiver. He forced the thought aside, his face betraying nothing.

"You're playing a risky game, Moretti."

Luca only shrugged. "Risky is what I do. But this—" he nodded toward the screen—"this isn't just some love letter. Judging by your face, I'd say it's something big."

Victor set the phone gently on the table. His eyes lingered on it, a flicker of reverence softening his otherwise hard expression. "This letter," he said, voice low and deliberate, "isn't just an artifact. It's a piece of a puzzle I've been chasing for years."

His gaze dropped back to the screen, to the signature etched in bold strokes at the bottom:

In loyalty and service,
Don Rodrigo Serrano
Captain of His Majesty's frigate Santa Teresa, Cartagena Station

Victor's pulse quickened—a rare betrayal of composure—before he steadied it. His ancestor. His blood. The diver had found a letter that tied his name to the very heart of the empire's pursuit of Elias Grey—one Victor hadn't even known existed.

Luca's smirk faltered, curiosity sharpening his eyes. "So, it's connected to Grey?"

Victor nodded slowly, his gaze distant but calculating. "Elias Grey didn't just steal treasure. He took something far more valuable. Something the Crown would have sacrificed anything to reclaim. This letter may be the key."

"What's more valuable than treasure?" Luca pressed.

Victor leaned forward, his dark eyes glinting. "Everlasting dominion. My family helped build an empire, only to be betrayed by it. This isn't about gold or jewels. It's about reclaiming what was stolen—our honor, our place in history... my place in history."

Luca tilted his head, lips curling. "And here I thought this was just about filling your coffers."

Victor's smile was cold, humorless. "Money is fleeting. Legacy endures."

"So, what's the plan?" Luca asked. "I've got photos of the map and the letter. Do you want me to keep tailing Morgan and his historian, or are we finally making a move?" His voice carried the eager edge of a predator itching for the hunt.

Victor's expression hardened, the calculating coldness returning. His hand twitched again. He reached for the amber vial, shook two more pills into his palm, and washed them down with a sip of cold coffee. The tremor eased—but only just.

"Patience isn't a suggestion, Moretti," he said evenly. "It's the difference between success and ruin. Impatience destroys empires—and I don't tolerate ruin."

The words hung between them like a blade.

Luca leaned back, drumming fingers lightly on the sofa. "Fair enough. But while you're playing chess, the rest of the world's playing poker. You want the whole puzzle? You'd better ante up for the pieces."

Victor's eyes narrowed, his smile thin as ice. "When the puzzle is complete, you'll have your reward. Cross me, and you'll find yourself discarded in the same shadows you skulk through."

Luca's grin flickered but never faded. He rose with a shrug, voice casual despite the tension heavy in the room. "Message received, boss. I'll be in touch."

The door clicked shut behind him.

Victor sat back, eyes fixed on the glittering harbor. He gripped the armrest again, holding until the tremor in his fingers passed. Rage and resolve warred inside him, but the resolve won. He would not let his body decide the end of his story. Not when Siecaza promised more than wealth, more than legacy—perhaps even deliverance from the disease gnawing at him from within.

"This time," he whispered, voice taut with conviction, "there will be no mistakes. The Corsair's legacy ends with me."

Chapter Ten

Under the Radar

The late-afternoon sun streamed through the windows of Isabelle's Key Largo apartment. The cluttered table between her and Jake was strewn with maps, a tablet, and notes gathered over the past few days. A ceiling fan stirred the heavy air, doing little to ease the weight of their conversation.

Jake leaned back, eyes fixed on a map of the southern Caribbean. "Getting there's one thing," he said, frustration simmering. "Not being followed—or stopped—that's the real problem."

Isabelle tapped her pen, thinking fast. "Chartering a boat or hiring a crew? Too obvious. We need to stay off the radar."

Jake smirked. "Low-key isn't exactly the vibe of an *archaeological expedition*."

"True," Isabelle replied dryly, a flicker of amusement cutting through her focus. "But I'll have to get used to stepping outside my comfort zone. What about your boat—*The Wayfinder*?"

Jake's smirk faded. "She's reliable, but she's built for salvage dives, not long blue water runs. We'd need to load extra fuel drums, provisions, spare parts—basically refit her."

"But she can get us there?"

"She can, if I tweak her fuel storage and rig a backup nav system," Jake said. "But those waters are rough—reefs, currents, weather. And that's before we factor in the guy who's been tailing us."

Isabelle frowned. "You really think he's still following?"

"I don't think—I know. Whoever he is, he's not giving up. And if he's funded, he could beat us there."

A long silence settled. Then Isabelle leaned in. "Alright. We keep it lean—no big crews, no obvious moves."

Jake tilted his head. "Go on."

She traced a route on the map. "Use smaller ports to resupply, keep moving. Stay unpredictable."

Jake chuckled. "You've got the spirit of a pirate, Professor."

"Hardly," she shot back. "You've got the skills to navigate. Let's use them."

He nodded slowly. "Then we strip the *Wayfinder*—make her faster, lighter. High-efficiency props, maybe extra jerry cans on deck. Give me a couple of days."

"Sounds good," Isabelle said, jotting notes. "But we can't ignore the tail."

Jake's grin turned wolfish. "Leave that to me. I've got a few tricks."

"Resourceful or reckless?" she teased.

"Depends on the day." He stood, stretching. "You handle provisions and route planning. I'll ready *The Wayfinder*. We leave as soon as she's seaworthy."

Isabelle met his gaze. "Jake, we're not just chasing a myth. If this is real, it could change everything."

Jake's voice softened. "Yeah. You've made that clear."

Their eyes held—resolve sparking between them.

"Alright, Captain Morgan," Isabelle said with a half-smile. "Let's make history."

Jake chuckled. "Now all I need is a barrel and a bottle of rum."

The *Wayfinder* swayed gently at the dock, gulls wheeling overhead. Inside the small cabin, maps and weathered charts covered the table.

"We've got a rough timeline," Isabelle said. "If we leave within a few days, we can reach the islands in about a week."

"Sounds good," Jake replied.

She gave him a look. "And how are we paying for fuel and supplies? I've got some savings, but not enough for everything."

"I'll figure something out."

"Jake, this isn't a 'figure it out later' situation," she said firmly. "We need gear, food, backup parts—it's going to cost."

"I know."

Her tone softened. "Preparation's not a luxury—it's how we survive. And let's be honest—you're not sitting on a secret fortune."

Guilt flickered behind his eyes. "I'll handle it."

"Please tell me that doesn't mean another job that'll get you in trouble."

He smiled thinly. "Trouble? Me?"

Isabelle's exasperated sigh filled the cabin, but she didn't press. "Just... don't make me regret trusting you on this."

"I won't."

She hesitated, watching him gather tools and charts. "Then I'll see you in the morning. Try to get some rest, Jake."

He managed a faint smile. "You too, Professor."

Isabelle gathered her things and stepped toward the hatch. Her footsteps faded down the dock, leaving only the hum of night insects and the creak of mooring lines.

Jake exhaled slowly, staring at the empty chair she'd left behind. Then he gathered his tools and stepped out onto the dock.

A few slips down, a skinny kid was coiling line under the yellow glow of a dock light. Eli looked up, pushing damp hair from his forehead.

"Evening, Jake. Burning the midnight oil again?"

Jake forced a faint grin. "Boat won't fix herself."

Eli nodded toward *The Wayfinder*. "She looks good. You heading out soon?"

"Soon," Jake said, checking the tie-downs along the rail. "Still a few things to square away."

Eli hesitated, studying him. "You okay? You look—"

Jake cut him off with a chuckle that didn't quite reach his eyes. "Just tired. Go home before the mosquitoes carry you off."

Eli smirked, slinging the coiled line over his shoulder. "Alright, Cap. See you in the morning."

"Yeah," Jake said softly. "See you then."

The kid's footsteps faded up the dock, swallowed by the quiet. Jake watched until the glow of Eli's bike light vanished into the street.

He stood alone now, the marina stilling around him, and for a moment he felt the weight of the decision he hadn't yet made.

He lifted his phone, thumb hesitating before pressing call.

"Jake Morgan," a gravelly voice drawled. "Didn't think I'd hear from you again."

"Not retired yet, Harv. Just need quick cash."

Harv chuckled. "There's a wreck off Dry Tortugas. Cargo didn't make the manifest—client wants it back, quiet-like."

"How quiet?"

"Quiet enough you don't mention it to the Coast Guard. Clean job: dive, recover, get paid. Five grand."

Jake hesitated, jaw tight. Through the cabin window, Isabelle moved over their charts. He looked away. *Just salvage,* he told himself. "When?"

"Yesterday. Don't screw it up."

The line went dead.

Jake stared at the phone. "Just one job," he muttered. Pops' words echoed: *No such thing as an easy wreck, boy.*

He shoved the phone into his pocket and looked out over the dark water.

The Gulf spread out like an endless sheet of black glass, broken only by the faint phosphorescence curling in his wake. Jake eased over the gunwale of the borrowed skiff, regulator between his teeth, the water swallowing him in a cold hush.

At thirty feet, the last silver trace of moonlight vanished. Darkness wrapped him tight, heavy and absolute. The beam of his headlamp pierced it—a narrow blade of white cutting through miles of suspended silt and drifting plankton. Bubbles streamed upward, soft explosions lost to the void.

He adjusted his buoyancy, descending slow. The hiss of his breath was rhythmic, hypnotic. Then—there. The seabed rose out of the gloom: sand rippled like windblown dunes, scattered shells glinting under his light.

A shape loomed ahead, ghostlike. Aluminum and shadow. The wreck.

The small twin-prop cargo plane rested at a list, nose buried in sand, one wing sheared clean. Torn metal creaked faintly as currents moved through it—a sound like a groan, alive in the dark. Jake hovered beside it, pulse steady, light sweeping the fuselage.

He brushed his hand along the skin of the plane. The metal was cold, slick with algae. In the cockpit, a reflection flashed—a face. He jerked the

light up—

The pilot sat motionless, still strapped in, head bowed. Skin waxy white, eyes open but unfocused. Hair drifted like pale sea grass in the current.

Jake froze. Every diver instinct screamed to leave. But he forced himself on, jaw clenched. *Just the cargo.*

He finned aft, the narrow corridor claustrophobic, his light bouncing off walls that seemed to breathe with the surge. Tiny fish darted past. His exhaled bubbles echoed like distant footsteps.

The cargo bay door loomed ahead, half-buried in sand. He worked the latch—metal protested, then swung free. A swirl of silt bloomed like smoke around him.

One crate. Red netting held it tight, too neat, too new. Jake frowned. The rest of the hold was empty—no scatter, no debris. Deliberate placement.

He cut the net, the knife's edge glinting. The lid creaked open.

Bundles stared back at him—pale, plastic-wrapped bricks, packed solid. *Drugs.*

The water pressed heavier. He felt his heartbeat in his ears. *Walk away.*

But then Isabelle's voice echoed in memory—her conviction, her trust. And Harv's, cold and transactional.

Jake looked back at the crate. *If I don't bring it up, someone else will.*

He knew what he had to do.

The phone rang twice.

"You get the cargo?" Harv demanded.

Jake kept his tone even. "You might want to double-check those coordinates. Nothing down there."

"Don't play me, Morgan."

"I'm telling you—it's gone. Either stripped or lost."

A dangerous pause. "Go back down."

"Not worth my time," Jake snapped, and hung up before the growl on the other end could land.

He exhaled hard, running a hand through his damp hair. "Hopefully he buys that." His gaze drifted to the old Toyota under the streetlight. "Now

I've got to find another way to make five grand."

He stared a moment longer, then muttered, "By dawn, the title's signed and the keys are gone."

The truck had been freedom—now it was fuel money.

Luca stepped from the shadows, cigarette flaring as Jake's Toyota rolled away. Smoke curled from his lips as he watched the taillights fade.

"So Morgan's moonlighting," he murmured. "Desperate men make mistakes."

He thumbed a message: *Morgan tangled with someone named Harv. Late-night dive. Will update.*

Sliding his phone away, he stared at *The Wayfinder* swaying at her berth. "Everything comes back to you," he said softly. "And sooner or later, so will he."

Morning sun spilled over the marina, glinting off calm water. Isabelle strode down the dock, satchel heavy with charts. On deck, Jake crouched beside the hull, welding torch hissing. Sparks jumped across his sleeve.

"I hope you got some rest last night," she said.

"Not really," Jake answered evenly, killing the torch. "But I solved our problem."

She studied him for a beat, catching the exhaustion in his eyes. "That sounds ominous."

Jake gave a faint half-smile. "You worry too much, Professor."

"Experience has taught me to," she replied, stepping aboard. "So—what kind of solution are we talking about?"

Jake wiped sweat from his brow and nodded toward the cabin. "Come inside. I'll show you."

He opened a cabinet and pulled out a thick stack of hundreds, setting it squarely on the table.

"Four grand. Enough to keep us moving if we're careful. Cash is simpler."

Isabelle froze. "Jake, this doesn't add up. You send me home for the night and show up with this? What did you do?"

He rubbed his neck. "I lined up a job, thought it might cover what we needed. It fell through. So I... found another way."

Her gaze drifted to the cash. Realization hit. "You sold the Land Cruiser?"

He nodded once. "Last night. Only thing worth anything besides *The Wayfinder*. We need her more."

She sank into a chair, emotion catching in her throat. "Jake, you didn't have to—"

"Yes, I did," he said firmly. "This is our shot. I'm not letting money stop us."

She studied him—exhausted but resolute. Admiration flickered beneath the worry. "Well," she said quietly, "between this and my emergency fund, we'll make it work. Just don't sell *The Wayfinder* out from under me."

Jake smirked. "She's not going anywhere."

Isabelle's smile softened. "Good. Then let's make this trip worth it."

Jake's shoulders eased. She spread a nautical chart across the table, tracing their route.

"You know," she said, "you didn't need to sell your truck to prove anything."

"This isn't about proving anything," Jake replied, steady. "It's about doing something that matters. No more waiting."

They bent over the chart together, shoulders nearly touching. Outside, *The Wayfinder* rocked in her berth. Inside, their quiet resolve set the course.

Across the dock, Luca nursed a beer at a restaurant table, *The Wayfinder* framed perfectly beyond the railing.

Update: Morgan repairing boat. Historian charting course. Departure soon.

His phone buzzed. *Destination?*

Unknown for now.

Not good enough. Follow. Sending men with a boat.

Luca's jaw tightened. *Unnecessary. I work cleaner alone.*

Not your decision. A second text followed: *Harv—who is he?*

Small-time criminal. Morgan tried for quick cash. Job collapsed.

Keep him out of my way, Victor replied.

Luca stared at the screen, irritation flaring. Then he opened another app—a blinking red dot pulsed on the map. The tracker he'd planted on *The Wayfinder* was live and steady.

As he signaled for the check, a thin smile curved his lips. "You may hold the leash, Victor," he murmured, "but this hunt belongs to me."

On deck, Jake tightened a line, casual but alert. From the corner of his eye, he watched the man at the restaurant rise and leave.

He'd already found the tracker that morning—tucked behind the control console, wiring just sloppy enough to give it away. For now, he'd left it live. Better they think he was unaware.

The cabin door opened. Isabelle stepped out, wrinkling her nose. "It smells like mildew in there."

Jake chuckled. "Gave the maid the year off."

"That implies you had a maid," she countered, crouching beside him. "Got anything to clean it with?"

He lowered his voice. "Our friend just left."

Her eyes sharpened. "How long?"

"All day. And they planted a surprise under the console."

"A tracker?"

He nodded.

She crossed her arms, thinking fast. "Then we use it. Let them think they're ahead while we stay in control."

Jake's grin returned, edged with approval. "You're starting to sound like me."

"You're rubbing off on me," she said. "So—what's the play?"

"Don't worry, Professor." Jake's smile turned sly. "When they see what I've got planned, they'll wish they'd stayed home."

CHAPTER ELEVEN

Under the Cover of Darkness

T he night air in the marina hung thick with saltwater and diesel, a humid heaviness that clung to Jake's skin. Water lapped against the hulls in a slow rhythm, masking the pulse hammering in his chest. Crouched on *The Wayfinder's* deck, he tightened the last bolt on the new winch; the wrench slipped in his sweat-slick grip. The unease that had followed him since the dive hadn't loosened—if anything, it was winding tighter.

A faint creak echoed from the dock.

Jake froze. The wrench stilled mid-turn as his instincts prickled. Slowly, he stood, scanning the dark through the dim cone of the marina lights.

Three figures emerged from the shadows—boots thudding against the planks, their shapes solidifying as they drew closer.

"Jake Morgan," Harv's voice rasped through the quiet, low and edged with menace. "We need to talk."

Jake's stomach sank. He forced a smirk anyway. "Harv. Didn't expect to see you tonight."

Harv's sneer flashed sharp in the faint glow, his two men flanking him like hounds straining at the leash. "You lied to me," he said. "Told me the cargo wasn't there. But my sources say you went down and destroyed it."

Jake's grip tightened on the wrench. "There was nothing worth recovering—just a rusted hull and bad luck."

"Bullshit." Harv's anger flared. "You cost me a fortune. And tonight, you're going to pay for it."

One of his men pulled a knife. The other cracked his knuckles, stepping forward.

Jake's mind ran the math—distance, reach, escape angles. No way out clean. "This really how you want to do this, Harv?"

Before Harv could answer, another voice cut through the tension—smooth, quiet, and cold as a blade.

"Three against one? That hardly seems sporting."

All heads turned. A figure detached itself from the shadows near the piling—a man moving with deliberate ease, hands in his pockets, dark eyes glinting under the lights.

Luca Moretti.

He smiled faintly. "Evening, gentlemen. Let's all take a breath, yeah?"

Harv frowned. "Who the hell are you?"

"Luca," he said simply, flicking open a switchblade with a practiced click. "A friend of Jake's. And I don't like the way you're talking to him."

Harv's sneer returned. "Friend, huh? Then you can die beside him."

He barked an order. The two goons lunged.

The first came at Luca, knife flashing. Luca sidestepped with fluid grace, caught the man's wrist, twisted. Bone popped. The knife clattered to the dock—and Luca's own blade followed through in a short, brutal arc. The man folded soundlessly, blood already spreading beneath him.

The second thug charged Jake. His swing missed; Jake ducked and brought the wrench around hard into the man's ribs. A dull crack, a strangled grunt. The man staggered, swung again—Jake slammed the wrench down onto his forearm, sending him howling to his knees, then drove a boot into his chest. He went down and didn't get up.

Harv fumbled for the gun at his belt. Luca was faster. He slammed Harv against the railing, the knife at his throat, steel drawing a bright bead of red.

"Don't," Luca whispered.

Harv's breath hitched. "Alright—alright. We can talk."

"Talk's cheap." Luca drove the blade in clean, severing the artery. Harv's eyes went wide; a wet gasp escaped as blood cascaded down his chest. He crumpled, fingers clawing uselessly at the wound before going still.

The last thug scrambled to his feet and bolted into the shadows, disappearing down the dock.

For a moment, the marina fell silent except for the lap of water and Jake's uneven breathing. He stared at the bodies, stomach twisting.

"Help me load them onto your boat," Luca said, voice calm as ever.

Jake blinked. "What?"

"You want to leave them here for the cops to find?" Luca's tone hardened. "Move."

Jake's hand trembled, bile rising in his throat. "Jesus, you just—"

"Move, Morgan," Luca snapped.

Jake obeyed, because his legs moved before his brain caught up. Together they dragged the bodies aboard *The Wayfinder*. The wet slap of canvas and the copper smell of blood filled the night. Jake tried not to look at their faces. He failed.

When the dock was clear, Luca pointed to the dark horizon. "We take them out far enough, weigh them down, and make sure they stay there."

Jake's voice came out hollow. "You've done this before."

Luca's eyes gleamed. "Long enough to know what works."

The engines rumbled to life. The marina lights receded as *The Wayfinder* slipped into open water. The hush of the Gulf swallowed them whole.

Jake's knuckles whitened around the wheel. He'd seen men die at sea before—but never like this. Never deliberate. Never by someone's own hands.

Behind him, Luca worked with unnerving precision—coiling rope, looping chain through belt loops and ankles, lashing cinderblocks like he was securing cargo. The rasp of rope on metal scraped against Jake's nerves, each sound a fresh reminder of how deep he'd sunk.

"Ready," Luca said at last.

Jake stared into the black water. "They don't deserve this."

"Sure they do," Luca said simply. Then he heaved the first body over the rail.

The splash cracked the silence. Ripples spread across the water like dark rings of consequence.

Jake's stomach clenched. He wanted to stop it—to do anything—but Luca was already moving to the next. Another splash. Another disappearance. The sea swallowed them without question.

When it was over, Luca wiped his blade clean with a rag, movements slow, deliberate—almost reverent. Jake leaned against the helm, sweat cold on his neck, pulse pounding. The metallic tang of blood still clung to his mouth.

The sea closed over the last ripple and went still.

For a long time, Jake just stared. His hands shook, the rope burns raw across his palms. The Gulf stretched endless and indifferent before him, a black mirror that didn't care what it hid.

He thought of Pops teaching him knots at the dock when he was a kid.

"Every knot has a purpose, Jake. A good one holds when it matters." Now those same hands had tied men to the deep.

"You're welcome," Luca said finally, voice dry. "They won't be a problem anymore."

Jake turned. "Why?" His voice broke between anger and disgust. "Why help me?"

Luca folded the knife, slipped it into his pocket. "Because I need you alive, Morgan. For now."

Jake stared. "You've been following me."

Luca smiled faintly. "Let's say I'm invested in what you're chasing. Maps, letters, old Spanish logs. You and the pretty historian—Isabelle Alvarez, right? You two are onto something."

Jake said nothing, but the silence gave him away.

Luca's smirk widened. "Thought so."

"Leave her out of this."

"You brought her in," Luca countered softly. "She's part of it now. So here's how this works: you keep digging, I keep you breathing. You find what's at the end, I take what I came for. Everybody wins."

Jake's jaw clenched. "And if I refuse?"

Luca stepped closer, voice dropping to a whisper. "Then someone else takes your place. And she won't survive the transition."

Jake's stomach turned cold. "You threatening her?"

"Just stating facts." Luca's smile never reached his eyes. "You find things. I make problems disappear. We'll make a fine team."

Jake met his gaze. "We're not a team."

Luca chuckled. "Call it a partnership of necessity."

They reached the marina as dawn bled across the horizon. Jake killed the engine. The silence that followed was heavy.

He tied off the last line at the slip, movements mechanical. His hands still smelled faintly of iron.

Luca stepped off the boat with his usual swagger, whistling as if nothing had happened.

"Hell of a night," Luca said. "Breakfast?"

Jake looked at him, disbelief curdling into anger. "Are you serious?"

Luca shrugged. "Why not? I'm starving."

Jake gave him a hard glare. "Get the hell off my dock."

Luca chuckled, entirely unbothered. "Suit yourself." He took a few steps up the pier, sunlight catching the dried smear on his sleeve. "You might want to scrub the planks before sunrise. Blood's tough to clean when it dries."

Jake didn't answer. He pulled the last cleat tight—again, though it was already secure. The ritual steadied his hands, barely.

"Good talk," Luca called back, whistling a jaunty tune as he disappeared down the dock.

Jake stood alone, listening to the water lap against the hull. Every ripple sounded like a heartbeat. He stared out at the endless blue—the same sea that had swallowed two men whole—and felt the chill crawl through him.

We'll make a fine team. Luca's voice echoed in his head. Jake let out a bitter laugh that died in his throat. He didn't feel like he was part of a team. He felt like a pawn.

Morning crept higher. Jake scrubbed the deck until the last trace of blood was gone, poured the dirty water overboard, and went below. Inside the cabin, the air was thick and stale. He sat, elbows on his knees, head bowed. The adrenaline had burned away, leaving only the exhaustion.

He reached for his phone and typed: *How soon can you be ready to leave?*

The reply came minutes later: I *can be there in a couple of hours. In a hurry?*

Jake stared at it. Then typed: Yeah. I'll tell you when you get here.

He tossed the phone aside and leaned back against the bulkhead, closing his eyes. Sleep came in fragments—half memories, half nightmares—until the sound of footsteps snapped him awake.

The cabin door creaked open, and sunlight spilled across the floor.

"Late night?" Isabelle's voice carried in, half teasing, half observant.

She wrestled two oversized cases through the narrow doorway and began unpacking, filling the small space with labeled containers and neatly wrapped tools.

Jake blinked, throat dry. "Are we heading to an archaeological dig, or did my boat turn into a cargo freighter overnight?"

Isabelle shot him a look. "This is essential equipment. I don't plan on improvising with duct tape and hope."

Jake sat up, forcing a smirk. "You sure you didn't bring your entire lab?"

"Every single thing here has a purpose," she said crisply. "You'll thank me later."

He raised his hands. "Alright, alright. I'll take your word for it."

The banter came easily, but Jake could feel the weight pressing underneath it. Every word was an act of control, a patch over the night's rot. Isabelle must've sensed it—her gaze lingered on him a second too long.

"You look like hell," she said quietly. "Something happen?"

He hesitated. "Radar issue. Took half the night to fix."

Her brow furrowed; she didn't buy it, but she let it go. "As long as it won't jeopardize the trip."

Jake's throat felt dry. "Everything's taken care of."

She studied him another moment, then turned back to her gear. "Good. Then help me make room, Captain."

He forced a grin. "Aye, Professor."

As they worked, the cabin filled with the comfortable noise of zippers, clinks of tools, and the muffled hum of harbor life. Bit by bit, Jake's breathing steadied.

Isabelle opened a small case, laying out delicate brushes and picks. "These are for artifact preservation," she said when Jake glanced over.

He picked up a magnifying glass, turning it over in his calloused hand. "You ever find anything worth all this trouble?"

Her smile softened. "Once, off Mozambique. A Portuguese astrolabe. It survived storms, shipwreck, centuries underwater. Cleaning it felt like resurrecting a heartbeat."

Jake nodded. "That's something. Most of what I pull up ends up as scrap or a payday."

"That's because you don't see the stories in them," Isabelle said gently. "Everything tells one."

He chuckled. "Maybe you should start writing mine."

"I already am," she teased.

For a heartbeat, their eyes met, and something in his chest loosened. Then Isabelle turned back to her kit, and the world steadied again.

By late afternoon, *The Wayfinder* sat loaded and ready. The marina air had cooled; long shadows stretched across the docks. Isabelle double-checked her inventory while Jake secured the last of the fuel lines.

"How long to *La Isla de Sombras* again?" she asked, stepping beside him at the rail.

"Eight days, if weather holds."

She grinned. "Good thing I came prepared."

Jake laughed softly, though his eyes stayed on the horizon—calm, blinding, and endless. Somewhere beneath that surface, two bodies slept in silence.

Isabelle nudged him. "What?"

He shook his head. "Nothing."

"So what about the tracker?" she asked. "We ditching it?"

Jake's smile returned, smaller now. "At the first refuel stop. Let them chase ghosts while we keep moving."

"Clever," Isabelle said, approving. "Think they'll catch on?"

"Eventually," Jake said, watching the light begin to fade. "But by then, hopefully we'll be too far ahead."

The sky deepened toward amber and gold, the day slipping quietly toward dusk. Isabelle stowed the last of her tools while Jake checked the lines one final time. The marina settled into that waiting stillness before evening.

He looked once more at the horizon—bright and empty—and exhaled slowly. Whatever waited out there, they were heading straight into it.

CHAPTER TWELVE

The Sea Beckons

The Wayfinder eased out of Boot Key Harbor as the sun slipped low over the horizon, bleeding soft hues of pink and orange across the water. The engine's steady hum blended with the rhythmic lapping of waves against the hull, a sound both familiar and foreboding in the stillness of evening.

Eli waited on the dock as *The Wayfinder* idled past the last slip, a coil of line slung over his shoulder. The evening light caught his sun-bleached hair, his faded marina shirt stirring in the breeze.

"Evening tide looks calm," he called, voice carrying easily across the water.

"Yeah," Jake said, one hand on the rail. "Figured we'd make use of it before the weather changes."

Eli nodded, that easy, quiet grin of his settling in. "Safe run out there. I'll keep an eye on your slip."

Jake hesitated a moment, then said, "Might be a while before I'm back."

Eli's grin tilted. "Where you headed this time?"

Jake's smile was small but genuine. "An adventure."

Eli laughed softly, shaking his head. "Then take me with you next time."

Jake huffed a short breath that passed for a laugh. "Sure thing, kid."

"I'll hold you to that," Eli said, stepping back as *The Wayfinder* drifted clear of the dock. "Bring her home the way you found her."

Jake gave a small salute, and Eli's wave lingered in the fading light until distance and sea swallowed the dock behind them.

Isabelle watched from the bow, a faint smile playing at her lips. "He looks up to you, you know."

Jake glanced over, brow creasing. "Eli? He's just a good kid. Helps out around the marina."

"Still," Isabelle said softly, her gaze following the dwindling shoreline. "Not everyone gets looked at that way. You give him something to aim for."

Jake's mouth twitched into a half-smile, though there was no humor in it. "Hope he aims higher than me."

Isabelle studied him for a moment, hearing more truth in the words than he probably meant to reveal. "Maybe," she said, her tone gentle. "But you could do worse than being someone worth aiming toward."

Jake didn't answer, only turned back to the helm as *The Wayfinder* cleared the breakwater and the open sea unfurled before them.

His hands rested lightly on the wheel, though his eyes weren't fixed entirely on the horizon. Isabelle stood at the bow, the breeze teasing strands of her dark hair as she gazed out to sea. For a moment, the fading light caught her in profile, turning her features to gold. Jake felt a tug in his chest—unexpected, uninvited—and looked away quickly, focusing back on his course as though the sea itself demanded his attention.

"Not having second thoughts, are you?" he called, his voice a shade too casual.

Isabelle turned, startled from her thoughts. A smile tugged at her lips. "Hardly. Just thinking about how this will read in my notes. The beginning always sets the tone."

Jake chuckled softly. "Setting the tone, huh? I figure the sea will handle that part for us."

"True," she said, stepping back toward him, her eyes catching the last threads of light. "But maybe documenting it will give future historians something to care about."

Jake nodded but didn't reply, though his gaze lingered a heartbeat longer than he intended before sliding back to the darkening horizon. Behind them, the lights of Marathon dwindled into distant pinpricks until there was only the vast night ahead.

For a moment, the peace of it all tempted him to believe they'd left their troubles on shore. But Luca's words from the marina returned, unbidden: *You don't have much of a choice.* Jake tightened his grip on the wheel. The sea wasn't just carrying them toward adventure—it was carrying them toward whatever waited in the dark.

Inside the cabin, Isabelle sat at the small table, her tools neatly arranged from earlier. A map spread out before her, she traced a route with her finger, her brow furrowed in concentration. Occasionally, she jotted notes in a worn leather-bound journal, her handwriting precise and methodical.

"First stop to refuel is Duncan Town," Isabelle called out, not looking up from the map. "It's about 380 nautical miles at a heading of one hundred and twenty-five degrees southeast."

"Aye, Captain," Jake replied with a playful salute as he double-checked the heading in the navigation system. "At this speed, we should get there in a little over two days, give or take."

Isabelle glanced up, meeting his gaze. Determination and commitment were etched into her expression. "I guess I better settle in, huh?"

Jake grinned, his tone light. "Hope you brought some playing cards."

"I guess I'll work on my solitaire game," Isabelle replied dryly, a faint smile tugging at her lips.

Jake leaned against the helm, his grin softening. "Why don't you try and get some sleep? I'll keep us moving until dawn. Tomorrow, I'll show you how to take over."

"You want me to drive the boat?" Isabelle asked, surprise and a hint of excitement lighting up her face.

"Yeah. I can't be at the helm twenty-four hours a day, and *The Wayfinder's* not fancy enough for autopilot," Jake said with a smirk. "It's either you or we stop every night and it takes us twice as long."

Isabelle arched an eyebrow, her expression skeptical but amused. "You sure you're okay staying up all night?"

Jake gestured toward the small coffee maker in the galley. "I'll get a pot of coffee going. That'll keep me upright."

Isabelle hesitated for a moment, concern flickering in her eyes, then stepped closer and laid a hand on his shoulder. "Alright. Don't overdo it, though."

The warmth of her touch caught him off guard — steady, genuine. For a heartbeat, Jake forgot the wheel beneath his hands, aware only of her nearness and the faint scent of citrus and sun on her skin. He covered the moment with a faint grin.

"I'll be fine," he said, waving her off a little too quickly. "Get some rest. You've got a big day as the new first mate tomorrow."

Isabelle rolled her eyes but couldn't hide her smile. She gathered her things and descended the steps into the forward berth, where she'd stowed her belongings earlier. As the door clicked shut behind her, Jake turned back to the helm, the open sea stretching out before him.

The quiet of the night settled around him, the weight of their journey pressing against his shoulders. With a deep breath, Jake poured himself a cup of coffee and settled in for the long night ahead.

Isabelle awoke feeling refreshed, the small berth filled with the muffled sounds of rushing water and the distant cries of seagulls. Sunlight streamed through the porthole, bathing the space in golden hues that danced across the walls. For a moment, she let herself savor the serenity before climbing the steps to the main cabin.

As she stepped into the cabin, she was greeted by the breathtaking sight of calm, crystal-clear blue waters stretching to the horizon. Numerous rocky islets dotted the seascape, their rugged silhouettes casting shadows across the water. On one of the larger islets, an abandoned stone lighthouse stood resolute, its weathered façade speaking of a time long past. Flanking it were a few crumbling stone block buildings, their edges softened by decades of exposure to the elements.

"Cay Sal..." Isabelle breathed, her voice a mix of wonder and excitement.

Jake stood at the wheel, his stance relaxed but steady. He glanced at her with a knowing smile. "Beautiful spot, isn't it?"

"Remarkable," Isabelle said, her eyes glued to the window as the lighthouse drifted past on the starboard side. "It was built by the British in 1839 to mark the southern entrance to the Florida Straits. The history here is incredible."

Jake chuckled, leaning slightly against the helm. "Do you dream about history too, or just recite it in your sleep?"

"You're hilarious," Isabelle said, shooting him a playful glare. Her expression softened as she turned back to the view. "I'm glad I didn't miss this. It's like stepping into another world."

Jake grinned, though the corners of his eyes sagged with fatigue. "Glad you think so, Professor." He stifled a yawn and rubbed the back of his neck. "Now, how about that crash course in seamanship..."

Isabelle straightened, her excitement shifting to determination. "I'm ready."

"Step on up," Jake said, stepping aside and motioning toward the helm with a flourish.

With a mix of enthusiasm and nerves, Isabelle took her place at the wheel. Jake guided her through the basics, showing her how to maintain course and speed, monitor changes in depth, and use the navigational system. Isabelle caught on quickly, her focus unwavering as she absorbed every detail.

After about forty-five minutes, Jake stepped back, observing her with an approving nod. "You've got it. Think you can hold the helm for a while?"

Isabelle glanced at the gauges, then out at the shimmering water ahead. She adjusted the wheel slightly, confidence growing with each passing moment. "Yeah, I'm good. Go get some sleep."

Jake's hand lingered on her shoulder, steady and reluctant to let go. "Wake me if you need me, okay?"

"I will," Isabelle promised, holding his gaze for a beat before her lips curved into a quiet smile.

Jake nodded with a satisfied smile and made his way to the bench seat on the opposite side of the cabin. He leaned back against the bulkhead, his body finally relaxing as his eyes drifted shut. Within minutes, his breathing had deepened, the exhaustion of the past few days catching up with him.

Isabelle remained at the helm, her fingers resting lightly on the wheel as the salty breeze flowed through the open window, tousling her hair. The serenity of the moment washed over her, the beauty of their surroundings filling her with a sense of wonder and freedom. She smiled to herself, marveling at the unexpected adventure she had found herself in.

For the first time in a long while, Isabelle felt truly alive.

The morning sun blazed down on the docks at Boot Key Harbor in Marathon, glaring off the sharp, angular lines of Victor's Sunseeker Predator 55. The yacht's glossy hull gleamed jet-black against the water, its profile low and predatory, built for both speed and spectacle. Wide teak decks stretched back to an open cockpit with plush seating, while tinted windows wrapped the saloon in mirrored glass, hiding its leather-and-chrome interior. Even at rest, it looked coiled to strike, its twin engines promising speed that left most boats in its wake.

Luca stood beside the luxury yacht, the heat barely registering as he studied the tracking app on his phone. The pulsing red dot showed *The Wayfinder* heading southeast, threading between Cuba and the Bahamas. He had watched as they slipped quietly out of Marathon just before sunset the night before. Sliding the phone back into his pocket, his jaw tightened.

"Alright, let's go," Luca ordered sharply, addressing the three men standing ready on the Sunseeker's deck.

The men moved immediately, their efficiency evident as they began prepping the yacht for departure. Each was dressed in tactical, weather-appropriate gear—black polos and khaki cargo pants—blending practicality with professionalism. Their movements were precise and coordinated, speaking to years of experience. These weren't hired thugs; they were seasoned operatives, handpicked by Victor Serrano for their competence and discretion.

Luca watched them work, his sharp gaze scanning for any sign of hesitation or error. He might not have chosen them himself, but he had to admit they knew what they were doing. Still, he didn't like sharing the chase. Victor's leash was always there—a constant reminder that the hunt was never entirely his own.

One of the men, a broad-shouldered operative with a close-cropped beard named Mateo, finished checking the mooring lines before turning to Luca. "Target's current location?" His tone was clipped, professional.

"Heading southeast between Cuba and the Bahamas," Luca replied curtly, irritation flashing at the needless question.

The second, Carlos—lean and wiry, his sharp eyes constantly scanning—slid into the cockpit and took position at the helm. "We'll close the gap in no time," he said, voice confident but measured.

"We'll maintain distance for now," Luca instructed. "People are easier to follow when they feel safe. Let them think they're ahead."

The third, Javier, dark-haired and watchful, moved methodically through the final checks on deck. He didn't speak, but his silence carried a steady assurance that made him no less dangerous.

The Predator's engines roared to life, and the yacht began to glide smoothly away from the dock, the sleek hull cutting through the water with effortless grace. Luca stepped into the cockpit, his boots striking the polished floor with purpose as he leaned over the navigation system.

"Cruising speed at twenty-five knots," Mateo reported from the helm.

"Good. Let's keep it steady for now," Luca replied. His dark eyes flicked to the horizon, scanning the water as the yacht picked up speed.

Pulling out his phone, he quickly typed a message to Victor: *Target is on the move. We're leaving the dock now. Will keep you updated.*

The response came almost instantly, concise and demanding: *Do not fail me.*

Luca smirked faintly as he slid the phone back into his pocket. Victor's constant oversight grated on him, but failure wasn't an option—not in Victor's world. He'd seen firsthand what happened to those who disappointed Serrano, and he had no intention of joining their ranks.

As the Predator gained momentum, the blue expanse of the sea stretched out before them, the hum of the engines thrumming in Luca's chest. The chase was on, and Luca was determined to stay ahead of every move Morgan tried to make. For now, he would play Victor's game. But in the end, Luca trusted one truth above all: in a hunt, only the predator who adapts survives.

The hum of *The Wayfinder's* engine was the only sound breaking the tranquility of the open sea. Two days had passed since they'd left Marathon, and the journey had settled into a steady rhythm. The warm sun blazed overhead, casting sparkling diamonds across the waves as the boat sliced through the crystal-clear water.

Isabelle leaned against the railing, the salty breeze tangling her hair as she stared out at the endless expanse of blue. The sense of adventure that had thrilled her at the beginning of the journey remained, though tempered now by the monotony of long hours at sea. She glanced toward the helm where Jake sat, his hand resting lightly on the wheel, his expression focused but relaxed.

"How's it feel to be a seasoned sailor?" Jake asked, glancing at her with a grin.

Isabelle smirked. "I wouldn't say seasoned, but I haven't run us aground yet, so I'll take it as a win."

Jake chuckled. "It'll happen sooner or later, don't worry. I think it's actually a requirement to be able to call yourself a sailor."

The playful banter eased the weight of their mission, if only for a moment. Isabelle turned back to the water, spotting a cluster of low-lying islands rising on the horizon.

"Is that it?" she asked, pointing ahead.

Jake followed her gaze and nodded. "Ragged Island—Duncan Town. We'll make a quick stop here to refuel, grab some fresh water, and stretch our legs. There's a small fishing community—good spot to lay low."

"Stretching my legs sounds amazing," Isabelle admitted. "Even the best adventure needs a pit stop."

Jake nodded, though his expression turned more serious. "There's one more thing I want to take care of while we're here."

Isabelle raised an eyebrow. "Tracker?"

He nodded. "If we're going to shake—" He stopped himself, jaw tightening, then finished, "—whoever's following us, we'll need to make it look convincing."

Isabelle's gaze sharpened. "You're still planning to put it on a fishing boat?"

Jake nodded. "If I find the right one, yeah. It'll buy us some time."

Her lips pressed into a thin line, but she nodded. "Alright. But let's be careful. We can't afford to draw attention."

Jake shot her a reassuring smile. "Don't worry. This isn't my first time working under the radar."

"Oh, I'm sure," Isabelle said, her grin widening. "Something tells me you've had plenty of practice."

As *The Wayfinder* closed in on Duncan Town Harbor, the details of the tiny settlement came into view. Colorful fishing boats bobbed gently in the shallows, their nets spread out to dry in the sun. Weathered houses in faded pastel hues lined the waterfront, their paint worn by salt and time. A few locals moved with easy rhythm—hauling in spiny lobsters, mending gear, or chatting in the shade of corrugated awnings. Behind the town, the flat salt ponds shimmered in the heat, a reminder of the island's past.

Jake throttled down the engine as they neared the dock, his movements precise and confident. Isabelle watched him, impressed by how easily he maneuvered the boat into position.

"Welcome to Duncan Town," Jake said as he stepped off the helm and looped the lines around a piling, steadying *The Wayfinder*. "Let's make it quick."

Isabelle swung her satchel over her shoulder with a nod. "I'll get the water and supplies. You handle fuel and your little tracker scheme."

"Deal," Jake said, flashing a grin. "Just don't let the charm of island life steal you away. I'd hate to have to track you down next."

She rolled her eyes, though the smile tugging at her lips gave her away. "Relax, Captain. You're not getting rid of me that easily."

The boat creaked as they stepped onto the dock, their footsteps blending with the sounds of island life. The air was heavy with the smell of diesel and fresh fish, and the sun bore down with unrelenting intensity. Jake's gaze swept over the harbor, his sharp eyes scanning for the right target—a boat that would carry the tracker far enough to throw off their trail.

"I'll meet you back here in an hour," Jake said over his shoulder as he started toward the far end of the dock.

"An hour," Isabelle repeated, watching him go before turning toward the small cluster of shops near the waterfront.

For both of them, Duncan Town offered a brief reprieve—but it also held the promise of what lay ahead.

The harbor bustled with activity as Jake walked along the weathered dock. The salty breeze carried the mingling scents of fish, diesel, and the faint aroma of coconut from a nearby shack. Locals moved with the efficiency of routine, hauling nets, mending gear, and unloading their catches.

Jake kept his pace casual, his hands tucked into his pockets. His sharp eyes scanned the boats lined up at the dock, their hulls painted in bright hues that had faded under years of sun and salt. He needed something big enough to stray far from the island but small enough not to stand out—a boat that would look natural traversing the open water.

He stopped near a medium-sized fishing vessel, its name *Sea Breeze* painted in peeling white letters on the bow. The boat looked perfect—sturdy, with a crew that appeared too focused on their work to notice a stranger lurking nearby.

Jake leaned casually against a nearby piling, pretending to check the messages on his phone. He waited, watching the crew unload their haul of spiny lobsters and grouper. They moved quickly, stacking crates onto a waiting truck. His window of opportunity was opening, but it wouldn't last long.

He slipped the tracker out of his pocket, its tiny red light blinking steadily. He moved toward the *Sea Breeze*, crossing the dock with purposeful ease, his movements calculated to blend into the bustle of the harbor.

As he approached the boat, Jake noticed a rusted ladder leading down to the deck. Perfect. With a quick glance around, he confirmed no one was watching and stepped onto the ladder, descending silently. His boots landed softly on the deck, and he crouched low.

The engine compartment sat at the stern, its fiberglass casing dented and streaked with oil stains. Jake knelt and secured the tracker on the underside of the casing with the adhesive backing, pressing it firmly into place. He double-checked its positioning—it was out of sight, but the signal would still transmit clearly.

A voice called out from the dock, sharp and unfamiliar. Jake froze, his heartbeat pounding in his ears.

"Hey, you down there! What're you doing?"

Jake looked up to see one of the fishermen standing on the dock, his arms crossed. The man's brow furrowed as he peered down at Jake.

Thinking fast, Jake plastered a sheepish smile on his face and held up his phone. "Sorry, didn't mean to alarm you! I thought this was the *Lucky Star*. Was supposed to meet a guy about some parts."

The man's frown deepened, but he relaxed slightly, scratching the back of his head. "The *Lucky Star's* two slips down."

"Appreciate it," Jake said with a nod, climbing back up the ladder. "Thanks, man."

The fisherman grunted in acknowledgment, his gaze lingering on Jake for a moment before turning back to his work. Jake strolled away, his heart racing, his every step calculated to look casual. One wrong move, and this could've gone sideways fast. Once he was far enough down the dock, he veered off and headed back toward *The Wayfinder*. The harbor's activity continued as if nothing had happened, the locals none the wiser to the small act of deception that had just taken place.

When Isabelle returned to *The Wayfinder*, she found Jake leaning over the chart table in the cabin, brow furrowed as he studied the next leg of their route. A cup of coffee sat forgotten beside him, the steam long gone.

"Everything go according to plan, Mr. Bond?" Isabelle asked, a playful smile tugging at her lips.

Jake straightened, meeting her gaze with a mischievous glint. "Of course, my dear Moneypenny," he said in his best Sean Connery impression, the accent rough but earnest.

Isabelle laughed, the sound bright and genuine. "You might want to workshop that accent," she teased, moving closer to glance at the chart. Then, with mock seriousness, she added, "Good thing I'm here. Every Bond needs a capable partner to keep him alive."

Jake smirked, leaning back against the bulkhead. "Capable partner, huh? Guess that makes you the real secret weapon."

Her grin widened, eyes flicking toward him. "Don't you forget it."

They shared a moment of levity before she set her satchel down and began stowing the supplies she'd brought aboard. "I got us enough water and provisions to last us through the next leg. Were you able to fuel up?"

"Yep," Jake said, tapping the chart with his finger. "She's all topped off and ready to go. We can make way whenever you're set."

"Good," Isabelle replied, reaching up to tuck a pack of paper towels into one of the higher cabinets. "Where's our next stop?"

"Either Haiti or the Dominican Republic. Once we get there, it's a straight shot to *Las Isla de Sombras*," Jake said, his tone shifting to business.

Isabelle glanced over her shoulder, curiosity sparking. "Haiti or the DR, huh? What's the deciding factor?"

"Weather," Jake admitted with a shrug, tracing a line on the chart with his finger. "East of the DR before turning south is the shortest run, but we'll be exposed to the Atlantic. Cutting south just west of Haiti gives us more protection—costs time, though."

His gaze snagged on the letters D.R., and his jaw tightened. For an instant, the chart blurred under the weight of an old memory—a search gone sideways, the kind you don't forget. He blinked it back and forced his tone lighter. "We'll see how it looks once we're out there."

Isabelle tilted her head slightly, sensing the hitch in his voice. She didn't press, only offered a small nod, filing away the reaction for later.

Isabelle leaned closer to the chart, her eyes scanning the two potential routes. "Makes sense. The Atlantic can be unpredictable, especially this time of year. The safer route might be worth the extra time."

Jake nodded, the faint hum of the boat's engine vibrating through the cabin as he folded the map. "We'll make the call once we get closer. No point stressing over it now."

She nodded, tucking away the last of the provisions. "Sounds like a plan," she said, sliding the cabinet door shut. "If you want to take us back into open water, I can hold the helm for a while so you can catch some rest before your night watch."

Jake raised an eyebrow, a smirk tugging at his lips. "You offering to take the helm again, Captain Alvarez?"

"I am," Isabelle replied, arching a brow to match his. "And this time, I swear I won't 'accidentally' veer off course."

Jake chuckled, shaking his head. "Bold words. Alright—you've earned your stripes. I'll get us clear of the harbor, then the wheel's all yours."

As he turned back to the controls, a grin lingered on his face longer than he meant it to. Isabelle caught it, her own smile flickering wider. She didn't call him out on it, but the glint in her eyes said she'd noticed—and that she wasn't about to let it slip from memory.

The Wayfinder glided smoothly out of the harbor, the open water ahead shimmering under the midday sun. Isabelle felt the familiar pull of excitement stir in her chest as the shoreline of Duncan Town receded into the distance.

"Alright, Professor, she's all yours," Jake said, stepping back from the helm with a mock flourish.

Isabelle slid into his place, her hands steady on the wheel as she corrected their heading. "You'd better rest while you can," she called over her shoulder, half-teasing. "Something tells me you'll need your energy before long."

Jake chuckled, stretching out on the bench. "If you need me, just yell. Or better yet, don't—waking up to a panic attack isn't my idea of fun."

Isabelle rolled her eyes, though a smile tugged at her lips. "Get some sleep, Morgan. I've got this."

Jake leaned back, the hum of the engines and the salt breeze carrying him toward sleep. The sound of Isabelle's steady voice lingered in his mind longer than he expected, a quiet reassurance against the uncertainty ahead. Above them, the sun hung high and bright, a silent witness as *The Wayfinder* pressed on into the unknown.

Jake floated in the dark, helpless. The muffled rumble drowned out the rasp of his regulator as the rocky tunnel closed in, squeezing tighter with every heartbeat. The water shuddered with a relentless force, shaking him like a rag doll.

"Jake... Jake!" Ryan's voice crackled through the comms, distant, desperate.

He tried to move, but the rock walls pressed closer, pinning his arms, crushing the air from his chest. Panic clawed at his throat. The voice came again, louder, frantic—yet he couldn't answer. The water pressed in, stealing every breath...

The world snapped back.

"Ryan!" Jake jolted upright, lungs burning, his breath ragged. The nightmare dissolved into the blurred outline of the cabin. His heart hammered as Isabelle's face swam into view, her hand firm on his shoulder.

"Jake! Wake up!" Her voice cut through the fog, sharp and urgent.

He blinked, struggling to orient. "What?!"

"Something's wrong with the engine," Isabelle said, breathless. The sputtering cough from the stern underscored her words, the machinery straining against failure.

Jake shoved himself upright, but Isabelle's eyes lingered on him for a heartbeat longer. She'd seen the terror in his expression, the name he'd cried out. Even as she turned toward the sound of the failing engine, concern etched her brow—Jake's nightmare had left more than just sweat on his skin.

Jake scrubbed a hand over his face, forcing the remnants of the dream into the back of his mind. The sputtering cough of the engine reached his ears, uneven and strained, and his stomach sank. "Damn it," he muttered, snatching his toolkit from its spot by the table.

"What's wrong?" Isabelle asked, close on his heels, worry still lingering in her eyes.

"Sounds like a loss of fuel pressure," Jake said, his tone clipped. He shoved aside the galley rug and heaved open the hatch in the floor, the hinges groaning. Hot, oily air rushed up as he grabbed the ladder and disappeared below. "Could be a loose connection in the fuel line... or a clogged filter. Happens more often than I'd like."

The compartment swallowed him in a haze of heat and metal, the thrum of the struggling diesel vibrating through the bulkheads as he set the toolkit down with a clatter.

Jake glanced at Isabelle and gestured toward the flashlight on the workbench. "Grab that and give me a hand."

She moved quickly, returning with the flashlight and crouching beside the hatch, her arm steady as she aimed the beam where he pointed. The cramped engine compartment vibrated with noise and heat, the smell of diesel thick in the air. Jake knelt low, his shoulders brushing the bulkheads as his hands worked along the fuel lines, checking clamps and fittings with practiced precision.

"This where the fuel enters the engine?" Isabelle asked, tilting the light to follow his movements.

"Close," Jake said, glancing up briefly. "This is the primary filter. If it's clogged, nothing gets through."

Her curiosity cut through the monotony of the task, and Jake found himself appreciating her sharp eye. She wasn't just watching—she was learning.

A few minutes later, his fingers brushed a loose hose clamp. He frowned, tugging lightly. The line shifted in his grip, barely holding on, the constant vibration of the diesel having worked it free over time.

"There you are," Jake muttered, relief threading through his voice. "Our culprit."

Jake reached for a screwdriver. "Loose clamp. Could've come off completely if we didn't catch it."

"So, this happens often?" Isabelle asked, her tone wry as she shone the light on the offending connection.

"More than I'd like," Jake admitted, a hint of a grin tugging at his lips. "Boats like this aren't exactly trouble-free."

Isabelle laughed softly. "I suppose even the best tools need maintenance."

Jake tightened the clamp and checked the rest of the connections, his fingers moving with practiced care. A moment later, the diesel caught steady, its hum smoothing into a strong, even rhythm. He leaned back on his heels, exhaling a satisfied sigh as the hot, oily air pressed close around them.

Glancing at Isabelle, he gave a short nod, the corner of his mouth lifting. "Not bad. You're a quick study."

"Thanks," Isabelle said, smirking as she handed him a rag. "Unfortunately, fixing engines wasn't part of the syllabus for marine archaeology."

"I imagine not," Jake replied, pushing to his feet and wiping his hands. His grin softened into something warmer. "Still—you handled it well. Didn't panic. Guess I'll keep you around."

Isabelle arched an eyebrow, her smirk easing into a genuine smile. "Glad to know I passed the test. Do I get extra credit for enthusiasm?"

Jake chuckled, shaking his head. "Careful, Professor. Keep this up and I'll have you rebuilding the whole engine by the time we hit port."

They shared a laugh, the tension breaking, before climbing back into the cabin. Isabelle spread her notes and maps across the table, while Jake slid behind the helm. The hum of the engine was steady now, a welcome reassurance that carried them back into the rhythm of the sea.

As *The Wayfinder* settled back into its rhythm, Jake kept one hand on the wheel, the steady thrum of the repaired engine vibrating through the deck. Every so often his eyes drifted to Isabelle at the table, her brow furrowed as she traced notes across the chart. There was something about the way she approached problems—curious, thoughtful, unafraid to dive in.

He shook his head, a faint smile tugging at his lips. For all the challenges waiting ahead, it felt good having her in his corner. She wasn't just sharp; she was steady—the kind of person who didn't flinch when things got messy.

The horizon ran like a clean line across the world. Jake kept them on it, the repaired engine a steady heartbeat underfoot. Somewhere astern, a faster heartbeat would find their wake—sooner or later. For now, he let the line and the woman at the table anchor him. Maybe, just maybe, they made a damn good team.

CHAPTER THIRTEEN

Crossroads of Risk

The sun hung high in a cloudless sky, casting a golden glow over the open water. *The Wayfinder* shouldered into a low swell at nine knots, its engine humming a steady rhythm that seemed to match the mood on deck. Jake, barefoot and shirtless, moved with practiced ease as he prepped the trolling rigs. A cool breeze carried the salty tang of the ocean, mingling with the sound of *Van Halen's Finish What Ya Started* drifting from the stereo mounted on the aft wall of the cabin.

He hummed along with the music, fully in his element. His hands moved with fluid familiarity, threading fresh ballyhoo onto a pair of hooks. With a smooth flick of his wrist, he cast the bait overboard, letting the line spool out before securing the rods in place. A faint sheen of sweat glistened on his sun-kissed skin, catching the light, and he wore an easy grin—the kind Isabelle realized she hadn't seen often enough.

From her spot near the cabin, she glanced up from the leather-bound journal she kept for her own notes. Her eyes lingered on Jake as he moved, every bit the seafarer, exuding a quiet confidence that was magnetic. The corners of her mouth turned upward into a smile before she even realized it.

The song shifted to a familiar tune, and Isabelle couldn't help herself. She tapped her pen on the table in time with the beat, and then, as the chorus hit, she sang along, her voice carrying over the gentle rush of the waves.

Jake froze mid-motion, turning to her with an exaggerated look of mock surprise. "Is that—are you singing?" he teased, a playful glint in his eye.

"Don't act so shocked," she shot back, her smile widening as she leaned against the cabin doorway. "It's a classic. You can't not sing along."

Jake chuckled, shaking his head as he adjusted the drag on one of the rods. "You keep that up, and you might scare off all the fish."

"Funny," Isabelle quipped, her voice dripping with faux offense. "Let's see you do better, Mr. Rockstar."

Before he could respond, the reel on one of the rigs suddenly screeched to life. Jake's grin spread wide as he jumped into action, grabbing the rod and leaning back with practiced skill.

"Fish on!" he called out, the thrill of the catch lighting up his voice.

Isabelle set her journal aside and stepped out, shading her eyes against the glare. "What is it?" she asked, her pulse quickening as much from his energy as from the reel's furious whine.

"Feels like a mahi," Jake replied, muscles taut as he worked the line. His focus was absolute, movements fluid and sure. Isabelle found herself watching him with a quiet admiration, drawn in by the strength and ease that came so naturally to him.

After a few minutes of tugging and maneuvering, Jake hauled the fish up over the railing.

"Mahi!" he announced triumphantly, holding it high for her to see.

She clapped, laughing. "Okay, you win this round. But I'm claiming credit for singing it into existence."

"Yeah, yeah," Jake said with a grin as he carefully unhooked the fish.

As he placed the catch into the cooler, Isabelle handed him a water bottle, shaking her head. "You're impossible, you know that?"

"And yet, you're still here," he shot back, grin never faltering.

The stereo shifted songs, and Isabelle laughed softly before humming along again, her voice threading through the steady rhythm of the sea. Jake leaned against the railing, the sun warm on his face, a fresh catch in the cooler, and Isabelle singing nearby. For a fleeting moment, it felt as though the rest of the world—the chase, the dangers waiting just over the horizon—didn't exist at all.

But as her laughter faded, Isabelle's gaze drifted back to the leather-bound journal lying closed on the table. Its pages were already filling with observations, sketches, and questions that had no easy answers. Whatever mysteries still lay ahead on Elias Grey's trail, she knew this moment of peace wouldn't last forever.

A few hours later, Jake stood at the helm, his hands resting casually on the wheel. "All right, decision time," he announced, eyes locked on the navigation display.

"About which route to take?" Isabelle asked, looking up from the book she'd been reading, curled comfortably on the bunk by the table.

Jake nodded. "We've got two options. We can either turn south now and head down the Windward Passage between Cuba and Haiti, or keep going past the Dominican Republic and cut south through the Mona Passage."

"Pros and cons?" she asked.

Jake tapped the screen, bringing up the weather overlay. "The Windward Passage is more protected—it'll keep us out of the worst weather, but it adds about a day. The Mona's shorter, but it's open water. We'd be taking a gamble with the weather."

Isabelle leaned forward. "What's the radar saying? How risky is it right now?"

"There's a system moving in from the east," Jake said, adjusting the range. "Still a long way off, but tropical waves build fast out here." He hesitated. "And we're not the only ones chasing this trail. Every day counts."

Every day lost was another chance for Luca—or someone worse—to catch up. The thought knotted his chest.

She studied him over the rim of her mug. "What's your gut telling you?"

Jake ran a hand through his hair, jaw tight. "My gut says we've got a better shot if we don't waste time. The Mona's faster, and if we're careful, we can stay ahead of the worst of it."

Isabelle set her mug down with a faint clink, her expression calm but resolute. "All right, sailor. I trust you. Let's go for the Mona Passage."

The weight of her words hit him harder than he expected. Trust wasn't something he was used to—not this easily, anyway. He gave her a quick nod, tension lingering in his shoulders. Turning back to the console, he entered the new heading with fingers that felt heavier than usual. No room for mistakes now.

Isabelle stepped up beside him, peering out at the open water. "Think we'll hit rough seas?"

Jake smirked faintly. "Let's just say I wouldn't put your coffee mug too close to the edge of the table."

She chuckled, but the weight of their decision hung in the air. Isabelle glanced at him again, noting how his eyes kept darting back to the radar.

"You know," she said, her voice light but steady, "every expedition in history involved risks. The important thing is that we're smart about them."

Jake's lips twitched into a half-smile. "Smart, huh? You've got a lot of faith in me for someone who hasn't seen me outrun a storm."

"I've seen enough to know you've got good instincts," Isabelle said. "And I'd rather take a calculated risk than sit around worrying about what might happen."

Jake looked over at her, the weight of her trust both steadying and unnerving. "Thanks, Professor. I'll do my best to make sure we get through this in one piece."

She gave him a reassuring nod before stepping back to the table. Jake focused on the horizon, eyes narrowing at the faint shift of the swell. The Mona Passage was their choice now, and it would test them both—because the sea had a way of punishing overconfidence.

Far to the north, the waters of the Bahamas gleamed under the midday sun, shifting from turquoise shallows to deep sapphire where the seafloor dropped away. Shallow reefs glimmered just beneath the surface, streaks of white sand breaking through like brushstrokes across the sea. The air was hot and heavy with salt—the kind that clung to skin and left a taste at the back of the throat.

Luca reclined in the cockpit of the *Sunseeker*, the polished teak deck warm beneath his feet and the steady vibration of twin diesels running up through the hull. Spray feathered off the bow and drifted aft in a fine mist, carrying the sharp tang of saltwater mixed with the faint bite of exhaust. Sunlight flared off the stainless rails and fittings, bright enough to sting the eyes when he turned his head toward the glare.

Above, a pair of frigatebirds wheeled lazily against the cloudless sky. Ahead, the horizon shimmered in the heat. All around stretched the beauty of the Bahamas—crystalline and serene—yet in Luca's eyes, it was nothing but a hunting ground.

The red dot marking *The Wayfinder's* position had shifted southwest after stopping at a remote island for two hours. Luca frowned, leaning forward; his instincts were on edge. "Why are you doubling back, Morgan?"

he muttered. When people deviated from predictable patterns, it was never a good sign.

He stubbed his cigarette out in the stainless-steel ashtray bolted to the deck, the faint hiss mirroring his irritation. Sitting upright, he turned to Carlos at the helm. "Increase speed to thirty knots. I want to get within visual range."

"Got it." Carlos pushed the throttles forward. The *Sunseeker* surged, cutting through the water with precision.

Within an hour they closed to within several miles of the tracker's position. Luca stepped onto the bow with binoculars in hand. The salty breeze tugged at his shirt as he scanned the horizon. To the south, a cluster of small fishing boats bobbed lazily; a sailboat cruised northwest with its canvas full. But Luca's focus locked on a single vessel: a medium-sized fishing boat, its weathered hull a patchwork of chipped paint and rust.

Through the glass he studied the men onboard—efficient, methodical, hauling crab pots. The vessel's name, *Sea Breeze*, was scrawled in peeling blue paint along the hull. Too ordinary. Too still. Luca's instincts flared.

"Bring us closer," he ordered, lowering the binoculars. "Keep it subtle—half a mile out. I want to see their faces."

Carlos adjusted course. Javier, at the radar console, glanced between the screen and Luca. "Still no deviation," he reported.

Luca's smirk didn't reach his eyes. "Because it's not them," he said flatly, tucking the binoculars under his arm. "Morgan's smarter than I gave him credit for."

"You think he planted the tracker?" Javier asked.

"I don't think." Luca's voice went cold. "I know." He drummed his fingers along the railing as his gaze flicked back to the radar. "Expand the range. I want every contact in a hundred-mile radius."

The screen filled with blips. "Two vessels moving south through the Windward Passage. Another three southeast, just north of Haiti," Javier read off.

Luca leaned over the console, eyes narrowing. "He's not going to backtrack. Time's too valuable," he muttered. "He'll cut through the Mona Passage. It's risky, but it's faster."

"What's the speed on the three contacts moving southeast?" he asked.

"Sixteen knots... twenty-one... and nine." Javier's finger hovered over the slower blip.

Luca's lips curved. "That's them." He straightened. "Get us within eight miles of the nine-knot contact. Radar shadow only—no wake overlap."

Carlos pushed the throttles. The *Sunseeker* accelerated; the water peeled away from the hull in foamy ribbons. Luca watched the horizon and the radar in the same split-second rhythm—data and sight feeding the same hunger.

"You think this Morgan's going to lead us to something big?" Carlos asked, half curiosity, half bravado.

"That's what Serrano thinks." Luca's answer was small and sharp. For a moment his thoughts flickered to Serrano's estate in Spain—the polished wood, the curated art, the way a man made his past into an argument for power. He respected the cunning; he resented the throne. Finding the prize first wouldn't just be a win. It'd be leverage.

"Full speed," Luca said. "We find it, we make him pay."

Thousands of miles away, under the fading glow of a Spanish sunset, Victor Serrano stood in the study of his estate overlooking Algeciras Bay. The last light of day slanted through tall arched windows, glancing off dark walnut paneling that gave the room its somber weight. A single brass lamp on his desk threw a warm circle across scattered documents, leaving the corners in shadow. Along the walls, shelves groaned with leather-bound volumes broken at intervals by portraits of ancestors staring down in stiff collars and polished armor. Their painted eyes caught the lamplight, unyielding and proud, though Victor read only failure behind the brushstrokes.

He paused beside the largest portrait, the figure of Admiral Don Rodrigo Serrano gazing forever toward an unseen horizon, as if still chasing the prize he could never seize. Victor's fingers brushed the frame, a gesture halfway between reverence and reproach. "You failed," he murmured, "but I will not."

Beyond the tall windows, the southern coast of Spain stretched toward the horizon, the Rock of Gibraltar rising dark against the amber sky. Olive groves and whitewashed villages dotted the rolling hills, their outlines softened by dusk, while the harbor lights of Algeciras flickered to life along the bay.

Victor's gaze, however, was fixed on the weathered parchment encased in protective glass at the center of the room. *El Poder Perdido*. The Lost Power. Its faded script, barely legible with time, seemed to whisper of stolen legacies and the promise of redemption. Slowly, his fingers traced the edge of the glass—hesitant, yet drawn by the gravity of what it represented. This was not sentimentality. This was history. His history.

A faint tremor passed through his left hand. He clenched his fist behind his back, forcing it to subside. Turning sharply, he crossed to the polished desk where an untouched glass of brandy waited, its amber surface catching the lamplight. The aroma of aged oak mingled with the faint smoke curling from a cigar in the ashtray. He ignored the drink for now, his eyes settling on another relic: a royal decree, yellowed and worn, bearing the crest of Spain—the double-headed eagle and a crumbling wax seal.

The words were etched into his memory: *You bear the stain of failure, a legacy unworthy of the crown. The treasure's loss will not be forgiven.*

His jaw tightened. He thought of Admiral Don Rodrigo Serrano—the family's once-great patriarch, entrusted with the crown's most sacred mission: recovering Elias Grey's stolen treasure. The mission had ended in disaster. Rodrigo's fleet vanished without a trace, swallowed by the sea. That failure had shattered the family's standing; their name, once synonymous with loyalty and naval prowess, became a whisper of disgrace. Political enemies and the Inquisition had finished the work, stripping titles, seizing estates, scattering survivors across Spain and the colonies.

For centuries, the Serrano's teetered on the edge of obscurity. But Victor would not let them fall. To him, the treasure wasn't just redemption—it was survival. Legends claimed its power could alter fate itself. Perhaps it could even deliver him from the truth gnawing at his nerves.

His phone buzzed on the desk. The name on the screen made his chest tighten: Dr. Herrera.

Follow-up on the new regimen — motor symptoms show slight improvement, but cognitive decline continues. We'll need to reassess dosage within the month.

Huntington's. The word carried the weight of a death sentence. Each day his body betrayed him a little more—tremors deepening, muscles beginning to stiffen, thoughts slipping like sand.

His hand trembled again as he reached for the brandy. He tightened his grip until the tremor stilled, staring at his distorted reflection in the amber liquid. The Serrano's had always been cursed—dragged down just as they climbed. Centuries ago, it had been the Inquisition. Now, it was a disease in his blood.

But he hadn't built an empire by surrendering. He had survived, fought, and conquered. He would not fail—not when the stakes were this high.

"Don Rodrigo may have failed," he whispered. "But I will not."

Victor turned back to the window. The bay shimmered in the last light, waves rolling toward the horizon like endless rows of opportunity. He raised the glass in a silent toast—not to the past, but to the future he intended to seize. Smoke curled from the cigar as he lit it anew, his gaze hardening. Somewhere out there, the treasure awaited. And with it, his redemption—and perhaps a second chance at life itself.

Out on the darkening seas, far removed from the elegance of Victor's study, *The Wayfinder* moved steadily through quiet waters. The hum of the engine was a soft undercurrent to the sound of the sea. In the small galley, Jake tended the stove where two fillets of mahi sizzled in butter, the savory aroma filling the cabin.

At the helm, Isabelle kept them on course. The faint glow of the instruments brushed across her features as she scanned the horizon.

"Smells good," she said, glancing back with a crooked smile. "Better than I expected from you—no offense."

Jake raised an eyebrow but didn't look away from the pan. "None taken. I'll have you know I'm a man of many talents."

"Clearly." She folded her arms and leaned against the helm. "What's your secret?"

"Fresh catch, a little butter, a little salt and pepper, and knowing when to flip it. Same as most things in life—timing and practice."

Isabelle chuckled. "Profound. You may just outdo yourself, chef."

Jake grinned faintly but kept his focus on the pan. The cabin seemed wrapped in its own cocoon of light and warmth, the night pressing in beyond the windows. Isabelle, lulled by the quiet rhythm of the boat, decided to test the waters of a different kind.

"What were you like as a teenager, Jake? Let me guess—rebellious, constantly getting into trouble?"

He laughed under his breath, plating the fish. "Define trouble."

"That's not a denial," she shot back. "Were you sneaking out at night, or just the kid everyone blamed because you looked guilty?"

Jake shook his head, grinning. "Bit of both. I wasn't much of a student, but I wasn't setting fires either. More the kind of kid who ditched class to go fishing or diving. My dad hated it. Pops, though? He called it 'practical education.'"

"Ah, the legendary Pops," Isabelle said warmly. "So you were the outdoorsy type even then?"

"Always." Jake slid the fish onto plates. "Couldn't sit still for long. School just... never stuck. I'd be staring out the window, thinking about the water. Pops used to tell me the ocean was calling, and I believed him."

"Did you ever get into anything serious?" Isabelle asked, her tone curious but cautious.

Jake hesitated, leaning back against the counter. "When I was seventeen, I got arrested for breaking into a salvage yard. There was this old dive boat I wanted—rusted out, engine shot. I figured I could fix it, make something of it. Problem was..." he rubbed the back of his neck with a rueful grin, "...I didn't have the money to buy it."

Isabelle paused. "You tried to steal a boat?"

"Borrow," Jake corrected quickly. "I thought I'd get it running, make some money, pay the guy back."

"And let me guess—it didn't go as planned?"

"Not even close." He laughed dryly. "Got caught before I made it out of the yard. Spent the night in a squad car. My dad was furious when he bailed me out. But Pops... he didn't yell. He just told me, 'If you want something, Jake, earn it. Don't take shortcuts.' That stuck."

Isabelle studied him, her expression softening. "And did it?"

Jake gave a half-shrug. "Mostly. I mean, here I am chasing treasure instead of stealing dive boats—progress, right?"

She shook her head, smiling. "I'll give you points for honesty. But I'm guessing that wasn't the last time you made your dad mad."

"Not by a long shot." His grin faded. "But I figured out how to do things the right way. Took me a few years, though."

"Well, here's to progress." Isabelle lifted her coffee in a mock toast. "And to not stealing any more boats."

Jake chuckled, plating the second fillet and sliding it across the table to her. "There's always tomorrow."

The Wayfinder pressed on into the night, the soft hum of the engine steady beneath the glow of the cabin lights. Isabelle settled at the table, offering Jake a smile of thanks as she caught the plate.

He sat opposite her, fork in hand. "So now that you know I was a teenage delinquent with a knack for bad decisions—what about you? What was young Isabelle like?"

She speared a piece of fish, her voice thoughtful. "Young Isabelle... she was curious. Always asking questions, always looking for answers."

Jake smirked. "Doesn't sound too different from now."

She laughed lightly. "Fair. But most of that came from my mom. She was... amazing."

Jake leaned forward, his grin softening. "What was she like?"

Isabelle set down her fork, fingers tracing idle shapes on the table. "When I was little, I'd sit in her workshop for hours, just watching. She melted silver, shaped gold—every piece had a story. She'd tell me how the Muisca people wore them as symbols of power or protection, a way to stay connected to their ancestors."

Jake stilled, listening intently.

"One time, I found this book in my dad's study," Isabelle continued, her voice quieter now. "It had a picture of a necklace they'd buried with one of their leaders. I showed it to her, and she recreated it—just for me. When she finished, she handed it to me and said, 'You're part of this story now. Wear it like you mean it.'"

Her lips curved in a wistful smile. "I still have that necklace. It's how I keep her close." She hesitated, then added softly, "Well... that, and this."

From her pocket, she withdrew the compass. "It was my father's," she said, turning it between her fingers. "He gave it to me after she passed. Said it helped him find his way when he couldn't see a path forward."

Jake extended a hand. "May I?"

She placed the compass in his palm. The brass felt smooth and cool, edges worn from decades of handling. He turned it over, studying the faint etching on the back and the glass face scratched by time. When he flipped the lid open, the needle wavered, hesitated—then clicked slowly north.

"The hand sticks sometimes," Isabelle said, a touch of fondness in her voice.

Jake nodded, thumb brushing the rim. "Old, but still true." He handed it back carefully.

After a moment, he reached for the leather cord around his own neck and pulled out the key.

"My turn," he said quietly. "This belonged to my grandfather. Pops called it a reminder to earn what you chase. I never found what it opens, but he said it wasn't about that—it was about remembering where you come from."

Isabelle smiled, eyes catching the faint etching near the barrel. "Looks like it's seen as much sea as you have."

"Probably more," Jake said, looping the cord back over his head. "Guess we both hang on to things that keep us pointed somewhere."

The cabin fell into a gentle stillness. Outside, waves lapped against the hull, and the stars pressed close above the dark horizon.

Jake's expression grew thoughtful, his usual easy charm replaced by something steadier. "Sounds like you got your curiosity and your sense of purpose from your mom."

"Maybe." Isabelle laughed softly. "She balanced my dad's academic intensity with creativity and heart. I think I'm still trying to live up to both of them."

Jake offered a small smile, genuine and unguarded. "Seems to me like you're doing a damn good job of it."

For a long moment, the only sound was the engine's hum and the clink of cutlery. Then Isabelle glanced at him, a flicker of unspoken connection passing between them.

"Thanks, Jake," she said quietly.

He smiled, a small, genuine thing, and gave a slight nod.

As they returned to their meal, the air between them felt changed—lighter, yet anchored by the stories they had shared. Invisible threads wove tighter in the quiet glow of the cabin, binding them to each other, whether either of them was ready to admit it or not.

Outside, the stars thinned behind a smear of cloud. Somewhere forward, a wave slapped hard under the chine and the wind found a higher note in the rails—the Mona was waking up.

Chapter Fourteen

Tempest and Shadow

*T*he *Wayfinder* lurched violently as the storm raged around them, rain hammering the deck in relentless sheets. Outside the cabin windows, the night was a blur of black water and whitecaps, each wave cresting higher than the last. The Mona Passage had chosen violence.

Jake's grip tightened on the helm as he fought to keep the bow head-on into the swells. The wind screamed through the radar arch, the boat groaning with each impact as if it might split apart. Jaw locked, he read the water, adjusting course with practiced precision—every move keeping disaster a hair's breadth away.

Behind him, Isabelle braced herself against the cabin table, knuckles white as *The Wayfinder* pitched hard to starboard. She had seen rough seas before—but nothing this furious. Nothing this alive with malice.

"Is it supposed to be this bad?!" she shouted over the storm's roar.

Jake didn't glance back, eyes flicking between the instruments and the black chaos beyond the glass. "Squalls in the Mona Passage don't play nice! Just hold on and—"

A metallic thunk cut through the gale. Something rolled across the deck with a teeth-rattling scrape.

Jake's stomach dropped. *No. Not that.*

One of their extra fuel drums had broken free of its straps, slamming against the railing with each violent tilt. Another wave and it would be gone—and with it, their hope of making landfall.

Before Jake could bark a warning, Isabelle saw it too.

"We're going to lose it!" she shouted, already lunging for the door.

Jake's head snapped toward her. "Isabelle, stop!"

But she ignored him.

The moment she yanked the door open, the storm pounced—wind

ripping it wide, rain and seawater blasting into the cabin, soaking her instantly. She staggered onto the slick deck, clutching the railing as the boat heaved beneath her feet. The world outside was pure chaos—water foaming over the planks, air a maelstrom of spray and darkness.

Jake swore violently, wrenching the wheel to counter a sudden gust. He couldn't leave the helm. Not now. If the boat turned broadside, they'd roll. *If I go after her, we're finished. If I don't...*

"Get back inside!" he bellowed, his voice cracking with fury.

Isabelle didn't listen. Her gaze locked on the fuel drum, now hammering the railing with bone-rattling force. They needed that fuel. She dropped to her knees, crawling forward as another wave broke across the deck, drenching her to the skin. Her soaked hands fumbled with the strap, fighting to loop it back into place.

Inside the cabin, Jake's pulse thundered. Every second she stayed out there, the storm had another chance to take her. His hands ached from clenching the wheel, the urge to abandon it almost unbearable. *Damn it, Isabelle—why now?*

The next wave made the choice for them.

The drum broke loose entirely, slamming into her side with brutal force. Isabelle gasped, stumbling back. The slick deck gave way beneath her and she slid toward the edge, seawater surging over her like an icy fist.

Jake's heart stopped. "Isabelle!"

She clawed at the railing, boots scrambling for traction, but the torrent threatened to tear her free. With a last desperate heave she ratcheted the strap, locking the drum in place—only for the storm to rise higher still.

A wall of water loomed above the bow, black and monstrous, and then came crashing down like a freight train.

The impact tore her loose.

Jake moved before thought.

He abandoned the helm—damn the risk—and hurled himself through the open door. Rain blinded him, salt stung his eyes, and then his body slammed into the railing as his hand caught Isabelle's wrist a heartbeat before she vanished into the sea.

The pull nearly ripped him over with her. His muscles screamed as the storm tried to tear them apart.

"Hang on!" he growled through gritted teeth, every fiber straining.

Her free hand flailed, searching for purchase, until her fingers finally closed around the railing. With a gasping, ragged effort, she clawed her way back onto the deck.

Then she collapsed against him—soaked, shaking, alive.

For a long moment, nothing but ragged breaths and the storm's howling fury filled the night.

Then Jake's fury broke through the adrenaline.

"What the hell were you thinking?!" he roared, gripping her arms as if afraid the sea would steal her again.

Isabelle coughed, pushing wet hair from her face, eyes burning with defiance. She didn't apologize.

Jake didn't let go.

Even as the helm sat unmanned, the storm raged on, threatening to finish what it started.

Twenty miles northwest, the *Sunseeker* rocked steadily at anchor off the north coast of Punta Cana. The wind had picked up, rippling across the bay, but here—sheltered from the teeth of the storm—the sea remained deceptively calm.

Luca stood at the helm, eyes fixed on the radar. The green blip of *The Wayfinder* crawled deeper into the chaos, its path jagged with frantic course corrections, its speed bleeding away. Morgan was fighting for his life out there.

"You're a stubborn son of a bitch, I'll give you that," Luca muttered, taking a long pull from a bottle of lukewarm water. It did nothing to wash away the taste of tension.

"He's either got balls of steel or a death wish," Carlos said, dragging on his cigarette. Ash scattered across the deck as he leaned against the console, smirking. "No way he makes it through."

Mateo, arms crossed, gave a low grunt. "Don't bet on it. The guy's a diver. They're used to staring down bad conditions."

Carlos scoffed. "There's bad conditions, and then there's the Mona Passage in a storm. Whole different animal."

Javier, ever the tactician, leaned forward, eyes narrowing on the screen. "Morgan's reckless, not stupid. If he pushed in, he believes he can thread it."

"Or he's just lucky," Carlos shot back, flicking his cigarette into the sea. He glanced at Luca. "Hell, maybe we don't even need to follow him. Let the ocean do the dirty work."

Luca's jaw flexed. "That's not an option."

Carlos arched a brow. "Why the hell not? Saves us a lot of trouble."

Mateo's frown deepened, his voice carrying more weight than usual. "Because if the storm swallows him, we'll never know where he was headed. Trail goes cold." He looked at Luca, reading him. "Right?"

Luca gave a slow nod. "Exactly."

He took another sip, eyes never leaving the screen. *The Wayfinder*'s signal pulsed—fragile but unbroken—inching forward against the storm's fury. Luca didn't like leaving fate in anyone else's hands, especially the ocean's. But for now, he had no choice.

If Morgan survived, Luca would be waiting.

If he didn't—then the game became something else entirely.

Out on the radar screen, the green dot flickered, still alive against the storm. Miles away, *The Wayfinder* fought on, every wave threatening to be its last.

By first light, the horizon broke open—Puerto Rico ahead. *The Wayfinder* rocked under the storm's dying breath. Rain still drummed against the windows, but the howling winds had quieted to a restless whisper. The sea remained rough, yet it no longer clawed at them with the same murderous intent.

Inside the cabin, Jake crouched in front of Isabelle, wrapping a towel around her trembling shoulders. She sat on the bunk near the table, soaked to the bone, her hands gripping the fabric as though it might anchor her. Damp strands of hair clung to her pale cheeks, but her eyes—dark and steady—hadn't lost their fire.

Jake ran a hand through his wet hair, adrenaline still coursing hot in his veins. He rubbed her arms through the towel, lingering longer than necessary, trying to coax the chill from her skin.

"You scared the hell out of me," he muttered, voice rough. He meant to pull away. He didn't.

Isabelle's fingers brushed his wrist for a heartbeat, fragile and deliberate. "Yeah, well... that makes two of us."

He rose, fetched a blanket from the locker, and draped it over her shoulders before crouching again. Her hands were ice. He took them in his, rubbing warmth back into her fingers, the callouses of his palms catching against her skin.

"I'll be fine," she said, though her voice trembled. She looked up at him, searching. "You let go of the helm for me."

Jake gave a short, humorless laugh. "What, you think I was gonna let you get washed overboard?"

"You could've lost control of the boat," she pressed, shivering still.

He didn't answer right away. The truth was, there hadn't been a choice. He'd seen her slip, and instinct had taken over. Everything else had vanished. He ran a hand across his face, exhaling hard. "Not much of a boat left to steer if my first mate's floating out in the damn ocean."

Isabelle gave a shaky laugh despite herself. "So I'm your first mate now?"

Jake smirked, though he kept hold of her hands. "Well, unless you're planning on abandoning ship..."

She shook her head. "Not a chance."

Their eyes met. The words landed heavier than either of them expected.

Jake finally let her go, moving to the galley. He poured steaming tea into a mug, the kettle whistling faintly over the muted roar of the sea. When he brought it back, he pressed it into her hands with quiet care.

Isabelle wrapped her fingers around the cup, sighing into the warmth. For a while, silence stretched between them. Not empty—charged. The storm had left behind more than just quiet seas.

"You scared me," Jake said again, softer now.

Her gaze lifted, unreadable for a moment, then softened. "Yeah...I scared me too."

He rubbed the back of his neck, forcing a crooked smile. "Let's make a deal. Next time we're in a storm like that, you stay inside the damn cabin."

Her eyebrow arched, some spark returning. "And if the fuel drums come loose again?"

"Then I'll be the one to tie them down," he shot back.

She smirked into her cup. "Aye-aye, Captain."

Jake chuckled, tension easing just a fraction. Outside, the sea rolled on, but the worst had passed. The air carried a promise of calmer waters.

For now, they had survived. Together.

By the time *The Wayfinder* eased into the marina at La Parguera, the sky was painted in soft strokes of pink and gold. The storm had long since passed, leaving the sea glassy and the air thick with humid warmth. The docks were quiet—just the chatter of fishermen prepping their boats and the distant thrum of an outboard fading across the bay.

Jake guided the trawler alongside the pier, hands steady on the lines as he secured them with the practiced ease of a man who had spent his life tying knots. Weariness tugged at him—an echo of the night's fight—but the sight of calm water felt like a reprieve.

Isabelle moved to step ashore, but the moment she straightened, a searing pain lit up her right side. She sucked in a sharp breath, clutching the railing as memory struck: the fuel drum slamming into her ribs, the storm, the sea, the fight to stay upright.

Jake caught it instantly. "What's wrong?"

"Nothing," she said quickly, though the word came out tight. She lifted her shirt just enough to see for herself—and winced. A deep bruise sprawled across her ribs, mottled purple and angry blue, the shape unmistakable from where the drum had struck.

Jake turned from the dock lines just in time to catch a glimpse. His jaw clenched. "Jesus, Isabelle." He stepped closer, gaze dark as he took it in. "That's not nothing."

She dropped her shirt, forcing a smile that didn't reach her eyes. "I'll live. Just sore."

"You should've told me sooner."

"And what would you have done?" she countered, one brow lifting despite the pain. "Turned the boat around? We had bigger problems last night."

Jake exhaled hard but said nothing. She wasn't wrong. Still, the sight of the bruise twisted something in him. "Fine. But you're taking it easy today."

Isabelle scoffed. "I'm not a porcelain doll, Morgan."

"No," he shot back, his tone firm, "but you don't have to be reckless, either. Take it slow. We're only here for fuel and supplies. No sense in making it worse."

Her retort died on her lips. She hated to admit it, but every step sent a dull ache through her ribs, and she knew by nightfall the bruise would be worse. She settled for rolling her eyes, though more out of surrender than defiance.

They refueled, resupplied, and checked *The Wayfinder* stem to stern, the simple tasks pulling them back into rhythm. By unspoken agreement, they kept conversation light. Both were bone-tired, both running on the frayed edges of adrenaline.

When everything was squared away, they gave in to exhaustion. Isabelle curled into the forward berth, the ache in her side dulled by sheer fatigue. Jake stretched out on the cabin's narrow bunk, one arm draped over his eyes to block the shafts of sunlight spilling through the windows.

The marina rocked them in a gentle cradle, waves tapping softly at the hull. Outside, La Parguera carried on with quiet life, but within the *Wayfinder*, silence reigned—deep, dreamless, and earned.

By dawn, the *Sunseeker*'s wake cut hard across the Mona Passage, its sleek hull hammering the swells as twin diesels roared beneath the deck. Spray whipped over the bow, flung high into the morning air, but Luca didn't ease back. At thirty-five knots, the yacht chewed up miles of open water—and he had no intention of giving Morgan any more breathing room than he needed.

The coastline of Puerto Rico stretched across the horizon, green ridges dropping into the blue Caribbean. La Parguera dozed along the southwestern shore, a sleepy port town just rousing to life. From a mile out, its marina was a clutter of masts and hulls, fishing boats rocking lazily in the calm after the storm.

Luca raised his binoculars, scanning the docks with surgical patience. The place looked unremarkable. But he knew Morgan. After a night like that, the man would need fuel, supplies, and a few hours of rest. Which meant he was here.

Mateo shifted at the helm, glancing over. "We sure about this?"

"They pulled in at dawn," Luca said without lowering the binoculars. "They haven't gone anywhere."

Javier studied the radar, brow furrowed. "Too many contacts this morning. The marina's crowded—we can't isolate one target."

Luca ignored the complaint. His gaze swept along the fuel docks, cataloging hull shapes and paint schemes. Patient. Exacting. And then—there.

The Wayfinder. Nestled between two larger boats, its dull lines and workboat paint trying to disappear into the clutter. Ordinary to anyone else. Not to him.

A slow smirk touched Luca's mouth. "Got you."

He snapped the binoculars shut and turned to the crew. "Near the fuel station. They'll move soon."

Mateo let out a low breath. "So we wait?"

Luca nodded. "We wait. They're headed southeast, and after last night they'll think they've shaken us. That's when they'll get sloppy."

Carlos leaned against the bulkhead, flicking his lighter open and closed. "Victor wanted us pushing harder. More pressure."

Luca's head turned sharply, eyes hard. "Victor wants results. We get them by being smarter, not louder." He looked back to the marina, his smirk sharpening. "You don't catch prey by charging. You let it think it's already free."

The *Sunseeker* idled just outside the harbor, engines rumbling like caged beasts. Luca kept his eyes fixed on *The Wayfinder*, a predator biding its moment.

All he needed was time.

That afternoon, sunlight poured through the portholes, carrying the scent of saltwater and fresh coffee. Isabelle groaned as she shifted upright, the dull throb in her ribs reminding her of the storm's brutality. She wrapped a strip of bandage Jake had found in the first-aid kit around her side, wincing before steadying herself.

In the galley, Jake was already up, mug in hand, charts spread across the table. He glanced up as she stepped in, eyes flicking briefly to her ribs.

"How's the side?"

"Still attached," she said wryly, pouring her own cup. "How long was I out?"

"Long enough to almost look human again."

She arched a brow but took the seat opposite, her gaze falling to the charts. "So, what's the plan?"

Jake traced a finger along a vast empty stretch of ocean off Venezuela's coast. "The archives put *Las Islas de Sombras* somewhere in here."

Isabelle leaned in, scanning the blank blue expanse. "That's a lot of ocean to comb through."

"Yeah," Jake admitted, leaning back. "But we've got one thing going for us. The logbooks talked about reefs and fog. If we're close, we'll know it."

She tapped the chart thoughtfully. "Unusual water color. Bird activity. Sudden depth changes. If the island hides behind fog most of the time, it won't show itself until we're right on top of it."

"Which means we take it slow," Jake agreed. "*The Wayfinder* isn't exactly equipped with cutting-edge nav tech."

"Or stocked with a Plan B," Isabelle muttered into her mug.

Jake smirked. "Backup plans are for people who expect to fail."

She rolled her eyes. "The Jake Morgan school of reckless optimism."

He grinned, but the expression faded as he folded the map. "Once we shove off, there's no turning back. No resupply, no safe harbors. Just us and whatever's waiting out there."

Isabelle met his gaze, steady. "Then let's not waste any more time."

Jake drained the last of his coffee and pushed to his feet. "Then let's get moving."

Half an hour later, *The Wayfinder* slipped free of its lines, gliding out of La Parguera's marina. Isabelle stood at the bow, the town receding behind them—the last familiar shore before the unknown.

Ahead, the Caribbean stretched vast and unbroken, its horizon shimmering like a mirage.

She turned back toward the helm, where Jake adjusted their course. His voice carried across the deck. "Alright, Professor. Let's go find that lost island."

The Wayfinder surged forward, her bow cutting the waves.

Together they sailed toward history—toward danger—toward whatever waited beyond the veil of legend.

CHAPTER FIFTEEN

The Sea That Swallows Islands

The Wayfinder pressed south into the Caribbean Sea, her diesel heart-beat steady beneath Jake's feet. The sea stretched unbroken, horizon dissolving where blue met blue. Somewhere ahead, if old charts and dead men's clues were to be believed, lay the cluster of islands they'd identified from the Spanish letter— the place Grey had vanished toward.

At the chart table, Isabelle had spread her notebook across the worn wood. Lines of her neat handwriting filled page after page—notes she'd copied from the FIU archives. Not Grey's words, nor his pursuers' desperate dispatches, but fragments from Spanish captains' logbooks: terse entries about sudden fogs, shoals that rose from nowhere, *false horizons* that tricked even seasoned pilots.

She ran a finger beneath one line and read aloud, her voice soft but clear over the hum of the engine.

"The horizon bent as if lifted by a hand, and a ship ahead disappeared into it as though swallowed."

She looked up, brown eyes steady despite the bruise of exhaustion around them. "Multiple captains described the same thing, Jake. Not just one."

He glanced back, one hand steady on the wheel. "An optical illusion."

"Maybe." She shifted, marking the margin of her notes, then winced as her ribs flared. The pencil stilled in her hand until the pain passed.

Jake caught it. "Easy."

"I'm fine." She sat back carefully, her expression stubborn. "We need these clues to help find this place. Our track could be off by a couple of miles in either direction. So keep an eye out."

His jaw flexed, torn between letting it go and calling her on it. In the end he only shook his head, a flicker of amusement breaking through. "Just let me know if you need anything, stubborn."

"Thanks." A faint smile tugged at her mouth. "Not stubborn."

Jake turned back to the helm, lips quirking despite himself. Beyond the bow the ocean rolled on—deceptively calm, as if it wanted to convince him nothing waited ahead. But his grip tightened on the wheel all the same.

"Alright," he murmured, eyes fixed on the horizon. "Let's see what your ghosts were warning about."

By late morning, the sea itself began to change.

Jake noticed it first at the helm—a shimmer across the bow where the water shifted from deep cobalt to pale green. At first it looked like sunlight playing tricks, but as *The Wayfinder* eased forward, the difference sharpened into a distinct seam—two bodies of water pressing together like mismatched panes of glass.

He throttled back, narrowing his eyes. "Shoals meeting the deep."

Isabelle pushed carefully up from her seat, one hand pressed to her ribs, and leaned over the railing. The color was unmistakable now: turquoise shallows feathering into ink-blue depths, a hard line slicing across the swell.

"Just like the journals described," she murmured.

A sudden upwelling surged to starboard—a patch of cold water rippling to the surface. Jake felt the temperature shift against his legs through the open cabin door, the kind of icy draft that didn't belong in the tropics.

He frowned, adjusting the wheel against the new tug in the current. "That's not normal."

Then came the birds. A line of frigatebirds and gulls cut across the sky, wings flashing in the morning light. Halfway through their arc, the formation bent sharply, veering wide—as though avoiding something unseen below.

Isabelle tracked them, flipping through her notes. "They saw more than birds breaking course. One wrote, *'The horizon bent as if lifted by a hand, and when it fell away the reef was upon us.'* Another called it a false horizon—sailors steering toward a line of sky that wasn't sky at all."

Jake glanced from her to the strange seam where turquoise pressed against cobalt. The horizon ahead did look odd—blurred, wavering—though whether it was light, heat, or something worse, he couldn't tell.

"False horizons," he muttered. "No wonder they wrecked."

Jake adjusted the throttle again, jaw set. Whatever it was, they were steering straight into it.

By mid-afternoon, the sea had settled into a deceptive calm—the kind that lulled sailors into believing nothing waited beyond the horizon. Heat pressed down on *The Wayfinder*, turning the cabin into an oven despite the small fans rattling above the chart table.

Isabelle leaned over her notes, sketching a line across the map, cross-referencing depths with the reports from the FIU archives. Her pencil slowed, then stilled as she drew a careful breath through her nose. The inhale caught, sharp with pain, and her hand pressed instinctively to her ribs.

Jake didn't ask this time. He ducked under the counter, pulled out the med kit, and set it on the table with quiet finality. Isabelle glanced at him, one brow lifting.

"Don't start," she said, trying to wave him off.

He ignored her, filled a plastic bag from the galley's icebox, and wrapped it in a cloth. "Humor me."

Before she could argue, he was already unwinding a roll of elastic bandage. "Lift your shirt."

She blinked, caught between protest and surprise, but the corner of her mouth broke into a grin. "Now who's being forward?"

"Touché," he said, tone firm but warm.

Reluctantly, Isabelle raised her shirt, exposing the dark bruise spreading across her ribs. She braced herself against the table as Jake sat on the bunk, face mere inches from her. The smooth brown skin of her midsection gleamed with sweat in the stifling heat, a bead slipping down her side. He fought to keep focus as he pressed the cold pack in place. She recoiled at the chill.

"Don't be a baby," Jake teased under his breath, securing the ice and wrapping the bandage snugly around her torso. His hands were steady, practical—but the closeness brought color to Isabelle's cheeks.

"There," he said, tying off the bandage. "Better than pretending it's nothing."

She exhaled slowly, a hint of relief softening her expression. "Thanks."

Jake gave a small nod, returning the kit. "Not stubborn," he said with a faint smirk. "Just reckless."

Her eyes narrowed, though her smile gave her away. "Determined."

"I think we're more alike than you'd like to admit."

She laughed softly, shaking her head. "Don't get ahead of yourself,

Captain."

Jake turned back to the helm, but the heat in the cabin no longer felt quite so oppressive.

By dusk the ocean seemed to exhale, flattening into a mirror. The last light of the sun smeared gold across the horizon, but the line between sea and sky blurred, wavering—as though the world itself couldn't decide where to end.

Jake eased back on the throttle, uneasy. The compass needle had begun to drift, twitching off their bearing before sliding back again. The depth sounder flickered once, twice, before steadying.

"Don't like that," he muttered, tapping the glass.

Isabelle closed her notebook, eyes on the shifting horizon. "You see that?"

He followed her gaze. The line of sky wasn't straight anymore. It dipped and rose, a faint distortion like heat haze but heavier, stranger. For a heartbeat the whole horizon seemed to lift, then fall again, leaving him disoriented.

"My abuelo told stories about this," Isabelle said quietly. "He called it *the sea that swallows islands whole.* Fishermen swore there were places where the ocean bent light, where land appeared and vanished like smoke."

Jake swallowed, fingers tightening on the wheel. "Not exactly the bed-time story you want when you're steering blind."

The sea lay flat and breathless, every ripple smoothed to glass. *The Wayfinder* cut through it without a sound. Even the engine's hum seemed muted, swallowed by the heavy air.

A low mist began to curl off the surface, spreading until it crept across the bow and swallowed the horizon entirely. A bead of moisture rolled down the rail, cold against Jake's fingers.

"This isn't weather," he said under his breath.

Isabelle wrapped her arms around herself, a shiver running through her despite the humid air. "No. This is something else."

The Wayfinder pressed forward, her wake vanishing into fog as though sliding across a veil drawn over the sea.

The fog thickened until the world shrank to the arc of the bow light. Jake throttled down, *The Wayfinder* crawling forward at idle, her wake erased behind her. Sound itself seemed swallowed—the diesel's hum muted, the slap of water against the hull gone. Even Isabelle's breathing felt too loud in the suffocating silence.

Then Jake heard it.

A low rumble carried through the mist—deep and steady. At first it could have been thunder, but no storm brewed. The sound grew until it became a roar, rhythmic, breaking.

"Surf," Jake muttered, tension hardening his jaw.

Isabelle frowned. "Out here?"

"Reef," he said grimly. "A big one."

Spray burst through the fog, droplets pelting the windshield. A gust carried the sharp tang of coral and crushed shell. Then, in the sweep of Isabelle's spotlight, a jagged wall of whitewater exploded into view—the reef rising like a fortress from the depths, surf detonating against it.

"Fuck!" Jake slammed the throttle into reverse. *The Wayfinder* shuddered as the screw churned against the current. The stern lifted and slewed sideways, the pull of water dragging them forward anyway. The reef loomed closer, every wave detonating like cannon fire against the coral.

"Jake!" Isabelle swept the beam left, then right—nothing but jagged teeth and crashing surf. Her heart hammered. "I don't see—wait..."

She pushed the spotlight farther to starboard. For a moment—only more whitewater. Then: dark water, a narrow ribbon threading between the reefs.

"There!" she shouted. "Starboard—forty degrees! Channel!"

"Got it!" Jake jammed the throttle forward and spun the wheel hard over. The diesel roared, *The Wayfinder* shuddering, foam boiling on either side as the current tried to wrench her broadside. A rogue swell slammed the bow, sending spray across the deck.

"Hold on!" he barked, fighting the wheel as the boat surged into the gap.

The hull lifted on a swell, then dropped into a trough, foam churning inches from the rail. For a heartbeat it felt as if the sea would crush them against the coral. Then, with a final surge, they burst through.

Silence.

The roar of surf fell away, replaced by a lagoon as still as glass. The spotlight swept wide—and Isabelle gasped.

Wreckage.

Dozens of broken masts jutted from the water like grave markers. Hulls split open on coral heads. Wooden beams draped in seaweed and coral protruded like skeletal ribs from the shallows. Some wrecks were ancient, half-consumed by the sea. Others looked far more recent—hulking iron shadows twisted by the reef's relentless grip.

"A graveyard," Isabelle whispered, raising her camera with a trembling hand. She snapped photo after photo, documenting the silent tomb around them.

Jake joined her at the rail, running a hand back through damp hair. "Jesus..."

They stood together in the eerie stillness, surrounded by centuries of ruin, until the fog stirred again—slowly, heavily—parting not with the drift of wind, but as though revealing something.

Beyond the graveyard, black cliffs rose sudden and sheer from the lagoon, jagged teeth silhouetted against the last glow of dusk.

Isabelle gripped Jake's arm, her hand cold against his skin. He covered it briefly with his own, steady and silent.

"We found it," Jake said quietly.

The mist closed again around them, but the silhouette of *Las Islas de Sombras* remained—stark and undeniable.

The *Sunseeker* idled just inside radar range, engines throttled low to keep noise to a minimum. The warm Caribbean night wrapped around them, but Luca barely noticed the humidity. His focus was on the blinking radar contact ahead—*The Wayfinder* had slowed to a crawl.

Luca stood at the helm, one hand resting on the console, the other flicking his knife open and closed in a steady rhythm. Tension hung thick in the cabin.

"They stopped," Carlos muttered from navigation, staring at the radar. "Or they're moving so slow it might as well be stopped."

Javier rubbed the back of his neck. "That means we're getting close to whatever they're looking for, right?"

Luca exhaled, watching the screen as if willing it to offer more. "No. It means Morgan's being careful. And if he's careful, that means it's dangerous as hell."

He stepped out onto the deck, raising binoculars. Beyond the bow, the night was an impenetrable wall of black, but in the distance the white crash of waves flickered under faint moonlight.

He lowered the lenses, jaw tightening. The passages east of Puerto Rico had been treacherous—but this felt worse.

Back inside, he leaned over the console.

"We could push forward," Mateo suggested. "The *Sunseeker* can handle it. We're faster and—"

"No." Luca cut him off sharply. "You want to take a high-performance yacht into a reef at night? Be my guest. I'll make sure your next of kin gets what's left of you."

Mateo clamped his mouth shut.

Carlos reclined lazily in his chair, taking a slow drag from his cigarette. "So, what? We just sit here?"

"We wait," Luca confirmed. "Let them do the hard part for us."

He pointed at the radar. "They're threading a needle through that reef. If we follow now, we risk tearing the hull—or worse, giving ourselves away." He shot Carlos a look. "You in a hurry to die?"

Carlos exhaled smoke and shook his head. "Not particularly."

Javier frowned. "So... when do we move?"

Luca studied the stationary dot caught within the radar echoes. A slow grin curved his mouth.

"At first light," he said, slipping the knife back into his pocket. "Once they've found a way through."

CHAPTER SIXTEEN

The Ghost in the Mist

They'd anchored in darkness, the cliffs little more than shapes against the stars. By morning, the mist had swallowed everything, and Jake eased *The Wayfinder* into the gray.

The cliffs swallowed the horizon by degrees until there was nothing left but stone and mist. Jake eased the throttles back and let *The Wayfinder* idle, hull nudging forward like a swimmer testing the water with his toe. The engine's note softened to a steady purr. Even that sounded wrong—muffled, as if the cove didn't just hold sound; it smothered it.

"Depth?" he asked, eyes fixed on the pale curtain of mist ahead.

"Thirty-two feet and getting shallower," Isabelle said, bent over the sounder. Her voice came out small in the hush. "The shelf rises fast toward the inside."

The cliffs pressed close, streaked black and copper with mineral stains, vines dangling like wet rope. The waterfall hung at the far end of the cove, a gauzy smear against the rock. It should have thundered. Instead it breathed—a long, wet exhale that couldn't quite reach them. Jake felt it more than he heard it, a vibration in the hull—tapping at the fillings in his teeth.

He rolled his shoulders, working a knot from his neck. "This place gives me a bad feeling, like it doesn't want us here."

Isabelle glanced at him from beneath the brim of her hat. "I feel it too." She looked out across the gray. "Like stepping into another world."

The mist folded in on itself, opening and closing without pattern. A pair of seabirds cut low across the water and vanished without a cry. Jake kept the bow steady, hands light on the wheel, reading the water the way he read currents while diving—through the helm, through the faint nudge at the keel. A cold seam slid along the hull, raising goose bumps on his arms.

He rubbed them, the motion pulling his necklace free from his collar. The small brass key swung and tapped his sternum: a soft, familiar knock.

He caught it with his fingers and held it there a second, thumb finding the grooves he'd traced since boyhood. Pops had worn it the same way. A key to something special, Pops would say, though he never knew what. Either way, it grounded him during uncertain times.

Jake let the key drop, bone-deep steadier than he had any right to be in this place.

"Keep tracking the bottom," he said. "If it comes up quick, I want to know before we chew the fiberglass up on rock."

"Will do." Isabelle bent back over the screen, camera hanging loose at her ribs. She shifted the strap a notch higher, easing it off the bruise that still lingered.

He let *The Wayfinder* continue to drift. The wake spread, met the cliffs, and crept back without a sound. He checked the tach, half-expecting the engine to have died without telling him.

"Twenty feet," Isabelle called. A beat later: "Eighteen."

Jake adjusted the helm to port, keeping the bow pointed into the current. "Good eyes. Don't let it sneak up on us."

The mist shifted near the mouth of the cove, and something vast began to suggest itself—lines before mass, geometry before details. A rise of hull where no rock should be; a rake of bow his brain first sketched as modern steel—then the angles settled, older, heavier.

A galleon.

It loomed half-sunken in the shallows, caught as if some hidden hand beneath the water still held it fast. The beakhead jutted like a broken tooth, masts sheared to stumps. Ropes sagged into black nets, rigging gone to rot. Not pristine—scabbed, breached, scarred—but standing. Standing when it should have been mulch and memory.

Jake let out a breath he hadn't realized he was holding. The key tapped his sternum once, twice, like a fingertip urging him to look harder.

"This thing," he said, voice low because loud felt wrong, "should be driftwood."

Isabelle lifted her camera, snapping quickly with the flash dialed low and angled off the surface to keep from blowing the mist. Her answer came soft, steady, her mind doing the work it needed to do. "Cold currents. Mineral spray. Shelter from storms." She swallowed. "Enough to slow the clock."

He took another breath, and the cove swallowed it whole. The key lay warm against his skin, and under the warmth he felt the cold rising from below, threading everything together.

Jake kept *The Wayfinder* well clear of the wreck, circling until he found a patch of deeper water where the anchor would bite. He cut the engine, and silence closed in again, heavy and smothering.

The vibration underfoot vanished, leaving only stillness. Without the diesel's hum, the cove revealed itself—water dripping against stone, the faint hiss of spray at the falls, and beneath it all a low, pulsing hush, like the whole place was holding its breath.

Isabelle stepped to the rail, camera lowered. "It feels... wrong without the engine."

"Feels like it's listening," Jake muttered. He scanned the cliffs, the water, the wreck half-shrouded in mist. For a moment he felt like a trespasser in someone else's grave.

Neither spoke. *The Wayfinder* rocked gently, chain taut on the anchor, the only living sound a gull crying faintly somewhere above—and even that was quickly swallowed by the gray.

At last Jake exhaled and nodded toward the inflatable. "Alright. Let's take the dinghy across."

He lowered the dinghy and gave the lines a final check. Isabelle passed down her satchel, then climbed in after him. *The Wayfinder* looked small, almost fragile, once they left her behind in the mist.

Jake set the oars in the locks and began to row. The dinghy glided toward the looming shape, each stroke loud against the hush. Isabelle sat forward, snapping quick frames—muted flashes, angled away—each click clapping where no one claps.

The galleon grew with each pull, no longer just a silhouette. Its timbers swelled dark from centuries of brine, swollen but unbroken. The hull rose sheer from the water, scarred by impact yet still defiant. Gunports gaped open along the sides, black and hollow, like a row of eyeless sockets staring across the cove.

Jake pulled the oars through the water, slower now, as if speed might offend the dead. "It's one thing seeing her from a distance," he muttered. "Up close, it feels like she's watching us back."

Isabelle lowered the camera, eyes fixed on the ruin. "Three hundred years, and she's still here. Not just a wreck... a monument."

"Doesn't sit right," Jake said, letting the dinghy drift the last few yards. He glanced at the hull, at the way mist clung to its scars, and felt the same prickling unease he'd had since entering the cove.

On the port side, a ragged ladder of timbers slanted down close to the waterline. Jake tied off to a rusted ring-bolt and gave the line a hard tug. Solid.

"You think it'll hold?" Isabelle asked.

"If it's lasted three centuries, it can take ten more minutes."

He climbed first, boots scraping on slick planks, the smell of salt and old wood thickening as he rose. Isabelle followed, lighter on the timbers, pausing halfway to frame a shot upward at the hull yawning above her. The reach pulled at her side; she grimaced and tucked an elbow in against her ribs before finishing the climb.

The deck spread beneath them, warped but intact. Cannons still sat in their ports, their iron mouths gaping, carriages fused to the planks by centuries of rust. Rigging lay in black tangles, sagging like nets abandoned by some long-dead fisherman.

Isabelle turned slowly, camera forgotten at her side. "Jake... it feels like we're walking through a grave."

He scanned the shadows of the forecastle and the open hatch below. His gut stayed tight, the silence pressing harder than the mist.

"I think we are," he said.

The door to the captain's cabin hung crooked on its hinges, the wood warped and swollen. Jake braced a shoulder against it and pushed. The hinges shrieked but gave, the sound ripping through the hush like a blade. Both of them froze, waiting, as if something might answer back. Nothing did.

Inside, the air was thick and stale. Mildew crawled across the walls in dark blooms. The narrow windows were crusted with salt, letting in just enough light to sketch the broken outlines of furniture: a desk slumped against one wall, a chair toppled on its side, a trunk sagging open with its lid half rotted through.

Isabelle stepped carefully inside, camera raised, but lowered it after one glance. "Smells like a tomb."

"Looks like one too," Jake muttered. He tested the planks beneath his boots, each step damp and complaining but holding.

A brass compass, green with corrosion, lay cracked on the desk. Beside it, the frame of a sandglass slumped sideways, its glass long gone. Quills rotted to splinters lay beside an overturned inkwell, dark stains feathered across the warped wood. A few scraps of parchment clung to the surface, fused into brittle sheets. Even a clay cup still sat in the corner, rim flaked but whole, as if its owner had only just set it down.

Isabelle lifted her camera, eyes bright despite the rot. "Think about it. Every historian dreams of this. A galleon like this should have been nothing but scattered timbers. Instead it's preserved in its own time capsule. Furniture, books, orders from Madrid... it's extraordinary." She took a shot—flash feathered, low—briefly painting every scar and stain in stark white before the shadows swallowed it back.

Jake lingered behind her, gaze roaming across the desk and then the dark corners of the cabin. Pops had filled his childhood with stories about pirates and treasure fleets, and now here he was, standing in the captain's quarters of a Spanish galleon. For a heartbeat, unease gave way to something else—excitement, raw and boyish, the kind he hadn't felt in years. Without thinking, he reached for the brass key around his neck and gave it a squeeze. *Wish you could see this, Pops.*

"Feels like stepping into one of those stories, doesn't it?" he said softly.

Isabelle turned toward him, surprise flickering into something warmer. "Exactly what I was thinking. Except this time we're the ones writing it down."

Their eyes held for a breath, the silence suddenly less oppressive, the ruin around them less like a tomb and more like a doorway. For that fragile instant, the discovery wasn't just history or legend—it was theirs, shared between them.

Then Jake's gaze slid back to the desk, the moment dissolving into the weight of caution. His eyes caught on one parchment pinned beneath a rusted knife. He worked it loose with care and handed it to Isabelle.

"What's it say?" he asked.

Isabelle took the fragile page, holding it by the corners. Her eyes narrowed as she traced the curling script that still clung to the parchment. She read softly, her voice low in the quiet:

"...nuestra flota lo acorrala. El corsario huye hacia la isla, y su suerte no puede durar. Por la gracia de Su Majestad, lo cazaremos y recuperaremos lo que ha robado..."

She paused, translating under her breath before repeating it aloud in

English, her tone hushed but steady:

"Our fleet presses him close. The corsair flees into the island, and still his luck cannot hold. By His Majesty's grace, we shall run him to ground and reclaim what he has stolen."

The writing ended in a dark blot where the ink had spilled and spread like a bruise.

Isabelle's breath quickened. "It's almost... triumphant," she murmured. "They thought they had him cornered."

Jake caught the faint brush of her shoulder near his, the warmth of her presence stark against the cold press of the cabin. He nodded toward the page. "Too fragile to carry. But it matters to you."

"All of this matters," Isabelle said, her voice hushed but urgent. She crouched beside the desk, her eyes moving from the ruined compass to the fused books, the brittle pages, even the clay cup. "Letters, instruments, every fragment—they're a record no one's touched in centuries. When we get back to *The Wayfinder*, I need to bring proper supplies. Catalog it. Do it right."

Jake scanned the dripping beams overhead, the shadows clinging to the corners. His jaw tightened. "If this place lets us come back."

The hush pressed in again, broken only by the slow drip of water from somewhere unseen. Isabelle raised her camera for one more shot, the click startlingly loud in the confined space.

Jake glanced at the door, instincts bristling. They had seen enough.

Back on deck, the mist pressed heavier, curling through the splintered railings and the skeletal rigging. The ship felt larger in silence, its shadows stretching into places unseen.

"Below?" Jake asked, tilting his light toward the nearest hatch.

Isabelle gave a tight nod and lifted her beam. "Let's be careful."

The hatch gaped black, its frame slick with mildew. Jake crouched first, testing the ladder with a hand. The rungs were damp but solid enough. He descended slowly, boots thudding into gloom, the air thick and sour with rot. Isabelle followed, her camera brushing against his shoulder as she eased down behind him.

Below, the light was meager—thin blades from the deck seams overhead, silver in the misty air. Jake pulled a flashlight from the gear bag clipped to his belt and swept the beam across the space. Hammocks hung limp between beams, sagging shapes like shrouds. Crates slumped in heaps, their edges swollen and blurred. The silence down here was different than above: heavier, closer—reverent.

"God," Isabelle whispered, her voice catching. She raised the camera and took a shot. The flash burst off warped planks, etching skeletal outlines of hammocks and dangling ropes before the dark reclaimed them.

Jake moved carefully, ducking under beams, scanning the shadows. "This is where they lived," he muttered. "What's left of them, anyway."

They passed a cluster of sea-chests, lids warped ajar. Most were empty, their contents long since rotted to nothing. One trunk still held scraps of cloth fused into a single leathery mass. Another was lined with rust where weapons had once been stored.

Isabelle crouched by a small tin box wedged between two beams. She pried it loose and brushed it clean, her breath quickening when she saw the seal still intact. Jake held the light while she coaxed it open. Inside lay a folded scrap of paper, browned but legible.

Isabelle read aloud, her voice hushed to match the place:

"...three ships lost to the reefs, and the sea still takes more each day. The corsair's men strike like ghosts, unseen, unheard, until they are among us. Some say the mist hides them, others that the cold weakens our bones and dulls our powder. God help us, for fear gnaws at us as surely as hunger..."

The words trailed into a blot, the last lines unreadable. Isabelle swallowed, the paper trembling slightly in her hands.

"They were terrified," she said softly. "Not just beaten in battle—haunted."

Jake's jaw set. "Grey didn't just fight them. He broke them."

The two of them stood there a moment longer, the hammocks swaying faintly as if some breath of air moved through the hold.

Finally Jake shifted, voice firm. "We've seen enough down here."

They climbed back up the ladder, the air growing marginally less oppressive as they emerged onto the deck. The galleon loomed silent around them, its timbers groaning faintly as if in protest. Jake didn't look back as they descended to the dinghy—he'd had enough of the dead ship.

The mist pressed close again as he rowed, the wreck fading behind them until it was only a shadow among shadows. Neither spoke, both listening to the soft slap of oars and the quiet hiss of spray off the cliffs.

Ahead, the strand emerged through the gray: barricades collapsed into heaps, the scar of cannon fire etched into the cliff face, and shapes scattered along the tide line.

The dinghy scraped gently against the shallows. Jake swung over the side, boots sinking into wet sand, and hauled them ashore. Isabelle followed, camera in hand, turning slowly as if the lens could somehow make sense of the scene.

The beach was a graveyard. Jagged piles of stone marked where the Spaniards had built hasty barricades, now slumped and scattered by centuries of storms. The splintered remains of a pier jutted into the surf, its supports scarred and broken as though cannon fire had chewed them away.

Farther up the strand lay bodies. Not bones, but leathery husks hardened by salt and time. Skin clung to bone like parchment, lips shrunk back from teeth in eternal grimaces. Their clothes hung in brittle tatters, but swords still rusted in their sheaths, muskets lay clutched in skeletal hands.

Some had fallen in lines behind the barricades, frozen in firing stances as if still aiming into the mist. Others lay twisted in flight, arms outstretched toward the sea, caught mid-scream, mouths warped open and sockets wide with terror.

Jake felt his stomach knot. "Three hundred years, and they're still here."

Isabelle lifted her camera, but her hands hesitated before she pressed the shutter. "Salt air, constant spray, no scavengers. The minerals in the mist..." Her voice was clinical, but softer than usual, as though she needed the explanation as much for herself as for him.

The shutter clicked.

Jake crouched by one corpse, careful not to touch. Salt had turned it into something between man and statue, the face frozen in anguish, a rusted bayonet jutting from its ribs. For a moment, with the mist shifting around them, it seemed like the figure might stir. He exhaled sharply and stood again.

Isabelle lowered the camera, staring at the line of hardened bodies behind the barricade. "We need to come back with the right gear. Document everything. This... this could rewrite parts of the history books."

Jake nodded, voice steady. "Then we'll come back. Do it right."

The mist thickened, dragging the light into pale ribbons. Sound felt smothered here, as if even the surf was holding back. Every step crunched over scattered stone and splinter, each echo magnified by the hush.

The beachhead stretched into ruins of what might once have been a Spanish camp—fire pits long gone cold, broken clay scattered like bones, shattered carts mired in sand. Whatever fight had happened here, it had ended in slaughter.

They followed the shoreline past the shattered barricades until the sand gave way to harder ground. The mist clung close, but shapes began to emerge—low stone fire pits, the outlines of huts or barracks built from palm and timber, clay jars splintered where they'd fallen centuries ago.

"This wasn't the Spaniards," Isabelle said quietly, crouching near one of the pits. Charcoal still lay black at its heart, undisturbed. She brushed her fingers over a shard of clay painted in a simple red stripe. "This was lived in. Organized."

Jake studied the layout. Even in ruin, it carried Grey's hand. Paths had been worn clear between structures. Supply carts sat grouped near the cliffside, wheels rotted to husks. Posts jutted from the earth where palisades had once stood, and higher up, he could see the remains of a platform lashed into the trees—an old watchpoint.

"Grey's men," he said.

The weight of it pressed in as they moved deeper into the camp. Here the air didn't feel frantic, like the beachhead. It felt heavy, purposeful, as though discipline lingered in the bones of the place.

Isabelle found a row of bunks, little more than wood frames now, leaning against each other in collapse. She knelt, brushing dust and salt away from a folded scrap tucked between the boards. The paper nearly disintegrated in her hands, but words remained in a shaky, uneven script:

"...I pray this letter finds you, my beloved. Grey is a good man, but the shadows grow longer each day. We follow him still, because he leads with more than gold. He makes us believe we can survive this. If fate takes me, know I gave my strength to him freely..."

Her voice faltered as she lowered the page. For a long moment, neither spoke.

Jake broke the silence, voice low. "Even with fear at their backs, they followed him."

Isabelle nodded, eyes roaming the ruined camp—palisade stumps, the blackened pits, the barracks crumbling under centuries of mist. "They weren't just hiding. They were building. They were prepared to fight, and to live."

Jake's gaze drifted to a splintered palisade post leaning against the edge of the ruins. Its surface was marked with a faint carving, nearly erased by salt and time. He traced the line with his thumb, heart tightening as the shape revealed itself—a serpent coiled around an anchor. Grey's mark.

The connection hit sharp, personal. Pops' stories had painted Grey as a phantom, a legend, but here he was—etched into the wood by his own hand, proof he had stood in this place. Flesh and blood, not myth.

Jake let his hand fall, breath steadying. "He left more than ruins," he murmured.

And his men had stayed with him until the end.

They left the camp behind and found a path cut into the cliffs. It wound upward through mist and dripping foliage, reinforced in places with beams now slick and black with age. The footing was treacherous—slabs of stone slimed with moss, patches crumbling where roots had broken through.

Jake went first, testing each step before shifting his weight. Isabelle followed close, one hand steadying herself on the rock wall, the other keeping her camera tight against her chest.

Halfway up, Jake paused. On a support beam driven into the cliffside, a faint carving caught his light. The wood was almost pulp with rot, but the lines still clung: a serpent coiled around an anchor.

He brushed his thumb across it, pulse ticking. "He wanted them to know he'd been here," Jake murmured. "Or maybe... he wanted someone else to follow."

Isabelle leaned closer, squinting. "Breadcrumbs," she said softly. "Centuries before us."

They pressed on. The trail narrowed, no wider than a man's shoulders in places, the drop yawning away beneath the fog. The mist thickened until the waterfall revealed itself in a rushing sheet, its roar strangely muted by the veil. Cold spray beaded their skin as they edged closer, the air dropping in temperature with each step.

Isabelle slowed, peering over the ledge at the rocks far below. Her knuckles whitened on the wall. The climb had woken a deep ache along her side; she kept one forearm snug to her ribs as she edged on. "I hate heights," she admitted, voice tight.

Jake offered a hand without hesitation. "Then don't look down."

She shot him a sidelong glance, nerves giving way to a flicker of a smile as she took his hand. Together they edged along the ledge until the trail ducked behind the falling water.

Mist lashed across them in gusts, cold enough to sting. Behind the curtain of water, a shadowed opening revealed itself—a mouth in the rock, framed by rough-hewn beams. Jake lifted the flashlight, the beam cutting through the gloom.

On the stone beside the opening, carved deep and deliberate, another serpent twined around an anchor. This one had endured, shielded for centuries by the spray. The lines were crisp, bold, as if Grey himself had just carved it.

Jake touched the stone, breath caught in his chest. "This way."

The flashlight's beam stretched into the dark, mist curling back as if reluctant to yield. He tightened his grip on Isabelle's hand, then stepped forward.

The world narrowed as they slipped behind the curtain of falling water. The roar dulled to a steady thunder at their backs, but the air inside was different—colder, sharper, the kind of chill that cut straight to the bone. Each breath misted in front of them, their lungs burning with the sudden drop in temperature.

The flashlight's beam swung over the rough-hewn opening. Wooden beams framed the mouth, black with age but still holding firm, their edges chewed by centuries of spray. Beyond them, the rock pressed inward, slick with moisture.

Jake ducked under the lintel, boots crunching on gravel, and swept the light forward. The mist thinned into shadow, the cavern beyond swallowing the beam in uneven gulps. The stillness here was heavier than outside, as though the cave itself resented intrusion.

Isabelle lingered at the threshold, arms crossed tight. "It feels like the cave is swallowing the light."

"That's because it is," Jake said, flicking the beam deeper.

He adjusted his grip on the flashlight, steadying the circle of light. He drew a breath, steadied himself, and stepped farther in.

CHAPTER SEVENTEEN

The Serpent Calls

The serpent mark was the last thing the light touched before they slipped into the dark. The tunnel narrowed, then widened again, leading into a cavern whose ceiling vanished into black. Stalactites gleamed with moisture, faint trickles dripping into pools that mirrored the light like shards of glass. The sound echoed, low and endless, as if the cave itself whispered back.

Jake angled the beam higher and stopped. On the wall above the first pool, gouged deep into the stone, were faint but deliberate scratches—two intersecting lines, then another set crossing them at an angle. A crude lattice, repeated three times down the wall.

He stepped closer, brushing the grooves with his fingertips. They weren't random. They had intent, rhythm—the kind of shorthand men used when they needed to communicate quickly.

Isabelle leaned in, brow furrowed. "Not a symbol I recognize."

"Not meant for us," Jake said quietly. "Grey's code. Warnings for his crew. Most likely."

Her gaze flicked to the black water. "So, they'd know where not to step?"

"Exactly. If we keep seeing these, it means we're walking through his traps."

The flashlight beam cut ahead into the dark. Mist curled back as if reluctant to yield, and the cavern swallowed them whole.

The passage widened into a chamber where the floor sloped downward into shadow. Water gleamed at the bottom, still and glassy, reflecting the beam back in fractured ripples. Across the chamber, a low stone opening gaped, half-submerged.

Jake tightened his grip on the flashlight. "Looks like that's our way through."

They edged down the slope, boots scraping slick stone. The air grew damper, colder, their breath pluming thicker. At the base of the slope the water lapped gently, deceptively calm.

Isabelle crouched, her light catching faint lines carved into the wall just above the waterline. "Here—Grey's code again." Two crossed lattices, cut sharp and deliberate.

Jake frowned. "Warning his men. Whatever's here, it's probably trouble. Watch where you step."

"Don't trigger the death mechanism—got it," Isabelle quipped, masking her fear with humor.

They stepped in together. The water surged against their legs, numbing them instantly and stealing their breath. Isabelle gasped at the shock, stumbling a half step before catching herself against the wall. Cold hammered the bruise like a fist, stealing the end of her breath.

Jake steadied her with a hand, then pushed forward, crouching lower as the ceiling pressed down. The beam trembled across wet stone, catching glints of mineral veins and sharp edges where the tunnel pinched.

His boot shifted against a slab that rocked under his weight with a muted clunk. Jake froze—but too late.

A low groan shuddered through the rock. Somewhere ahead, gears or counterweights shifted, stone grinding against stone. A hidden sluice had opened. The water stirred, then surged upward in a sudden swell.

"Jake—" Isabelle's voice snapped taut.

"I know." He braced against the wall as the water climbed his chest. It wasn't a natural flood—it was deliberate, a channel designed to drown them once the trigger stone was disturbed.

The ceiling pressed lower, the air thinning to a narrow strip above the rising surface. Isabelle's breath came fast and shallow, panic sharp in her eyes. "We have to turn back—"

Jake swept the beam wildly. Grey's code flashed at him—crossed lattices etched not upward but downward, cut into the rock just above the surface. His stomach clenched.

"Not back," he said. "Down."

Isabelle stared at him, water lapping at her chin. "You can't be serious—"

The flood surged higher. They had seconds of air left. Jake seized her wrist, pulling her close. "It's the only way. Trust me."

He drew one last breath, shoved the flashlight into the crook of his arm, and plunged them both under.

The cold crushed around them, stealing heat, stealing thought. The beam shook across the black water, catching the lattice marks again—this time etched deeper, arrows pointing toward a narrow hole in the chamber wall, just wide enough to squeeze through.

Jake kicked hard, dragging Isabelle with him. She thrashed once, panic jolting through her, but he held fast, forcing them both into the gap. The twist sent a hot spike through her ribs; she clamped down on the pain and kicked.

Stone scraped Jake's shoulders, lungs already screaming, then the passage spat them out into a pocket of air.

They broke the surface together, gasping raggedly. The chamber beyond was small but dry, the floor slick with centuries of mineral build-up. Water spilled in behind them, churning as the flood filled the chamber they'd escaped.

Isabelle clung to him, her breath shuddering. "That was insane."

Jake pressed his back to the stone, lungs burning, heart hammering. "Grey built it that way. Anyone who panicked... drowned. Only those who trusted made it through."

Isabelle stared at him, water running down her face. She said nothing, but the look she gave him answered anyway.

For a moment, neither moved. Then Jake pushed himself upright, extending a hand to her. "Come on. We're still not clear of all this."

She took it, her fingers cold but steady. Together they turned toward the narrow tunnel ahead, leaving the roar of the drowning chamber behind.

The new tunnel stretched ahead, narrow but mercifully dry. Their boots slapped against slick stone, each step sending echoes running off into the dark. Jake's lungs still burned from the flood; Isabelle's gasps matched his, ragged and uneven.

She managed a weak laugh, brushing water from her hair. "Remind me never to go cave diving again."

Jake gave a breathless grunt that might have been a laugh, but his eyes stayed fixed on the beam of his light. He wasn't ready to believe they were safe.

The tunnel angled upward, its walls rough-hewn but unnaturally straight. Wooden braces propped sections of ceiling, lashed with corroded iron bands. Isabelle slowed, brushing her fingers over the marks. "These aren't natural. Grey's men cut and reinforced this. He engineered the cave."

Jake swept the light along the supports. Deep cracks webbed the beams, wood splintered and dark with age. "And he didn't just reinforce it. Look—" He nudged one beam with the back of his knuckles. It shivered loose dust, far too brittle for its size. "This is a setup—another trap."

The roof seams were already spidered, fine lines running through the stone as if waiting for a nudge; the smallest jar would carry.

Isabelle said nothing, but the way she hugged her light tighter spoke louder than words.

They pressed on, stepping carefully. Isabelle aimed her light lower, illuminating the floor. That's when Jake froze. A thin strand ran taut across the stone, ankle-high from one beam to the other. In the beam of his light it looked almost like a cobweb, but the dark, tar-stiffened fibers gave it away—old cordage, brittle with age, yet still strung tight as if Grey himself had tied it yesterday.

Isabelle's voice was low. "If that goes, the whole passage might come down on us."

"Exactly," Jake said, his eyes never leaving the line. "So don't touch it."

They edged past the trip line, holding their breath as though even that might set it off. Jake's light swept the far side, clear stone waiting ahead. Relief pricked through the tension.

Then a crack echoed above. A fist-sized stone, loosened by the stress in those hairline seams, jarred free from the ceiling and struck the cord dead center.

The line snapped.

The groan that followed was deep, guttural, like the cave exhaling. The sound rolled through the supports, wood answering with a long, splintering creak. Dust sifted down in fine threads, stinging their eyes and throats.

"Don't move," Jake said, jaw clenched.

They froze, every breath loud in their ears. The creaking swelled—one beam bowing, then another. The first failure sent a shock of vibration down the line; a second beam loosened and slumped inward, knocking a cascade of pebbles that skittered past their boots.

"Run!" Jake snapped.

He shoved Isabelle forward as a timber split with a sound like a rifle shot. They bolted, feet slipping on gravel, the flashlight bouncing wild arcs across the ceiling as more supports cracked in succession. Each collapse fed the next: a rotten brace let go, its fall upsetting a neighboring post, which in turn forced a stone seam to unseat. The tunnel became a stuttering avalanche—first small showers of grit, then falling slabs, then a thunderous cascade that chased them down the corridor.

Jake lunged, hauling Isabelle through a narrowing gap just as a slab the size of a table smashed where she'd been a heartbeat before. Dust filled the air, a choking gray that turned breath into sand. Isabelle coughed and spat; Jake dragged her forward, hands slick with grime.

They slammed out into a jagged pocket of space—less a room than a carved notch—just as the roof behind them convulsed and gave. The passage they'd come through folded down into a heap of stone and timber with a sound that rattled their teeth.

They lay there, heaving, grit in their mouths, heartbeat hammering in their ears. Isabelle pressed her forearm to her ribs and fought for smaller breaths that didn't stab her like a knife. Jake angled the light back; the tunnel was gone—a ragged wall of rubble, nothing but a raw seam where air still whispered through. No path. No retreat.

"No going back," he said hoarsely, the words scraped from him by sand and strain.

Isabelle sat up, coughing, eyes bright with anger and fear. "He wanted to erase the trail," she rasped. "He didn't just trap people—he tried to bury them with no trace."

Jake's shoulders tightened, the stress turning to an edge in his voice. "All we can do is keep moving. Find this treasure and then get out of here." His tone was practical, clipped—but close to breaking.

"That's assuming there is a way out now," she said, looking back at the pile of rubble where a tunnel used to be.

The words hung in the stale air, heavier than the dust. Jake snapped before he could stop himself. "Well, what do you want to do? Just sit here?" His voice was sharper than he meant, bouncing too loud off the stone.

Isabelle didn't flinch, though her eyes hardened. "You think Grey and his men built a back door in case of an accidental trigger? I doubt it." Her voice cracked as she lowered her head. "Oh god, we might die in here."

Jake's jaw worked, but no answer came. For a moment the weight of her words pressed against him harder than the rubble. She could be right. The certainty he'd been clinging to slipped, leaving doubt hollow in his chest.

He dragged a hand down his face, exhaling hard. Then he set his hand on Isabelle's shoulder, steady and sure. The touch lingered, grounding them both. When he finally spoke, his voice was lower, less sure. "Look, our only option is forward. Let's deal with what's in front of us—not what we can't change now."

Isabelle's gaze lifted. Slowly, she placed her hand over his, holding it there. The gesture was small but unshakable, a silent promise that neither of them would face this place alone.

They stayed like that for a breath longer, two damp, dust-caked figures in the dark, before Jake finally shifted the light toward the tunnel ahead. Isabelle's hand slipped from his only when they began to move, both carrying the weight of that touch forward into whatever Grey had left waiting.

The next stretch of tunnel was mercifully still. Their boots crunched on loose grit, each sound magnified in the hush. Water dripped somewhere deep in the stone, a slow, steady rhythm that seemed to count the seconds as they passed.

Neither spoke. The cave demanded their silence. Their breaths rasped in the stale air, fogging in the cold, and every so often the flashlight beam caught the glitter of mineral veins or the black mouths of abandoned side shafts. Nothing moved, yet the tunnel felt alive, listening.

Isabelle adjusted her pack against her shoulders, the leather creaking loud in the quiet. Jake's fingers brushed the brass key at his chest, steadying himself with its familiar weight. For the first time since entering the caves, there was no immediate threat pressing down on them.

But the stillness was no comfort. It was the kind that lingers before storms, holding its breath. Both knew it wouldn't last.

The tunnel narrowed, then widened abruptly into a cavern that looked too regular to be natural. Pillars rose in uneven rows, cut from the living stone, their faces scarred by chisel marks dulled with time. Some leaned like tired sentries; others lay toppled in heaps of rubble. The ceiling above sagged low and heavy, shadows layered thick between the columns.

Jake slowed, sweeping the beam across the hall. "Feels different," he muttered.

The words dropped flat, swallowed by the air—no echo, only a muffled hush, like speaking underwater.

Isabelle's brows drew together. "Sound is wrong here." She pressed her palm to one of the pillars. "The way it's cut—it deadens everything. Some ancient builders used tricks like this to unnerve people. Grey must have borrowed the idea."

Jake shifted uneasily, boots crunching grit. "Can't even tell how big it is. Feels like something's waiting."

The flashlight beam slid over the floor. Between the bases of the pillars, faint grooves formed a grid, shallow lines scored into the stone. Isabelle crouched, studying them. She traced one with her fingertip, then glanced up at the nearest column. A faint lattice carving caught the light, shallow but deliberate.

Her lips pressed thin as she checked the next pillar, then the next. Each bore the same mark, always aligned with certain squares in the grid. She squinted, mentally mapping.

"They line up," she murmured. "Pillars marked with Grey's sign, and the grooves—like a chart. The safe squares match his mark." She tapped one tile with her boot. "This one. It fits."

Jake frowned, sweeping the beam wider. "And the others?"

She pointed to hairline fractures spiderwebbing the ceiling above. "Step wrong, and the ceiling comes down. He engineered the grid to collapse the hall on intruders."

Jake's grip on the flashlight tightened. "Wonderful."

She drew in a breath, then carefully shifted onto the first marked square. It held. She tested her balance, then looked back at Jake. "It's deliberate. A path through. But we have to follow it exactly."

His brow furrowed, jaw tight. "You sure?"

"As sure as I can be," she said, voice steady but low.

Jake searched her eyes for a beat, then swore under his breath and stepped onto the same square. "Alright. Lead the way, Professor."

The hush pressed harder as they moved, every shift of their boots a whisper, every shallow breath a burden.

Halfway across, Jake's boot grazed the edge of an unmarked square. A faint tremor shivered up through the floor; a dusting fell from the ceiling above the wrong tile—just a whisper of powder, but enough to make the danger visible. Isabelle's hand shot out, grabbing his sleeve. Her eyes locked on his. "Careful."

He froze, muscles taut, before carefully shifting back onto the correct tile. His breath hissed through his teeth. "Thanks."

She gave a single nod and led on, her focus sharpened by the stakes. Step by step, the hall yielded.

At last, they reached the far side. Isabelle paused beneath the final pillar, her hand brushing the stone as though reluctant to leave it. "This place wasn't just about killing intruders. Grey wanted them to feel the weight of every step. Fear was part of the design."

Jake swept the light back across the hall, shadows swallowing the path they'd taken. "Yeah, it's working."

They slipped into the narrow tunnel beyond. With distance, sound returned—water dripping, stone settling—but the memory of that suffocating silence clung to them as tightly as the dust.

The passage sloped down, then leveled into a cavern that stopped Jake cold. Unlike the rough tunnels behind them, this place had been shaped. The walls were smoothed flat in patches, scarred in others where steel had bitten deep. And everywhere—layer upon layer—the stone was carved.

Jake swept the beam across them and felt his throat go dry. Spirals. Serpents. Circles with veins jagged through their centers. The same marks repeated again and again, as if someone had hacked at the stone in fits, unable to stop themselves. Some were sharp and deliberate, others shallow, as if scratched in a fever. The chamber felt less like a workshop and more like a cell—obsession written into every wall.

Isabelle stepped closer, breath visible in the chill. "He carved all this himself?"

Jake's voice came out hoarse. "Or tried to stop himself from carving it."

He angled the light lower. Between the etched spirals, the stone had blackened in patches—as if scorched. One mark drew his eye in particular: a handprint, seared into the rock, its edges blistered and fused. The fingers splayed wide, the outline darker toward the palm, like something—or someone—had burned straight through flesh to reach the stone beneath.

Jake crouched, the hair along his arms lifting. "That's not soot. It's fused—melted."

Isabelle knelt beside him, eyes wide. "How is that even possible?"

"I don't think it is," Jake murmured.

She reached out, hesitated a breath from touching it. "Grey... whatever he took—it did this to him."

Jake straightened, the key at his chest cold against his skin. "Or he did it trying to understand it."

He lifted the flashlight again. Across the chamber, more evidence of desperation emerged: broken chisels half-buried in dust, scraps of torn parchment scattered like shed skin, streaks of soot smeared by a shaking hand. One corner of the cavern wall bore words gouged directly into the rock—Spanish, jagged and uneven, as if carved mid-madness.

Isabelle read them softly:

"It watches even in silence. The glass breathes. The sea answers its call. God forgive what I have done."

The words hung there, raw and final.

Jake said nothing. The silence pressed until Isabelle exhaled shakily and turned toward the far side of the cavern.

The light caught on a dais, its surface crowded with brittle scraps of parchment. She hurried forward, her fingers trembling as she eased one open. The ink had bled and browned, but the words still clung to the page:

"...a stone of black glass, smooth as if forged by no hand, round and near perfect. Its surface bends the world in reflection, as though it warps the very air about it. Veins of gold lie within, spirals breaking like lightning across the dark, serpent lines curling outward into shapes of teeth or binding. Rings encircle it—one traced in gold, the other set with emeralds that gleam at points as precise as a compass. More green stones shine against the black, placed as though by design, their light caught like stars against the night. It weighs more than any orb of its size, and grows colder by the day. The Spaniards whispered of it in dread, yet still they sought it. At night, I dream of drowning though no water touches me. It is no common treasure. I fear it was never meant for men to bear..."

Isabelle's breath caught, her eyes shining as she traced the faded script. "Jake... this is it. He was writing about the treasure. About Siecaza."

Jake's stomach churned. Pops' pirate tales had never sounded like this. These weren't the words of a captain boasting of spoils—they were the confessions of a man unraveling.

"Look," Isabelle said quietly, pointing to another sheet half buried beneath the rest. Its ink had run like blood, but a sketch remained—rough, frantic lines of a sphere surrounded by sigils and annotations. At its edges, Grey's handwriting wavered: *"balance... blood... the tide answers."*

Jake stared at the drawing. "He wasn't stealing treasure. He was trying to solve it."

Isabelle turned, the flashlight beam skating across the walls. More spirals.

More serpents. More feverish circles carved atop older ones, the stone scarred white with overwork. She moved slowly, methodically, until the light froze on a carving unlike the rest.

A hill rose from the stone, sharp-etched, and on its crest stood a church—arches and a tower unmistakable even in rough lines. Not frantic like the others. Intentional.

Isabelle stepped closer, brow furrowed. "This one's different," she murmured. "Not madness. Deliberate. It looks... so familiar." She shook her head, frustrated. "I can't place it."

She slipped her notebook from her satchel, kneeling by the wall. In the quiet, her pencil moved with steady, practiced strokes, tracing every line of the carving. She shaded the hill, marked the tower, pausing now and again to check her angles. When she finished, she studied the page with a small nod, as though she'd captured something vital even if she didn't yet understand it.

"I'll figure it out later," she said softly, closing the book and tucking it away.

Jake hovered beside her, uneasy. The rest of the carvings screamed of obsession and unraveling. But this—this was clear, purposeful. "Whatever it is," he said grimly, "it meant enough for Grey to mark it here."

A sudden chill rippled through the air—sharp enough to draw breath from their lungs. The flashlight's beam flickered, weak for a moment, then steadied again.

Isabelle turned, eyes searching the dark. "Did you feel that?"

Jake nodded once. "Yeah." He didn't say it out loud, but the thought crawled in anyway: *The serpent calls.*

Before Isabelle could respond, a sound broke the hush. Faint, but unmistakable: the echo of voices. Boots scuffed stone—two... maybe three.

Jake killed the flashlight instantly, plunging them into black. He reached for her hand, his whisper tight against the dark.

"Someone's here."

CHAPTER EIGHTEEN

Predators in the Fog

The first light of dawn bled across the horizon, soft and gray, turning the sea into a rolling sheet of pewter. Mist clung low over the reef channel, draping the jagged coral teeth in shifting veils. Every few seconds a wave broke against the outcroppings, white spray erupting like breath from some half-submerged beast.

The Sunseeker Predator Fifty-Five edged forward with the precision of a blade sliding between ribs. Her hull whispered against the current, throttled down so low the twin diesels purred instead of roared. At the helm, Mateo sat hunched forward, shoulders tense, eyes locked on the shifting water ahead.

"Too shallow," Carlos muttered from the co-pilot's seat. "We scrape once and we'll open her belly."

"Hold your tongue," Mateo growled, never looking away from the reef. His knuckles whitened on the wheel as he feathered the throttles, nudging the yacht through the fog.

Behind them, Javier bent over a small screen patched to the drone feed. He had replayed the footage twice already, watching how Jake's trawler, The Wayfinder, had crept through the same passage the night before. The overlay flickered faintly on his tablet—the trawler's course line traced against the reef like a ghost trail, shifting in and out of clarity as mist drifted past.

"Port, three meters," Javier said calmly. "That's where he turned."

Mateo obeyed with a slight twist of the wheel. The Predator's bow edged left, grazing the line of foam where hidden coral clawed beneath the surface. The mist closed in tighter, swallowing sound until only the hiss of water against steel remained.

At the stern rail, Luca stood motionless, watching. His black windbreaker snapped lightly in the breeze—the only sign of movement. He had not spoken since they entered the channel, but his presence weighed heavier than the fog itself.

Every eye flicked to him between tasks, as if measuring whether his silence meant calm or condemnation.

The Sunseeker Predator Fifty-Five crept forward another ten yards.

Carlos swore under his breath as the depth sounder pinged—three feet under keel. Too close. "This is madness," he muttered. "He threads a fishing boat through, fine, but this—"

"Quiet," Luca said at last. His voice was soft but it cut through the cabin like a knife.

The men obeyed instantly.

Javier raised his head from the tablet. "We're still on his line. He knew the reef. Probably scouted it."

"No," Luca replied, eyes narrowing at the gray horizon. "He guessed. And the sea let him through."

The words hung heavy. Luca's expression did not change, but the mist seemed to close tighter, the reef teeth leaning in around them like jaws.

Another swell surged against the channel mouth, sending spray across the deck. Mateo steered into it, the Predator's bow rising before dropping with a muted thud. The engines growled, then steadied again to a whisper.

The reef walls narrowed. To starboard, a spire of coral jutted above the water, slick and black. To port, the shoal shimmered just beneath the surface, pale teeth waiting to rip steel. The Sunseeker Predator Fifty-Five slid between them by less than the length of an arm.

Javier checked the feed again. "Ten meters ahead, then he bent starboard. Past that—open water."

Mateo exhaled through his teeth. "If he was wrong—"

"He wasn't," Luca said. "Morgan has instincts. Like a shark. He can smell his way through currents others can't even see."

Carlos gave him a wary glance. "Then why do we follow him into this? Why not wait in the open sea?"

Luca finally turned from the rail. His gaze fixed on Carlos with the cold stillness of a predator measuring prey. "Because sharks don't wait in open water," he said quietly. "They follow blood into the reef. And Morgan bleeds a trail he doesn't even know he leaves."

Carlos looked away.

For a breathless moment, all sound vanished but the hiss of water under hull. Then the fog thinned. The channel widened into a hidden lagoon, still as glass. Palm silhouettes rose from the inner shoreline, their reflections wavering on the water.

Mateo eased the throttles back further. "We're through," he whispered, relief breaking across his face.

Luca said nothing. His eyes scanned the lagoon, already seeking the next sign of Morgan's passage. He raised a hand slowly, as if scenting the air.

"Find his boat," he ordered.

Mist drifted low across the lagoon, softening the palm silhouettes along the shore. Anchored near the beach, The Wayfinder rocked gently, her white hull dulled by sea spray and dawn light.

But it was not the only ship in the cove.

Beyond her, half-shrouded in fog, loomed the wreck of a Spanish galleon.

Carlos leaned over the Predator's bow rail, staring. "Madre de Dios..." His voice was half a curse, half a prayer. "That's a galleon."

Mateo spat over the side. "She shouldn't even be here. The sea should've eaten her long ago."

Javier adjusted the drone tablet, as though seeing her through both screen and mist. "Grey left her here," he said quietly. "Not by accident. A message. Or a monument."

Luca's gaze fixed on the wreck, his face carved from stone. "The sea buries what it wishes. Sometimes it remembers." He let the words hang, then turned back to The Wayfinder.

"Take her. Quietly. No splashes. Leave her floating long enough for Morgan to see the truth before she goes under."

Carlos's grin widened. "Understood."

The tender splashed into the water and angled toward the trawler.

Carlos vaulted over The Wayfinder's aft rail first, landing soft on the deck. He listened—no footsteps below, no voices. He signaled, and Mateo followed.

They moved fast. Carlos ducked into the cabin, scanning the galley, the berths, the helm. Empty. The smell of diesel and stale coffee lingered, but no trace of life.

Mateo went below, wrench in hand. He worked quickly at the bilge pumps, loosening lines, slicing hoses. Carlos found a through-hull fitting and cracked the valve just enough. A slow, invisible seep would begin—unnoticed until it was far too late.

Within minutes the sabotage was done. The hoses lay open, fittings cracked, the slow seep of seawater already starting its work. The Wayfinder still floated serene, bobbing gently as if nothing had changed.

Carlos climbed back into the tender, wiping his hands on a rag. "She'll go down quiet. Hours, maybe. By the time they return, she'll be kissing sand."

Mateo swung the rope off the cleat and followed him. "Then they'll know."

"They'll know nothing," Carlos said with a smirk. "They'll be too busy drowning with her."

The tender nosed back through the fog toward The Sunseeker Predator Fifty-Five. On The Wayfinder, water dripped unseen into her bilges—the first breath of her slow death beginning beneath the calm surface. The ripples from the tender's wake faded quickly, swallowed by the mist that hung over the lagoon.

By the time they reached the Predator, the fog had thickened again. Luca stood at the rail, watching the cliffs that rose like dark ribs above the water. Somewhere beyond them, Morgan's trail climbed toward the island's heart.

"Gear up," he said at last. "We go ashore."

Minutes later the team moved out, boots finding purchase on wet rock as they followed the narrow ledge toward the ruins.

The mist clung heavier along the cliff base, weaving through broken arches of stone and half-collapsed walls. The air smelled of brine and rot, old iron leaching from hidden things buried long ago.

Luca led the way, boots crunching on wet gravel. Behind him, Mateo and Carlos kept their rifles slung, eyes scanning the ruins as they moved. Javier brought up the rear, the drone tablet strapped across his chest like a shield, though no signal would pierce the rock above.

They followed the trail Morgan and Alvarez had taken. It was easy to read—the scuffed earth where boots had slid on damp stone, handholds darkened by recent touch, palm fronds bent in passing. Prey always left a trail when they hurried.

The ruins themselves were stranger. Half-choked staircases climbed the cliffside, their edges carved with eroded symbols that caught what little light filtered through the mist. Spanish barricades still blocked certain passages, heavy timbers bound with rusted iron.

Bodies slumped against some of them—not skeletons, but leathery husks. Skin clung taut to bone, faces shriveled and eyeless. Their faded uniforms hung in tatters, colors long since bled to gray. The air around them was sharp with the scent of damp stone and dried leather, preserved by the island's peculiar curse.

Carlos froze at one barricade where two corpses still leaned upright, skulls canted back toward the sky as though watching for salvation. "Santo Dios..." His voice dropped to a whisper. "They shouldn't look like that. Not after centuries."

Luca studied the scene with a detached eye. The shriveled flesh still bore the marks of blade work, ragged tears where throats had been opened. "Grey killed them here. Left them for the survivors to see."

Mateo spat. "Bastard."

"Strategist," Luca corrected. He crouched, brushing away dirt to reveal faint scratches on the stone—serpents and spirals, half-carved, half-gouged. His gloved hand lingered over one, almost reverent. "He understood the hunt. Fear weakens a man faster than hunger."

The mist thickened again as they climbed higher. The sound of surf below faded, replaced by the drip of water through stone and the muffled beat of their own footsteps. Every corner seemed alive, every shadow a watcher.

Ahead, the path narrowed beneath a collapsed arch where the cliff face had split. Beyond it, the light dimmed to a dull gray and the air thickened—cool, mineral, and close. Luca ducked through first, feeling the shift as the open ruins gave way to the cave system. The echoes changed too, from the sigh of wind to the slow heartbeat of dripping water. They were inside the island now.

A low tremor rolled through the ground beneath their boots—followed by a faint, distant cry that froze them where they stood.

"Jake!" The voice echoed through the tunnels, muffled by stone but unmistakable. Isabelle. Her scream tore through the rock, raw with fear.

Carlos swung his rifle toward the sound. "That came from up ahead!"

Luca's expression hardened. "Move."

They ran, boots splashing through shallow water. The air filled with a faint grinding roar—the sound of stone collapsing somewhere ahead. Dust spilled from the ceiling in soft streams, filling the air with the dry sting of grit.

"Trap," Javier muttered. "They set one off."

The tremor faded, leaving silence and settling dust.

Luca steadied himself, head tilted toward the darkness, listening. "They're alive," he said finally.

Mateo glanced back, uneasy. "Then they're close."

"Closer than they should be," Luca said. "Grey's hand still guards these halls."

A few yards ahead, the tunnel forked. The left path was caved in completely; the right was narrowed to a vent where slabs had shifted, leaving only a crawlspace.

Javier pressed a glove to the fissure. A faint breath of air stirred against his hand. "It connects. Same direction they went."

Luca crouched, running a finger through the fresh dust. "They made it through before the collapse."

He looked up. "We follow."

Carlos eyed the narrow gap. "That's not a tunnel. That's a coffin."

Luca gave a thin smile. "Then crawl like the dead, and you'll fit."

One by one, they stripped down their packs and squeezed into the fissure. Stone scraped ribs and shoulders, dust filling mouths and eyes, but no one stopped. The scent of brine and earth thickened the deeper they went.

When they emerged on the far side, the air was cooler, almost still. Their lights swept over a cavern supported by leaning pillars, the floor carved with faint straight lines—a shallow grid cut into stone.

Mateo's voice dropped. "What the hell is this?"

Javier angled his light downward. Wet bootprints crossed the tiles in a careful pattern. "They were here. Look—still damp."

Luca crouched, tracing one with a gloved finger. "Grey's design. A chart—puzzle or trap. And Morgan already solved it."

He rose, placing his boot squarely in the first wet print.

Mateo exhaled, then followed his lead, stepping carefully where the damp trail wound between the pillars. Javier came last, keeping the beam steady on the path ahead.

The silence was smothering—no echoes, no insects, only the soft drip of water and the shuffle of their own boots.

At the far side, the footprints vanished into a narrow passage chiseled with spirals and serpent motifs. Luca's torch cut across them, revealing the same stylized patterns from the old dispatch sketches—the mark of Grey himself.

He smiled faintly. "We're close."

"Kill the light," Jake whispered.

Isabelle clicked off her flashlight, plunging the chamber into total blackness. Jake pulled her low behind a toppled stone table near the wall. Dust scraped under their palms as they crouched in the dark, listening.

Boots scuffed against stone. Voices—low, cautious. A beam of white light cut into the chamber, swinging across the etched walls. Several more followed.

Jake held his breath as the beams passed over the plinth at the center, then crawled across the carved serpents etched into the far wall. The light moved in a steady rhythm, a hunter's sweep.

The crunch of boots grew louder. Close. Too close.

A figure rounded the table's edge—his rifle up, his torch beam spilling over the stone.

Jake pounced.

He slammed into the man, wrenching the rifle sideways and driving him back against the wall. The weapon barked once, muzzle flash searing the dark. Isabelle let out a scream, the round smacking uselessly into stone. Jake shoved harder, pinning the man's chest with the rifle, his own teeth bared in the struggle.

Then cold steel pressed to Jake's temple.

"Enough."

Luca's voice was calm, steady, inches away. His pistol dug hard against Jake's skull, flash light painting his face in stark angles.

"Let him go, Morgan," Luca said softly.

Jake froze. He felt Isabelle's sharp intake of breath behind him, the weight of her fear. The man squirmed under his grip until Jake eased off. The rifle clattered to the floor.

Two more figures loomed behind Luca, rifles leveled, beams of light slashing across the chamber. Isabelle raised her hands slowly, her face pale in the glow.

Luca didn't move the pistol. "It's time to pay up."

Jake straightened slowly, hands open. He kept his eyes locked on Luca's. "That's a hell of a way of showing gratitude."

"Gratitude?" Luca's smile was thin, humorless. "I told you once—I don't save lives for free. I invest in them."

"What?" Isabelle's voice broke between disbelief and anger. "You know this man, Jake?"

Luca tilted his head, pistol never wavering. "Didn't he tell you? He owes me. If not for me, Morgan would be rotting at the bottom of Boot Key Harbor. But we took care of those guys, isn't that right?"

Jake's jaw clenched, silence damning. He couldn't form the words.

Isabelle's voice cracked, raw. "You knew him? And you didn't tell me?"

Her eyes burned, but she didn't push—not with Luca's gun still raised. There was no point now. If they lived through this, she would get answers.

Luca's pistol never wavered. "Enough. You're out of options, Morgan. Tell me where Grey hid the treasure."

Jake forced a smirk. "A deal's a deal, I guess. You save my life—I lead you to the treasure."

Luca's gaze sharpened. "Then show me."

Jake turned slowly, sweeping his light across the wall. The spirals and serpents coiled in the glow, their carved lines converging toward a narrow fissure in the rock.

"There," he said. "Grey wasn't mad—he was marking a path with these markings. The treasure's not in this chamber. It's in a vault... down a tunnel we passed earlier. He buried it behind the trap so no one could reach it without knowing the pattern."

From the corner of his eye, he gave Isabelle a tiny shake of his head—a silent warning. Play along.

She caught it, her face pale but voice steady. "He's right. Grey always left layers of defenses."

Luca studied the carvings, then Jake, then Isabelle. Silence stretched. His smile was thin, sharp. "A vault," he murmured. "Of course." He lowered the pistol a fraction, hunger deepening in his eyes. "Then you'll take us there."

Flashlight beams bobbed as they filed out. Two of Luca's men went first, rifles up. Luca and the other flanked behind, boxing Jake and Isabelle in the middle like prisoners being marched to the gallows.

For a while, only the scrape of boots and the drip of water filled the silence.

Luca's voice cut through, calm, conversational. "You've come far, Morgan. I almost admire it. But you've always been reckless. Never thinking more than a step ahead."

Jake didn't look back. "Did you say hi to my friends on the fishing boat?"

The pause behind him was brief but telling.

Luca's smile carried in his voice. "Clever. Cost me a day I didn't intend to lose. But all you bought was time—and time always runs out."

They walked on. The tunnel widened until the chamber with the tiled floor and sagging ceiling opened before them. Dust still hung faintly from the cracks above, silence pressing flat and heavy, swallowing even their steps.

The lead man lifted his light. "This way." He stepped carefully onto the damp trail of bootprints that still marked the safe path. The others followed.

Jake leaned close to Isabelle, whispering, "Stay sharp." His hand brushed hers—a small, deliberate signal.

Her jaw set. She didn't know what he planned, only that it would be dangerous. Still, she gave the faintest nod.

Jake measured the distance—ten steps to the middle, where the ceiling sagged heaviest. His chest tightened.

"Keep moving," Luca ordered from behind.

Jake clenched his jaw.

Now.

He shifted sideways, planting his boot hard on a tile just outside the safe path.

The stone groaned beneath him. A crack split the silence like thunder.

"Down!" Jake grabbed Isabelle and lunged forward as the ceiling gave way.

The chamber roared. Stone slabs let loose from above, pillars split in showers of grit and dust. The sound was deafening—like the island itself was tearing apart.

Luca's reflexes were fast. He seized Isabelle's arm, yanking her back as debris thundered down. The pull spun all three of them around, dragging

Isabelle between them.

"No!" Jake shouted, wrenching for her. Isabelle twisted, planting her boot hard into Luca's chest and pushing with all her might. The kick tore her free, sending her sprawling toward Jake just as another block of stone slammed into the floor where she had stood.

Jake hauled her into his arms and rolled clear of the collapse.

A scream ripped through the chamber. Carlos hadn't moved fast enough.

He was pinned beneath a fallen slab the size of a wagon, his flashlight skittering across the tiles before the light went dark. His legs kicked wildly, boots scraping stone, while the weight of the block crushed his chest flat. The scream pitched higher, then cut off in a wet, choking gasp. Dust billowed, swallowing the sight of him—but the silence left no doubt.

Isabelle's hands flew to her mouth. She staggered against Jake, eyes wide, horror carved deep across her face. "My God..." Her voice trembled. She'd studied death all her life—excavated bones, brushed dirt from skulls—but never like this. Not a man screaming as he was crushed. Not inches away.

Jake gripped her arm, steadying her, his own face tight. "Don't look."

But the sound lingered anyway.

The collapse thundered on, stones smashing pillars into splinters, air filling with grit so thick it clawed the lungs. Then, just as suddenly, it stilled.

A jagged wall of rubble split the cavern in two.

On the far side, Luca and his remaining men stood coughing in the haze, their beams slicing through the dust.

On Jake and Isabelle's side, only silence. The path back to Grey's chamber yawned behind them—dark, final.

Jake's chest heaved. They'd tried to trap Luca's crew—but instead they had cut themselves off.

Across the collapse, Luca's laugh echoed, low and mocking. "Well played, Morgan. You freed yourselves... straight into a tomb. Guess I'll go find the vault now."

The light from Luca's side faded as the dust thickened, leaving Jake and Isabelle half in shadow.

Jake pressed a hand to her shoulder, steadying her as her breath came sharp and uneven. "We'll find another way," he whispered. "Hopefully, Grey left a back door."

Isabelle shook her head, dust streaking her face, voice breaking between fear and anger. "You don't know that. You don't know anything, Jake. You gamble, and people die." Her eyes flicked to the rubble where Carlos's scream had been cut short. "You nearly got me killed."

Jake's throat worked. He wanted to argue, to defend himself—but the weight of the chamber, the smell of dust and stone, pressed the words down. "I know," he said quietly. "But right now we need to find a way out."

For a moment she just stared at him, torn between fury and the fragile thread of trust she still clung to. Then she looked away, her silence louder than anything she could have said.

Behind them, the spiraled carvings on Grey's walls seemed to writhe in the half-light, watching.

For a long moment, neither moved. The air hung thick with dust and the faint trickle of settling stones. Then Jake pulled his pack tighter and stood. "Let's go back and check the walls in Grey's chamber for a way out," he said.

Isabelle hesitated, wiping grit from her face. She didn't answer, but after a moment she lifted herself off the ground, her flash light beam cutting thin through the haze.

They retraced their steps through the short passage, the floor littered with debris from the collapse. The air grew heavier the farther they went, thick with the scent of damp stone and old decay. When they reached the chamber, their lights caught the spirals and serpents that covered every surface, the carvings seeming to twist in the flicker of the beams.

Jake began working the nearest wall, running his hands over the symbols, pressing against any that felt loose or uneven. "He had to leave himself another way out," he muttered. "Grey wouldn't box himself in."

Isabelle moved slower, methodical, her scholar's eye catching details Jake's haste missed. She studied the patterns, searching for anything inconsistent, anything that didn't fit.

Minutes passed before she froze. "Jake," she said quietly.

Jake turned. She crouched near the far corner, tracing the edge of a carved spiral with her fingertips. "These lines—look. Everywhere else, Grey's patterns are perfect. But here..." She pointed to a faint break in the groove, barely visible in the dust. "It doesn't connect."

Jake knelt beside her, running his palm over the surface until he felt it too—a subtle seam hidden within the carving. "Feels hollow," he said.

Together they pressed. The stone resisted, then shifted with a deep, scraping groan. Dust spilled from the edges as a narrow opening appeared, revealing a crawlspace beyond.

Cold, ocean air flowed from the gap.

Jake angled his light inside. The tunnel was rough, claustrophobic, hacked straight through the rock with uneven strokes.

He glanced back at Isabelle. "You found it."

"What would you do without me?" she said—more serious than sarcastic.

Jake slung off his pack. "Well, it's the only direction left." He dropped to his knees and slid inside, his light cutting through the dark throat ahead. Stone scraped his shoulders as he crawled forward.

Isabelle lingered a heartbeat longer, sweeping her light across the carvings one last time. The spirals and serpents twisted in the half-shadow, seeming almost to shift with her movement. Her breath came quick and unsteady. "What have I gotten myself into...?"

Then she ducked into the tunnel, and the chamber vanished behind them.

On the far side of the collapse, Luca stood with his light angled toward carvings on a near wall. Dust streaked his coat, his expression calm, almost satisfied.

"Clever," he murmured, studying the marks. "He thought he could bury us and take the treasure for himself."

Mateo stepped beside him, coughing. "You really think the vault's there?"

Luca smiled thinly. "Grey wouldn't carve lies into stone. Morgan just didn't look deep enough." He turned, motioning for Mateo and Javier to move ahead. "Let's see where the truth leads."

He disappeared into the tunnels, his beam slicing through the dust like a blade, leaving the sealed passage behind him like a grave.

Far below, in the still lagoon, *The Wayfinder* rocked gently at anchor. Her stern rode an inch lower in the water, unnoticed beneath the soft veil of fog—the first quiet sign that something was dying.

CHAPTER NINETEEN

Against the Current

The passage twisted downward, the air growing colder and damp. The scent of earth thickened with every step. Water dripped somewhere ahead—steady, hollow—echoing like the pulse of the island itself.

Then came another sound: a distant rush, the pull of an unseen tide.

A faint silver glimmer flickered ahead.

Jake quickened his pace. "I think I see an exit up ahead."

They ran.

The tunnel curved once more, and then the world burst open into wind and moonlight.

A cliff—too close.

They skidded onto loose stone, momentum carrying them forward. Gravel slid beneath their boots. Jake hit the ground hard; Isabelle's cry echoed beside him. The slope wouldn't stop pulling.

He clawed for purchase, nails scraping rock. His other hand shot out, grabbing Isabelle's arm.

They slid—closer, closer—until friction caught. Rocks spilled into the dark void below as they stopped with their boots hanging over empty air.

For one suspended breath, neither moved.

Then they dragged themselves back, chests heaving, hearts pounding.

They sat on a high escarpment overlooking the sea. Below, a cove—a mirror of shifting fog and moonlight, the tide surging faintly against stone. Wooden pilings jutted from the water like blackened teeth. A narrow pier reached into the mist, its beams slick and broken—a ghostly remnant of another age.

A hidden cove.

Elias Grey's escape plan.

Isabelle's voice came soft, breathless. "This is how they got out."

Jake wiped a streak of grit and sweat from his face. "Grey planned for everything," he murmured. "The Specter could've sailed straight from here, hidden in the fog—a vein he read like a map. The Spanish never would've seen her."

He pointed toward the faint outline of the pier below. "That's where she was tied up."

Isabelle took a cautious step toward the edge, scanning the descent. "We can climb down if we—"

A voice cut through the night.

"Not so fast."

Jake froze. His blood turned cold.

Up on the ridge above them—Luca. Half-silhouetted against the moonlight, pistol raised, his smirk cutting through the haze.

"Leaving so soon?" His voice carried over the wind. "And after everything we've been through?"

Jake's pulse hammered. Sheer drop behind them. No cover. No way out.

Luca cocked the pistol. "Don't move. You had me with the vault. Now you're going to tell me where the treasure really is."

Jake's hand found Isabelle's wrist. He glanced once toward the dark water below.

No choice.

Their eyes met—a silent understanding.

A nod.

They jumped.

"No!" The gun cracked, the sound splitting the night.

The night air turned into a howl as they plunged into the dark.

The roar of the ocean surged up to meet them, swallowing the fading echo of Luca's gunshot.

Jake tried to knife straight down—feet first, arms crossed—but the shot tore him wide.

Impact.

The water hit like concrete. The shock tore through him, stealing his breath, freezing every muscle for a split second before instinct dragged him back.

Pain. White-hot, searing.

His left arm wouldn't move. His mind caught up a heartbeat later—Luca had fired. A deep, pulsing burn radiated through his bicep, hot blood mixing with the cold sea.

He was sinking.

The current gripped him, pulling hard, dragging him down into blackness. His lungs burned. He kicked against it, forcing his body upward, the weight of his wound threatening to haul him back into the depths.

Above—movement.

Isabelle.

She broke the surface first, gasping, spinning in panic. "Jake!"

He pushed through the dark water, bursting into open air with a ragged inhale. Salt and iron filled his mouth. Isabelle's hands found him instantly, gripping his shoulder.

"You're bleeding," she said, breath trembling.

Jake shook his head, teeth clenched. "We have to keep moving."

Adrenaline overrode everything—pain, exhaustion, fear. There was no time.

From the cliffs above, Luca's voice echoed across the cove. "Impressive!" The sound carried on the wind, mockingly, close enough to chill the blood.

Jake and Isabelle turned, treading water. The shoreline loomed near—bare rock and no cover. They'd be visible targets within seconds.

"Out past the point," Jake said, breath sharp. "Go."

Isabelle hesitated, eyes catching the dark tendrils of blood spiraling through the water around him. Moonlight shimmered off it—black against silver.

"Jake—"

"Go." His tone left no room for argument.

She nodded once.

Together, they pushed away from the cove, striking out toward the open water, the current tearing at their limbs, the cliffs shrinking behind them into the dark.

The cold wrapped around them like a vice, sharp and numbing. Each stroke sent a fresh lance of pain through Jake's injured arm, but he gritted his teeth and kept moving. The water burned the wound; the tide's constant pull tried to drag him under.

Beside him, Isabelle's breathing came fast and ragged. The cold, the exhaustion, the throb in her ribs—all of it closing in. She clutched her side once, sharp and instinctive, before pushing through the water again.

"Keep going," he muttered, barely above the lapping waves.

Luca's voice still echoed faintly from the cliffs behind—shouts drifting, growing weaker but not gone.

They swam low, barely breaking the surface, letting the dark swells hide them. Jake's gaze fixed on the cove's mouth ahead, but the adrenaline was thinning. Sharp aches knifed through his body; his arm felt like it was on fire.

Then he felt Isabelle falter.

Her strokes grew uneven. Slower.

"Isabelle," he called over the water. She kept moving, but her limbs were sluggish, her form breaking down.

"I'm—" she gasped, fighting to stay afloat. "I'm okay."

But she wasn't.

Jake lunged toward her, looping his injured arm across her chest before she could protest.

"Jake..."

"Shut up," he gasped, kicking harder, dragging them both with his good arm. Pain tore through the wound, a searing burn with every stroke. His fingers went numb, but he clenched his jaw and held on. He had to.

Isabelle struggled weakly, pride warring with exhaustion. "You're hurt," she choked out, trying to push him off.

He didn't answer—just ground his teeth and swam for both of them. Every muscle burned. His legs turned to lead. The cold, the exhaustion, the blood in the water—it all threatened to pull them under.

But he kept going.

Through the dark.

Through the pain.

Through the relentless pull of the sea—of gravity.

Until finally—the cove's entrance loomed ahead, a break in the black water where the swells bent and rolled, promising a way out.

Jake pushed forward, dragging Isabelle with him, breath ragged. Each pull sent a fresh wave of pain through his wounded arm, but he didn't stop. He wouldn't stop.

"The open water beyond the point—that's our only chance," he muttered through clenched teeth. "If we make it there, we're out of his sight."

"Come on, Izzy," slipped out before he could stop it.

Her eyes flashed—surprise, then something softer—before the next swell shoved them on.

A wave surged behind them, lifting them dangerously close to the jagged rocks along the point. Jake twisted, shielding Isabelle with his body. The swell crashed—white spray erupted—but at the last second, the current shifted. The water rolled them past the rock face, shoving them toward open sea.

The drag of the undertow lessened. He kicked harder, lungs burning, vision tunneling.

Then—his foot hit something solid.

For a split second he thought it was debris—then realized it was the seabed.

He lunged forward, hauling Isabelle with him. His hands and knees scraped wet stone as he dragged them from the surf, every muscle screaming, his arm on fire. He didn't stop until they were clear of the waves.

They collapsed together on the shore, gasping. Isabelle's body shook violently from exertion, her fingers clawing into the crushed-shell beach as if the sea might try to take her back. Her breaths came shallow and quick.

Jake rolled onto his back, sucking air, chest heaving in sharp, uneven gasps. Salt stung like fire against his wound; blood trickled down his arm in slow, dark rivulets that glistened in the moonlight.

For the first time, he allowed himself to see it. A dull haze crept into the edges of his vision. Dizziness set in—blood loss catching up, draining what little strength he had left.

For a long moment, neither of them spoke.

The night was eerily quiet. Only the soft slap of water against the rocks and their own ragged breaths broke the silence.

Isabelle turned her head toward him, face pale in the moonlight. "You—" she swallowed hard, forcing the words out. "You're bleeding."

Jake exhaled sharply, pushing himself up onto an elbow. "I noticed—you're welcome, by the way."

Isabelle let out a weak breath—something between a laugh and a scoff—but her hands were still trembling.

He forced himself upright. The throbbing in his arm had become a deep, relentless burn that crawled up into his shoulder. His fingers barely responded, his grip unsteady—but he couldn't afford to dwell. They weren't safe yet.

"We need to keep moving," he said, getting to his feet.

Isabelle groaned but followed, still unsteady. "Jake—wait...a second."

"We don't have a second." He gripped her arm and hauled her up. "Luca's not gonna stop. We need to get back to The Wayfinder."

She swayed, nodded, brushed wet hair from her face.

They turned toward the treeline, moving carefully along the narrow strip of beach, keeping to the shadows. The ground was uneven—wet stones shifting underfoot—but they stayed low, stayed silent. Jake stumbled over a ridge of coral rubble; Isabelle caught his arm, steadying him.

Behind them, beyond the point, Jake could feel Luca's presence. Hunting.

The main cove came into view. The wind was calmer here, the water gentle and dark, lapping softly at the shore. For a heartbeat, Jake let himself believe the worst was over.

Then he stopped. Something was wrong.

The silhouette of *The Wayfinder* should have been there—anchored in the moonlight, her familiar shape waiting like a promise.

But she wasn't.

Jake's pulse spiked. His exhausted body locked, every muscle rigid.

No.

He staggered forward a few steps, eyes scanning the dark water, desperate, searching. Hoping he was mistaken. Only rippling moonlight and black waves answered.

And then—he saw it.

A soft glug-glug rose from the deep. A thin stream of bubbles broke the surface, shimmering briefly before vanishing into the dark.

His stomach dropped. *The Wayfinder* was gone.

He stood frozen, breath caught. She had been more than fiberglass, metal, and wood.

She had been freedom. Livelihood. Family. The last piece of his life that was truly his. Now she lay in the black depths, silent and dying. The old diesel-and-salt smell he'd lived with for years seemed to lift off the water and vanish.

A shadow moved beside him. *Isabelle.*

She'd seen it too. Her hand found his—steady, grounding. A silent acknowledgment. A quiet understanding.

He didn't move. He didn't want her to see the hurt.

His jaw clenched; his pulse roared. For a heartbeat, he considered diving—as if he could haul her back, undo what had been done.

He knew better.

His fists curled. He shoved the grief down, burying it where it wouldn't slow him. *Survival first. Grief later.*

When he finally spoke, his voice was low and controlled. "We need another way off this island."

Isabelle nodded, fingers tightening briefly around his before she let go.

He drew a sharp breath and turned from the sinking wreck. *Forward.*

They moved low along the tree line, shadows swallowing them. A vessel rode at anchor near the pier remnants—a Sunseeker Sunseeker 55, its sleek hull catching ghostly slivers of moonlight where it bobbed. For the first time since the fall, Jake felt a pulse of hope. A boat meant a chance.

But they weren't alone.

A faint ember flared in the dark. A cigarette. The glow outlined a face in profile—one of Luca's men—lean, bored, a hand settled on his hip. A pistol sat in a holster; a shotgun hung across his torso. A guard who hadn't yet bothered to worry.

Jake exhaled through his nose, voice low. "One guy. We take him out, the boat's ours."

Isabelle's eyes flicked to the pier and back. "How?"

She didn't let him answer. A short, incredulous scoff. "Oh, right." Flat. "You know all about getting rid of people."

The words landed like a stone.

Jake went still. It cut deeper than anything on the island. He found her face hard in the low light—no accusation, just the fact of it. He didn't need the rest of the sentence to know what she meant.

The moment stretched, full of everything unsaid.

He forced his jaw closed. "That's not fair."

"Isn't it?" Isabelle breathed. "You kept that from me, Jake."

"I'm ashamed of it, Izzy," he said, the truth out quick and blunt.

Fury burned in her eyes. "Don't call me that."

Jake felt the pit of his stomach fall. "I thought I could get some quick cash to help pay for this trip, but when I got down to the wreck, you know what I found?"

Isabelle's brows lifted a fraction, but she stayed silent.

"Drugs," he said quietly. "This guy wanted me to bring up a stash he'd lost. I couldn't do it. I wasn't going to drag that poison ashore and feed it to the people I grew up with."

"That doesn't make you a saint."

Jake dropped his gaze, shaking his head. "Of course not. But when the guy who hired me came to kill me for it... Luca, who'd been watching me, stepped in. He killed them. Not me."

Isabelle looked away toward the cove below, considering. "What happened after that?"

Jake hesitated, the next part sour in his throat. "We loaded the bodies onto *The Wayfinder* and dumped them in the ocean. I didn't think I had a choice. You have to believe me."

She blew out a small, exasperated breath, rubbing her arms as if the memory chilled her. The wind off the cove carried silence between them.

He held her gaze. "I didn't kill anyone. And I'm not planning on killing anyone now."

For a long beat she said nothing, the weight of his confession hanging between them. She searched his face—looking for the lie or the omission—and for a heartbeat he braced for whatever would follow. Instead, she swallowed the words in her throat and gave a small, curt nod.

He let out a tight breath. He drew in the night air, tasting salt and iron before focusing on the task ahead. The tension between them thinned but didn't vanish.

"Are we good?" he asked, careful.

She hesitated, flexing her fingers around the strap of her satchel. "For now." Tension still in her shoulders.

The silence that followed was brittle but necessary—an uneasy truce born of exhaustion and truth. Wind hissed through the palm fronds, carrying away what neither of them said.

Jake's gaze swept the shoreline, catching the faint ember of a cigarette near the pier—one guard, maybe more. His voice dropped, business returning to its edge.

"There's no time to unpack it. One shot, one clean window," he said, scanning the water. "We need to move."

He studied Isabelle a moment longer, noting the tension still coiled in her shoulders. Then, without another word, they fell into motion.

He scanned the boat, calculations running. A straight run would be suicide—the guard was armed, and one crack would summon Luca. They needed a diversion.

He turned back to Isabelle. "You're going to make him come to you."

Her brow drew down, tone clipped but steady. "How?"

He looked toward the water, measuring distance. "Swim out and call for help. Sound like you're from a capsized boat."

Isabelle blinked, forcing the last of the argument down. "You want me to fake drowning?"

"Not drowning," he said, voice low. "Desperate. Make him move closer—make him think somebody needs him."

Understanding crossed her face, wary but focused. "And while he's distracted..."

"I'll come up the swim platform and knock him out." Flat, no flourish.

She held his stare, then nodded. A flicker of something passed between them—not forgiveness, not yet, but resolve.

"All right, let's do this," he said, offering a fist. She hesitated, then bumped it.

A brief, almost-smile—agreement said more than words. Time to move.

They slipped into the cold water. The chill stabbed into muscles already raw from the earlier plunge. Salt burned his wound; blood tasted like iron. Every stroke narrowed his margin left.

They moved carefully, barely disturbing the surface, breaths slow and measured. Every ripple could give them away. A trace of lingering tension remained—a thin current running beneath their cooperation.

Jake fought to keep his strokes steady, but the pain had shifted—no longer sharp, now a dull, relentless ache grinding at his strength. His heart pounded too fast. The edges of his vision ghosted black.

Not now. Forward.

The boat loomed closer. The faint glow of the guard's cigarette sent embers into the dark—the only sign of life aboard.

Jake flicked a glance at Isabelle. She met his eyes, gave a small nod, then angled away, strokes slow and deliberate, finding her mark.

He watched her a half-second longer than he should have, the echo of guilt still tugging beneath the adrenaline, then turned for the swim platform.

Isabelle's voice rang out, sharp and frantic. "Please! Help me! Our boat—it capsized! My boyfriend—I don't know where he is!"

The guard jerked at the sudden voice from the darkness, then cursed, flicking his cigarette into the water as he stepped to the rail. "Who the hell is out there?" Sharp, skeptical.

"Please! Help me!" Breath hitching like she could barely keep her head up.

"Shit..." he muttered, leaning forward.

Jake reached up to the platform with his good hand, fingers finding slick fiberglass. He paused, chest rising and falling, steeling himself. Then, slowly, he reached with his injured arm.

Pain flared, sharp and unforgiving. Muscles refused to cooperate. His fingers barely closed around the edge, grip weak.

He gritted his teeth and hauled himself up anyway, staying low, silent. One mistake and it was over.

"I—I don't know where my boyfriend is! The current pulled us apart!" Isabelle's voice wavered perfectly, panic threading every word.

Jake found a fire extinguisher clipped to the bulkhead and unlatched it.

The guard exhaled in frustration, stepping closer. "Hold on, chica. I can't see a damn thing—"

The first swing cracked hard against the man's temple, staggering him. He windmilled, knees dipping. Jake stepped in and drove a second, shorter blow. The guard folded to the deck with a dull thud.

The world tilted. Darkness crept at the edges. Jake caught himself on the rail before he tumbled backward into the water, then forced breath through his teeth until the deck steadied.

"Remind me to never piss you off," Isabelle said, treading water, eyes wide.

Wincing, Jake managed a grin and reached down with his good arm to help her up. Too winded to waste words.

He rolled the guard onto his stomach, checked for a breath, and slid the shotgun out of the sling. The man groaned faintly—alive, but out cold. Jake hesitated, then met Isabelle's eyes. No discussion was needed.

Together, they dragged the limp body to the stern. The deck lights cast a pale wash over the guard's face as Jake hooked an arm under his shoulders and Isabelle grabbed his legs. One, two—heave. The body slipped soundlessly into the dark, floating out into the cove.

For a moment, neither spoke. The ripples spread and vanished beneath the boat's shadow. Jake's chest rose and fell, the motion tight, restrained. Isabelle's gaze lingered on the widening circles before she turned back toward the helm.

"Think you can get the engines started?" Jake asked, voice thin.

"How hard can it be?" Isabelle pivoted into the cockpit.

Jake staggered forward, hand on the rail, making for the bow. At the windlass control he thumbed the switch. Chain rattled up, links streaming wet through the roller. He guided the last feet with his good hand.

"Keys—thank you," Isabelle muttered as she found them on a lanyard. The diesels turned, then caught with a deep, powerful rumble.

Jake slid into the captain's seat, scanning the panel. Isabelle killed the cabin lights; the world snapped to silhouettes and starlight.

Jake eased the throttles. The *Predator* answered, gliding for the mouth of the cove.

Isabelle pushed wet hair back. Jake shot her a sidelong look, smirking.

"You never mentioned a boyfriend..."

"Yeah. Six-foot-five. Navy SEAL. Really wish he was here," she deadpanned.

Jake blinked. "Wait—seriously?"

She held his gaze, then smirked. "Shut up and drive."

He brought the *Sunseeker* into a slow drift over the spot where *The Wayfinder* had gone down. His fingers tightened on the wheel before he exhaled and turned away.

"I need to grab a few things," he said, already peeling his shirt.

"Jake, you're in no condition to swim again."

He barely glanced at his arm, dark stain spreading down his bicep. Shoes off. "Won't take long."

"Jake—"

He was already over the side.

The cove swallowed him, surface rippling as he kicked deeper. For a beat, the pain went distant. The weight of his wound, the chaos—all of it dissolved into the quiet pull of the deep.

The Wayfinder loomed below, resting on the seafloor like a fallen warrior. Moonlight filtered in silver shafts, painting the wreck in a pale, underwater dusk.

He hovered, staring down. His chest tightened. It wasn't just a boat—it was years of work, sacrifice, dreams built and lost.

He sank a little farther, as if drawn. As if to say goodbye.

He slipped through the open cabin hatch. Inside, everything was in disarray—floating debris, loose gear shifting with the currents. He moved fast, grabbing what he needed: a waterproof case tucked under the bench, a drybag with their clothes, a coil of line, a compact tool roll. The bags he and Isabelle had packed were still secured.

His lungs burned. He kicked hard, vision tunneling as he surged for the surface.

Breaking through, he gulped air, body screaming protest. The pain flared; he pushed through, swimming to the platform.

Isabelle leaned out, grabbing the bags as he hauled himself aboard.

"That was reckless," she said, eyes flicking to his arm.

"Yeah," he muttered, slumping against the rail. "Didn't want to leave your sundresses behind."

"Ass—" she started, a reluctant grin forming.

A gunshot cracked through the night.

Another followed, sharp report echoing off the water. A round sparked off the stern rail.

"Go, go, go!" Isabelle shouted, ducking as another round slammed into fiberglass.

Jake didn't need the encouragement. He slammed the throttles forward.

The *Sunseeker* roared, surging into the channel.

On shore, Luca and another man burst from the tree line, sprinting for the pier, weapons raised.

"Don't let them leave!" Luca bellowed, firing again.

Jake locked on the water ahead. The reef lay close, a black smudge. He gripped the wheel with his good hand, hunting the break.

Another shot cracked, chewing fiberglass astern. Splinters blew past Isabelle as she crouched lower, one hand braced on the seat while the boat tore through the dark, flashing past the looming shadow of the Spanish galleon's bones.

He scanned desperately. The reef stretched wide, impossible to read. His vision kept swimming; depth skewed. Was the break closer, or was that the blood loss?

"There! Starboard—see the slick line where the swell doesn't crest!" Isabelle jabbed a finger.

He didn't hesitate. Wheel over. The *Sunseeker* canted hard.

A subtle dogleg. He tried to correct, but his grip slipped, movements slow.

No room for mistakes—

The world lurched.

Impact.

A sickening scrape tore along the hull as the *Sunseeker* kissed the reef's edge. The deck shuddered. Pain exploded in his arm, hot and blinding.

"Hold it!" Isabelle yelled.

He wrenched the wheel back. The boat lurched free. Somewhere aft, an alarm chirped—bilge. A low vibration rose underfoot, starboard shaft complaining.

They were still moving.

Luca reached the end of the beach, still firing, but the *Sunseeker* slid out of range.

Jake exhaled, jaw locked, as they cleared the reef and took open water. The bilge pump whirred again, a throaty gurgle spitting overboard.

They had made it—far enough.

The *Sunseeker* surged into the swell, leaving the island shrinking into darkness. A low thrumming persisted through the deck plates—starboard, damaged but driving.

Jake tried to keep his grip firm, but his hands wouldn't cooperate. His fingers trembled on the throttles. He blinked hard; the world tilted.

Not yet. A little farther. He wanted distance before Luca found another way to come.

Only when the island was a black smear on the horizon did he let out a breath. His grip slackened—not by choice. His fingers felt thick, slow, as if they weren't his own. He tried to ease back cleanly; the motion came sluggish, unsteady. The engines held a steady hum, the bilge cycling again—another spit of water overboard.

Isabelle exhaled a breath she didn't realize she'd been holding. Alive. Somehow.

Her gaze flicked to Jake—and dropped.

"Jake—oh my God."

He turned, brow folding. Face pale.

She pointed. "Your arm. I thought you scraped it on the rocks when we jumped, but—" she swallowed—"you're shot."

He blinked, as if seeing it for the first time. His left bicep was a mess of torn skin and slick, dark crimson, blood dripping to his elbow. His fingers twitched, distant, numb. A fresh wave of dizziness washed through him; the world tilted.

Shit.

This time he knew he wasn't going to fight it off.

His vision tunneled. The edges blurred. The engine hum faded to a distant drone. His pulse roared, his body finally cashing a bill he'd been ignoring.

Too much blood loss. Too much strain.

The deck tilted. *No—the deck was steady*. His knees weren't.

"Jake!" Isabelle lunged, catching him as he sagged. She hauled him toward a bench. "Stay with me. Jake, look at me."

He tried to speak—fine—but the word stuck. Light smeared. Her face ghosted.

Blackness seeped in.

His weight settled. Breathing shallow. Face chalk-white.

"Jake?" Panic surged. She pressed two fingers to his neck. Pulse—too fast, too weak—but there.

She exhaled sharply, shoving fear aside. *Fix him first. Panic later.*

She spun for the cabin, tore open compartments. *Useless, useless—*

Cold plastic under her fingers. A first-aid kit.

Relief flared—then she saw the slosh. Water skimming the cabin sole, creeping higher with each swell.

Shit. Think.

Automatic pumps should've kicked on. Maybe they had—maybe not enough.

She raced back up, eyes raking the panel. There—*BILGE PUMP OVERRIDE.*

She slammed the switch. A mechanical whirr shivered through the hull. Seconds later, a wet gurgle blasted overboard.

Working. For now.

She grabbed the kit and a foil blanket from the ditch bag, then knelt beside Jake. He was slumped where she'd left him, breathing shallow. Too pale.

She ripped the kit open. Gauze. Saline. Suture set. Not ideal for a seawater wound—but she had to stop the bleeding.

She pressed a thick pad of gauze to the entry, another to the exit, lifting his arm to slow the flow. Blood seeped fast, then less. She flooded the wound with saline, washing salt and grit.

"Figures," she muttered. "The one time I get to stab you with a needle and you're too out of it to complain."

Her hands trembled; she stilled them by force. Years ago on the Yucatán, a dive partner and a coral head—hours from help. It had been her or no one.

She set two wide, interrupted stitches to tame the worst of the bleeding—knowing it wasn't ideal on a dirty wound—then packed fresh gauze and wrapped it tight with an elastic bandage, building a firm pressure dressing.

"Okay." She pressed fingers to his neck again. *Warm. Pulse still there.*

She pressed a water bottle to his lips. "Small sips," she whispered, though he was barely conscious. She set it within reach and brushed damp hair from her face.

"You're a pain in the ass, you know that?" she said softly. "But you are not allowed to leave me like this."

The bilge cycled again—another gurgle overboard. The low shaft vibration thrummed underfoot, steady as a worry.

Now the boat.

The island was quiet.

The chaos of the night had faded to the rhythmic crash of waves and the whisper of wind through the jungle. Mist thinned, revealing the skeletal pier where the Sunseeker had been moored—before Morgan and Alvarez took it from under them.

Luca stood at the end of the ruined dock, watching the last trace of the stolen boat slip toward the horizon. A dull ember flared at the tip of his cigarette as he took a slow drag, his face unreadable.

Behind him, Mateo cursed, kicking at damp sand. "They got away," he muttered, tight with frustration.

Luca exhaled, smoke curling. Slowly, a smirk tugged. "They won't get far."

He glanced toward the beached tender, knowing it would never make an offshore chase.

He flicked the cigarette into the dark water. "Hand me the satellite phone."

He already knew who would answer.

CHAPTER TWENTY

Into the Deep

T he low hum of the Sunseeker's twin diesels was steady—a fragile reassurance against the chaos of the last few hours. Beneath it came the softer, more ominous sounds: the hiss of waves brushing the hull, the hollow clink of something loose rolling across the deck, and the relentless rhythm of water shifting below her feet.

The yacht rocked gently on the swell, the motion slow but unpredictable, as if the sea hadn't quite decided whether to spare them. The air smelled of saltwater and fuel, cut through by a faint electrical tang from the overworked bilge pump.

Isabelle exhaled sharply, her hands still smeared with Jake's blood. He remained slumped where she'd left him, propped against the corner bench of the aft cockpit. The dim glow from the overhead LEDs painted his skin in cold tones of blue and gray. The bandages around his arm were tight, but dark patches of red had already begun to seep through. His breath came shallow, uneven—but steady enough to keep her from falling apart completely.

He needed warmth.

She pushed herself upright, boots squelching faintly against the damp deck. Every movement drew a dull ache from her legs, stiff from waning adrenaline. The night air pressed close—warm, heavy, and laced with the metallic scent of blood and seawater.

She turned toward the stairs leading below deck, gripping the stainless-steel railing for balance as the hull tilted beneath her. The *Sunseeker's* interior was sleek and foreign, all soft leather and polished teak—luxury designed for champagne afternoons and sunlight, not survival in the dark.

It was nothing like the research vessels she'd worked on, or *The Wayfinder's* sturdy practicality. This boat was indulgence incarnate—every curve meant to impress; every surface built for comfort rather than necessity. And now, it was bleeding slowly into the ocean.

The standing water on the lower deck had drained away, but the automatic bilge pump cycled again—a whirring grind followed by a hollow gurgle, then silence. About forty seconds later, it would start again. The sound was mechanical and steady, but to Isabelle it felt like a ticking clock. Somewhere below the waterline, the reef strike had opened a wound in the hull they couldn't afford to ignore.

The pump hummed again, echoing through the deck plates.

They were still losing ground.

Her fingers trailed along the paneling as she descended the narrow stairwell, using the polished teak walls to steady herself. The air below was cooler, heavy with the mingled scents of salt, fuel, and damp upholstery—a faint reminder that the ocean was pressing against every inch of the hull.

The hum of the engines dulled to a low vibration through the soles of her boots. Down here, the world felt sealed off—no wind, no waves, just the quiet, claustrophobic stillness of luxury trapped in survival mode.

She paused at the bottom of the stairs, eyes adjusting to the soft amber glow spilling from recessed floor lights. The lower deck stretched before her in muted elegance: pale leather upholstery, chrome fixtures, glossy cabinetry that caught glints of light with each sway of the hull. It was beautiful in a cold, impersonal way—too perfect, too sterile.

Where would they keep blankets?

Her gaze drifted across the space until she spotted a door ajar near the forward bulkhead. She crossed quickly, the slight list of the boat forcing her to brace against the frame as she pushed it open.

A stateroom. The air inside was untouched—cool and faintly perfumed, as if the yacht's owner had never actually slept here. The bed was neatly made, the linens pristine, the pillows squared and stacked like a showroom display. Isabelle's throat tightened. The contrast between this immaculate comfort and the chaos outside felt obscene.

She strode forward and tore the comforter from the bed, the crisp fabric whispering as she dragged it behind her through the corridor. By the time she reached the cockpit, her pulse was pounding again.

Jake barely stirred when she wrapped the comforter around him, tucking it close beneath his chin. His skin was cold against her fingertips.

"Stay warm, okay?" she murmured—soft, automatic, the words meant more for herself than for him.

She lingered for one heartbeat longer, searching his face for any sign of change. *Nothing.* Then she turned away.

The bilge pump kicked on again, its hollow whine echoing through the deck. The boat was still sinking.

Her pulse hammered as she turned back toward the cabin. If there was something—anything—she could use to patch the hull, it had to be below deck.

She retraced her steps, moving past the stateroom and deeper into the narrow passageway leading toward the stern. The floor tilted beneath her with each swell, the motion unsteady and unpredictable. Every door she passed was a guess. She flung open cabinets, checked beneath counters, tore through the galley and salon—polished wood and chrome flashing in the beam of the overhead lights—until she reached a compact storage compartment near the engine room.

This has to be it.

The air back here was hotter, thick with the tang of diesel and oil. The low thrum of the twin diesels vibrated through the walls, constant and alive. She yanked open a storage hatch, hands slick and trembling as she rifled through the contents—flashlight, spare fuses, oil filters, coiled lines. Nothing useful.

Then her fingers brushed something solid wedged behind a set of tools. A rectangular plastic case. She pulled it free, turning it over in her hands. The label was faded, but the words were still legible—bold and merciless:

UNDERWATER REPAIR EPOXY — FAST CURING

Her breath caught.

She popped the latches with shaking fingers. Inside: two putty sticks, gloves, a folded instruction sheet.

She unfolded the paper fast, scanning the directions:

Mix the two compounds. Apply directly to the damaged area. For leaks below the waterline, use from the exterior for best results. Hold until initial cure.

She froze.

From the exterior.

The words hit her like a blow to the ribs.

She had to go into the water.

The cabin suddenly felt smaller, the air thick and hot in her lungs.

Isabelle swallowed hard, the instruction sheet trembling in her grip.

No. No, no, no.

She'd spent years in the water—diving shipwrecks off Florida, mapping submerged ruins in the Caribbean—always with clear visibility, controlled depths, safety lines, a team at her back. Places where the sea was calm and predictable, where light still reached.

This was different.

This was open water.

At night.

Her gaze dropped to the instructions again.

For leaks below the waterline, use from the exterior for best results.

She read it twice. A third time. As if the words might soften, or rearrange themselves into something less impossible.

They didn't.

Her stomach twisted.

She traced a finger over the ink, pulse thudding in her ears. There had to be another way—patch it from the inside, slow the leak, anything.

Then the hull lurched. A fresh swell hit broadside, sending a faint glug... glug... glug from somewhere below. Water where it shouldn't be.

No. You know better.

I have no choice.

The weight of it settled cold and heavy in her chest. She stuffed the instructions back into the case, grabbed the flashlight, and forced her legs to move.

Get up there. Just move.

As she climbed the stairs, cooler air hit her skin—sharp, briny, real. She drew in a deep breath, heart still pounding, and turned toward the only thing in sight that could stop her.

Jake.

He lay where she'd left him, swathed in the comforter, skin pale in the dim glow. His chest rose and fell, slow and shallow.

If he were awake, he'd handle this.

She could almost hear him—Jake's calm, unbothered voice on *The Wayfinder*, laughing through the spray while patching a stubborn leak. "Patching holes is part of the lifestyle," he'd said then, grinning like it was nothing.

It's not nothing now.

And this wasn't the Keys. This wasn't daylight in a harbor with tools and time. This was black water, an open sea, and a dying boat.

He can't help. It's just me.

For a moment—just a heartbeat—she thought about shaking him awake, just to hear his voice. But she knew better.

And the bilge pump's dull whine below —rougher sounding now then before— reminded her: the clock was still ticking.

Her jaw set. *It's just me.*

Her movements became mechanical. If she thought too much about what she was about to do, she'd stop herself.

Boots first.

She planted one foot on the seat beside Jake, yanking off the waterlogged leather, then the other. Each one hit the deck with a dull slap, leaving dark prints against the teak. Her jacket followed, then her soaked-through outer shirt. The night air clung to her damp skin, warm but heavy, tasting of salt and oil.

She went to the helm, reached for the throttles, and clicked both gears to neutral, watching the white churn aft flatten as the props wound down to stillness. No spinning metal below her feet. She drew a breath she hadn't known she was holding.

She turned, gaze drawn back to Jake as if sheer willpower might wake him. The blanket rose and fell with each shallow breath, but he didn't stir.

She was running out of time.

The bilge pump cycled again—its low whine cutting through the stillness like a countdown.

Isabelle forced herself aft, each step heavier than the last. The motion of the boat made her legs feel foreign, like she was walking through someone else's nightmare.

At a stern locker she flipped the latch. Inside a shallow bin: a basic dive mask and a coiled lanyard. She looped the lanyard through the flashlight's tail and clipped it to her wrist, then cinched the mask down hard.

She reached the swim platform. It gleamed under the deck lights, a slick patch of fiberglass hovering inches above blackness. She stepped onto it, bare feet slipping against the wet surface as the boat rocked beneath her. The gentle rhythm made her feel unsteady in a way that had nothing to do with motion.

The ocean stretched out below—a vast, lightless void. Deep. Endless.

Waiting.

She gripped the edge of the platform, knuckles whitening. Her reflection shimmered faintly in the ripples, fractured and ghostlike.

Her breath caught. A phantom chill crawled up her spine, prickling her skin despite the humid air. Rationally, she knew the water near the equator wouldn't be cold—but her body didn't care about logic. Fear had already rewritten the rules.

The silence pressed in, thick and heavy. The boat suddenly felt too small. The world, too wide.

She clenched her jaw.

Just get in. Find the damage. That's all.

Her body refused. Every instinct screamed against it.

She squeezed her eyes shut. Inhaled. Exhaled. Once. Twice.

Three... two... one...

Then—before her mind could rebel—she pushed off.

The water swallowed her whole.

The light from the boat vanished instantly, snuffed out like a flame.

Silence. The kind that wrapped around her like a second skin, pressing in from all sides—heavy, endless, alive.

She forced herself deeper, every kick heavy, her chest already too tight, her lungs too aware of the air she'd left behind. The flashlight carved a thin, trembling cone through the dark, a fragile circle of pale light. Beyond it—nothing.

She swept the beam along the hull, searching for damage.

But her eyes kept flicking to the dark beyond. Too quiet. Too empty. Which meant something had to be there.

A knot coiled in her stomach, a primal instinct firing deep and old. Her back felt exposed. Her legs dangled like bait.

An image rose unbidden—a great white emerging from the void, jaws unhinged, closing around her spine before she even knew it was there.

Her pulse spiked.

She twisted sharply, jerking the flashlight into the black.

Nothing.

Just water. Empty. Waiting.

She was burning through oxygen too fast. She had to calm down.

Focus.

She turned back to the hull, forcing her beam to stay on the fiberglass.

Another image tried to climb the ladder of her thoughts—something rising from below, taking her ankle, dragging her down—but she shoved it away.

Her grip on the flashlight slipped; the beam jolted. Panic flexed.

Go.

She broke.

She kicked hard, shoving for the surface, her legs burning, arms trembling, the light knocking against her wrist on its lanyard.

Too fast. Too desperate.

Her head burst through the surface. She gasped, choking on air like she'd been drowning.

She clawed at the swim platform, hauling herself up with weak, numb arms. Her lungs burned. Her heart slammed against her ribs.

She wasn't okay.

Her hands shook violently as she pressed them against the slick fiberglass. Tears blurred her vision, hot against her cold skin.

I can't do this.

The thought lashed through her like a whip, tearing through everything she was holding together.

And suddenly—she hated it.

Hated the fear. Hated how it had gripped her like a vice, drowning her before the ocean even had the chance. Hated that she was sitting here, gasping for air, instead of fixing the damn boat.

"Come on, Izzy," she growled under her breath, pressing the heels of her palms into her eyes. "You don't get to fall apart now."

Her breath shuddered, raw in her chest. Her body wouldn't stop shaking. Her mind frayed at the edges.

She curled her hands into fists and squeezed her eyes shut.

She wasn't supposed to be here. She was an archaeologist, not a survivalist. She worked in controlled conditions, mapped shipwrecks with a team, had backup, had support, had rules to follow—

Not this.

Not alone, in the black void, patching a sinking boat with nothing but a lump of putty and lungs already aching.

Jake would have done it.

If he were awake, he'd tell her to breathe. He'd know what to do. He'd patch the hull without hesitating. He would've been fine.

But Jake couldn't help right now.

And she was the only thing keeping them alive.

She drew in a deep, shaking breath. Held it. Let it out slowly.

Another. Slower.

The trembling in her limbs didn't stop, but something colder began to take root beneath the terror.

Not calm. Not bravery.

Resolve.

If she didn't do this, they were going to die out here.

No one else was coming. No one else was going to fix this.

She wasn't ready.

But she had no choice.

She pressed her forehead against the wet fiberglass of the swim platform, the cool, sharp scent of salt filling her lungs. The deck vibrated faintly under her palms, a muted reminder of the engines idling, waiting.

One more breath.

And this time, she wouldn't surface until she found the damage.

Below her, the black water stretched out—endless and waiting.

Her bare toes gripped the slick fiberglass of the swim platform. Her hands still trembled. Her pulse was still too loud.

But this time—she didn't hesitate.

She clenched the flashlight between her teeth, tightened the lanyard at her wrist, grabbed the edge of the platform, and pushed off.

The ocean swallowed her again.

No looking around.

She locked the beam on the hull the instant she submerged, keeping it steady, refusing to let it wander into the black.

Nothing else existed. No abyss. No monsters.

Just the boat. Just the job.

She kicked deeper, following the thin cone of light along the hull. The fiberglass stretched pale and smooth in the dark, ghostly beneath her light. Tiny flecks of sediment drifted through the beam like slow-falling snow.

Then—

There.

A jagged crack, eight inches long. Its edges splintered and raw, the water pushing through it in a rhythmic pulse—breathing in, breathing out—like the boat itself was wounded.

She steadied herself, bracing one hand against the hull.

Not catastrophic. Yet.

But if they ran the engines hard again, or if the seas picked up...

Her lungs tightened.

She ran her fingertips over the fracture, testing the edges. The current was stronger than she'd expected—an invisible force sucking at her skin, drawing her in.

The pressure in her chest sharpened, lungs screaming for air.

She kicked off the hull, light bouncing, and drove upward.

Break the surface. Breathe.

Her head broke through the water. She gasped, dragging air deep into her chest, coughing against the salt.

Her arms trembled as she gripped the swim platform.

The leak was small. *Fixable.*

She just had to mix the epoxy.

She hauled herself onto the platform, chest heaving, saltwater streaming from her hair. The world spun slightly. Her heart thundered against her ribs.

But she'd done it—she'd found the wound.

And she was still breathing.

She had survived the second dive.

Now came the hard part.

Isabelle ripped open the kit, her fingers still shaking.

Inside—two tubes. One white, one gray.

Mix equal parts. Knead together. Apply directly to the damaged area. Hold until it grabs—about ninety seconds.

She forced herself to breathe. *Ninety seconds. Underwater, that might as well be forever.*

No time to think.

She squeezed equal amounts of the putty into her palm and mashed them together—mixing, folding, kneading. The material softened under the friction, heat blooming against her skin as the colors merged into a uniform gray.

The chemical reaction had started. The clock was ticking.

She shoved the putty into the waistband of her leggings, clenched the flashlight in her teeth again, tightened the mask strap, and slid back into the water.

The darkness swallowed her one last time. She hoped.

She forced her body downward, every kick steady, her vision locked on the hull. The sleek fiberglass curved into the abyss, fractured where the crack gaped open like a wound still breathing.

She pulled the putty free and pressed it hard against the fracture.

The water fought her.

It resisted, clawing at her fingers, trying to claim the opening as its own.

She shoved harder, forcing the epoxy deep into the seam. The putty spread under her fingertips, warm and pliant, molding to the curve of the hull. She smoothed the edges, sealing the flow until the pressure against her palms began to fade.

Her lungs screamed.

Now came the worst part.

She had to hold it.

She flattened both palms over the patch and pressed, muscles trembling with effort.

One... two... three...

The seconds dragged.

Thirteen... fourteen... fifteen...

Her pulse pounded in her ears, a low, violent drumbeat.

Twenty.

Not yet.

Thirty.

Almost there.

Her vision narrowed, tiny sparks flashing at the edges.

Forty-five... forty-six...

The burn in her chest turned to fire. Every instinct screamed for air.

Eighty-seven... eighty-eight... eighty-nine—

She broke. *Surface. Now.*

Kicked off the hull, driving for the surface, arms heavy, every muscle blazing. The flashlight swung on its lanyard, its beam slicing through the dark in frantic, stuttering flashes.

She burst through the water, gasping, choking on air like it was the first breath she'd ever taken.

The night rushed back in—wind, salt, the low hum of the bilge.

Her arms shook as she grabbed the swim platform and hauled herself aboard.

She collapsed onto her back, chest heaving, saltwater pooling beneath her.

For a long moment, she just lay there, staring up at the stars—bright, sharp pinpricks against the black. Her lungs burned, her hands throbbed, and her heartbeat still roared in her ears.

Then, beneath it all, she heard the faint hum of the bilge pump. A low whir... a gurgle... and then—nothing.

It cut off.

She waited, counting the seconds in her head.

Ten.

Twenty.

Thirty.

Normally, it would've cycled back on by now.

It didn't.

The silence stretched, heavy and absolute.

Then she exhaled, the sound breaking into a shaky laugh—half disbelief, half relief. It built quietly, trembling in her chest until it broke free, louder this time, unsteady and raw. The laughter caught in her throat, twisted, and turned to something else entirely.

Tears welled up, hot against her salt-streaked cheeks, mixing with seawater she hadn't noticed still clinging to her skin. They came fast—tears of joy, exhaustion, everything she'd been holding back since *La Isla de Sombras*, since the caves, since the moment Luca had pressed a gun to Jake's head and she'd thought it was all over.

Her breath hitched. She pressed a trembling hand over her mouth, half-laughing, half-sobbing, unable to stop either.

The sound of the sea filled the silence around her—gentle, rhythmic, alive.

She'd done it.

The patch was holding.

The boat wasn't sinking anymore.

For the first time all night—they had a chance.

And for the first time, she had saved them.

The polished conference table gleamed under the soft, recessed lighting, but it wasn't profit-and-loss slides on the screen—it was a site plan. A digital blueprint of Black Tide's Algeciras Cold Chain Terminal stretched wall to wall: reefer racks in neat grids, a new cross-dock finger jutting toward the quay, and a row of high-capacity blast freezers annotated negative thirty degrees Celsius in red.

Victor leaned back, fingers steepled, as the operations director traced a laser across the plan. "Phase II adds one hundred twenty reefer plugs on the west apron, dual-circuit ammonia with CO_2 cascade in the main room, and a pharma corridor sealed to GDP standards. Redundancy is N plus one on compressors and power—two diesel gensets plus battery buffer to cover the switchover."

Victor's gaze flicked to a narrower module shaded blue. "And the quarantine vault?"

"Negative-pressure, independent scrubbers," she said. "Temperature integrity to within half a degree. If a container alarms, we can isolate without compromising the corridor."

A slight tremor touched his ring finger; he folded his hands to still it. "Fire suppression?"

"Inert gas in the freezers, dry pipe in the dock. No water near cartons. We also specified rapid-close doors to minimize thermal loss during peak."

He considered the airflow vectors rotating on the model. "Dock cycle time?"

"Target is eight minutes door-to-door. We'll pre-chill the staging lanes."

"Good," Victor said. "Speed is a kind of mercy."

The legal lead cleared her throat. "Community advisory board wants written assurance on ammonia risk."

"Give them truth," Victor replied. "Risk exists. Control exists more."

He let the map spin, the cold geometry of it catching in the glass. "Approve the west apron and the pharma corridor. Hold the blast tunnel until I see the grid study. If Spain sneezes, I don't lose a warehouse."

"Yes, sir."

His phone buzzed once on the table. *LUCA.* Victor's eyes didn't leave the blueprint. "We're done," he said softly. "Execute Phase II." He stood, took the call in the corridor, and didn't bother with a greeting.

"Tell me."

Luca stood at the water's edge, the satellite phone cold in his grip. The jungle behind him hissed with cicadas and the distant call of something unseen, but his focus was locked on Victor's voice.

"They escaped and treasure is not here," Luca said, blunt. "The *Sunseeker's* damaged—we can't use it to pursue. We're stranded."

Silence on the line. Not the kind that meant anger—Victor didn't show anger. This was the kind that meant he was deciding who to blame.

Finally, Victor spoke, voice unreadable. "Status of the others?"

Luca's jaw tightened. He hesitated—a flicker that could get a man killed. Then he forced the words out. "Carlos didn't make it."

A longer pause followed. Luca could hear Victor thinking: processing, calculating.

At last Victor exhaled, clipped and cold. "He was my nephew. His father will not be happy."

Luca rolled his eyes under his breath. He hadn't liked Carlos much—careless, entitled. That explained a lot.

"Yeah," he muttered. "Figured."

Silence stretched. Victor wasn't amused. "What now?"

Luca squared his shoulders, forcing his voice to stay level. "We need an extraction."

A beat. Then Victor: "A helicopter will be there in an hour." Short. Precise. No wasted words. No anger. Far worse than yelling.

Just as Luca thought the call was ending, Victor's tone sharpened. "Who was driving when the *Sunseeker* was damaged?"

Luca's grip on the phone tightened. He knew what Victor was really asking. He could have lied—said Carlos was at the wheel, pinned it on the dead. But Victor would know. So, Luca didn't bother.

"Does it matter?" he said instead.

A long pause. Then Victor let out a quiet, humorless chuckle. "No. It doesn't." Then ended the call abruptly.

Steps approached. Mateo stood nearby, watching like a dog waiting for a command. Javier shuffled, still dazed and wet, thumb rubbing his split lip into a line of red.

"What's the damage?" Mateo asked.

Luca let out a slow breath and lowered the phone. "We have an hour."

Javier grunted, massaging the back of his head. "Then what?"

Luca looked out where the *Sunseeker's* wake had dissolved into the night—white on black, the last ribbon of their escape. He clenched his jaw.

"Then," he said, voice hard as flint, "we hunt them down."

The *Sunseeker* drifted, silent and still, rocking gently on the open sea.

The horizon had begun to smolder with the first traces of sunrise, the deep navy of the night peeling away into streaks of orange and violet. The engines were quiet—Isabelle had shut them down hours ago.

They were low on fuel anyway. No sense in wasting what little they had.

She leaned back in the captain's chair, one leg draped over the armrest, the other stretched out, bare toes resting on the console. The bottle of tequila she had found in the galley sat loosely in her grip, half-empty—nursed over the last hour.

Not drunk. Just enough to take the edge off, to loosen the coil that had been wrapped tight around her chest ever since she'd clawed her way out of the water.

She tilted her head back, staring up at the stars that were still clinging to the sky. She should have been proud of herself. She'd done what she had to—what Jake would've done. But now that it was over, the adrenaline was gone, leaving nothing but the weight of everything that almost went wrong.

She had patched the hull.

She had kept them afloat.

She had done something she never thought she could.

Instead, she just felt tired. Her limbs were heavy, her skin sticky with salt, her hair still damp from earlier. She rolled the bottle between her fingers, then lifted it to her lips, letting the burn settle in her chest.

A laugh pushed at her throat, dry and humorless. Who the hell drinks tequila after almost drowning? The answer, apparently, was her.

Her gaze flicked toward Jake. Still out cold.

The blanket she had wrapped around him had slipped slightly, exposing his bandaged arm. The wound was bad, but he was alive. His chest rose and fell, slow and steady.

Her fingers tightened slightly around the bottle. For hours, she had been waiting for him to wake up. Now that she had a moment to breathe, she wasn't sure if she wanted him to. Because the second he did, everything would start again. They still had to get moving, find fuel, figure out their next step. For now, she just wanted one more minute of quiet.

She lifted the bottle again—a soft rustle from behind her made her freeze.

A low groan.

She turned her head sharply. Jake's fingers twitched beneath the blanket. His brow furrowed, a flicker of movement in his half-lidded eyes.

Then—his gaze found her.

Isabelle exhaled sharply and sat forward, placing the bottle down without thinking.

She was on her feet in seconds, moving toward him, heartbeat suddenly too fast.

"Jake?!"

His eyes were unfocused, blinking against the light. His throat bobbed, his lips parting like he wanted to speak but couldn't quite form words yet.

Isabelle knelt beside him, pressing a hand lightly to his forehead—warm, but not burning.

Her chest tightened anyway.

A slow blink. His breathing shallow, uneven.

"Hey, come on—stay with me." Her hands moved fast, grabbing the bottle of water she had set beside him earlier. She cracked the cap and pressed it to his lips. "Drink."

Jake obeyed without protesting, taking slow sips. Some of the color returned to his face, but he still looked too pale. Too weak.

She hated it.

"You scared the shit out of me," she muttered.

Jake's eyes flicked toward her, studying her through the haze of exhaustion.

His gaze dropped briefly—to her bare shoulders, the damp tank top, the way her hair was still tangled from seawater. Then back to her face.

"...You look like hell," he croaked.

Isabelle let out a dry, breathless laugh, shaking her head. "Yeah?" She arched a brow. "That's rich, coming from you."

Jake huffed weakly, but even that seemed like too much effort.

His left arm throbbed, sharp and heavy, but—he could move it. That was a start. His jaw tightened as he looked down at the bandage around his arm. "You patched me up?"

Isabelle shot him a look. "What, you thought some kind of magical first-aid fairy came while you were passed out?"

Jake managed the barest smirk. "...Just checking."

He shifted slightly, trying to push himself up—but Isabelle moved fast. "No, no, no—" she pressed a hand against his shoulder, keeping him down. "You are not doing this right now."

Jake scowled. "We need to—"

"Go nowhere," she interrupted. "We're low on fuel, and you're—" she gestured at him "—basically held together with duct tape."

Jake blinked, disoriented. "Where... are we?"

Isabelle leaned back, glancing toward the horizon where the first light touched the waves.

"Drifting," she said quietly. "Somewhere in the South Caribbean Sea."

Jake's brow furrowed, but he nodded faintly, eyes focusing on the bottle sitting across on the console.

"...Tequila?"

Isabelle exhaled heavily, rubbing her fingers against her temple.

"You almost died... I almost died..." she muttered. "A glass of wine was not going to cut it."

Jake snorted, but the sound was weak. He let his head rest against the cushion, eyes drifting toward the soft glow of morning over the horizon.

"...How bad?"

Isabelle's lips pressed together. "Bad."

Jake closed his eyes. Nodded once.

"But you're awake," she added, quieter. "That's good."

Jake cracked his eyes open again, watching her. The humor in her voice was forced. For the first time, he really looked at her. The exhaustion was there, deep in her eyes, buried under the sarcasm. She had been waiting for him to wake up. And she wasn't okay.

Jake exhaled slowly. "...You alright?"

Isabelle didn't answer right away. For a second, he thought she might brush it off.

Then—she let out a slow, heavy breath, rolling her shoulders like she could physically shake off the weight of the last several hours.

"No," she admitted.

Jake nodded. "...Yeah."

Silence.

Then—Isabelle huffed a laugh, shaking her head. "Well, now that you're awake, you're gonna explain why you drove our stolen getaway boat into a goddamn reef."

Jake choked on a laugh.

Isabelle grinned, despite herself, and handed him the tequila bottle.

Jake took it without hesitation.

Yeah. They were going to be fine.

Then—*thump, thump, thump.*

The low, rhythmic pulse of rotor blades cut through the quiet, a distant sound that sent a shiver down Isabelle's spine.

She was the first to hear it, her gaze snapping to the horizon. A dark speck, just visible in the growing dawn, was closing in fast.

Jake stirred, his voice hoarse. "Is that what I think it is?"

Isabelle's jaw tightened. "Maybe it's not them." But even as she said it, she didn't believe it.

Jake let out a dry, humorless breath. "We're not that lucky." He shifted, trying to push himself upright. "I've got to—"

"No, you're in no condition." Isabelle shoved him back down, her grip firm. He was too weak to fight her.

His jaw clenched. "We can't stay here, Izzy."

The sound of her nickname—rough and familiar on his voice—pulled a small, unbidden smile from her, brief but real. She'd snapped at him the first time he'd used it, but now it landed differently. She tightened her grip on his shoulder, steadying both him and herself, surprised by how much she liked the way it sounded coming from him.

"I know."

Her pulse hammered as she spun toward the helm, turning the ignition keys for each engine. The *Sunseeker's* twin diesels rumbled to life beneath them, a deep mechanical growl that vibrated through the deck. She threw the throttles forward. "Hold on."

The yacht surged ahead, slicing through the waves, its bow lifting before leveling out as it gained speed.

But the helicopter kept coming. It banked sharply, tracking them. Any hope that it was a coincidence vanished.

"They're following," Jake called from the bench, his voice strained.

"I see it." Isabelle kept her eyes locked ahead, knuckles white on the wheel.

Jake exhaled hard. "Fuel?"

Isabelle's eyes flicked to the control panel. "Fifty gallons."

Jake swore under his breath. "We can't keep this up for long." He sank back, thinking fast. Luca must have called for a pick-up. That meant the helicopter had already burned fuel getting to the island—maybe they couldn't keep this up either.

The thump of the rotor blades grew louder, the deep bass vibrating through the air, sending a shudder through Isabelle's chest. She stole a glance over her shoulder.

The helicopter swept in low on their port side, a logo gleaming under the morning light—sleek and ominous against the dark fuselage.

Black Tide Global.

Jake's brows furrowed. The name clawed at his memory. He'd seen it before—but where?

Then his stomach dropped.

Key West. The auction house. The business card. The man with the charming voice and cold, dead eyes. Victor Serrano.

Jake clenched his teeth. It wasn't just Luca and his thugs anymore. They'd been caught in something much bigger.

Beside him, Isabelle leaned forward, eyes narrowing as she locked onto the cockpit.

Luca was there—strapped into the co-pilot's seat, sunglasses flashing the ocean below. One hand gripped the overhead handle; the other lifted in a lazy, mocking wave. Even from this distance, Isabelle could feel the smugness radiating off him.

Her pulse roared in her ears. A slow, humorless grin spread across her face. Then she lifted one hand off the wheel—and flipped him off.

Jake choked on a weak laugh. "Christ, Izzy."

The helicopter lingered a moment longer, as if considering them. Then, as if amused, Luca muttered something to the pilot.

The aircraft pulled up sharply, banking out of sight.

Isabelle's fingers tightened around the wheel.

"Where the hell—" Jake started, pushing himself up slightly.

Then—

It dropped right in front of them.

A hundred yards ahead.

Low.

Blocking their path.

The *Sunseeker's* bow plowed forward, engines snarling beneath the deck.

The helicopter hovered just feet above the water, its downwash sending sharp sprays of saltwater slapping against the windshield.

The side door slid open.

Two men stood inside.

Armed.

Jake swore. "Shit."

One man braced a foot against the edge of the doorway, his rifle steady. The other stood beside him, shouting something inaudible over the roar of the rotors.

Isabelle didn't slow down.

Logic screamed at her to. But after everything—the caves, the drowning, the panic, the sinking boat, the fight for every single inch of survival—she was done being hunted. She was not stopping.

Her jaw locked. Her fingers tightened on the throttle.

Jake saw it. "Izzy—"

She ignored him.

The helicopter loomed ahead, daring them to turn away.

She didn't.

She aimed straight for them.

Let them move. Let them back down.

Jake braced against the bench, swearing under his breath, torn between concern and pure, reckless admiration.

The two men stiffened as the boat did not slow. One man waved an arm, shouting. The other's grip on his rifle tightened.

They expected her to turn.

She didn't.

Then—for half a second—doubt hit her. Her breath caught. The helicopter was too close. They weren't moving.

At the last second, instinct took over—her throat locked up, her body bracing, a scream tearing from her lips as she ducked low.

And the helicopter pulled up.

The roar of the rotors swept over them, deafening. A wall of wind and pressure slammed against the *Sunseeker* as it tore past. The water churned violently where it had been hovering.

The yacht ripped through the opening.

Isabelle exhaled hard. Her heart slammed against her ribs, her breath shaking.

The helicopter took up the chase once more, but it had fallen back nearly half a mile before the pilot managed to get the nose back around.

Jake and Isabelle both watched it, their bodies tense, bracing for round two.

Then—suddenly—it veered south, banking away.

Isabelle exhaled again, her grip on the throttle loosening as tension bled from her shoulders. She slumped back into the captain's chair, letting her head fall against the headrest, and finally pulled the throttles back slightly.

"Hell of a move," Jake offered from his spot on the bench, still stretched out, still too pale—but watching her with something close to admiration.

She huffed a tired smile but didn't have the energy to gloat. "We need fuel." Her voice was rough from exhaustion.

Jake shifted slightly, wincing, but forced himself to focus. "What's close?"

Isabelle studied the map on the navigational screen, blinking through the haze of fatigue. "About thirty miles south of Grenada," she said, glancing back at him.

Jake nodded slightly. "Bring the throttles back until the RPM gauges read two thousand. We'll be running on fumes, but we should be able to make it to a marina."

She adjusted the throttles accordingly, feeling the *Sunseeker* ease into a steadier cruising speed. Then she adjusted their heading, bringing the bow around toward Grenada.

A long silence stretched between them—just the sound of the engines humming beneath their feet, the spray of saltwater against the hull.

Then, finally, Isabelle let out a breath, shaking her head slightly. "Just so you know... I'm going to need some serious R&R after this." She glanced at Jake, dead serious. "We both are."

Jake let out a weak chuckle, closing his eyes against the rising sun. "No argument here."

Then, after a beat, he opened them again, turning toward her with a look she didn't like. "Oh, by the way," he said, voice dry but laced with something heavier. "I think I know who's really after the treasure."

Isabelle frowned. "What?"

Jake exhaled through his nose, running a hand over his face. "And you're not going to like it."

Isabelle's stomach twisted at the tone in his voice. She straightened slightly. "Who?"

Jake's fingers curled loosely against the armrest, the rising sun catching the exhaustion in his features. "Victor Serrano."

The name hit like a drop of ice water.

Isabelle's blood went cold. Her hand tightened on the wheel. For a heartbeat, she didn't move—didn't breathe. Then, softly, almost to herself: "...Victor Serrano."

The engines droned on, carrying them east into the rising light—toward safety, or the next storm.

The Sikorsky's blades were still winding down as Luca stepped onto the tarmac, peeling off his headset and tossing it into the cabin. The morning heat pressed down on him—thick with jet fuel and salt air—but he barely noticed. His mind was already locked on the next move.

Mateo and Javier trailed behind, stiff and silent. The pilot was already coordinating refueling with the ground crew, but it would take time. Not much—an hour, maybe—but enough for Luca to think two steps ahead.

His phone buzzed. *Victor.*

Luca exhaled sharply and answered.

"Tell me something useful." Victor's voice was clipped, cool.

Luca didn't hesitate. "We made visual contact before we had to divert to refuel." He ran a hand through his hair, already anticipating the next question. "But I know where they're headed."

"Where?"

"They were running on fumes when we broke off. Closest place to refuel is Grenada—St. George's Marina. Maybe a smaller dock nearby, but that's their best bet. They wouldn't risk pushing farther."

Victor let the pause stretch, weighing the words.

Then his voice came, colder. "You told me the treasure wasn't on the island."

"It wasn't," Luca said quickly. "But they might know where it is."

A beat of silence. Heavy.

"Explain."

Luca pressed on. "They escaped with whatever they found in the caves. Could be something that points to the real location. Either way, they've got information we need."

Victor exhaled, slow and deliberate. "Then find out what they know."

Luca's jaw tightened. "We will."

Victor's tone shifted, cutting like a blade. "How bad is Morgan?"

"Injured," Luca said. "He won't move fast."

"So, they're desperate."

Luca nodded, though Victor couldn't see it. "Exactly."

Another pause. Then Victor's voice softened, dangerous in its calm. "You have contacts in Grenada. Use them. And, Luca—"

Luca's grip on the phone tightened. "Yeah?"

Victor's voice dropped an octave. "Don't fail me again."

The line went dead.

Luca exhaled slowly, tucking the phone away before turning back to Mateo and Javier.

Mateo raised a brow. "Victor pissed?"

"Victor's always pissed."

Javier smirked, then winced, touching his temple. "Yeah, but this feels extra."

Luca shot him a look. "Do I look dead to you?"

Javier snorted softly. "Fair point."

Luca turned back toward the helicopter, watching the ground crew finish the refueling.

Jake and Isabelle thought they'd gotten away.

They were wrong.

Victor set the phone down, the faint hum of the terminated call still ringing in the silence. Beyond the glass wall of his office, midday light washed across the Port of Algeciras, glinting off container cranes and the whitecaps of the bay. In the distance, the Rock of Gibraltar rose pale and immovable against the horizon.

He turned toward the console on his desk. The global map glowed softly, threads of sea routes pulsing like arteries. One small red pin blinked in the Caribbean.

La Isla de Sombras.

He studied it for a long moment, then hit the intercom button and spoke without looking up. "Send a recovery team."

His assistant's voice answered through the intercom, calm and efficient. "Standard recon?"

Victor's eyes stayed on the map. "No. Full survey. Every carving, every trace. Anything bearing Grey's symbols or Spanish naval markings comes directly to me."

A brief pause. "Understood."

Victor leaned back in his chair, the faint tremor in his hand barely visible as he reached for the glass of water beside him. The surface rippled once before going still.

He stared out over the harbor. Luca would chase the living. Victor would chase the dead. One of them would find what Elias Grey left behind.

CHAPTER TWENTY-ONE

A Fragile Haven

The *Sunseeker* limped into the glassy bowl of Secret Harbour Marina, its once-sleek hull scuffed and salt-streaked—the last twenty-four hours written across its skin. Morning light slid over the green hills and pastel villas of L'Anse aux Épines, turning the water a bruised turquoise. Halyards ticked against masts in a loose metallic chorus while a pelican skimmed the surface and folded into a dive. The air carried the sweet-spice breath of land—nutmeg and wet vegetation—braided with diesel and sun-warmed varnish.

Isabelle eased the *Sunseeker* toward the fuel dock, hands steady on the wheel despite the grit in her eyes and the knot lodged between her shoulders since the helicopter. She doubted it would loosen anytime soon.

Jake hadn't moved since they cleared the headland. He lay on the bench with his eyes half-lidded, breathing steady but shallow, the fizz of adrenaline long gone. What remained was weight—blood loss, bone-deep fatigue—and the slow, patient roll of the marina cradling them both.

As she maneuvered into the slip, the world around her felt disarmingly calm. A dockhand in a faded blue polo with a Grenadian flag patch stepped onto the pier, motioning her forward. Isabelle eased the throttles back; the diesel rumble softened to a murmur, and the *Sunseeker* glided toward his outstretched hands, the water parting in slow, glassy ripples. She barely had the energy to toss the lines.

"Morning," he greeted, looping the ropes over the pilings with the ease of long habit. His gaze swept over the scuffed hull, the streaks of salt, then to Jake—pale and unmoving on the bench.

"You look like you had a rough night," he said.

"You have no idea," she muttered.

The dockhand—his name tag read Lennox—secured the last line and stepped closer. "Fuel's available. Need anything else?"

Isabelle hesitated. Normally she'd be wary of asking for help, but Jake was in no shape to move, and she wasn't about to leave him alone.

"Yeah. A doctor. Preferably someone local and discreet."

Lennox's brows lifted, but he didn't pry. "There's an old doc up in L'Anse aux Épines. Retired from General Hospital a few years back. People still go to him. Name's Dr. Baptiste."

"Do you think he'd come here?"

"For the right price, maybe. I can give him a call."

"Please." She slipped him a few folded bills. "Tell him it's urgent."

Lennox nodded. "I'll see what I can do. Need anything else? Water, food?"

She glanced at Jake—still too pale—and back at him. "Yeah. Just the essentials."

He disappeared down the dock, phone already out. The sun glanced off the water in shards of white light; a pelican landed near the pilings, sending ripples across the mirrored surface. Isabelle sat back at the helm, listening to the quiet rhythm of the waking marina — the slap of water against hulls, a distant gull's cry, the low thrum of a generator coming to life — normal sounds that felt impossibly far from the night they'd survived.

Jake stirred beside her, fingers twitching beneath the blanket she'd tucked around him.

"Where ... are we?" His voice was hoarse.

"Secret Harbour," she said softly. "Grenada. For fuel and rest. A doctor's coming to check on you."

Jake cracked one eye open, a weak smirk tugging at his lips. "Didn't know you cared so much, Izzy."

"Shut up."

A knock on the hull made her rise. Lennox was back, and beside him stood a tall, wiry man in his sixties—dark-skinned, silver hair cropped close. A rumpled linen shirt, sleeves rolled, a well-worn leather satchel over one shoulder.

"Dr. Baptiste," Lennox introduced.

The doctor's sharp eyes moved from Isabelle to Jake, taking in everything with one glance. "Let's see what we're dealing with."

He set his bag beside Jake and went to work, movements efficient but unhurried. Isabelle hovered nearby, arms crossed.

Baptiste peeled back the bandage. Jake barely reacted, though his jaw tightened.

"Who stitched him up?"

"I did."

"Not bad. A little uneven, but clean."

He probed the wound with careful fingers. Jake hissed through his nose but didn't pull away. "You were lucky," Baptiste murmured. "No infection yet. Keep it that way."

He pulled out a sealed IV pack, spiked the bag, and set the catheter. "He's dehydrated. Lost more blood than I like." The cabin filled with small, precise sounds—the tear of plastic, the click of metal, the faint rush as saline began to drip.

Jake's eyes flicked toward Isabelle. "I hate needles."

"You hate a lot of things."

Baptiste adjusted the line, unfazed. He set a small amber bottle beside Jake. "Antibiotics. Twice a day. No skipping doses. No drinking." His glance landed on the half-empty tequila bottle near the helm.

Jake managed a weak grin. "That one's not on me, doc."

Isabelle rolled her eyes. "How long until he's ... functional?"

Baptiste's eye brows furrowed, "functional?"

"Able to move. To help," Isabelle clarified, gesturing to the rest of the boat.

"You want the real answer or the reckless one?" He asked with a smirk.

"Reckless," Jake muttered.

"Few days to move without tearing something. A week if you want to do it right."

Isabelle's jaw tightened; she nodded. They didn't have a week.

Baptiste handed her packets of electrolyte powder. "Fluids, food, rest. In that order."

Jake shifted, wincing. "Rest is boring."

"Better than dying, son." Baptiste checked the IV once more. "If there's fever or swelling, call me."

"Thank you," Isabelle said quietly.

He waved her off. "You paid for discretion. You'll have it." Pausing at the deck edge: "Wherever you're headed, try not to end up needing me again."

He stepped off the boat. Isabelle stood listening to the slap of water against the hull, the faint shimmer of heat rising off the harbor, knowing they wouldn't be that lucky.

The *Sunseeker* had gone still. The IV bag hung above Jake's bench, the slow drip marking time in the hush. Warm air pressed close. Isabelle rolled her shoulders, trying to shake the ache that had settled deep in her muscles. For the first time in days, she wasn't bracing for impact.

Jake was stable. They had fuel. And for the moment, no one was trying to kill them.

From the helm, she watched him sleep—the color returning to his face, breathing even and unbroken. The IV had done its job. For once, he looked almost peaceful.

She stepped closer, adjusted the blanket, fingers brushing his cheek. Warm skin, rough stubble. Relief hit hard and quiet. She withdrew her hand before he stirred, pulse quickening at the foolish tenderness of it.

"I'm gonna take a shower," she murmured.

The stateroom's head was small but clean—polished chrome, warm teak, soft light pooling across the mirror. She peeled off her salt-stiffened clothes and caught her reflection: new bruises shadowing the faded ones along her ribs — the ghost of every hit and fall she hadn't had time to feel. For a long moment she studied the exhaustion in her eyes, the small tremor in her hand.

"Remember why you're doing this, Izzy," she whispered, then stepped beneath the rainfall shower.

Heat poured over her shoulders, cutting through the chill that had lived in her bones since the island. She braced her hands against the wall and let the salt, the sweat, the fear wash away. She had patched the hull. She had kept them afloat.

But the thought of how close they'd come—to sinking, to losing him—tightened her chest.

They were alive. For now.

When she finally shut off the water, the air smelled faintly of soap, almost foreign after so much salt and blood.

Back on deck, Jake still slept, chest rising in an easy rhythm. He had scared the hell out of her. She brushed damp hair from his forehead and whispered, "Don't die, okay?"

He didn't stir.

She retreated below, dropped onto the bed, and for the first time in days, Isabelle slept.

Luca stepped out of the vehicle and rolled his shoulders, scanning the marina with a practiced eye. The flight from Port of Spain had been short, but exhaustion clung to him—too little sleep, too much frustration, and the gnawing fact that Jake and Isabelle had slipped away again.

The air smelled of fuel and brine. A few charter captains hosed down their decks; fishermen hauled in the last of the day's catch.

"They didn't make it farther," Mateo muttered. "If they were smart, they stopped here."

Luca spotted a dockhand coiling rope near the pier's edge and walked toward him. "You work here?"

Lennox glanced up. "That's what it says on my shirt."

"We're looking for a Sunseeker Predator fifty-five. Came through this morning," Luca said, extending a couple of bills between two fingers.

Lennox's eyes flicked to the money, then back to the man holding it. He studied Luca's face, weighing the calm against the edge beneath it. "Lot of boats come through," he said at last.

A fisherman called over, "Saw one like that—came in early, tied up by the fuel pumps."

Luca flicked him the bills. "Appreciate it." When he turned back, his eyes lingered on Lennox—a look that carried the kind of chill people remembered—then he strode toward the fuel dock.

The Sunseeker sat silent in its slip, sunlight glinting off the wet hull.

"That's them," Mateo said.

"So, what now?" Javier asked.

"No need to rush," Luca replied. "They're injured. They'll stay put. We

wait." A faint smirk pulled at his mouth. "They'll have to move eventually."

A few fishermen lingered nearby, smoking and talking low. Luca handed
one of them a folded slip of paper and a couple of bills. "Call this number
if that boat moves."

Then he turned away, eyes still on the *Sunseeker* — a predator waiting
for its wounded prey to stir.

The hum of the *Sunseeker's* systems was the first thing Isabelle noticed as
she stirred, the quiet rhythm grounding her before she even opened her
eyes. The cabin was dim, the only light spilling from the hallway in a thin
line across the floor. The air carried a faint scent of salt and something
clean—detergent, maybe. The sheets were cool against her skin, and for
the first time in days she felt warm. Dry. Safe.

She blinked, disoriented for a heartbeat before memory fell back into
place. Grenada. The marina. Jake.

A slow breath left her lungs. Her muscles were sore but no longer
trembling; the shower had helped more than she'd expected. It had been
the first real comfort since the island—the hot water washing away the last
chill of the ocean, of fear itself.

The towel she'd wrapped around herself had loosened, barely clinging as
she rolled onto her side. She inhaled, steady and quiet. She'd slept. Actually
slept.

But reality waited.

A glance at her watch—past eight p.m. She groaned, pushing upright
until her feet met the cool deck. Then she saw the bags Jake had dumped
near the door. A dark puddle spread around them, seawater still dripping
from the fabric.

She let out a dry chuckle. "Fantastic."

Laundry could wait. Food first.

She pulled on her salt-stiff leggings and tank, tied her damp hair into a
bun, and stepped out of the stateroom. The air outside was soft and heavy
with salt, the marina alive with muted sounds—distant music from a bar,
the faint clatter of dishes, the gentle lapping of water against the docks.

Jake was still stretched out on the bench in the cockpit, right where she'd left him, though now he looked more aware. His eyes found her as she approached.

"You're up," he murmured, voice rough with exhaustion.

"So are you."

He managed a weak smirk. The IV bag beside him hung empty, but there was color in his face again.

"You feeling human?" She asked.

"Getting there."

She carefully peeled away the tape and slid the catheter from his arm. "You don't need this anymore."

"Thanks." He flexed his fingers, then looked her over, a faint grin tugging at the corner of his mouth. "You look... refreshed."

"I look like hell."

"A little," Jake said, a hint of a grin tugging at his mouth.

"Whatever. You need food. So do I."

His stomach growled in agreement.

"I'll see what I can find," she said.

"Not going anywhere." He paused, then added, "You good?"

It wasn't a casual good—it was *are you really okay?*

"...I will be," she said finally.

"Be careful."

"I'm getting food, not smuggling contraband."

"Yet."

She shook her head, smiling despite herself, grabbed some of their remaining cash, and stepped onto the dock.

The Secret Harbour Marina Restaurant & Bar was a low-lit haven tucked between rows of yachts, its open windows spilling music and the smell of grilled seafood into the night. Inside, the scent of spice and salt wrapped around her like warmth. The place had settled into that quiet lull after the dinner rush—crew lingering over drinks, laughter low and unhurried.

"Takeout?" the woman at the counter asked.

Isabelle glanced up at the handwritten specials board, blinking away the fog of fatigue. "Yeah—uh, two grilled fish with rice and vegetables. And something sweet?"

"Banana bread's fresh tonight."

"Perfect."

A few minutes later, Isabelle walked back along the docks with the warm bag in hand. The air was cool and clean. She wasn't fully rested, but she felt a little more like herself. And for now, that was enough.

The Sunseeker bobbed gently in its slip. Jake's eyes lifted as she climbed aboard.

"I thought you left me for dead."

"Thought about it," she said with a faint smile.

She unpacked the containers—grilled fish, rice, vegetables, thick slices of banana bread—and handed him a fork. They ate in companionable silence, the only sounds the scrape of plastic and the lap of water.

Finally, Jake leaned back. "Catch me up. What'd I miss?"

"While you were bleeding all over the deck, I was busy keeping this thing from sinking."

"From the reef," he muttered, remembering.

"Yeah. When I went below for a blanket for you, I found water. A lot of it."

"That bad?"

"Bad enough we wouldn't have made sunrise if I hadn't done something."

He exhaled, guilt shadowing his face. "What did you do?"

"Kicked the bilge pumps on, stitched you up, then found the underwater repair epoxy."

"You patched the hull?"

"I wasn't about to let us sink."

Jake shook his head slowly. "Izzy, that's... incredible."

She shrugged. "Just followed instructions."

"You got in the water. Alone. In the dark."

"It wasn't my first choice. But it had to be done."

"I should've—"

"There was nothing you could've done. If our places were switched, you'd have done the same."

"Still. I hate that you had to."

"Me too."

He studied her, voice softening. "You saved my life."

Isabelle froze, fingers tightening on her napkin. His eyes held no teasing—just gratitude. When his fingers brushed hers, light but warm, she turned her hand over, letting the moment settle.

"Thanks," he murmured.

"Don't make me do it again."

They ate the rest in silence—comfortable, but charged. Then Isabelle's brow furrowed.

She looked up again. "Promise me—no more secrets."

Jake met her gaze. "It was a mistake. I won't do that to you again."

He pushed his container aside, exhaustion dragging at him. "I need a shower."

"Think you can handle that?"

"I'm injured, not helpless," he said, pushing himself upright. The motion drew a sharp breath through his teeth, and he caught the railing before the deck could tilt under him.

"You just stopped yourself from face-planting."

"I paused. Big difference."

She smacked his good arm. He chuckled—low, tired, but real—and disappeared below deck.

Isabelle leaned back, eyes closing to the hum of the marina. Then she remembered the soaked bags. Groaning, she headed below to start the laundry.

The rhythmic churn of the washer filled the cabin, oddly comforting after days of chaos. When the first load finished, the clean scent of detergent replaced salt and damp.

Jake had been gone a while.

"You still alive in there?" she called.

A pause. "Yeah. Just... taking my time."

"You mean sitting on the bench because you got dizzy?"

"...Maybe."

"Don't make me come in there."

A pause. Then — "Oh no," he called, mock-dramatic. "Another dizzy spell! Someone strong and incredibly smart should come check on me."

Isabelle laughed. He was fine.

When he finally emerged, a towel around his waist and damp hair curling at the ends, he looked better—still pale, but alive.

"You took forever," she said, tossing him folded clothes.

"It's called self-care, Izzy. You should try it."

"Smart-ass."

She stretched, fatigue dragging through her shoulders. "I'm crashing."

Jake nodded, hand brushing the doorframe as he turned toward the other stateroom.

"Get some rest, okay?" she called after him.

He looked back, smiling just enough to reach his eyes. "You too."

They both slept.

Morning spilled across the marina in slow, golden light. The air was warm and still, carrying the faint aroma of coffee and diesel from the docks. Gulls wheeled lazy arcs above the masts, and the slap of water against hulls kept a steady rhythm below. Isabelle sat on the aft bench, fingers wrapped around her mug, the heat seeping into her palms while the weight in her chest refused to lift.

The companionway creaked. Jake climbed up from below, his arm in the sling Baptiste had left for him, a second mug steaming in his good hand. Sunlight caught the stubble along his jaw and the tired squint in his eyes.

"Sleep well?" she asked.

"Like the dead."

"Yeah, you're not far off."

He watched her, sensing what lingered beneath the quiet.

"Jake," she said, setting her mug down. "We need to talk."

"That's never a good start."

"I need you to be honest. How far are we willing to take this?"

"You want to go home."

"I don't know." She drew a breath. "We've lost *The Wayfinder*. You nearly bled out. And for what? We don't even know what we're really chasing anymore. Treasure? History? Siecaza? What if it's something that shouldn't be found?"

Jake listened, silent.

"If we turn back, we disappear. Victor doesn't have to find us."

He exhaled slowly. "You're right. This trip's already taken its pound of flesh."

His voice dropped. "I've always just kept moving — even when I shouldn't. That's how I lost my friend Ryan. We were diving a wreck off the Dominican Republic after a storm. The current was still bad, visibility down to nothing. I should've called it."

He rubbed a hand over his jaw, eyes distant. "He got trapped when part of the hull collapsed. I could hear him over the radio, calling my name, but I couldn't get to him." His voice thinned, barely above a whisper. "By the time I reached the breach, his line had gone slack."

Silence settled between them—only the faint slap of water against the hull filling it. Isabelle watched him, the weight in his expression cutting deeper than she expected.

She hadn't seen this side of him before—the wear beneath the bravado, the quiet self-reproach. For once, she didn't try to fill the space with words. She reached out instead, her hand finding his, fingers curling gently around his calloused knuckles.

"You couldn't have saved him," she said softly. "You did what you could."

Jake's gaze stayed fixed on the water. "Maybe. Doesn't change how it feels."

Isabelle hesitated, thumb brushing over his hand. "You've been carrying that alone for a long time."

He gave a faint, uneven breath that might've been a laugh. "Feels like several lifetimes."

"Then maybe it's time you stop running from it," she said, voice low. "You don't have to keep moving just to outrun ghosts."

For a long moment, neither of them spoke. The quiet between them wasn't heavy—it was understanding. The first real one they'd shared.

Finally, Isabelle leaned back, her gaze drifting toward the water. "So we agree continuing isn't great for our health," she said, trying for lightness but not quite getting there.

Jake's mouth twitched. "That's fair."

"But if we stop, they won't," she went on, the thought tightening in her chest. "If we turn back, they'll take whatever Grey took—and I don't trust them with it."

Jake nodded slowly, the fog of memory still clinging to his eyes but focus returning.

"So... what if we find it first? Not for the money. To keep it out of their hands."

He met her eyes. "Grey was afraid of it. That means something."

"This is a terrible idea," she said.

"Yep."

She sighed, gaze drifting toward the open sea. "A little farther."

Jake's smirk returned. "A little farther."

The decision settled between them like the tide turning—quiet, inevitable.

CHAPTER TWENTY-TWO

The Passage South

The restaurant at Secret Harbour Marina was busier than the night before. The midday crowd had claimed the shaded deck that overlooked still blue water, where sails rippled lazily against their masts and laughter drifted over the soft clatter of silverware. The scent of grilled fish and island spices carried on a breeze that smelled of sea air and sunbaked teak—warm, clean, touched with the sweetness of flowering hedges along the pier.

At a small table near the railing, Isabelle sat with her notebook open, sunlight sliding across the page in shifting stripes. Beside it lay the page from Elias Grey's journal—its ink faded, the edges brittle with age. She'd spent most of the morning studying it, copying every line beside the sketch of a church façade from the chamber wall that refused to leave her mind.

Jake sat opposite her, his left arm still bound in the sling, a glass of water sweating beside his good hand. The exhaustion hadn't left him, but the sharp edge of pain had dulled to something he could manage. He watched her work, half-smiling.

"You're doing that thing again," he said softly. "World disappears until you solve it."

"Hmm?" she murmured without looking up.

He smirked. "Exactly, that thing."

Isabelle ignored him, tracing a line along her sketch with the side of her pencil. Two towers rose on either side of an ornate façade. A curving pediment crowned the structure, a cross etched above the central arch. Three portals lined the base—grand, symmetrical, deliberate. The style was Iberian, but the flourishes weren't Spanish.

She frowned. "This isn't Caribbean. The carving's too refined, too... Portuguese."

Jake leaned forward, curious despite himself. "So Grey had been farther south?"

"Maybe," she said absently. Something about the proportions tugged at her—familiar, intimate, like a half-remembered melody.

Then memory flickered: sunlight on pale stone, the smell of roasted coffee drifting through narrow streets, her father's voice echoing across a plaza. *See the curve there, Izzy? That's the shift from Baroque to Rococo. Lighter. More human.*

Her breath caught. "Wait."

Jake straightened. "What?"

"I know this place," she said, a small smile breaking through. "I've been there."

"You have?"

She nodded, excitement building. "My dad took me to Rio when I was fifteen. He was lecturing on colonial trade routes—dragged me through every old church in the city. I remember standing right here." She tapped the curved pediment on the sketch. "The Church of Our Lady of Mount Carmel. In the old quarter of Rio de Janeiro."

Jake studied the drawing. "You're sure?"

"Positive. The twin bell towers, the triple doors, the pediment—everything matches. But look—" she pointed to the shading around one arch, "—Grey's version is simpler. The ornamentation wasn't finished yet. The structure's the same. The bones never changed."

For a moment she wasn't in Grenada anymore but fifteen again, standing beside her father on uneven tiles, sea air thick with coffee and candle wax drifting from open doors. He'd laughed when pigeons scattered across the square, his hand resting on her shoulder as he explained how the Portuguese imported faith and architecture in the same breath.

Jake's voice pulled her back. "So Grey was there."

She nodded. "It makes perfect sense. Rio was a major colonial hub by the mid-eighteenth century—Portuguese governors, merchants, Spanish envoys passing through. If Grey was hiding from the Spanish, that church would've been the perfect place to bury something in plain sight."

Jake's eyes flicked over the sketch, then to her face. "Then that's our next stop."

The certainty in his tone steadied something inside her. The past few days—the firefight, the chase, the exhaustion—blurred into background noise. What remained was purpose.

She smiled faintly. "Rio." The word tasted like memory and promise at once.

He nodded, unfolding a chart with his good hand. "Let's see how far it is."

She exhaled, tucking the page back into her notebook. "Alright, Captain. How bad can it be?"

Jake traced a rough line south across the expanse of blue. "From here to Rio de Janeiro... about thirty-three hundred nautical miles."

Her eyes widened. "That's—"

"—a long way," he finished, a tired grin tugging at his mouth.

She leaned back with a low whistle. "So we're not exactly around the corner."

"Nope."

For a while they just sat there, listening to the murmur of conversation and the hush of waves against the hulls below. Isabelle closed her notebook, fingers resting on the worn cover.

Her father's voice lingered—*History always circles back, Izzy. The stories you chase will one day chase you.*

Maybe he'd been right.

She looked up at Jake, whose eyes were fixed on the map but distant, thoughtful. "We're really doing this," she said quietly.

He smiled. "Looks that way."

She felt the pull of a grin. "Then we'd better figure out how to get there before your arm falls off."

Jake chuckled, folding the map. "Practical as ever."

"Someone has to be."

Their laughter mingled with the sea outside—soft, contented, almost ordinary. For the first time since the island, the tension between them eased—not gone, but tempered into something familiar.

Isabelle glanced once more at the sketch lying between them, the faint lines of Grey's hand connecting centuries across the page.

The bones never changed.

Neither, she thought, did the need to see what lay beyond the horizon.

The breeze had shifted by the time their plates arrived, bringing the hum of outboards from the harbor. The air carried grilled snapper and roasted plantains; around them, the marina's rhythm went on—dockhands calling, a steelpan echoing faintly from a bar down the pier.

Isabelle stirred the ice in her glass. Her mind was already miles ahead. "So," she said finally, "we take the Sunseeker—straight shot down the coast."

Jake looked up from the chart, somewhere between amusement and dread. "I wish."

"What do you mean? We have a boat. We know where we're going. What's the problem?"

He rubbed his jaw, bracing for the explanation. "The *Sunseeker's* not built for that kind of trip. Performance yacht, not a long-range cruiser."

"So we stop for fuel."

Jake exhaled. He tapped two points on the map—Grenada and Brazil—his finger tracing the ocean between. "Izzy, do you have any idea how far that is?"

She squinted. "Thirty-three hundred nautical miles?"

"Yeah. The *Sunseeker's* range is only a couple hundred miles per tank. That means a dozen-plus refueling stops."

"Okay... but there are ports along the way."

"Sure, but we'd need thousands of gallons of diesel—well into five figures. Just in fuel."

That got her attention.

"Five figures?" she repeated.

He nodded. "Give or take."

Isabelle sat back, staring toward the harbor where sunlight glinted off the sleek hull below. "You're telling me we can't use the one thing we actually have going for us?"

"Not unless you've got a secret trust fund I don't know about."

She smirked. "Impressive math skills, by the way."

"Comes from years of calculating how close I can get to running out of fuel before I have to call for a tow."

The smile faded as he looked down at the chart. "That's not even counting food, docking fees, and supplies. We'd bleed ourselves dry before we reached the Amazon."

For a long moment only the murmur of the crowd and the slap of halyards filled the air. Isabelle drummed her fingers on the table. "...So what do we do?"

Jake's gaze followed a fishing skiff gliding into the marina. "We find another way."

"That's not a plan."

"Not yet."

She sighed. "Alright, plane tickets. Fast and easy."

He shook his head. "The second our names hit a manifest, Luca and Victor's people will know exactly where we're headed."

"Then what's left?"

He hesitated, thinking. "A cargo ship."

"A what?"

"Freighters run between the islands and South America all the time. If we can find one bound for Brazil out of the Port of St. George's, we might be able to pay our way onboard."

"Like passengers?"

"More like stowaways with permission. Off the books—no paperwork, no manifest. Safer, cheaper, and once we're in Brazil, we can disappear."

"How cheap?"

"A few hundred bucks, maybe more. Depends on the captain."

She ran a hand through her hair. "And you think you can find someone willing to take us?"

Jake gave a half-smile. "You're looking at a guy who's spent his whole adult life dealing with people who don't ask a lot of questions."

"Comforting."

"It's a gift."

Silence settled as the breeze shifted. She glanced toward the docks. "And we just... leave the Sunseeker sitting there?"

"We could leave it with Lennox, the dockhand," Jake said. "Hell of a tip for the guy."

"Let's not drag him into this."

"Yeah. You're right."

They ate in small bites after that, not out of appetite but to keep their hands busy. Around them, the easy hum of the marina felt almost mocking—normal life moving on while theirs tilted toward the unknown.

When the plates were nearly empty, Isabelle met his eyes. "Alright," she said. "So we head to the Port of St. George's."

Jake folded the chart, tucking it under his arm as he stood. "It's our best shot."

She tossed a few bills on the table. "Then let's go find ourselves a ship."

Jake smiled faintly. "Guess we're hitching a ride."

"You make it sound almost fun."

"What? You're not having fun, Izzy?"

She laughed. "I don't think fun is the word I'd use."

They turned toward the sunlit dock, their shadows stretching long across the boards as laughter faded behind them. The sound of the sea followed—a steady reminder of everything ahead and everything they'd already survived.

From the shaded patio of a small café across the marina, Luca watched Jake and Isabelle step into the sunlight. They paused near the boardwalk, laughter passing between them, before Jake adjusted the sling at his shoulder and started toward the marina office.

"They're leaving," Luca murmured.

Across from him, Mateo tilted his chair back. "Looks like it."

Javier, a table away, glanced over his phone. "They went back to the *Sunseeker* a few minutes ago—came out with bags. They're not taking her, though?"

"Doesn't look like it," Luca said. He watched as they crossed the dock toward the main gate. "Wherever they're going, it's not close. Get someone down here to secure the *Sunseeker*."

Mateo arched a brow. "You think they'll be back for it?"

"Doesn't matter," Luca said, slipping his phone away. "I don't like leaving loose ends."

"Maybe they're giving up—going home."

"I wouldn't count on it with these two." Luca set down his untouched drink. "Let's see where they go."

At the end of the pier a taxi pulled up. Isabelle spoke to the driver while Jake loaded their bags. The trunk closed, the door slammed, and the cab pulled away into the bright Grenadian afternoon.

"Where do you think they're headed? The airport?" Javier asked.

"Maybe. Could be another port."

"So what's the play?"

"We find out where that cab's headed. Check the main routes—the airport, the Port of St. George's, the ferry terminal. If they're leaving Grenada, it'll be through one of those."

Mateo rose with him. "And if we lose them?"

Luca slipped on his sunglasses, scanning the road where the taxi had vanished into the palm-lined hills. "Not an option."

He started down the boardwalk with Mateo and Javier falling in beside him, their footsteps matching the measured rhythm of his stride. Behind them the chatter of the marina carried on—bright, untroubled, unaware that the calm had just been broken.

The taxi rattled through the narrow streets of St. George's, climbing past rows of faded stucco before dropping toward the harbor. The city opened suddenly—a bowl of turquoise water ringed by green hills and red-tiled roofs. Cargo cranes towered over the docks, their long arms frozen mid-swing against the glare of the late-afternoon sun.

The driver hummed softly to the radio. The breeze off the harbor mixed sea spray with the dry tang of rust and machine oil—the scent of a city that never truly slept. Isabelle leaned her forehead against the window, watching forklifts weave between warehouses, dockhands shouting over engines, gulls circling overhead.

It was chaos, but a functional kind of chaos.

Jake adjusted the strap of his sling, his good hand resting on the duffel at his feet. "You sure about this?"

"Not even a little."

He smiled faintly. "Good. Then we're on the same page."

The driver stopped at a row of corrugated-metal buildings. The heat hit them the second they stepped out—thick, humid, tasting of iron and brine.

Jake handed the driver a few bills, then glanced toward the docks. "Alright. Let's find someone bound for Brazil."

Isabelle shaded her eyes. Massive container ships loomed offshore while smaller freighters rocked lazily against the piers. "There must be a hundred ships here."

"Then one of them is bound to say yes."

They wove through stacks of pallets and coils of rope. Workers moved constantly—loading crates, checking manifests, shouting in a mix of English and Creole. Isabelle stayed close, her notebook tucked in her bag. A few dockhands gave them curious looks—two outsiders with no clear purpose.

Their first few inquiries went nowhere.

"Passengers?" a bearded man scoffed. "Ain't no cruise ships here."

Another waved them off before Jake finished his sentence. "Cargo only. No room for extras."

By the fifth rejection Isabelle's patience was fraying. Sweat gathered along her temples; the clang of metal on metal grated.

"This was your big idea," she muttered.

"You doubt my legendary charm already?"

"I'm starting to."

"Don't worry. Someone here's got a price."

"Let's hope it's one we can afford."

They rounded the corner of a warehouse, and the noise thinned. Near the end of the pier, a smaller freighter sat moored apart from the others—a weathered vessel with peeling paint and a faded name stenciled across its bow: *Mariana's Resolve.*

Jake slowed. The ship wasn't pretty but it was sturdy, the kind of workhorse that had seen every ocean and was still afloat. "That one."

A man stood on the gangway, barking orders to two deckhands hauling crates. Older, broad-shouldered, sun-creased, his hair streaked with gray but thick—authority in every movement.

Jake called up. "Captain?"

The man looked down. "Who's asking?"

"Jake Morgan. This is Isabelle. We're looking for passage to Brazil."

"Not a damn cruise ship," the man said, voice gravelly from years of shouting over engines.

"Didn't think it was."

That earned a dry chuckle. "Then what exactly are you hoping for?"

"We can pay," Isabelle said. "We just need transport—quietly."

The captain eyed them, noting Jake's sling and the weariness behind their faces. "Name's Vasquez," he said. "Captain of the *Mariana's Resolve.*"

"Good to meet you, Captain."

"Headed to the Port of Santos," Vasquez said after a moment. "Five, six days if the weather holds. You got cash?"

Jake pulled out a small stack of bills. "Enough to buy us a corner to sleep in and maybe some food."

Vasquez considered it, then jerked his head toward the gangway. "Come aboard. We'll talk."

Jake shot Isabelle a quick look—half cautious, half triumphant—and followed.

The ship creaked beneath their feet, the smell of oil and open water stronger now. Up close the *Resolve* showed its age—rust along the rivets, paint flaking—but it felt honest, built to endure.

"Stay close," Vasquez said. Crewmen glanced up as they passed. He led them through a narrow door and up a short flight of steps to a dented cabin.

"Your room," he said simply.

Inside were two narrow bunks, a tiny desk bolted to the wall, and a round porthole looking out toward the harbor. Cramped, but clean.

Isabelle dropped her bag on a bunk. "Not exactly first class."

"Beats sleeping on the dock," Jake said.

"Galley's down one level," Vasquez added. "You eat when the crew eats. Don't be late. Stay out of the way, don't touch what isn't yours, and if something happens, keep your mouths shut. We leave on the tide—engines are already warming."

"Understood," Jake said.

The door clanged shut behind him.

Isabelle groaned, collapsing onto the bunk. "Perfect. Traveling with a schedule as flexible as the ocean."

Jake smiled. "Relax, Izzy. It's part of the adventure."

"You keep saying that like it's supposed to make me feel better."

She lay back, listening to the distant creak of lines and the muted thud of cargo being stowed somewhere above.

An hour later, the ship shuddered as the engines turned over and the air below deck grew warm with motion.

Warm evening air met them as they climbed to the deck. The harbor lights of St. George's twinkled behind, already shrinking. Isabelle leaned on the rail beside Jake, breathing deep.

"Hard to believe Grey made this kind of journey with nothing but wind and stars," she said.

"He had a knack for impossible odds."

"So do we, apparently."

"Guess we're in good company."

They stood in silence, watching violet dusk melt into sea and sky. The ship rolled gently, alive with its own rhythm.

"You ever notice how the sea sounds different at night?" Jake asked.

She listened. "Like it's whispering."

"Never sure if it's talking to us or warning us."

"Maybe both."

They fell quiet again, the wake glowing faintly astern—a pale trail dissolving into dark.

"You ever think about what we're doing?" Jake asked. "Chasing a man who's been dead three hundred years?"

"All the time," she said. "But then I think about why—what it might mean to return what was stolen. And suddenly it doesn't feel so crazy."

"Yeah. Maybe he'd approve."

"You think about him a lot, don't you? Grey."

Jake smiled softly. "Maybe more than I should. With all the stories Pops used to tell... feels like I'm chasing a ghost who might help me understand myself."

"Maybe that's why you're the one who found all this," she said. "Maybe the trail was always meant for you."

He laughed quietly. "That's a little poetic, even for you."

"Yeah," she admitted, smiling. "Felt a little cheesy when I said it."

The sea stretched endless ahead, a smooth, dark expanse that reflected the starlight in shards of silver. Behind them, Grenada had become a smudge on the horizon.

A couple of hours later, after a quick dinner with the crew, the ship had settled into its night rhythm.

Moonlight slipped through the small porthole, pooling across the floor. The *Resolve* hummed softly beneath them—a steady pulse through the hull.

Isabelle lay on her side, eyes open to the shimmer of water outside. Sleep wouldn't come. Every time she closed her eyes, the day replayed itself—the sketch, the port, Vasquez's clipped tone. Across from her, Jake lay on his back, one arm behind his head, the sling folded beside him. His breathing was too even.

"You can't sleep either," she whispered.

He smiled faintly in the dark. "Not yet."

"What were you thinking about?"

He hesitated. "Home. The Keys. Pops in a chair that should've collapsed ten years earlier, telling stories like they were gospel."

"About Silas. About Grey," she guessed.

"And my dad," he said quietly.

He hesitated, then began.

"Our family ran a salvage business down in Marathon—*Morgan Marine.* Pops started it after the war, and my dad took it over when he got out of the Coast Guard. By the time I came along, it was what we did. Summers, weekends, after school—I was the kid scraping barnacles and coiling lines while the other kids were out fishing."

Isabelle watched him quietly.

"My dad expected me to take it over someday," Jake said. "He never said it like an order, but it was there in everything—how he'd talk about new contracts, or what upgrades we'd make 'when you're running things.' He wanted me to keep it alive. Keep it ours."

He drew a slow breath. "Thing is, I didn't want to inherit it. I didn't want my world to shrink down to one dock and one name painted on a hull. I told myself I'd take a season away—crew on other boats, see some open water. Just a year to clear my head."

"And you didn't come back," Isabelle said softly.

"Not for a long time." He gave a small, hollow laugh. "By the time I did, there was nothing to come back to. The boat was gone, the shop was empty, and the sign was already taken down. He'd sold everything. Said he couldn't keep it running without help, and he wasn't wrong."

Isabelle's gaze stayed on him, steady but gentle.

"He didn't yell," Jake went on. "Didn't throw a punch or a plate. Just looked at me like he didn't know who he was talking to anymore. We had dinner that night and barely said ten words. That silence pretty much stuck."

He rubbed his thumb along the edge of the blanket. "We talk sometimes—holidays, birthdays. Safe stuff. He asks if I'm working. I say sure. We don't touch the real things. I think part of him still blames me for letting it go, and part of me knows he's right."

The ship creaked softly around them, a long, slow exhale.

"You wanted more," Isabelle said after a moment. "That's not a crime."

"Maybe not," he said. "But I wanted it at the wrong time. Wanted the world when he needed me home. Some choices you can't undo."

"Then make different ones now," she said quietly. "That's what you're doing."

He looked at her then, something unguarded flickering across his face. "You really think so?"

"Yeah," she said. "I do."

He was quiet.

"My dad used to say history belongs to the people who do the work and the people who keep it honest," she added. "Your family did the work. Maybe what you're doing now is the other half."

"Doesn't fix a closed shop."

"No. But you're not done yet."

He turned his head. "You really think any of this could make up for it?"

"I don't think that's how it works," she said. "But I think facing the right direction counts."

His mouth tugged at one corner. "You're bossy in the dark."

"You know I'm right."

He exhaled, something in it loosening. "I left because I wanted a bigger life," he said. "Then I stayed gone because I didn't know how to go back."

"Maybe that's the part you've already started fixing," she said. "You didn't run when it got ugly. Not on the island. Not here."

He let the silence sit. The ship's heartbeat filled the edges.

"My dad told me once," she added, "that returning something stolen is a way of returning a piece of yourself, too. Seems like you found the right kind of bigger."

Jake's smile lingered. "Careful, Alvarez. You almost sound like you believe in me."

"Almost," she teased.

They drifted into that gentler quiet.

"Thanks," he said finally.

"For what?"

"For not pretending it's nothing. And for not pretending it fixes everything."

"Spoken like a realist."

"Someone has to be."

His breathing eased; the weight in the room lightened. Isabelle watched him a moment longer, then rolled onto her back.

Southward, the *Resolve* pressed into open water, its wake a pale seam unspooling behind them. Inside the little cabin, two bunks held, the dark held, and for the first time in days the night felt like a place to rest instead of a map to solve.

The ship carried them through the dark, the hush of the sea a quiet promise in the walls.

CHAPTER TWENTY-THREE

Southward Shadows

The mess smelled of coffee grounds, frying oil, and diesel—the perfume of a ship at work. The *Mariana's Resolve* rumbled beneath Jake's boots, a steady vibration that matched the slow clink of cutlery against metal trays. Morning light knifed through the narrow portholes and flashed across mugs, tin plates, and the sweat-shined forearms of men who'd been up since before dawn.

Captain Vasquez sat at the head of the table, big shoulders bent over a newspaper that looked like it had already crossed the Atlantic twice. Torres, the first mate, shoveled eggs with the indifference of someone who'd learned long ago to eat before the next alarm bell. The cook—Pez, short for Pérez—moved between the galley and the table with an ease that suggested he could find his footing in a hurricane.

Jake slid into the empty seat across from Vasquez. His arm had been freed from the sling that morning; it ached but it moved, which was good enough. The captain poured him a mug of something black and aggressive.

"Still walking, el buzo," Vasquez said. "Good sign. I thought you might stay in that bunk forever."

"Couldn't sleep through all this peace and quiet," Jake said, managing a half-smile.

Laughter rippled down the table. Pez dropped a plate in front of him—plantains, eggs, and something that might once have been sausage. It tasted better than it looked.

A moment later Isabelle appeared at the doorway, notebook tucked under her arm. The crew made room automatically, their conversation pausing the way men do when a new variable enters the room. She gave a polite smile, nodded thanks, and took the open seat beside Jake. Sunlight caught the ends of her hair, still damp from a quick shower.

Vasquez raised his coffee in greeting. "Welcome to my kingdom, profesora. Eat fast before Pez remembers he's charging for seconds."

Isabelle smiled. "I'll try to keep up." She opened her notebook half out of habit, then hesitated when she realized every eye was on it. She closed it again, cheeks coloring.

Torres grinned. "Planning the next exhibition already?"

Jake leaned back in his chair. "She just likes to take notes on how many times sailors stare at her 'notebook.'" He made exaggerated air quotes, and the table broke into laughter. Even Pez nearly spilled his coffee.

Isabelle shot him a look that was half amusement, half warning. "Careful," she said, smiling despite herself. "I take excellent notes."

Conversation shifted to weather and ports. Vasquez complained about customs officers in Trinidad; Pez countered with stories about pirates off Aruba that no one believed. It was ordinary talk, and it felt good.

Then Ramires, the youngest of the deckhands, spoke up between mouthfuls. "Saw two patrol boats in St. George's yesterday. Matte-black hulls, no flags. Locals said they were corporate security. Someone mentioned Black Tide."

The name landed like a coin dropped into a glass. The chatter thinned.

Vasquez snorted. "Those bastards show up everywhere now—say they're guarding cargo, but nobody trusts a company with guns and no colors. Not since what happened in Curaçao."

Jake looked up. "What happened in Curaçao?"

Vasquez lowered his mug, eyes narrowing at some memory. "Research freighter out of Cartagena. University job—moving colonial artifacts and survey samples to a conservation lab in Europe. Good people aboard, from what I heard. Halfway to Willemstad, they radioed for assistance—main engines dead, steering shot, whole power grid failing one system at a time." He shook his head. "Black Tide had a vessel in the area and answered the call. Hauled alongside, offered to 'secure the cargo' while the crew waited on repairs."

Torres muttered, "Let me guess—the engines came back to life once the crates were gone."

Vasquez gave a dry laugh. "A miracle of modern engineering. By the time port authority reached them, the ship was running fine—but empty. No damage, no distress record, no cargo. Black Tide filed a report saying they'd never made contact."

Pez spat into the sink. "And nobody did a damn thing."

"Not a thing," Vasquez said. "Company lawyers buried it faster than a storm anchor. The university's insurance called it mechanical failure. Everyone walked away clean."

Silence hung for a moment, heavy and close. Jake kept his face still, but heat crawled up the back of his neck. Beside him, Isabelle's fingers tightened on her mug. She didn't look at him immediately—only after Vasquez turned back to his newspaper did her eyes find his.

One glance was enough: *They're still out there.*

Torres broke the silence. "Anyway, that's their problem. Ours is keeping this crate afloat till Brazil." The table laughed again, forced but functional, and the easy rhythm returned.

When breakfast wound down, Vasquez tapped the table with a calloused finger. "If you've got business in Brazil, finish it quick. Things move strange down there these days—new money, old ghosts." He winked and pushed away from the table.

The crew filtered out toward their duties. Isabelle lingered to help Pez clear plates despite his protests. Jake watched her for a moment—how easily she moved among strangers, how she thanked the cook in Spanish that carried a hint of melody from another coast. He realized he was smiling and quickly busied himself with stacking cups.

On deck, the day had sharpened into heat. The sky was the kind of blue that made distance feel infinite. The *Mariana's Resolve* cut through it at a steady twelve knots, engines thrumming beneath the soles of his boots. He leaned against the rail with his coffee, watching the wake stretch out behind them—white foam dissolving into blue until even the memory of Grenada vanished.

He thought of the word Vasquez had used: ghosts. Maybe that was what they were now, sliding south between storms and silence, trying to stay ahead of the living and the dead alike.

From somewhere below, Isabelle's laughter drifted up—light, surprised, alive. Jake closed his eyes and let the sound carry on the wind.

Then came a clang from the companionway and Torres's voice, rough over the engine hum: "Morgan! You know your way around a wrench?"

Jake looked down toward the open hatch. "Depends on what's broken."

"Pump mount's shaking itself loose. Could use another pair of hands."

Jake set his mug on the rail, the last of the coffee gone cold. "On my way."

He swung down the ladder, the air thickening with heat and oil as the noise rose to meet him.

The engine room of the *Mariana's Resolve* was a world apart—no sunlight, no breeze, only heat and vibration. The air shimmered, thick and oily, drumming to the slow heartbeat of the ship's twin diesels. Pipes ran like arteries overhead, sweating condensation that dripped in rhythmic taps onto the steel deck.

Jake followed Torres down the narrow catwalk, ducking instinctively under a valve line. The first mate carried a wrench the size of a crowbar and a cigarette tucked behind his ear.

"Loose mount bolt on the secondary pump," Torres said over the engine roar. "You look like a man who knows a spanner from a spoon."

"I've been called worse," Jake said.

They reached the aft bulkhead where a bracket rattled under the vibration, the sound almost lost beneath the diesel roar. Torres crouched beside the pump housing and jabbed a finger at a trembling support plate.

"See that? The mount bolt's walking itself out. I can't hold the housing and torque it at the same time."

Jake nodded, bracing himself against the bulkhead. "I've got it. You keep it steady."

Torres jammed his shoulder against the pump assembly, muscles straining as the metal shuddered beneath him. "All right—hit it!"

Jake leaned his weight into the wrench. The first turn fought back, shrieking against the threads. He gritted his teeth, shifted his stance, and forced it another half rotation.

"Hold—almost—there," Torres grunted.

The bolt bit home with a heavy *clack*, vibration smoothing to a steady thrum.

Torres stepped back, rolling his shoulder. "That's it. She'll stop dancing for now."

Jake exhaled, sweat running down his temples. "Guess that counts as a duet."

Torres grinned through the haze. "Not bad for a passenger."

"Guess I'm not most passengers."

Torres grinned. "You sound like Vasquez. He was born on a freighter, I think. Been running this line longer than I've been alive."

Jake wiped sweat from his brow, glancing along the rows of gauges.

He liked the place's predictability. Everything here made sense—cause and effect, pressure and release. Not like Grey's trail, with its half-answers and riddles.

They climbed back toward daylight, passing through a hatch into the corridor where cooler air drifted in from the deck vents. The sudden quiet after the engine room made his ears ring. Jake leaned against the bulkhead for a moment, eyes half-closed, feeling the pulse of the ship through the steel.

He thought of Isabelle bent over her notes in the small cabin they shared—a single desk, two bunks, stacks of papers she refused to stow. Probably sketching again, tracing those serpent markings from the chamber walls. She worked with the same intensity she'd had since Grenada, but he'd seen the difference now: less urgency, more purpose. Maybe that's what survival did—it burned away everything except what mattered.

He made his way topside, blinking against the glare. The air felt thicker this close to the equator, sunlight a weight pressing against his shoulders. Vasquez stood by the rail, talking to Torres, and nodded in Jake's direction. "Pump's good?"

"Good as it'll get."

"Then you've earned your dinner." The captain turned his gaze to the horizon. "We'll cross the current tonight. Looks calm now—but I don't trust that color."

Jake followed his line of sight. The water looked different here—darker, heavier, the long rolling swells running from east to west like the earth's breath. Flying fish scattered in silver flashes as the bow cut through. It was beautiful in the kind of way that made you wary.

When Vasquez left, Jake lingered. The hum below blended with the hiss of wind over the rail. It reminded him of dives he'd made in wrecks where light barely reached, surrounded by groaning hulls and the sound of his own breath in the mask—pressure on every side, the world shrinking to the edge of his vision.

He realized, not for the first time, that the feeling wasn't so different up here.

The ocean stretched in every direction, endless but never free. Someone always charted the course, owned the cargo, decided where you'd make port. Even Grey, with all his daring, had been chased to the world's edge by men who called his freedom theft.

Jake rested his forearms on the railing, staring south where the clouds thickened on the horizon. Somewhere beyond them lay Brazil—and another set of devils waiting to be found.

The island no longer looked like a secret.

Floodlights burned against the jungle, bleaching the palms into pale silhouettes. Generators thudded by the shoreline, their hum blending with the steady hiss of the surf. Canvas tents stamped *BTG / Research & Recovery Division* lined the path toward the cavern mouth, their sides bulging with gear and plastic crates.

Inside the cave, Elias Grey's chamber had become an operating theater.

Laser scanners spun on tripods, mapping the walls with intersecting beams of blue light.

Cables and sensor lines crisscrossed the floor where Jake and Isabelle had once knelt in the dark.

The carvings glared back under the floodlights—serpents, spirals, broken sigils—no longer mysterious, only catalogued.

Dr. Adriana Cortez moved through the chamber with surgical precision, voice clipped and steady as she dictated into her recorder. "Section C, upper register: European overlay on pre-Columbian base. Severe surface disruption. Cause—fire or chemical agent."

Her radio crackled. "Dr. Cortez, surface team reports the galleon secure. Salvage underway."

"On my way," she said.

At the mouth of the cove, floodlights turned the sea into liquid glass.

The Spanish galleon still rested there, half-submerged where Elias Grey's trap had pierced her hull three centuries before. The bow lay deep in silt, but her stern rose intact above the surface—decks straight as a stage, rails still crowned with gilded trim that caught the halogen glare. Time had not destroyed her; it had preserved her, embalmed by still water and secrecy.

Now she was crawling with people.

Black Tide crews clambered over the railings, their helmets flashing in the light. Divers moved through the flooded lower decks while others hauled dripping crates to the surface and passed them to the men above.

Every artifact was tagged, photographed, and sealed in plastic before being lowered into the boats circling below. The once-still cove now churned with noise and movement.

From the beach, Cortez watched through binoculars, her voice clipped over the open channel. "Strip it clean. All of it. If it's not nailed down, bring it in."

The teams obeyed.

In the captain's quarters, technicians pried open chests and drawers, laying out their contents in neat rows: gold escudos, brass compasses, fragments of parchment too brittle to unfold. The cracked compass Isabelle had handled lay inside a transparent case, tagged Artifact 14–A. Another pair worked near the mainmast where skeletal forms still slumped against the gunwale—Spanish soldiers frozen where the blast had thrown them. They photographed each uniform fragment, clipped tags to jawbones and epaulettes, then eased the remains into labeled containment bags.

On the boats below, operators stacked the crates in tight rows before ferrying them toward shore, where the floodlit beach gleamed like a staging yard. The labels all read the same:

PROPERTY OF BLACK TIDE GLOBAL.

A young technician, watching the ship's hollowed decks above, muttered to his partner, "It's like watching someone rob a grave."

Cortez heard him. "We're not grave robbers," she said evenly. "We're preserving history. You'd rather all this continue to rot out here in the elements?"

"No, ma'am," the technician answered quickly, embarrassed.

Cortez turned back, eyes still on the ship. "That's what I thought."

She handed the binoculars to an aide. "Tell Rafiq to prep the next LiDAR run."

Back inside the chamber, Cortez found the tech team waiting.

"Run the LiDAR again," she said. "Higher resolution. I want every contour."

A low whine filled the air as scanners swept the walls in slow arcs, projecting ghostly blue grids across the carvings. On the monitors outside, the stone rendered itself into pixels and polygons—serpent spirals, fractured sigils, faint etchings buried under soot.

Rafiq, the youngest analyst, paused mid-scroll. "Dr. Cortez... look at this section—lower left quadrant."

She joined him at the screen. A pattern had emerged: an archway flanked by twin towers, the faint outline of a bell and cross etched above. Architectural, not symbolic.

"Portuguese Baroque," Cortez said softly. "Early eighteenth century."

Rafiq keyed a search through their visual archive. A progress bar crept across the display, reflecting in his glasses. Then the system chimed, lines of text appearing beneath the image:

MATCH DETECTED — *Igreja da Ordem Terceira do Carmo, Rio de Janeiro (18th cent.)*

For a moment, the camp went still. The scanners hummed on, indifferent.

Cortez straightened, jaw tightening. "Package and transmit all data. Flag priority for Algeciras."

Outside, the satellite uplink dish rotated toward the sky. A green light blinked once, twice, then steadied—sending centuries of history, stripped and digitized, halfway across the world.

She watched the indicator glow, then turned back toward the cove. Dawn was threatening on the horizon as she supervised the final crate being sealed. "Load everything onto the launch," she told the logistics officer. "We're done here."

The generators drowned out the surf. The chamber, beach, and galleon all lay empty now—stripped of artifacts, meaning, and voice. Only the serpents remained, their carved heads glinting under the floodlights as if they were watching the thieves at work.

Cortez turned away first. The uplink's green light faded behind her as the feed reached across the ocean—to Algeciras.

Algeciras, Spain — Black Tide Global Headquarters

Dr. Ana Velasquez leaned over her monitor in the data lab, the three-dimensional model of Grey's chamber turning slowly under her cursor. The Rio church façade glowed bright within the digital ruins, annotated in white text. She ran a cross-check, verified the match, then tagged the file for executive review.

Minutes later, upstairs in his glass-walled office, Victor Serrano opened the report himself. The image filled the screen: a ghost of a church drawn into stone, spiraled by serpents, pulsing with soft blue light. Reflected in the glass, his face looked pale and weightless, eyes burning with something feverish.

He whispered, "South."

A smile touched the corner of his mouth. "Of course he went south."

The warning signs came long before the first wave.

By late afternoon, the air had gone heavy and the light turned green around the edges, the way it does when the sky can't decide whether to break or hold. The horizon blurred into a wall of steel-gray vapor, its edges flickering like a slow fuse.

Jake noticed it first. Years on the water had tuned him to the quiet before weather—how the wind shifts pitch, how the gulls vanish. He felt it in his gut before the barometer confirmed it.

He was tightening a cleat line on the aft deck when Isabelle appeared beside him, tucking a loose strand of hair under her cap.

"Barometer's dropping," she said.

"Yeah—I can feel it," he said. "She's spinning fast."

Thunder murmured across the open sea, a low roll that made the rigging tremble.

Vasquez's voice carried from the bridge: "Secure all gear and batten what you can—we'll take her bow-on till it passes."

The deck came alive. Torres and two other crewmen sprinted along the rail, lashing down drums and hauling canvas over exposed cargo. The wind picked up so fast it seemed to pull color out of the world around them.

Jake moved aft to double-check the lashings, boots slipping on the wet steel, pain already tightening his arm. Isabelle followed without being told, her hair plastered against her face.

"Get back inside before it hits," he told her.

"Not a chance." She looped another tie-down, jaw set. "You'll need another pair of hands."

He started to argue, but the first blast of rain hit—a hiss that became a roar.

The squall arrived like a curtain dropping.

Wind howled through the rigging; the deck canted sharply as the first swell struck. Water sheeted across the steel, turning every step treacherous. The ship groaned, rolling into the waves, spray hammering the windows of the bridge.

Torres came pounding down the deck from the port side, shouting over the wind. "The aft winch is jammed—Vasquez wants it clear before it takes a line with it!"

Jake nodded and moved to meet him. Together they braced against the railing, rain hammering their faces as the ship rolled.

The jam wasn't small; the steel drum shuddered under tension, cable humming like a live wire. If it parted, half the stern gear could go with it—maybe even the railing.

Jake grabbed a winch handle, locked it into place, and threw his weight against it. The metal shrieked as it gave an inch, then seized again. His injured arm flared white-hot; he gritted his teeth and shoved harder.

Another shriek—and then it broke free, the winch spinning under his grip, spraying salt water and rust. The cable whipped once, hard enough to leave a welt if it caught skin.

"Get that brake set!" he shouted over the wind.

Torres dove for the lever, teeth flashing white through the spray. "Got it!"

Jake eased the load back onto the drum, the cable hissing as tension bled out. The vibration faded from a violent tremor to a steady rhythm. The fairlead stopped chattering; the lead held fair.

A second wave slammed the hull broadside. Jake's boots slid out from under him. He grabbed for the rail instinctively—and his left arm took the weight.

Pain detonated through his shoulder. For a heartbeat he couldn't breathe; the world shrank to the taste of salt and the white stab of agony.

Torres lunged to steady him. "You good?"

Jake nodded, breath ragged. "Keep moving!" He caught a line with his good hand, helping Torres lock it off just as another surge rolled beneath them.

Isabelle's voice cut through the storm. "Jake! The hatch!"

They slammed the hatch closed together, the sound swallowed by the wind. For a moment they stayed there, braced in the narrow space, breath mingling, salt water running down their faces. Her eyes locked on his—close enough that he could see his reflection flicker in them when the lightning flashed.

"You don't quit, do you?" she shouted over the storm.

He grinned, breathless. "Not while you're watching."

Lightning split the sky, turning the sea silver for an instant before plunging it back into darkness. The rain came sideways now, driven so hard it stung their skin. The ship climbed a wall of water and then dropped, the low rumble of the engines rising into a wild shriek as the props tore free of the sea.

Torres cursed as a coil of rope slid toward the scuppers. "Grab it!" he shouted.

Jake dove, caught the rope just before it whipped overboard, and pinned it with his boot. The motion jarred his arm again; the world tilted. He nearly lost his footing, but Isabelle was there, catching his arm and hauling him back against the rail.

"Got you!" she yelled.

He wanted to tell her to get below deck, but the words wouldn't come. Instead, they fought side by side as the rain thickened, securing loose gear, checking lines, shouting warnings. The deck felt alive beneath them—groaning, flexing, defying the sea with every shudder.

At one point Vasquez's voice blared from the bridge loudspeaker: "Hold fast! She'll ride it out!"

Jake glanced up. Through the driving rain he saw the captain silhouetted against the lightning, one hand gripping the rail, the other steady on the throttle—defiance incarnate.

The worst of it lasted nearly an hour.

By the time the wind began to shift, Jake could hardly feel his fingers. The rain softened from knives to needles, thunder rolling farther off. The crew moved slower now, shoulders bent, checking lashings. The deck was littered with debris—splintered wood, tangled rope, a bent bucket spinning in the scuppers.

Jake leaned on the rail, breathing hard. His clothes were soaked, his arm throbbing, but the pain had dulled into something distant and familiar—proof that he was still here.

Isabelle appeared beside him, drenched, cheeks flushed from the cold. Her hair clung to her neck, her hands trembling from adrenaline. When she saw him watching, she laughed—a short, incredulous sound that dissolved into a smile.

"Progress," she said. "I didn't almost get washed overboard this time."

"We'll make a sailor out of you yet."

She laughed, shaking her head. The sound cut through the lingering wind like sunlight through clouds.

Vasquez emerged from the bridge, cigar somehow still wedged between his teeth. "Every ship needs a storm to prove she floats," he called. "You two just proved your worth."

Torres raised a tired salute. "Captain, next time, I quit."

"You quit," Vasquez said, "you swim."

The crew's laughter was thin but genuine. The tension broke, carried off by the retreating thunder.

Jake and Isabelle stood together at the rail as the light returned, thin gold spilling between the clouds. The sea still heaved, but it had lost its malice—rolling now like something tired of fighting. The air smelled clean again, rinsed of salt and smoke.

They stood in silence for a while, the rhythmic slap of water against the hull the only sound. The sun broke through in shards, laying a molten path across the sea.

Jake looked out at the light breaking through the clouds. "Used to think the calm was the reward," he said quietly. "Now it just feels like the warning."

Isabelle studied him. "Maybe the calm parts are just where we catch our breath."

He huffed a quiet laugh. "I was hoping for a little positivity."

"I'm a realist."

The last gust swept the deck, warm and clean. Isabelle pushed her wet hair back and leaned on the rail beside him. For a long moment neither spoke. The sky ahead was clear, a deep, impossible blue stretching toward the curve of the earth.

Jake's arm ached, his muscles heavy, but the engines settling back into rhythm felt like a heartbeat. For the first time in days, he let himself believe they might actually make it.

He glanced at Isabelle, intending to thank her or tease her—he wasn't sure which—but she caught his look and smiled first. It was small, tired, and perfect.

In the cabin, Isabelle re-wrapped his arm tight and pressed a blister pack into his palm. "Two now, two tonight," she said. He didn't argue.

The *Mariana's Resolve* cut forward through the long, rolling swell.

Behind them the storm faded into nothing, and ahead the horizon brightened with promise.

Rain lashed the glass walls of Victor Serrano's office, turning the city lights of Algeciras into a smear of color. Thunder rolled over the Strait of Gibraltar, its echo softened by the thick-paneled silence of the room. Beyond the window, the Mediterranean gleamed black and restless, mirroring the storm that pressed against the coast.

Inside, only the monitors glowed. On the central screen, the carvings from Elias Grey's chamber turned slowly in ghost-blue relief. The outline of the Rio de Janeiro church—Our Lady of Mount Carmel—hung like a beacon amid the serpentine patterns.

Victor stood motionless, one hand resting on the desk, the other hovering near the glass. The reflection of the church façade overlapped his own face, the twin images blurring together each time lightning flared outside.

The phone buzzed. *Luca Moretti.*

He answered without greeting. "Tell me you have them."

Static crackled, followed by the sound of rain hitting metal.

Luca's voice came through strained but steady. "Nothing yet. We're sweeping flight logs and passenger manifests leaving Grenada. They may have hitched a ride on a cargo ship under the table."

Victor's gaze stayed fixed on the map, his knuckles whitening against the desk.

"Once again, I've done your job for you, Luca," Victor said, his voice low but cutting. "They're moving south."

There was a pause, just the hiss of interference between them. "South?" Luca repeated.

Victor tapped a key. The projection of the church expanded across the screen, its twin towers rising from digital shadow. "My team on the island found this—carved into the chamber wall. Grey's next destination. Igreja da Ordem Terceira do Carmo, Rio de Janeiro. That's where they're going."

"Brazil?" Luca said, incredulous. "That's thousands of miles away."

"Distance is irrelevant. Direction matters," Victor replied. "Begin repositioning assets. Use our people in Belém and Santos."

Luca hesitated. The faint roar of wind came over the line. "We've still got half the crews combing the Windwards. You want me to pull them mid-sweep?"

"I want results," Victor snapped. "Stop chasing their wake and get ahead of them."

Silence hung on the line, then Luca said, "This had better be worth my time, Victor. I don't chase fairy tales."

"That isn't your concern."

The tone in Victor's voice cut the air like a blade. He adjusted the cuff of his sleeve, concealing the tremor that had begun to pulse in his right hand. "Find them, Luca. Before they find it and disappear again."

Static flared, swallowing Luca's reply. Then: "Yeah. I hear you."

The line went dead.

Victor stood alone in the hum of the monitors. The rain outside had thickened to sheets, sliding down the glass in silver veins. The reflection on the window fractured—the church's carved towers, the serpent spirals, his own thin outline dissolving between them.

He reached toward the screen, tracing one trembling finger along the rendered façade. "South again, Elias," he whispered. "Always south."

Lightning split the clouds above the Strait, filling the office with white light for an instant before plunging it back into shadow. When it faded, Victor's reflection lingered faintly against the glass—half man, half ghost—watching the storm roll in.

The coast appeared with the dawn—a pale green smudge through morning haze. The *Mariana's Resolve* rode the calm swells toward the Port of Santos, her decks streaked with salt and sunlight. After days of storms, the air felt impossibly still, the horizon a sheet of molten gold.

Santos woke around them as they approached: cranes swinging in wide arcs, trucks grumbling through narrow lanes, dockworkers shouting in Portuguese over the drone of engines. The smell of diesel and roasted coffee mingled with sea air and something faintly sweet, like rain on hot pavement.

Jake and Isabelle stood by the rail, bags at their feet. For the first time in days, neither spoke. The simple sight of land—hills veined with roads, roofs catching the light—was enough.

Vasquez joined them, his cap pulled low against the glare.

"You two heading inland?"

"Rio," Isabelle said.

He gave a low whistle. "Careful on that road. The closer you get to Rio, the more sharks you find that don't swim."

Jake smiled faintly. "Seems to be a theme lately."

Vasquez's grin was brief but genuine. "You need another ride, you know where to find me."

They shook hands, then stepped onto the gangway as the ship settled against the dock. Behind them, cranes and trucks descended on the *Mariana's Resolve*, stripping her of cargo and reloading her with fresh. Forklifts hissed and clattered across the deck while Vasquez barked orders in three languages. The ship looked smaller somehow, swallowed by motion and noise, but steady as ever amid the chaos.

The port gave way to city streets thick with traffic and humidity. Vendors pushed carts of fruit and coffee along the sidewalks; music spilled from open doorways. They stopped at a small café near the waterfront—two chipped cups of strong coffee, a plate of warm bread, a chance to think.

Isabelle spread a folded map of Brazil across the table, smoothing its creases with careful hands. "We can follow BR-101 up the coast," she said, tracing the route with her finger, "or cut inland toward São Paulo and loop back east. The coastal road's slower but quieter—fewer checkpoints, fewer questions."

Jake raised a brow. "You sound like a proper smuggler."

She smiled without looking up. "We might as well be."

He leaned back, watching her trace the line north. "You're quite the navigator."

"My father taught me," she said softly. "He used to bring home old maps from the university and spread them across the kitchen table. He'd trace the routes with his finger and tell me every line was a choice someone made—every wrong turn a story waiting to be found."

Jake listened, the din of the café fading behind her voice.

"When he took me to Rio as a teenager," she continued. "He called it a conversation between worlds—stone from Europe, hands from Brazil. He said history never builds in one language."

Her eyes stayed on the map, but her voice had gone quiet. She reached into her pocket and drew out her father's compass, rubbing a thumb over its weathered brass.

Jake nodded slowly. "She'd be proud of you."

Isabelle looked up and smiled faintly. "You think so?"

"I know so."

For a while they sat in silence, the sound of waves and passing traffic filling the space between them. Outside, sunlight shimmered off the wet cobblestones.

By midday, they'd arranged transport—a supply truck hauling packaged coffee and produce north toward Rio. The driver was broad-shouldered and genial, amused by their accents and light luggage.

"Eight hours, maybe nine," he told them. "Road's good till the mountains."

Jake helped load their bags into the back while Isabelle double-checked the route on the map. The driver laughed. "You two tourists or smugglers?"

"Something in between," Jake said, climbing in beside him.

The truck rumbled out of Santos after lunch, climbing into the hills where rainforest pressed close to the road. Mist hung in the trees; waterfalls cut bright seams through the green.

They wound through switchbacks and tunnels, passing roadside stands where children sold coconuts and fruit to passing cars.

For hours the rhythm of the road carried them—the hum of tires, the steady vibration through the cab. Conversation drifted in and out. Isabelle asked the driver about the towns they passed; Jake watched the sky darken over the Serra do Mar.

When rain came, it came fast—brief squalls that blurred the windshield and left the world shining afterward. Somewhere near Ubatuba, the driver turned up the radio, and tinny samba filled the cab. Isabelle laughed, a sound that made Jake smile despite himself.

Night fell as the road curved inland. The first lights of Rio de Janeiro appeared beyond the hills—a scatter of gold across the dark sea, growing brighter as they descended.

The driver whistled low. "Welcome to Rio."

They climbed down stiff-legged, thanking him as he pointed them toward a narrow street lined with small hotels. The city pulsed around them—car horns, distant music, the smell of salt and gasoline.

Jake watched the truck's taillights fade down the street. "Funny how everything keeps moving," he said.

Isabelle nodded. "That's how things survive. Keep moving, keep changing."

He smiled. "Guess people aren't much different."

They turned toward the lit windows of a modest inn, the sound of the sea still faint in the distance. Ahead, somewhere beyond the rooftops, waited the church Elias Grey had drawn three centuries ago.

CHAPTER TWENTY-FOUR

Echoes Beneath Rio

The first warmth of sunlight slipped through the wooden shutters, striping the walls in gold. Outside, the city was already awake—the clatter of carts over cobblestone, the sing-song calls of vendors hawking coffee and pão de queijo, the distant clang of church bells folding over one another like waves. Somewhere below, someone was laughing, the sound bright and fleeting.

The fan above the bed turned with a lazy rhythm, stirring the scent of salt air and old wood. Isabelle sat at the narrow desk beside the window, hair still damp from her shower, dark strands curling against her neck as they dried. She wore a simple linen blouse tucked into khaki trousers, rolled at the ankles—her usual field uniform softened by the quiet of the morning. A mug of coffee cooled at her elbow, next to her scuffed leather satchel and an open laptop whose casing still showed faint salt stains.

It was a small miracle the computer still worked; it had been sealed in a watertight case when *The Wayfinder* went down. The machine hummed quietly now, its glow mingling with the sunlight that spilled through the shutters.

On the screen: a sepia-toned photograph of Igreja da Ordem Terceira do Carmo—the Church of Our Lady of Mount Carmel. Its twin bell towers rose like sentinels over Rio's colonial core, their baroque ornamentation caught halfway between grandeur and decay. Isabelle's brown eyes, alert and intent, flicked between the image and her notes laid out beside her, where she had carefully copied Elias Grey's carving.

"The proportions are wrong," she murmured, half to herself. "Grey's drawing matches the original façade—before the 1750s expansion. He saw it before the rebuild."

Behind her, the bedsprings creaked. Jake stirred, sitting up slowly, rubbing a hand over his face. His sandy-blonde hair was tousled, and the morning light traced the faint stubble on his jaw. His arm was freshly bandaged, the white gauze stark against his sun-browned skin. Even in rest, he carried a quiet, sea-worn strength.

"You've already been at it for hours?" he asked, voice rough with sleep.

She didn't look up. "Research doesn't sleep."

He gave a short laugh, standing to stretch, the hem of his T-shirt tugging across his lean frame. "Neither do archaeologists, apparently."

Isabelle's mouth curved faintly. "Occupational hazard."

Jake reached for the mug she'd set out for him, taking a long sip as he crossed to the window. The shutters opened to a view of tiled rooftops and laundry lines strung like bunting between the buildings. The morning haze curled around the distant hills, and the scent of frying oil drifted in from the street below.

He absently lifted the brass key that hung from the cord around his neck. The metal caught the light as he turned it between his fingers, tracing the grooves with his thumb—half comfort, half promise. *I'll find it, old man. I'm getting closer.*

Behind him, Isabelle tapped a final note into her document, then opened a new email draft.

To: Dr. Ana Oliveira

Subject: Quick question — Carmo catacombs & early chapel footprint

Her fingers hovered over the keyboard for a moment.

Ana—

Desculpa o aviso em cima da hora. I'm in Rio for a few days reviewing notes on the early 18th-c. façade at the Carmo. A drawing I'm working from suggests the pre-1750 proportions, and I'm trying to understand how the undercroft/crypts align with that earlier footprint.

Would you have a few minutes to sanity-check me and point me to any cross-sections from the restoration teams? I can bring the sketch that's puzzling me.

If you're free, could we grab a quick coffee across from the Carmo late morning (around 10:45–11:00)? If today's impossible, any pointers or a contact on the team would still be a huge help.

Obrigada,

Isabelle

She hesitated, then hit send.

For a moment, only the soft hum of the fan and the city's morning noise filled the room. Then Isabelle's phone vibrated on the desk—a new message.

Ana Oliveira: Of course, querida! I'm near the Centro this morning—11:00?

Isabelle smiled to herself. "That was fast," she murmured.

Jake's reflection flickered in the glass of her laptop screen. "So what's the plan? We heading out?"

"Yes — we are going to meet a colleague of mine that may have some insight on the layout of the church in Grey's time," she said, closing the laptop and slipping it into her satchel.

Jake smiled faintly. "You really think there's something under there?"

Her gaze met his, steady and certain. "I don't think Elias Grey went to all the trouble of carving that picture for nothing."

Jake leaned against the window frame, the key at his chest catching a sliver of sunlight. "Seems odd, though, doesn't it? For a man trying to hide something, why leave a clue like that?"

Isabelle hesitated, tapping a finger thoughtfully against her satchel. "His journal page mentioned that the treasure was... affecting him. Maybe he couldn't help himself. Or maybe," she added quietly, "it was a call for help."

The air between them stilled—not heavy, but charged, humming with the weight of what might come next.

Isabelle stood, looping the satchel's strap across her shoulder. The morning light caught in her hair, bringing out a deep chestnut sheen. "Let's go find out."

The square was alive with morning color. Jacaranda petals drifted through the air like slow-moving snow, gathering in violet patches between the cobblestones. From their table beneath a faded umbrella, Isabelle and Jake could see the baroque façade of Igreja da Ordem Terceira do Carmo rising across the street, its white stone warmed to honey by the late morning light. A pair of pigeons wheeled above the twin bell towers, the same towers Grey had once sketched more than two centuries ago.

The café smelled of roasted coffee and baking sugar. A soft breeze drifted lazily through the shaded courtyard, stirring the scent across the worn mosaic tiles. Isabelle had spread her notes across the small table, her handwriting looping neatly between sketches of Grey's carvings. She looked more at ease than she had in weeks—the tension in her shoulders replaced by the bright focus that always came when she was solving a puzzle.

Jake watched her, a faint smile tugging at the corner of his mouth. "You look like someone who's about to rewrite history," he said.

"Maybe just footnote it," she replied without looking up, though a small smile broke through.

A woman's voice called Isabelle's name, warm and clear. "Isabelle! Finalmente!"

Dr. Ana Oliveira crossed the courtyard with an easy stride, her shoulder-length hair caught in a loose twist, reading glasses perched on her head. She wore a light linen jacket over a simple blouse and carried a tablet under one arm. Her face broke into a smile as she reached their table.

"It's been too long," Isabelle said, standing to hug her.

"Too long, and too far," Ana replied in lilting English. "Your message sounded mysterious."

Isabelle smiled faintly, catching Jake's gaze. "Just a curiosity. I think the original structure may predate the surviving records."

Ana raised a brow and sat, flagging the waiter for coffee. "Ah, the old historian's trap—finding what isn't supposed to exist." Her attention shifted to Jake. "And you must be the diver."

"Jake Morgan," he said, offering a handshake. "Mostly I lift anchors, not history."

Ana laughed softly. "You're in the right company for dangerous hobbies."

Jake shot Isabelle a sidelong glance. "Yeah, who would've thought archaeology was so dangerous?"

Isabelle looked away, though a smile tugged at her lips. "Jake's a friend who agreed to come along on this little expedition."

Ana's grin widened, teasing. "How romantic."

Jake beamed. Isabelle blushed.

Their coffees arrived—small porcelain cups, thick and dark. Across the square, the church bells tolled eleven, their sound rich enough to vibrate the café's glassware. Ana turned her tablet toward them, swiping through a collection of architectural scans and sketches.

"The Carmo has been rebuilt three times since 1700," she explained. "Each fire, each flood, each new bishop wanted something grander. But beneath it all—" she zoomed in on a cross-section of the foundation "—the same footprint remains. The earliest structure was a Carmelite chapel from around 1710, maybe earlier. There are records of a crypt, possibly catacombs. They were sealed after a flood in the 1800s."

"Sealed," Jake repeated. "Meaning filled in?"

Ana shook her head. "No—simply walled off. Too unstable to use. And now, too bureaucratic to reopen."

Isabelle leaned closer to the tablet. "Can you zoom in here?" she asked, pointing to a faint annotation on the blueprint—a serpent curling into a circle. "That symbol. It matches a carving we found."

Ana frowned, squinting. "Ah, that. The restoration teams assumed it was a stonemason's mark. There are dozens like it on the lower walls. They even found one carved into the column bases near the left transept."

Jake's eyes met Isabelle's. "Left transept," he murmured.

Ana caught the exchange, curiosity flickering across her face. "What exactly are you looking for, Isabelle?"

"Patterns," Isabelle said quickly. "Architectural continuities. The way religious symbolism carried over through reconstructions."

Ana smiled knowingly but didn't press. "Well, if your curiosity gets the better of you, tread carefully. The Carmo has its secrets. Some of them still bite."

When they parted, the afternoon light had turned softer, slanting between the rooftops. Isabelle watched Ana disappear into the crowd and then looked back toward the church. The bells were silent now, the square quieter except for the chatter of vendors and the slow roll of passing cars.

"You think she'd help us if she knew what we're really doing?" Jake asked.

"She already did," Isabelle said. "Now we know where to look."

They crossed the street together, stepping through the shadow of the bell tower as they reached the church doors. The bronze handles were cold beneath Jake's fingers. He pulled one open, and the world changed.

Inside, the air was cool and close, steeped in the scent of candle wax, incense, and damp stone. The noise of the street outside faded to a distant murmur as the heavy doors closed behind them, the thud carrying through the sanctuary. Rows of wooden pews stretched toward a high altar framed in gold leaf and shadow.

Sunlight spilled through tall, arched windows, striking the motes of dust that hung suspended in the air. The glass caught the light in blues and reds—saints and martyrs rendered in fractured color that shimmered across the marble floor. A soft chorus from a hidden choir loft carried through the nave, the harmonies echoing against vaulted ribs painted with scenes of angels and stormy seas.

Jake slowed, taking it all in. His boots clicked against stone worn concave by centuries of footsteps. "Feels older than it pretends," he murmured.

"It is," Isabelle whispered. Her gaze moved across the gilded columns and the flaking frescoes that climbed toward the ceiling. "Half of this ornamentation was added a century after Grey's time. But underneath..." She trailed off, fingertips brushing a pillar's base where newer plaster met rougher stone. "You can still feel the bones of the original chapel."

They passed a side chapel glowing with candlelight—silver votive lamps swaying gently, reflecting halos across the carved faces of saints. Beyond, a confessional stood half open, its wood dark and polished from generations of hands. The faint smell of incense thickened as they neared the altar, mingling with something older, earthier, that seeped through unseen cracks in the floor. A breath of cool, faintly salty air threaded along the tiles, as if drawn from somewhere below.

Jake glanced toward the far end of the nave. "Left transept?"

Isabelle nodded, lowering her voice. "That's where Ana said they found the mason's mark. On the plan it anchors the north arm."

"Great. What's a transept?" Jake whispered, almost sheepish.

Isabelle caught his eye and grinned. "When a church is laid out like a cross, the short arms perpendicular to the nave are the transepts."

"Ah. Thanks."

She smiled as they started forward again, the faint echo of their footsteps mingling with distant prayer. Her eyes scanned the floor and walls, every uneven seam or discoloration a possible clue. Jake's gaze stayed lower, instinctively reading the ground the way a diver reads a wreck—searching for the unnatural in what time has tried to disguise.

Near the left transept, Jake noticed a pattern on the floor: a serpent curled around a cross, half-buried under a candle stand. Similar to Grey's motif.

He nudged one tile with his boot. The faintest hollow tone answered. Isabelle looked up sharply.

Jake glanced around—the nearest parishioner was kneeling several pews away, head bowed. He bent down, pretending to tie his bootlace, and pressed again. The hollow echo came a second time.

Her heart quickened. "That's not solid foundation," she whispered.

"Maybe a shaft or old access tunnel," Jake replied quietly.

A sacristan appeared from a side door, broom in hand, and the two straightened quickly. He offered a polite nod, suspicious eyes lingering only a second before moving on.

When he disappeared behind the altar, Isabelle exhaled.

Jake smirked. "You really think this is the spot?"

She nodded. "Grey left the mark for a reason. Whatever's down there, it's been sealed for centuries."

He tilted his head toward the exit. "Then maybe we come back when no one's watching."

She gave a small, determined smile. "Tonight."

The square had emptied hours ago. Streetlights burned in yellow halos along the cobblestones, their reflections trembling in the shallow puddles left by a brief rain. Across the street, Igreja da Ordem Terceira do Carmo stood in silence, its façade washed pale beneath the lamps, twin bell towers cutting dark shapes against the low clouds.

Jake and Isabelle lingered in the shadow of a narrow alley, dressed in dark, practical clothes that blended with the night. Jake had swapped his sun-bleached shirt for a dark long-sleeve T-shirt, soft with wear, sleeves pushed up just enough to move, the bandages on his arm hidden beneath the fabric. Isabelle wore black trousers and a fitted olive jacket, her hair tied back, a small satchel slung across her chest. They looked less like tourists now and more like people who didn't want to be seen.

The air was heavy with the mingled scents of wet stone, exhaust, and rain-soaked earth. A passing taxi hissed along the slick street, its taillights painting red streaks across the puddles. Isabelle adjusted the strap of her bag, her voice barely above a whisper.

"Are we really doing this?"

Jake's eyes stayed on the church doors. "You said it yourself—Grey left something here. Might as well see what's so important that the Church decided to bury it."

She hesitated, then nodded. "Ana's layout mentioned a service entrance behind the sacristy."

Jake's mouth ticked up. "Good. Saves us the trouble of breaking in through the front."

They crossed the empty square, their footsteps soft on the wet stones. The echo of the city was distant now—muted engines, a dog barking somewhere far off, the rhythm of their own breath. Around the rear of the church, the walls rose close and dark, broken only by the outline of a small arched door set into the stone.

A heavy iron lock secured it. Jake knelt, pulling his multitool from his pocket, the metal glinting faintly in the streetlight.

"Since when do you know how to pick locks?" Isabelle asked, keeping watch over her shoulder.

"Learned it back home," he said with a shrug. "My dad kept the salvage shed locked, and I got tired of waiting. Curiosity's a bad habit."

He worked quietly, fingers steady, the faint scrape of metal on metal barely louder than the night. Then—footsteps. Muffled and quick, from somewhere down the alley. Isabelle froze, breath caught.

"Someone's coming," she hissed, voice sharp but low.

Jake's hand tightened on the lock. For a second they only listened, hearts thudding loud enough to drown the city.

The footsteps drew closer, then veered away, passing the alley mouth and fading with a thin, jangling echo of a metal gate. A gust of wind followed, stirring the wet leaves near their feet.

Jake exhaled slowly, jaw tight. He adjusted the pick, tried the tumbler once more, and a soft, satisfying click answered.

He looked up, flashing a grin that was half relief, half mischief. "Guess curiosity still pays off."

"Let's just hope it doesn't get us arrested," Isabelle muttered.

Jake eased the door open. The hinges groaned softly, a sound far too loud in the stillness. A rush of cold, stale air spilled out, carrying the scent of wax, stone, and something older—dust, maybe, or damp earth touched by salt.

He glanced back once to make sure the alley was empty. "Ladies first," he whispered.

Isabelle shot him a look that was half exasperation, half nerves, then slipped past him into the darkness. Jake followed, pulling the door gently closed behind them until the thin strip of streetlight vanished.

Inside, the world contracted to cones of light from their flashlights. The nave stretched ahead in shadow, pews reduced to vague outlines, gilded altars glimmering dimly where candlelight clung to their edges. A few votives still burned near the front, tiny islands of gold in a sea of dark.

Every sound seemed amplified—the soft echo of their footsteps against the cold tile, the drip of water somewhere deep within the walls, the quiet rustle of Isabelle's jacket brushing stone. A faint hum of distant ventilation masked their movements.

"It feels different at night," she whispered. "Like it's holding its breath."

Jake cocked his head toward her, brow furrowed. "You've never broken into a church at night before?"

Isabelle shot him a look, the corner of her mouth twitching. "Do you hear yourself?"

He grinned faintly. "Good point."

They moved cautiously along the aisle, their flashlights sweeping over ornate carvings and statues. The angels and saints looked spectral in the dim light, their painted eyes catching the glow just enough to seem alive.

They made their way toward the left transept—the same corner where they'd found Grey's serpent mark earlier that afternoon. Isabelle's pulse quickened as the familiar candle stand came into view, its wax drippings hardened into pale ridges. Jake slid a folded bit of cloth beneath its foot to dampen any scrape, then crouched.

His light skimmed the floor. "There it is," he murmured. The serpent carving glimmered beneath a thin film of dust.

Jake ran his hand along the seams of the tile, fingers finding a slight depression. "There's a ring here."

He looked up at her. "You sure about this?"

Her eyes met his, steady and dark in the glow. "Elias Grey went to incredible lengths to hide what he found. I don't think he meant it to stay lost forever."

Jake nodded once. "No turning back now."

He gripped the ring and pulled. The sound that followed was low and deep, a grinding groan that rolled through the church like distant thunder. Dust fell in a soft veil from the vaulted ribs as the stone slab shifted, revealing a square opening and a tight spiral of steps leading down into the black.

Cold air rose from below—damp, heavy, carrying the scent of age and something metallic. A faint draft moved along the tiles toward the opening, as if the church itself exhaled.

Jake angled his flashlight down. The beam disappeared after a few turns, swallowed by darkness. "Smells like a century of bad air," he muttered.

Isabelle's voice was barely audible. "This must lead to the original crypt."

"Only one way to find out."

The stairway twisted tightly, slick with condensation and worn smooth by centuries of feet. Their lights barely cut the dark, revealing glimpses of carved crosses and Latin inscriptions etched into the damp stone walls. The air was colder here—still, heavy, thick with earth and a mineral tang.

Isabelle followed close behind, her voice echoing softly off the curve. "Grey must've come this way. These carvings—some of them match the ones on the map margins."

Jake's boot slipped slightly, scattering a fragment of stone that clattered down the steps and vanished into the dark. He steadied himself, glancing back. "Are you saying Grey helped design these passages?"

She swept her light across a weathered relief of intertwined serpents. "Based on the markings in the margins, I'd say so. He wasn't just following old tunnels—he was shaping them."

The stair let them out into a low crypt supported by rough arches. Water dripped rhythmically from the ceiling, pooling in shallow depressions across the floor. A plain altar stood at the center, its edges softened by time, a serpent-and-circle carved deep into its face. Around the perimeter, relics lay half-buried in silt—rusted candlesticks, broken statuary, fragments of coffins long decayed.

Isabelle stepped toward the altar, running her fingertips across the carving. "This isn't just a crypt," she whispered. "It's a sanctuary."

Jake swung the beam toward the far wall. A faint gleam broke the monotony of stone. Set into the masonry was a dull iron plate, square-edged and weathered, its surface embossed with a serpent coiled around an anchor—the mark of Elias Grey. Moisture traced thin rivulets down its face, catching the light like veins of mercury.

He stepped closer. "Looks sealed."

Isabelle joined him, eyes wide. "It's his mark. Elias left this."

Jake brushed the dust away, tracing the lines with his thumb. "Then this is the next step."

The flashlight trembled in his hand; a low vibration rippled through the floor. Somewhere beyond the walls, water sighed.

"Did you feel that?" Isabelle breathed.

"Yeah," Jake said quietly. "Let's make this quick."

He wedged the multitool into the crack between the plate and the stone, prying gently. Grit rained down. The plate shifted a fraction, revealing a thin slit of darkness beyond. The air through the gap was colder, metallic, with a whisper of salt.

Isabelle steadied the light over his shoulder. "Careful."

Jake glanced up, a flicker of humor breaking through the tension. "You really think I'd—"

The beam hiccupped, fluttered. The metallic tang surged; a breath of wind licked across their cheeks. Jake's fingers were still braced against the iron, feeling the give of it, the faint tremor of something moving in the dark beyond.

The flashlight sputtered once, twice—then went out.

Darkness swallowed them whole.

Chapter Twenty-Five

The Corsair's Labyrinth

The street outside the Church of Our Lady of Mount Carmel lay nearly silent. From the shadow of a parked delivery truck, a man watched the church. He stood with his back to the wall, cigarette ember cupped in his palm, eyes fixed on the rear door near the old sacristy.

Two figures moved there—a man crouched by the iron handle, a woman standing close behind, her head turning every few seconds to scan the empty street. The man worked quickly, tools glinting faintly in the lamplight. They froze as a late-night walker passed, then a soft click carried across the stones. The door gave.

The watcher drew a slow breath as the pair slipped inside, the door easing shut behind them.

He lowered the cigarette, crushed it under his shoe, and lifted a small microphone to his mouth. "They're in," he murmured. "The foreigner picked the lock. No lights, no alarms."

Static hissed before a smooth, measured voice answered, "You're certain it's them?"

"Positive. Same couple from the pictures you sent."

A pause. Then: "Have the men hold a one-kilometer perimeter around the church. Based on what I've seen, they might surface anywhere."

"Understood."

"We'll be there shortly."

The line went dead. He let the microphone hang and looked back at the church—its pale façade washed in amber light, high windows black and unblinking. A faint unease prickled the back of his neck, colder than the night air.

He exhaled, muttering in Portuguese, "Que Deus tenha piedade de quem perturba o descanso Dele." *May God have mercy on those who disturb*

His rest.

The ember faded. The plaza fell quiet again.

For a heartbeat, there was only darkness.

The scrape of metal on stone fell away, leaving only the sound of their breathing. Somewhere behind them, water dripped in slow, uneven rhythm—patient as time itself. Jake's pulse thudded in his ears.

"Jake?" Isabelle's whisper barely carried. The echo came back thinner, warped by the narrow walls.

He fumbled for the flashlight, slapped the casing once, twice. The beam snapped to life—a trembling cone that cut pale arcs across the chamber. The light found the serpent-etched iron plate again, its surface slick with condensation. A smear of red glistened near the edge where he'd slipped the blade.

Beside him, Isabelle's light joined his, dust and mist drifting through their beams like ash. The air was cool and heavy, thick with the scent of wet stone and old decay.

"What was that?" Isabelle asked.

"It like someone doesn't want us down here."

Jake wedged his multitool beneath the plate again. Metal screamed against stone, a grating wail that carried down unseen corridors as he tried to wrench open the plate. Isabelle flinched, covering her mouth as flakes of rust and powder fell in a slow haze.

Then came the hiss—a thin exhalation, stale and cold. It smelled of sealed earth and time.

"Something's behind it," Jake murmured.

He leaned his shoulder into the plate. The hinges groaned, and a gust of trapped air spilled into the room, swirling dust through their lights. When it finally gave, the plate swung outward with a dull clang, revealing a tight passage hewn straight into the bedrock.

Their beams reached only a few feet before being swallowed by black. The tunnel walls were slick with moisture, carved with faint reliefs—crosses intertwined with serpents, symbols half-lost beneath lichen and age. A phrase was barely visible in the grime: *Veritas sub umbra.*

"'Truth beneath the shadow,'" Isabelle translated softly.

Jake ran a hand along the damp threshold. "Grey's handwriting all over this," he muttered. "Looks like you were right."

Cold air drifted from the passage, heavy with minerals and the sweet rot of time. Somewhere deep within, a hollow space seemed to breathe.

They exchanged a look—a flicker of trust in the half-light—then Jake nodded toward the opening.

"Right behind you," he said quietly.

Isabelle slung her satchel higher and stepped closer. The tunnel's mouth yawned at chest height, just wide enough for her to squeeze through. Jake crouched beneath it, lacing his fingers into a foothold. She braced a hand on his shoulder for balance and slipped her boot into his waiting hands. He winced as her weight tugged against his bandaged arm but didn't let go, steadying her until she caught the edge and pulled herself into the passage.

Stone scraped her shoulders as she wriggled forward, her flashlight beam trembling ahead into the dark.

When her boots disappeared, Jake hauled himself up after her. The rock was slick beneath his palms, cold enough to sting. His chest pressed against stone as he forced his way inside, breath echoing in the confined space.

Behind them, the iron plate swung shut with a hollow clang that reverberated through the walls, sealing away the sound of the world above.

Their twin beams crawled ahead, carving thin seams of light into the dark as they moved deeper into the Corsair's labyrinth.

The passage pressed tight from the start.

Jake dropped through the opening after Isabelle, landing in a crouch on slick stone. The air down here was cooler, thick with the smell of minerals and damp earth. Above, the square tunnel they'd crawled through gaped like a wound in the wall, its edges beaded with moisture.

Isabelle steadied herself beside him, brushing grit from her palms. Their flashlights swept across the narrow corridor ahead—just tall enough to stand upright now, though the ceiling hung close enough to catch the edges of their beams.

"Guess we found the express route," Jake muttered, flexing his sore arm.

The walls closed in as they started forward, their shoulders brushing damp stone. Water traced slow veins down from the ceiling, merging into a shallow channel along the floor. Every sound—each step, each breath—echoed back at them, multiplied in the dark.

"Elias Grey's idea of interior design?" Jake murmured.

"He built it to be heard as much as seen," Isabelle replied softly. "Every sound tells a story—who's coming, where they step."

He glanced back at her. "You think he really put that much thought into it?"

"You don't carve a place like this without knowing what you're doing."

The corridor bent sharply and opened into a small chamber where three arched passages branched into darkness.

Jake swept his light across them. Each looked the same—same curve, same damp sheen, same promise of getting lost forever.

"Well," he said quietly, "left, right, or damned either way?"

"They're identical," Isabelle murmured, scanning each in turn.

He listened—only the slow drip of water somewhere ahead. "We could mark our path, try one at a time. You did bring the breadcrumbs, right?"

"Left them in my other pants. If Grey built this, it won't be random. There'll be a pattern or a test."

Then Isabelle's light caught something faint above the left-hand arch—a shallow groove, half-swallowed by grime.

"Wait. There's something carved here."

Jake brushed away black residue. The outline of a lion beside an anchor emerged.

"Some kind of crest," he said.

"Old merchant seal," Isabelle offered. "Or a port mark."

"Port Royal used the Lion and Anchor," Jake said. "Could be coincidence."

She aimed her light at the other arches. One bore a cross, another a pair of wings—same depth, same hand.

"He made every path look true," she whispered. "But if you knew him, you'd know which mattered."

Jake's jaw tightened. "Pops always said Elias was from Port Royal."

He stared once more at the lion and anchor—the emblem of merchants and thieves alike—then stepped through that arch, the darkness swallowing his light.

A few yards in, Isabelle froze. Her beam caught a faint metallic glint stretched across the corridor at knee height.

"Jake—stop."

He halted. The light revealed a dust-furred tripwire strung taut between the walls. Jake crouched, following it to a niche cut in the stone. Inside, rusted iron spikes hung ready to drop.

He exhaled. "Simple but effective."

"Eighteenth-century mechanics," Isabelle murmured. "He used what he had."

"So... did we pick wrong? Why trap this one?"

"Maybe not wrong," she said. "Just another layer of protection."

Jake eased the wire loose. The spring shuddered but held. Dust drifted from the ceiling.

"Eyes peeled," he muttered, pocketing the multitool.

The next stretch was smoother—almost unnaturally so. The layer of dust looked wrong. Footprints behind them stood out clearly; ahead, the floor was broken—a gaping pit where the stone had collapsed. He crouched at the edge, light catching rotten timbers and rusted iron half-buried in dark water.

"Looks like time—or someone—tripped this one already."

"Whatever he built, it didn't age kindly," Isabelle said.

"I'm not sure that's good or bad."

They edged along the narrow ledge, the smell of old water and rust following them until solid ground returned.

They had gone perhaps twenty steps when the walls began to tremble.

A low vibration swelled from above—a groan of shifting stone. A single pebble dropped between them and cracked against the floor.

"Move!" Jake shouted.

They ran. The sound rose into a deafening roar as the corridor gave way behind them, stone exploding into dust and thunder. Isabelle stumbled; Jake caught her arm, yanking her forward as the air filled with grit and the sting of powdered limestone.

When the noise finally died, the passage behind them was gone—swallowed by rock and silence.

Jake coughed into his sleeve. "You alright?"

"I think so," she managed.

He glanced at the sealed corridor. "Well we aren't going back that way."

The tunnel sloped downward, air thickening until it opened into another junction chamber—larger, ceiling lost in shadow. Three arches waited ahead, symbols dulled by centuries.

Jake swept his light across them. "More symbols."

A serpent coiled in a circle, a pair of crossed oars, and an anchor wrapped with a serpent.

Jake studied it. "The Specter's flag. Pops had it in his workshop."

Isabelle looked up. "Then maybe this is the next step in his story."

Jake nodded slowly. "From where he came from to what he commanded."

He aimed his light toward the Specter's arch. "Let's hope the old man's ship still leads the way."

They stepped beneath the emblem. The air changed—colder, drier, tinged with the faint sweetness of decay. The walls turned smoother, deliberate.

Jake lowered his voice. "Feels different down here."

"Because it is," Isabelle said. "This wasn't carved for defense."

The passage narrowed, then opened into a circular chamber. The floor was uneven, a mosaic of shattered flagstones and glittering shell fragments. Rows of alcoves lined the walls, each holding what remained of long-decayed bodies—some in tattered cloth, others reduced to bone and shadow. Rusted cutlasses and pistol barrels rested across skeletal arms; a few still bore trinkets of brass or tarnished gold.

Jake's light lingered on one alcove. "Crewmen."

Isabelle approached another, voice soft. "He buried them down here."

Silence pressed close. Water dripped somewhere distant.

"Why hide them here?" Jake asked.

"Not to hide—to remember," she said. "Look—the alcoves form a ring."

Between each recess, faint carvings repeated: anchors, serpents, compass points—Grey's private litany.

"He must've used this place after the others were gone," Isabelle murmured. "He wasn't sealing something in—he was saying goodbye."

Jake's light found the far wall—an iron door, half-swallowed by calcite and shadow. Its surface bore the serpent-and-anchor motif, grooves blackened by age.

He approached. "Grey's banner."

"It's sealed," Isabelle said, studying the hinges crusted with mineral deposits. "Hasn't opened in centuries."

Jake crouched. "There's a recess here—square, like something fits."

"A lock?"

"Possibly." He glanced at the ring of alcoves. "You think the key's buried in here?"

"If Grey buried his men, maybe he left one to guard it."

Jake met her eyes. "Then we find who."

They started near the door, working slowly. Jake lifted loose stones and collapsed timbers, careful not to disturb the dead. Most were reduced to pale fragments, the occasional glint of a buckle or blade.

The smell grew stronger—earth, mineral, decay that no time erased. Dust drifted like smoke.

"Nothing mechanical," Jake muttered.

"Maybe not mechanical." Isabelle had paused at an alcove near the door. Her beam fell across a collapsed skeleton—one arm folded on its chest, the other outstretched toward the floor. "Look at the femur."

She brushed away grime. A shallow etching emerged—a serpent's tongue curling from the bone toward the knee.

Jake leaned in, brow furrowed. "You've got to be kidding me."

"It's the serpent," she whispered. "He made the key part of the man."

Jake stared at the hollow sockets above the carved bone. "You think this was one of his crew?"

"Probably. Someone he trusted—or someone who volunteered."

He exhaled. "If this is the key, it's not exactly what you want to use."

"Elias Grey didn't make anything easy."

Jake crouched beside her. "You sure?"

"No. But it fits his logic. Iron corrodes down here—bone holds detail."

For a long moment they stood over loyalty turned to legend. Then Jake lifted the femur with a soft crack of dust and centuries-old air.

He turned it in his hand, carved notches catching the light. "Might actually work."

Isabelle stepped to the door, beam steady on the square recess. "If it's meant to, it will."

Jake fit the notched end into the recess. It slid with a dull scrape. He twisted.

A heavy click echoed through the chamber. Ancient gears groaned to life. Dust rained from above as bolts withdrew one by one.

The iron door shuddered, then eased inward, releasing a breath of cold air—metallic and still.

Jake looked at her. "Guess we found our way in."

"Or our way out," Isabelle said quietly.

He pushed the door wider, hinges screaming as the sound carried like a sigh through the bones of the dead.

The beam of Jake's flashlight swept a small circular chamber, barely twenty feet across, walls polished and etched with faint reliefs—ships at sea, storms, spirals of wind twisting toward a central figure: a man on a cliff, holding a sphere that bent the waves around him.

Below the carving, a single line had been chiseled into the stone: *Not all treasure is meant to be found.*

Isabelle's breath caught. "Elias Grey..."

A spiral pattern ringed the floor, leading to a stone dais. Upon it sat a sealed chest, its surface darkened by soot and salt, the serpent-and-anchor motif filled with faint gold leaf.

Jake brushed away dust. "From what Pops told me, Grey's hoard wouldn't fit in something this small."

"Siecaza," Isabelle said, kneeling opposite, reverent.

He tested the rusted latch. It groaned but held. "Rusted."

"Try the blade."

He worked the multitool tip beneath the hinge. With a strained creak, the latch gave. Dust billowed, carrying the scent of oil-soaked wood and silk.

Inside lay a bundle wrapped in oilcloth atop a silk-lined interior molded with a shallow hemispherical depression—as though something round had once rested there.

Jake lifted the bundle and peeled back the fabric. A leather-bound journal rested within.

"Grey's handwriting?" he asked, easing the cover open.

Isabelle studied the ink under her beam. "It's his. Same loops as the page from *La Isla de Sombras*." Her thumb traced the last line, faint under grime. "Dated months after he reached Rio."

"What's it say?"

She read softly: *They came sooner than I expected. I was betrayed. The Spaniards know where I have gone. What I could move, I have hidden. To those who may one day follow, I leave this, that they might understand.*

"He knew he was running out of time," she murmured.

"Still trying to protect it," Jake said.

She turned the page. "He mentions another route—'*south, where the winds carve the world's edge and the sea runs cold.*'"

"South... around Cape Horn," Jake said.

"Or the ports nearby," Isabelle added. "Somewhere he stopped before sailing on."

"Punta Arenas," Jake murmured.

A low tremor rolled beneath their feet. The dust on the chest rippled.

"You feel that?" he asked.

Another shudder. The walls groaned.

"Opening the door must've weakened the structure," Isabelle said, standing quickly.

Jake slid the journal back into the oilcloth, tying it tight and tucking it under his arm.

The tremor deepened—dust falling in steady streams as carvings cracked like porcelain.

"We have to move—now!"

He pulled her toward the door as a slab crashed onto the dais behind them.

They stumbled into the antechamber, coughing. The rumble built to a roar. Stone rained from above. Jake clutched the bundle to his chest; Isabelle's light flickered through clouds of grit.

"Keep going!" he shouted.

They dove through the threshold just as the vault gave a final, thunderous collapse. The serpent sigil splintered and vanished into shadow.

Silence followed—thick, suffocating. Then came the sound of water, faint but rising—from somewhere deep below.

Jake turned, breath ragged. "We've got to find another way out before this floods."

Isabelle nodded, the image of the chest's vacant cradle burned in her mind.

They raised their lights. The first drops slipped through cracks—thin rivulets snaking down the walls, pooling at their feet. Within seconds, the puddles spread.

Jake swept his beam along the seams. "Fracture feeding from the bay. We'll be swimming soon."

"Which way?"

"If water's coming in, it's going out somewhere too. We just have to follow the current."

They backtracked through the rising water, boots splashing in quick, echoing strides. Ahead, the tunnel pinched to a jagged crack in the rock. The air had turned sharper—saltier—the smell of the tide thick in their throats.

"This way," Jake said, crouching low and easing through.

The passage beyond was rougher, cut from raw limestone that glittered with damp crystals. The floor was slick with moss, the air colder. Tiny crabs skittered for cover as their lights swept over the walls.

"Old drainage tunnel," Jake muttered. "Probably feeds straight to the bay."

"Hopefully still does," Isabelle said as another tremor shook the stone.

They pressed on, hunched beneath the low ceiling. The muffled roar of moving water grew louder ahead.

The tunnel sloped downward, twisting through the rock until it opened into a flooded gallery where collapsed beams jutted at angles. Moonlight shimmered through the water beyond, refracted in shifting silver bands.

"There," Isabelle breathed. "Moonlight."

Jake waded forward, the cold biting his legs. "Tide's coming in."

The gap ahead was barely three feet high, half-filled with churning seawater. Beyond it glimmered open air.

"We've got one shot before it fills," Jake said. "Ready?"

Isabelle tightened her grip on her satchel. "Go."

Jake ducked into the narrow channel, pulling himself through as water surged against him. Salt burned his eyes; his shoulder scraped stone. The tunnel pitched downward, the roar of the sea growing louder until it swallowed everything.

Jake shoved forward as the current took him. Cold slammed into his chest, the light ahead flaring white—

—and the world broke apart in water and sound.

CHAPTER TWENTY-SIX

Ghosts in the Bay

The world broke open into mist and saltwater.

Jake hit the shallows on his knees, salt burning his throat, the catacombs still echoing in his ears. A surge rolled him sideways. He got an arm under Isabelle, dragging her toward the dim shoreline where the bay breathed in slow, steady rhythm. Pebbles ground against his palms. His lungs worked like rusted bellows—pull, catch, cough, repeat.

They collapsed onto gritty sand, gasping. The air smelled of brine and old stone, the sour edge of the tide heavy in it.

He blinked stinging salt from his eyes and tried to take in the shore. The beach was narrow—no more than twenty yards deep before it met the cracked line of an old seawall. Mangroves had claimed the gaps between the stones, their roots spilling toward the water like black ropes. To the east, a wooden pier jutted into the bay, its pilings dark with algae and barnacles. Farther still, faint lights marked a service road and the skeletal outline of a dock crane. Between him and the pier stretched open sand and scattered debris—just enough cover if they moved low.

Behind them, Rio's harbor lights bled through the fog—a dirty pearl smearing the sky. The city's hum pressed faintly through the mist, and from the bay ahead came another sound that didn't belong—an engine idling on the water. A spotlight cut a slow white arc through the mist.

"Izzy, get up," he rasped. "We have to move."

Isabelle coughed into the crook of her arm and nodded, eyes watering. Jake pulled her upright and they staggered together through the shallow wash, the mud sucking at their feet.

Voices broke the night—close, male, alert.

Flashlights lanced through the fog, sweeping the waterline and the base of the seawall. Two figures moved in a deliberate grid, beams slicing back and forth. Radios crackled at their shoulders, Portuguese fast and clipped.

Jake tensed, not understanding. Isabelle whispered in his ear. "They said they're moving east."

He nodded once and guided her toward the broken section of seawall. They dropped behind it, pressing into the damp shadow.

Even at a distance, Jake could see the dark tactical gear—the same kind the men on La Isla de Sombras had worn.

Black Tide, he thought. Serrano's people.

A beam flared against the stones and slid away. Jake pressed his cheek to the cold concrete. Salt stung his eyes. He could smell wet grit and the faint sour drift of harbor trash.

Isabelle's lips brushed his ear, and a wave of warmth cut through the cold. "They were waiting for us?" she whispered.

Jake kept his voice a thread. "Or watching. Someone probably saw us slip into the church and called it in."

The warmth of her breath startled him more than the words. For an instant, the danger and the nearness blurred together, then the world shrank back to fog and stone.

Victor didn't have to be fast, Jake thought—only everywhere.

The engine offshore shifted pitch. Through a break in the fog, Jake caught a flash of the vessel—a black RHIB nosing through the chop, its hull low and hard against the water. The spotlight widened, swept once across the haze, then vanished again as the mist swallowed it whole.

From behind the seawall, the bay looked like hammered lead under the hovering light. Beyond it, the mountains crouched against the horizon—dark, massive, steady.

A radio cracked again, a burst of static and words. Isabelle tilted her head, listening. "They're checking the rocks," she whispered, worry threading her voice.

Jake slowed his breathing. Panic got you found. Found got you dead.

He counted rhythms: one pair of boots moving left, another pacing closer; the engine's drone; the spotlight's arc—eight seconds wide, always pausing near the pier's pilings.

He touched Isabelle's forearm, felt the tremor beneath her skin. A mixture of fear, cold, and exhaustion. He squeezed once. She nodded.

When the nearest beam slid away, he pointed: along the seawall, then toward the tangle of mangroves ahead and mouthed, *Go*.

They moved.

Keeping low, they followed the jagged wall until the mangroves began to close around it. Jake led, shoulders hunched, staying within the dark seam of shadow. Wet grit shifted beneath his feet. He froze. The footsteps beyond remained steady. He moved again.

Isabelle matched his rhythm, quick and silent. They slipped between the roots where the mangroves had overtaken the wall. The air changed—dense, still, heavy with decay.

Through the web of branches, Jake saw the two searchers split their pattern. One went higher along the embankment, stride efficient, military. The other stayed near the water, his light grazing the shallows and bouncing back into his face. Thirty feet. Maybe less.

Another burst of radio static. Isabelle listened. "They're going to search another stretch."

Jake nodded. The RHIB's engine hummed a steady rhythm out on the water. He could picture its pilot pacing them—slow, patient, letting the shore patrol drive prey toward open water.

He leaned close. "When they pivot, we move to the next cover. Stay low. Don't give them a silhouette."

She nodded. "How many?"

"Two on foot. One RHIB. Probably more behind."

"And Victor ahead," she said, half a whisper, half a breath.

The tide lapped softly against the roots. The spotlight slid over the mangroves, turning their leaves to dull metal, then moved on. One operative turned at a retaining wall and said something into his radio. The other mirrored him.

"Now," Jake breathed.

They slipped from the mangroves and dropped beneath a collapsed section of the seawall—a concrete slab that had fallen years ago and now leaned over a hollow of silt. They crawled inside, grit biting at their forearms. Jake pulled Isabelle in beside him, the space reeking of rust and damp stone.

Footsteps passed six feet away. A flashlight scoured the slab above, bleaching it white for a heartbeat, then fading. Jake held his breath until darkness settled again.

The radio crackled. Isabelle caught the words. "They're saying it's clear.

Checking the pier."

The RHIB's light swung wide and found the pier pilings, holding there. The engine burbled, a lazy predator's breath.

Jake's arm throbbed. The sling might have been gone, but his arm felt like borrowed machinery—unwilling, but functional. He flexed his fingers. They answered. Good enough.

Isabelle's breath touched his cheek. "We can't stay here," she whispered. "If they call in more—"

"We won't." He nodded toward the pier. "We'll move along the shadow—look for a boat, debris, anything that floats."

Her eyes glimmered faintly. "You think like a salvage rat."

"Not sure if that's a compliment or an insult."

Her mouth twitched—half smile, half pain.

The footsteps receded toward the pier. The RHIB's light swept across a raft of trash—plastic, crates, a deflated buoy—before moving on.

Jake pressed his palm into the mud to rise and felt the drag of something fibrous. Fishing line. He brushed it aside and found a torn net half-buried. Nets meant boats, once. Maybe still.

He touched Isabelle's shoulder, pointed toward the pier's deeper shadows. She nodded. He waited through the next sweep of light, then moved.

They slid out low and fast, the pier's supports towering like black trunks above them. Barnacles rasped his hip when he clipped a piling. He caught his breath, tasted iron, kept going.

A gull cried once—offended—and vanished into fog.

Under the pier, the world narrowed to sound: the hollow clap of tide against wood, the hiss of water through gaps, the distant hum of the patrol's engine. Light fractured through the lattice of beams, slicing across their faces as they moved. Jake saw the searchers' boots beyond, dark stumps pacing in rhythm. He matched their tempo, freezing when they paused.

At the far end, the ground rose into a hump of rubble and mangrove. Beyond that, the shoreline curved away—out of the patrol's sight line.

A radio flared, sharp. Isabelle froze, breath catching. "They found our footprints," she whispered, more to herself than him. Her fingers clenched in the mud. "Merda."

Jake's gut went cold. Two drags from the water, then staggered prints across softer sand. He pictured a flashlight tracing each step, slow and patient.

The engine revved, spotlight swinging back toward their tracks.

Options flickered through his head. Fight—suicidal. Hide—temporary. Run—loud but maybe fast enough.

He chose.

"When the light sweeps left," he whispered, "we cut right past that rubble and use the bend. Then we lose the prints in the shallows. Stay in the waterline."

Isabelle nodded once, calm despite the tremor in her breath. "Right behind you."

They waited. The beam found the prints, turning the sand white, then drifted left, widening its arc toward the pier.

Jake moved.

They sprint-crouched along the rubble, keeping low. Grit shifted beneath their feet, quiet as whispers. The light flared behind them, sliced by the pier's ribs.

They reached the curve and dropped into a gouge where the tide had chewed the bank away. The water washed in and out, erasing itself. Jake stepped into it and pulled Isabelle after him. Cold water climbed to their calves. They moved sideways, matching the tide's rhythm so each step disappeared as soon as it formed.

Behind them, voices rose—frustrated, clipped. Another burst from the radio. The spotlight swept back and forth, slower now, hungrier.

Jake kept his eyes on the bend ahead, where the shoreline disappeared behind a tumble of stone. Isabelle's hand found the back of his shirt for balance.

The light passed again, slow and methodical. Jake matched its rhythm, counting under his breath.

Seven. Eight. Pause.

On the lull between sweeps, they reached the break and slipped into its shadow. The noise behind them softened. Not safe—just quieter.

Isabelle leaned against the rock, breath sawing. She wiped salt from her lips with the back of her wrist. In the dim light, her eyes looked almost black.

Jake scanned the fog ahead—mangroves, rubble, and the broken hull of something wooden half-buried in the mud. The shape was warped, ribs jutting through the tide like bones, but it might still float.

"There," he said quietly. "That'll have to do."

They moved toward it, keeping low, the sound of the patrol fading behind them.

The shape loomed out of the fog—a cracked fishing skiff, its hull half buried in the tide-slick mud. One side had collapsed inward, ribs jutting like broken spars. The other still curved whole enough to dream of floating.

Jake crouched beside it and ran a hand along the planks. The wood felt water-swollen but solid under the slime. "She's taken on a few decades," he muttered, "but she'll do."

Isabelle peered over his shoulder. "That will float?"

"Doesn't have to float well. Just long enough." He jerked his chin toward the water. "Tide's turning. We row east, across the bay."

They worked in silence, prying away the sand that held the hull. Every motion drew a squelch from the mud and a stab from Jake's arm. Isabelle used both hands to lever against a root, hair hanging wet across her cheek. The tide crept higher, sliding between their knees, black and cold.

"Almost," Jake whispered, shoving with his good arm. The hull rocked, groaned, and stuck again.

Isabelle kicked at the silt. "It's wedged."

He scanned the ground, found a length of rotted rope tangled in mangrove roots, and looped it through the bow ring. Together they heaved. The mud released in a sucking gasp and the boat lurched free, water rushing into the hollow it left.

A faint voice echoed from the pier—Portuguese carried thinly over the water. Isabelle froze. "They're circling back."

Jake looked up. Through the fog, the RHIB's searchlight shimmered like a pale moon, closer than before. "Then we move."

They dragged the skiff into the shallows, hearts hammering. The bow dipped into the chop; for a heartbeat it seemed the whole thing would vanish, then it bobbed back up. Jake steadied the boat while Isabelle climbed in, then pushed off and slid in after her. It wobbled, creaked—but held.

"Find anything to row with?" he whispered.

Isabelle handed him a cracked oar she'd pulled from the mud. "One and a half."

He smiled thinly. "Nice." He looped the rope around a length of drift board, tying it to the oar's broken end—a crude second paddle.

From beyond the pier came the thrum of the RHIB's engine. The searchlight swung in a broad arc, washing the fog to silver.

Jake dropped to his knees in the stern and began to row—short, silent strokes. Each pull tore at his arm. The skiff crept forward, soundless except for the soft splash of wood against water.

The fog thickened over Guanabara Bay, swallowing the skyline behind them. Ferries would cross here by daylight, but now the channel was empty and still. The current tugged west, drawing them faintly back toward the city. Each pull on the oar felt heavier than the last. Somewhere in the gray distance, a ship's horn sounded—low, patient, directionless.

Farther out, the engine note of the RHIB rose. The beam widened.

"Stop," Isabelle whispered.

Jake froze. The RHIB materialized through the fog, no more than thirty yards off their port side. The light carved the water in front of them, dazzling white. Prop wash slapped against the surface, rocking their little boat.

Isabelle's hand found his sleeve; he could feel her breath quicken beside him. The beam slid past at ten yards, the glare turning the mist to molten glass. Radio chatter crackled through the stillness.

Jake counted the pulses of the engine. *One... two... three... four.* The searchlight veered left, chasing ghosts along the pier.

He waited another heartbeat. Then: "Go."

He paddled, barely stirring the water, but the skiff inched east, away from the sound. The engine faded, swallowed by fog.

Minutes stretched thin. Only the hiss of tide and the groan of wet wood marked their passage. Jake kept the strokes small, conserving motion. His arm burned; Isabelle reached for the oar.

"Let me."

He hesitated, then nodded. She rowed in measured rhythm—steady, efficient, the same calm she used when decoding maps. Each dip of the blade drew them farther from the lights behind.

Through the mist, dawn began to seep—soft gray bleeding into black. The far shore emerged by degrees: cranes, ship masts, and the faint smell of diesel. Ponta d'Areia, maybe, Niterói's shipyards.

Jake exhaled slowly, the first full breath since the catacombs. "You row like you've done this before."

"My abuelo used to take me out on his boat, the *Magdalena*," she said softly. "It was a lot nicer than this heap—but rowing is rowing."

He smiled faintly. "Good thing one of us still remembers calm water."

They fell silent again. Behind, the RHIB's light flickered once more and vanished.

Jake took the oar back, muscles trembling. "Almost there."

The fog had begun to thin, and faint lights winked through the gray—shoreline lamps, maybe, or windows half lost in the haze. Each pull dragged more than it moved, the skiff groaning with every stroke. Then, at last, the bow scraped against something solid.

He exhaled, chest heaving, and let the tide carry them the last few feet until the hull settled crooked in the shallows. The water lapped softly at the boards. The darkness had thinned to a gray that hinted at morning.

Isabelle was already moving. She swung her legs over the side and splashed into knee-deep water, dragging the bow higher onto the beach. Her boots sank in the mud. "Help me with this before it floats back out." Jake waded after her, arm burning. Together they heaved until the skiff wedged in the sand above the waterline.

They stood there for a moment, neither speaking. Diesel and brine filled the air. Gulls called somewhere out in the haze—the first sound of the living world since the tunnels.

Jake wiped the back of his wrist across his mouth. "We made it."

"For now," Isabelle said. Her voice came out low, rough around the edges.

They pulled the skiff farther under the remains of a small pier—its boards half-collapsed, ropes dangling like cobwebs. Jake found a heap of old nets and threw them over the hull, disguising the shape. When he was done, it looked like any other forgotten wreck along the working shoreline.

He leaned against one of the pilings, breath coming slow, the adrenaline finally leaving him. His arm throbbed in deep, steady pulses. Isabelle crouched nearby, brushing silt off the soaked satchel that held Grey's journal. She glanced toward the bay, the last ripples smoothing out where they'd come from.

"Do you think they'll look this far?" she asked.

Jake shook his head. "Not for a while. They'll think we drowned before we cleared Rio."

"That's comforting," she murmured.

He managed a tired grin. "It's all I've got."

For a while they just listened—to the slow lap of tide, to the distant clang of metal from the shipyards waking. Somewhere inland, a radio crackled faintly from a fisherman's shed, a song muffled by static. The world had resumed without them.

Jake straightened. "We should get moving before we're too tired to."

They left the pier and followed a narrow strip of sand toward the faint outline of low buildings. The ground turned from wet grit to gravel, then to cracked pavement. Fish stalls lined the edge of a narrow street—awnings dark with dew, tables stacked with empty crates. A cat darted from beneath one and vanished into a heap of nets.

Ahead, the town was waking—first the rumble of trucks, then the faint chatter of early vendors setting up for the day. The sounds reached them like echoes from another world.

Jake's steps grew uneven. Every few strides, his boot scuffed instead of landing cleanly. Isabelle noticed and slowed her pace to match his.

"Your arm," she said quietly.

"Still attached," he muttered. "That's enough."

She gave a faint smile, more weary than amused. "You said the same thing about the boat."

"Worked, didn't it?" He aimed for a joke; it landed dry. The world swayed a little, the kind of sway that came after too many hours of motion. Isabelle steadied him with a hand on his back. He didn't pull away.

They passed a shuttered warehouse, its doors tagged with fading graffiti. The street beyond curved uphill toward a cluster of old stucco buildings. A faded placard above one read *Pousada da Baía*—letters half lost to salt and time.

Isabelle looked up at it. "That might be the closest thing to a bed we're going to find."

Jake followed her gaze. The windows were dark; a single light burned behind the curtained front desk. "Fine by me," he said.

They crossed the empty street. The door creaked when Isabelle pushed it open, and the smell of old linen and sea drifted out to meet them.

Behind the counter, a half-awake proprietor stared at them through a haze of cigarette smoke. He didn't speak—just blinked, as if two drowned ghosts had wandered in from the bay.

Jake and Isabelle traded a look, then followed the man's gaze downward. Whatever had passed for clean clothes hours ago was now a wreck. Jake's dark shirt clung to him like a second skin, stiff with salt and torn from shoulder to cuff. His trousers were caked in mud halfway to the knees, boots trailing sand and bits of eelgrass. Isabelle's olive jacket was streaked brown and gray, the fabric frayed at the seams; her once-black trousers looked dredged from the harbor, and her hair hung in soaked, tangled ropes that dripped steadily onto the tile.

Jake broke the silence first. "How do you say shower in Portuguese?"

Isabelle's mouth twitched, then spread into a weary smile. "Let's hope it's up for the task."

Jake turned back to the proprietor. "We'll try not to ruin the sheets."

The man just grunted, slid a key across the counter, and reached for his ashtray.

The hallway was narrow and uneven. Their footsteps echoed softly on the tile.

The room was small but clean enough—peeling plaster, one narrow bed, a wooden chair, and a window facing the water. Pale light pressed through the curtains, turning the air a muted gold.

Jake closed the door and slid the bolt. For a long moment, neither spoke.

Then Isabelle exhaled and let the satchel drop to the floor. "One small bed," she murmured.

Jake leaned against the wall, the weight of the night catching up all at once. "You wanna be the big or little spoon?"

A ghost of a smile tugged at her mouth. "In your dreams, sailor."

Isabelle crouched beside the satchel and began pulling out its contents—the soaked map case, the wrapped bundle of Elias Grey's journal, a few scattered notes. She laid them on the chair by the window where the light was strongest. The paper had gone limp and translucent around the edges, ink feathered but still legible.

Jake pushed off the wall and crossed to the small bathroom alcove. The faucet groaned once before producing a thin stream of rust-colored water that slowly cleared. He cupped his hands, rinsed the grit from his face, and caught his reflection in the cracked mirror—pale, hollow-eyed, a smear of mud streaked across his jaw. He looked less like himself and more like something the tide had forgotten to take back.

Behind him, Isabelle peeled off her ruined jacket and draped it over the bedframe. Her shirt beneath was torn at the shoulder, exposing a scrape already darkening with bruises. She noticed him watching in the mirror and smiled faintly. "You look worse."

He found a small first-aid tin under the sink and brought it to the bed. "I think we make a matched set."

She sat while he cleaned a cut on his forearm, the antiseptic bite making him hiss through his teeth. "Hold still," she said, taking over when he fumbled the bandage with one hand. Her touch was sure but gentle, practiced from days of fieldwork. With a strip torn from a towel, she knotted a makeshift sling and set his arm across his chest. He didn't argue.

Jake nodded toward the journal pages drying in the window light. "Think they'll make it?"

"Mostly." She turned one gently between her fingers. "Grey wrote on thick stock. He must've expected weather."

"Smart man," Jake muttered.

"He had to be," she said softly. "To keep it hidden this long."

For a while, neither spoke. The only sound was the faint ticking of the wall clock and the muted slap of waves against the seawall outside. The morning light thickened, pale gold spilling across the floorboards and climbing the walls.

Isabelle brushed a strand of damp hair from her face, then leaned toward one of the pages where the ink had held truest. Her brow furrowed. "Here," she said, pointing. "This line—it wasn't clear before."

Jake joined her, leaning close enough to smell the salt still clinging to the paper. The words were faint but readable: *South, where the winds carve the world's edge.*

She looked up at him. "He meant Patagonia, didn't he?"

Jake nodded slowly. "Punta Arenas. World's end winds."

The name hung between them for a moment, heavy with distance and possibility.

Isabelle exhaled, a mix of relief and resignation. "Then we go south."

Jake glanced toward the window, where the sunlight had begun to burn through the last of the fog. "After a few hours of sleep."

She smiled—the first real one since they'd surfaced from the tunnels. "Hours? How about days?"

"Tempting."

Jake sat on the edge of the bed, boots still on, feeling the floor sway beneath him like the deck of a ship. The adrenaline was gone, leaving only exhaustion. Isabelle stretched out beside the window, one arm over her eyes, the open pages fluttering faintly in the sea breeze.

The world outside brightened, gulls calling somewhere over the water. For the first time in what felt like forever, neither of them moved.

CHAPTER TWENTY-SEVEN

The Weight of the Words

The room smelled faintly of linen and sun-warmed wood.

Isabelle woke to a dim wash of gold slipping through the wooden shutters, the light soft and forgiving after the suffocating dark of the catacombs. She wore a loose linen shirt borrowed from the innkeeper, the sleeves rolled past her elbows, and the hem brushing the tops of her thighs. They'd arrived at the inn with nothing but the clothes on their backs, and the clean fabric felt almost luxurious against her skin. Her damp hair curled in uneven strands against her neck. For a moment she couldn't tell if the sound she heard was the rush of memory or the murmur of the bay beyond—until a gull cried somewhere past the balcony and the world steadied again.

Her body ached in places she hadn't known could hurt. Every movement recalled the fight through the flooded passage—the crush of water, the scrape of stone, Jake's hand closing around hers in the dark. She let herself breathe until the throb behind her eyes eased.

Their clothes hung over a chair, still damp from washing. They'd barely managed to shower before collapsing, scrubbing away mud and grime that had clung like a second skin. The innkeeper hadn't asked questions, only passed them towels and a key with sympathetic eyes. Isabelle remembered the clean sting of soap, the swirl of gray water down the drain, the sense of shedding another layer of fear.

Jake lay beside her on the narrow bed, close enough that she could feel the slow rise and fall of his breathing. His bandaged arm rested between them, the gauze white against sun-bronzed skin. The sheet had slipped low around his waist, revealing the rough canvas of old scars across his chest and shoulders. Some were pale and thin, the marks of years spent working salvage and sea, others newer — reminders of the danger that seemed to follow him. She wondered how many stories were written there that he'd never told.

The brass key hung against his chest, catching the fading light with a dull glint. In sleep, the tension had drained from his face; the lines of strain and determination softened until he looked younger, almost peaceful — not the man who had fought his way through a collapsing tunnel, but someone momentarily unburdened.

She moved carefully, not wanting to wake him, bare feet whispering over the cool tile. On the small chair by the window sat Elias Grey's journal, the leather cover wrinkled and water-marked but intact. The ink had bled along the edges of some pages, yet the words endured—tight, deliberate, the handwriting of a man who weighed each thought before setting it down.

She traced the indentation of one letter with her thumb before opening it. Her eyes lingered on the first page, but instinct guided her deeper. She turned to the back, where the final entries clustered together in darker ink and hurried script.

The last page was dated November 1718.

"His handwriting changes here," she murmured under her breath, running a fingertip over the uneven lines. "It must have been written right before he disappeared again."

The ink was pressed hard into the paper, as though Grey had written against the clock. Isabelle drew in a quiet breath and began to read the words softly to herself.

November 8th, 1718

The sea grows colder. The wind carries voices from the horizon—men of Spain, relentless in their pursuit. Their ships hunt me still, though months have passed since the capture of La Fortuna. They will not rest while breath remains in their lungs, or the treasure eludes their grasp.

I have moved the treasure again, deeper than before, to a place the tides themselves may one day forget. Not for wealth, nor for glory, but for mercy. It is not only a trove of wealth I carry—it is a burden that corrupts the soul of any man who covets it.

I have seen what it does. The treasure bends will and reason alike. It whispers in the dark and weighs upon the heart and mind like stone. To those who seek it, I leave these words: what you chase is not salvation, but shadow.

Should you find these pages, know that I write not to tempt, but to warn. The Spaniards would see the world burn to claim what they do not understand. I have done what I must to keep it from their hands. If my end comes soon, let this journal be both map and mercy to the one who follows. Not all treasure is meant to be found.

— E.G.

When she finished, Isabelle let the journal rest open across her lap. The faint evening light caught the edges of the page, turning the ink a deep bronze. A breeze stirred through the shutters, carrying the scent of wood smoke and distant rain.

She sat there for a long moment, staring at the words. *Map and mercy.* The phrase circled through her thoughts, heavy with meaning.

She closed the journal gently, pressing her palm over the cover. "He knew what he was doing," she whispered to herself. "And he knew what was coming."

Outside, the gulls wheeled over the darkening bay, their cries thinning with the wind.

The mattress shifted behind her.

Jake stirred, exhaling a quiet breath as he blinked awake. "You're at it already?" His voice was rough with sleep, low and dry.

"I couldn't help myself," she said softly. "You need to see this."

He pushed himself upright, wincing as his arm adjusted in the sling. "What is it?"

"The last entry," she said, handing it to him. "It's dated November 1718."

Jake frowned, rubbing sleep from his eyes. "Didn't he attack La Fortuna around March that year?"

Isabelle nodded, "Eight months later, he was still running."

Jake gave a small nod of acknowledgment as he scanned the page, though he didn't read aloud. "He sounds... desperate."

"He was," Isabelle said. "But not just from fear. From responsibility. He knew the Spanish were closing in, so he moved the treasure again. Not for glory—he said for mercy."

Jake looked up at her slowly. "That doesn't sound like any treasure I've ever heard of."

"No," she said. "It doesn't."

She rose and crossed to the small window, the journal still in her hands.

"He said it bends will and reason alike. That it whispers in the dark. Whatever he took—it's what the Spanish were chasing. And he left this journal so whoever came next would understand what they were really after."

Jake rubbed his thumb along the edge of the brass key that hung from his neck. "You think this is really Siecaza."

"I do." She turned back toward him, her expression thoughtful, re-solved. "Every clue we've found, every risk he took—it all points to that. Grey wasn't protecting his gold. He was protecting everyone else from this."

Jake's gaze shifted toward the bay, where the last light of day trembled across the water. "So, why'd the Spanish want it so badly?"

"That's the question." She began to pace again, the dying light catching in her hair. "They knew enough to fear it, but not enough to stop. Maybe they thought they could control it—or use it."

Jake frowned slightly, his brow furrowing. "Like a weapon?"

Isabelle paused, considering. "Maybe—yeah."

The word hung there between them, heavier than the air in the small room.

Jake watched her for a moment. "And Grey didn't just hide it. He made sure no one could follow unless they understood what they were walking into."

"Exactly." She stopped beside the bed. "This isn't a map. It's a warn-ing—and maybe a test of intent."

For a long moment, neither of them spoke. The only sound was the muted churn of the bay and the rhythmic creak of the fan above.

Jake finally broke the silence. "What about Grey's famed treasure trove? Where is that in all this?" He rubbed his face, sighing. "Sorry, I'm trying not to be the asshole looking for the payday, but I was sort of counting on that—you know?"

Isabelle studied him, reading the conflict behind his words, and nodded. "He would have needed vast resources to do what he did in the catacombs. I'd guess wherever Siecaza went, so did the real treasure."

Jake nodded appreciatively, the admission softening something in his expression.

"There's a lot to go through in there," Isabelle said, gesturing toward the journal. "We'll find more answers."

She could see the gears turning in his head and gave him the silence to process it. The glow from the window had faded to a dull amber, filling the room with a kind of quiet that felt heavier than exhaustion.

Finally, she spoke again, her voice gentle. "You still with me?"

Jake looked up, caught off guard by the question. Then a faint grin tugged at the corner of his mouth. "So, say we get to the end of this whole thing — you take Siecaza back to its home, and I take the gold back to mine, right?"

Isabelle took a step closer and backhanded him lightly across his good bicep. "No. We take Siecaza back, and we take the gold home," she said, unable to hide her smile.

Jake tried to dodge, but the slap landed squarely, and he feigned injury before breaking into laughter. Isabelle laughed too, and for a moment the small room was filled with something they hadn't felt in days — ease, lightness, the reminder that they were still alive.

Then Jake reached out, taking her hand in his. His thumb brushed her knuckles, warm and careful. "But in all seriousness," he said quietly, "I'm with you."

Isabelle's heart kicked in her chest, her cheeks flushing before she could school her expression. "Good."

Their laughter faded into a comfortable silence as the last of the daylight slipped through the shutters. Outside, the bay lights shimmered across the water like scattered coins, and the night gathered around them — soft, steady, and full of unspoken promise.

For the first time in what felt like days, they both simply breathed. No running, no hiding — just quiet and the sound of the sea beyond the window.

By the time the lamps flickered on across the bay, the world outside had folded into twilight. The air carried a cool edge now, tinged with rain and the faint smoke of cooking fires drifting in from the harbor.

The small room glowed softly in lamplight. Isabelle sat at the narrow desk near the window, Grey's journal open in front of her. Jake was across the room, one foot propped on a chair, scanning a map he'd borrowed from the innkeeper. Between them, the silence felt purposeful rather than tired — the stillness of minds beginning to work again.

"He kept meticulous records," Isabelle said after a long stretch of quiet, flipping through a page with care. "Ship routes, ports, provisions... even the names of his crew. But then it changes. The tone, I mean."

Jake looked up from the map. "How so?"

"Here." She turned the book toward him, running her finger along the inked lines. "The handwriting gets sharper — rushed. And there are these short passages about dreams, or maybe visions — *'shadows that follow even in daylight.'"*

Jake leaned forward, nodding toward the journal. "When did he write that—about the dreams?"

Isabelle flipped back a few pages, scanning the margins. "August of 1718."

"So, probably around the time he got to Rio after leaving La Isla de Sombras," Jake said. "He was already thinking about his escape route—and having dreams about it."

Isabelle traced the line of Grey's hurried script with her fingertip. "He mentions the *'treasure'* influencing his mind. Maybe that was part of it too."

Jake's brow furrowed slightly. "If Siecaza could reach him even then..."

She nodded. "Then maybe it never really let him go."

They both sat in silence for a moment, the only sound the low hum of the ceiling fan and the faint patter of rain against the shutters.

Finally, Jake exhaled through his nose, the weight of it grounding him. "You think he wanted whoever followed him to find all this?"

"I think he knew they would," Isabelle said. "And he wanted them to understand what they were chasing before they did something they couldn't undo."

Jake leaned back against the wall, the map still folded in his hands. "Sounds like a man who'd seen too much of what it could do."

She nodded. "He was trying to leave a legacy — not of gold, but of understanding. Maybe that's what he meant by mercy."

Jake rubbed at his jaw, thinking. "And we're following that same trail."

"Not for gold," Isabelle said. "For truth."

He smiled faintly. "Speak for yourself. Truth's a little harder to cash in."

She shot him a look that softened into a smile. "You're incorrigible."

"Just honest." He set the map down on the desk beside her notebook. "If we're going all the way to Punta Arenas, we'll need to be smart about it. Serrano's probably already got people watching the major ports."

Isabelle nodded, already reaching for her pen. "Then we avoid them.

Smaller stops, connecting routes if we can find them. We can buy tickets with cash — no IDs, no trail."

Jake rubbed the back of his neck, thinking. "So, still no planes."

"Right. Too easy to track," she said, leaning over the map he'd spread on the desk. "Buses will take us part of the way south." She ran a finger down the faded highway lines. "Rio to São Paulo, maybe Curitiba, then here—Porto Alegre."

Jake followed her hand, nodding. "And after that?"

"We'd have to cross into Argentina," she said, eyes narrowing as she studied the map. "From there, maybe more buses or a car through Patagonia... eventually to Punta Arenas."

Jake leaned on the desk, considering the distance. "That's a long haul."

"It keeps us off the grid," Isabelle said. "Once we get far enough south, we'll blend in with the people heading toward the research stations or fishing ports."

Jake gave a small nod. "We'll need to travel light. Buy what we need on the way, ditch what we don't."

"Guess that means we aren't going back for my laptop?" Isabelle asked, though she already knew the answer.

Jake shook his head. "You saw how many guys they had out there just on the beach. We'd be spotted in an instant going back to the inn."

Isabelle nodded, exhaling through her nose, then looked back down at the map. "The slower route is safer now. Serrano's people won't expect us to go overland."

A faint smile tugged at Jake's mouth. "Guess we're taking the scenic route."

"Think of it as retracing Grey's path—just on roads instead of currents," she said.

He grinned. "If we can stay off the grid, I'll take whatever moves."

Jake glanced at the window, where the lamplight met the first sheen of rain. "We'll need to leave before dawn."

"Agreed." She marked a final note in her journal, then closed it gently. "Punta Arenas," she said quietly, almost to herself. "The port at the world's end."

Jake met her eyes, his tone steady. "Then that's where we're headed."

Outside, thunder murmured over the bay, and the reflections of the harbor lights shivered in the water like restless stars.

The rain had thinned to a fine mist by the time Jake stepped onto the narrow balcony. The boards creaked softly under his bare feet. Beyond the railing, the bay stretched out in shifting layers of silver and black, the lights of anchored boats wavering on the water like fragments of broken glass.

He braced a hand on the railing, taking in the humid air. It carried the smell of wet stone and diesel from the docks, a reminder that the world kept moving no matter what they'd survived. Behind him, the muffled sound of pages turning marked Isabelle's steady presence — her quiet ritual of rereading Grey's words, trying to decode the man's mind one line at a time.

Jake's eyes drifted toward the far end of the waterfront. A black SUV sat idling near the seawall, headlights off, its shape just visible beneath a flickering streetlamp. He frowned. Maybe it was nothing — a late arrival from the ferry road, a delivery driver waiting out the rain. Still, something about the stillness of it made his pulse slow in that old, deliberate way.

He watched for a long moment, long enough to see a shadow shift inside the vehicle, the faint glow of a cigarette ember blooming and dying in the dark.

Jake exhaled quietly, jaw tightening. He pushed off the railing and went back inside.

Isabelle looked up as he closed the balcony door behind him. "What is it?"

"Could be nothing," he said. "But there's a car down by the seawall — no lights, just sitting there."

She set the journal aside, her voice low. "Serrano?"

"Could be," he said. "Or someone who works for someone who works for him."

Isabelle's brow furrowed. "You think they tracked us here already?"

Jake nodded his head. "Possibly. If they connect the footprints they found last night with the idea we crossed the bay, then—yeah, they could be here."

She rose and crossed to the window, parting the shutters just enough to glance outside. The bay lights reflected in her eyes, sharp and watchful. "Then we should definitely be ready to go before dawn," she said softly.

Jake nodded. "Guess it's a good thing I'm already packed," he said, gesturing around the near-empty room with a half-smile.

Isabelle let out a quiet chuckle, the sound brief but genuine.

"A few hours of sleep," Jake added, "then we move."

Outside, thunder rolled far out over the bay — low and distant, like the slow turn of something coming closer.

Jake lingered at the window a moment longer, watching the lights tremble across the black water, each reflection fading and reforming until they were impossible to tell apart.

Behind him, Isabelle watched his silhouette against the glass, the faint glow of the harbor outlining his shoulders. For the first time since the catacombs, the weight of what they carried pressed in again — not fear, but purpose. She closed her eyes briefly, steadying her breath. Whatever waited at the world's end, they were already bound to it.

CHAPTER TWENTY-EIGHT

Five Days South

They left Ponta d'Areia before dawn dressed as people the world looks past—borrowed shirts, caps low, shoes still damp from the night before. The oil-stained paper sack between them held two rolls, two coffees, and Elias Grey's journal wrapped in salt-stiff leather. Cameras watched from dark domes along the terminal wall. Jake noticed them but tipped his brim lower and said nothing. The less their faces remembered, the better.

The bus climbed into cloud as the sea fell away behind them. Waterfalls stitched silver down the jungle cliffs, vanishing as quick as breath. They passed villages where roosters ruled the dawn and children waited beside painted walls for the day to begin. Isabelle sat with her hands folded around the journal.

When she finally opened it, the pages rasped like dry leaves. She read softly, the engine's hum filling the pauses between words.

August 3, 1718 — Rio de Janeiro

The brothers of the Carmelite order received my donation with grace. The masons extend the chambers into bedrock as I have drawn. The traps are set; the walls are marked in symbols only I read. By next month the lower vault will be sealed, and the orb will sleep beneath holy stone.

Jake huffed a laugh. "Buy a church, hide a miracle."

"Donations built chapels all the time," Isabelle said, but her smile was real. Then she winced when he nudged her—bandages tight beneath a shirt two sizes too big. He apologized. She threatened his arm with exactly the amount of sincerity he deserved. The air between them lightened by a hair.

By late afternoon the road wound south through freight yards and valleys washed in bronze light. Near dusk, the bus rolled past the wide brown river dividing Brazil from Argentina. Border posts came with stamps and perfunctory smiles; the café smelled of frying oil and rain. Isabelle's Spanish was steadier than Jake's, but fatigue blurred them both into silence.

They crossed into Argentina under sodium lamps, the night thick with mist. At some point Jake tucked a blanket across her lap without waking her, and at some point she woke and let it stay.

By the next evening the bus had rattled south through endless flatlands until the map gave up on names. The light turned pewter; the plains stretched to the horizon like a thought with no end. The engine coughed once, then again, and died as if it had decided to quit the journey before they did.

The driver swore softly, tried the ignition twice, and called someone who didn't sound optimistic.

"Replacement in the morning," he said in accented English. "Nearest town—General Roca. Fifty kilometers."

Jake stared down the highway. A pair of distant lights burned beneath a corrugated awning—barely a rumor of civilization.

"We're not known for our patience," he said.

"Or good decisions," Isabelle replied, already on her feet.

The "station" was a rusted glass box with two pumps and a clerk half-watching a muted telenovela. The air smelled of diesel and instant coffee. Isabelle asked if the old Hilux outside still ran. The clerk shrugged, produced a key, and named a price that mixed skepticism with opportunity.

"Cash only," he said.

Jake peeled off damp bills. The clerk slid a handwritten receipt across the counter and waved them toward the door.

Outside, the Hilux looked like it preferred dying to quitting. It started on the second breath.

"Is it stealing if we don't bring it back?" Isabelle asked, half under her breath.

"Temporarily borrowed," Jake said.

"That the legal term?" she murmured, climbing in. She angled the vents away from the cracked windshield and cinched her satchel tighter. The journal rested against her chest like a small, defiant heart.

The next two days became a geography of wind and wire. South turned into definition—the pampas flattening to a vocabulary of fences and sky. They traded the wheel when shoulders knotted and spoke only when silence started to feel like surrender.

They followed Route Three through Comodoro Rivadavia, San Julián, and Río Gallegos—towns strung like beads on the spine of the highway. Fuel stations blurred into memory. Isabelle reread the Río entry once, tracing Grey's script, and neither of them said his name again.

Morning came in pewter light. The world thinned, color draining from the grass until only wind and wire remained.

"Empty's got its own kind of beauty," Jake said.

"Like the sea."

"Colder," Isabelle answered, steering into a squall that vanished five minutes later as if the sky had changed its mind.

By the fifth night, the wind sang through the door seals and the truck replied in rattles. They stopped for fuel at a lonely outpost where the attendant looked half-asleep and fully bored. Jake slept with his cap low; Isabelle drove with her jaw set and the journal pressed against her hip like a promise.

The Strait announced itself first by smell—kelp and cold iron—then by sound, the water moving like muscle beneath a lid of cloud. Gulls found them again, crying like things that remembered the world before maps.

Punta Arenas rose from the fog as scattered light pinned to a black shore. The Hilux coughed, thought better of it, and, mercifully, rolled to a stop at the overlook on its last goodwill. Below them, the water shimmered with the kind of calm that only follows distance.

"End of the road," Jake said, hands slack on the wheel.

"Or the beginning," Isabelle replied, eyes still on the water. She set her palm on Grey's journal. The leather was cold.

Near General Roca, two days and an entire patience reservoir behind, Luca stood beneath a tin awning that shook in the wind and set two fingers on a station counter.

"Two nights ago," he asked in patient Spanish. "This couple—did they rent your truck?"

The attendant didn't remember until a few folded bills suggested it was a good story to recall. He opened an app. A red dot pulsed on a map near Punta Arenas.

"Dios mío," the man said. "They didn't say—"

"They didn't need to," Luca said. He stepped back into the wind and called ahead for fuel, for a waiting PC-12, for the kind of silence money buys. The road south was one line only, and lines end.

"They'll run out of road," he murmured, gloving his hands.

CHAPTER TWENTY-NINE

The Edge of the World

The wind off the Strait cut like a razor. Jake crossed his arms, trying to hold on to what little warmth he had left. The Hilux sat a mile behind them on the ridge, hood still propped, fading into the violet dusk. The last of the engine's heat had bled away an hour ago. Now it was just another piece of wreckage at the world's edge. The attendant at the service station wouldn't be happy, he thought.

Beside him, Isabelle walked with her collar turned up, hair whipped loose from its braid. She kept one arm clamped around her satchel, the other buried in her coat pocket. Their breath condensed in the frigid air.

Below, Punta Arenas stretched along the water, its lights trembling like distant sparks in the wind—fragile, defiant, and alone against the dark. Beyond, the Strait of Magellan rolled under a pewter sky, the horizon swallowed by mist.

"Civilization," Jake muttered. "Or something close enough."

Isabelle's laugh was a dry puff of steam. "I'll take close enough, so long as it has heat."

They followed the sloping road down, gravel crunching beneath their boots. The wind never eased; it shoved at their backs as if hurrying them downhill. When they finally reached the first row of houses, Jake felt the strange vertigo of being among people again—wood smoke, the faint thump of a radio somewhere, the barking of a dog that sounded bored rather than feral.

The streets were narrow and half-deserted. Tin roofs rattled overhead. Murals of saints and sailors flaked off the stucco walls, and every corner smelled of saltwater and fish.

A painted sign creaked above a doorway: *Hostal del Faro.*

Warm light bled through lace curtains.

Isabelle tilted her head toward it. "Looks open."

Jake pushed through the door, bell jangling. Heat and the smell of stew wrapped around them. An older woman in a wool shawl appeared from behind a counter, wiping her hands on an apron.

"Buenas noches," Isabelle said. "Do you have a room for tonight?"

The woman studied them a moment—their travel-stained clothes, windburned faces—then nodded, smiling kindly. "Sí. Small, but warm."

Isabelle's relief was visible in her shoulders. "Gracias." She glanced at Jake, then back to the woman. "Cash okay?"

The innkeeper nodded and disappeared briefly behind the counter, returning with a brass key attached to a polished wood float. "Tea and soup in the café," she said, her smile wry, like she'd said it a thousand times before.

Isabelle smiled back, replying, "Perfecto."

They climbed a narrow staircase that groaned beneath them. Their room was small: two narrow beds, a cracked mirror, a single window facing the bay. A heater ticked in the corner.

Jake exhaled, a long, exhausted sigh. Watching Isabelle thank the innkeeper—her voice steady despite the day—had steadied him too. She'd been the one to keep them moving when the truck gave out, the one who stayed practical when all he wanted was to curse the cold. It struck him that she could make even this—half-frozen, hungry, standing in a stranger's hallway—feel almost bearable.

She rubbed her hands together and blew into them. "We're not exactly dressed for this," she said, teeth chattering between words and stepping close to the heater.

Jake tugged at the sleeve of his thin shirt. "Tomorrow we'll find a shop. Coats, gloves, maybe socks. How nice does a warm pair of socks sound right now?"

That earned the smallest laugh from her—soft, tired, but real. "Ugh—so good."

For a moment they just stood there, the heater's warmth starting to thaw the deep freeze that had settled in their bones. Outside, the wind moaned against the shutters, a sound like water rolling over stone.

Downstairs, the smell of food drew them back to life. Isabelle caught it first—garlic, onions, something simmering—and gave him a look that said let's move before dying of starvation. They followed the narrow stairs to a small café at the back of the inn.

A cast-iron stove glowed behind the counter, throwing red light across the room. Two dockworkers sat at a corner table, their voices low over a deck of cards. The innkeeper ladled stew from a pot that looked older than the building and gestured toward a pair of seats near the window.

"Dos platos," Isabelle said, settling into the rhythm of the place. The woman smiled and grabbed two more bowls from a cupboard beside the stove.

Jake sank onto the bench and flexed his stiff hands. "Remind me to stop judging diners that only serve one thing," he muttered.

"I was just thinking the same," Isabelle said. "If it's hot and it's not coffee, it's perfect."

The stew arrived a minute later—thick with potatoes, carrots, and some kind of fish that fell apart in the spoon. They ate in silence at first, the kind born of exhaustion and the comfort of actual food. Heat crept back into Jake's fingers.

Isabelle finished half her bowl before she spoke again. "Feels like we finally outran everything," she said quietly. "At least for tonight."

Jake nodded, eyes on the harbor lights trembling across the black water. "And we only had to come to the edge of the world to do it."

A gust hit the windows, rattling them in their frames. The innkeeper chuckled from the stove. "The wind never sleeps," she said without looking up.

Isabelle smiled faintly. "She's not wrong."

Jake broke a piece of bread in half and handed it across the table. "Here's to one night of hoping she will be, though."

They ate until the bowls were empty and their shoulders started to relax. Isabelle leaned back against the wall, eyes half-closed.

For a long moment neither spoke. The silence wasn't uncomfortable; it was the kind that comes when words have been used up.

When they finally stood to leave, Isabelle thanked the innkeeper in Spanish and asked about breakfast. The woman promised coffee at dawn and wished them buen descanso—a good rest.

Upstairs, their room felt warmer now, the air thick with the faint scent of stew and smoke. Isabelle turned down the lamp until the room was half-dark, letting the silver of the harbor spill through the window.

She drew the curtain partway, looking out at the lights on the water. "He really did come this far," she said. "It's strange thinking we're tracing the same horizon."

Jake eased down on the bed, boots still on. "He probably went even farther," he said, voice rough with fatigue. "And hopefully tomorrow we figure out how or why."

The heater ticked, wind pressing softly against the glass. Isabelle pulled the blanket over herself and reached to switch off the lamp.

"Tomorrow," she whispered.

Jake let the sound of the wind fill the silence. It carried the scent of the sea and something older, a whisper caught between the centuries. He closed his eyes and listened until the world went quiet.

Morning came late and gray. The light that crept through the curtains was thin, filtered by clouds. Jake woke to the smell of coffee and the hollow note of a ship's horn rolling in from the harbor.

The room had grown cold overnight. His breath fogged faintly as he sat up and pulled on his shirt. Across the room, Isabelle stood at the narrow mirror, hair still damp from washing, trying to coax warmth into her fingers.

"Good morning," she said, catching Jake's eyes in the mirror.

"Morning," he replied gruffly, looking away with a sheepish half-smile.

"How'd you sleep?"

"Like I hadn't slept in a week," he said with a grin.

"Me too," she murmured. "At least I didn't have to fight you for the covers this time," she added, teasing.

Jake rubbed his eyes and smirked. "You don't have to lie—you know you missed me."

She shook her head, smiling despite herself.

"So," he said, swinging his legs over the edge of the bed, "what's the plan this morning?"

"Coffee," she said, voice rough with sleep. "That's the first priority."

He chuckled. "Finally, a plan I can get behind."

Downstairs, the innkeeper greeted them with two steaming mugs and a plate of bread. She looked them over—travel-stained clothes, thin shirts, tired faces—and clucked her tongue.

"Demasiado frío para eso," she said. *Too cold for that.*

Isabelle laughed and answered in Spanish, "Where can we buy something warmer?"

The woman pointed toward the waterfront. "Mercado Central. Two blocks down. Tell Diego at the clothing stall I sent you. He'll give you a fair price."

The morning wind met them like a living thing—sharp, unrelenting, and alive with the scent of the sea. It pressed down the narrow street and chased ribbons of mist between the rooftops. Their boots scuffed over cobblestones still slick from the night's frost as they made their way toward the waterfront.

The Mercado Central wasn't much to look at—just a crooked row of stalls huddled against the wind, canvas awnings snapping like sails. Vendors were still setting up, stamping their feet to keep warm, the air filled with the mingled smells of bread, roasting coffee, and brine.

A man selling wool sweaters called out, "Buenos días!" as they passed. His breath rose in clouds. Isabelle smiled and returned the greeting, switching easily into Spanish.

They found the clothing stall the innkeeper had mentioned—a narrow booth overflowing with oilskins, scarves, and knit caps strung from hooks. The shopkeeper, a wiry man with weathered skin and a knitted cap pulled low over his ears, looked up from folding a stack of sweaters.

"Ah, you must be the ones María sent," he said in halting English, his grin quick and genuine. "She said you came walking in from the road. Brave, or crazy."

"Maybe a little of both," Jake said.

The man laughed and gestured to the racks. "Then you need proper clothes. Here, try these."

He handed Jake a heavy oilskin jacket, the dark canvas creaking as he lifted it. Jake slid it on—the fit was loose but warm. Isabelle found a gray wool coat, long enough to fall past her knees, and a soft scarf dyed the blue-green of the Strait. The air in the stall smelled faintly of lanolin.

Jake grinned, tugging the collar of his new jacket. "Almost looks like we're not lost anymore."

"Almost," she said.

The shopkeeper chuckled, counting out their change. "Now you look like Magellan's crew," he said. "Just... try not to sail away in this wind."

Jake took the last of their Chilean pesos, folded into a neat stack, and slid it into his pocket. The man nodded toward the sea. "Wind from the south today. Bad for fishing, good for leaving. Safe travels if you decide not to stay with us a while."

Outside the market, the cold didn't bite as deep. Their breath still rose white in the air, but the wool and oilskin held the warmth close. They walked along the quay, passing crates stenciled in faded Spanish and ships moored tight against the piers. The horizon was a smear of steel-gray water and distant mountains, the kind of view that made the world feel both enormous and small.

Isabelle tucked her gloved hands into her coat pockets. "It's strange," she said. "Standing here, you can almost feel how close he was—Grey. Like the past isn't finished with this place."

Jake adjusted the collar of his jacket against the wind. "Then shall we see if the records remember him."

They followed the curve of the waterfront toward the Archivo Marítimo Regional, a squat building of pale stone with narrow windows that looked out on the harbor. The sign above the door was sun-bleached and crooked, letters barely legible from years of salt air.

As they reached the steps, the wind seemed to ease, the sound of gulls fading to a distant echo. Isabelle looked back toward the market, the stalls now glowing gold in the morning light. Then she turned to Jake, her breath clouding the air between them.

"Ready?" she asked.

Jake nodded. "Let's find the ghost of The Specter."

They stepped inside.

The air inside the Archivo Marítimo Regional smelled of dust and leather—like paper that had forgotten sunlight. The front desk was empty except for a brass bell and a ledger signed by a handful of visitors, most of them researchers or students.

Isabelle brushed her gloved hand across the cover of the ledger. "Feels like we're interrupting ghosts," she murmured.

Jake glanced around. The building wasn't large, just a handful of rooms with peeling plaster walls and narrow windows that let in strips of colorless light. A sign in Spanish read: *Archivos: 1700–1800.*

A door creaked open deeper inside, and an older man in a sweater vest appeared, blinking at them from behind wire-rimmed glasses. His hair was silver, combed neatly back, his expression patient in the way of someone who had spent a lifetime among books.

"Buenos días," he said. "Are you researching something historical?"

Isabelle smiled and switched to Spanish. "Sí, señor. We're looking for records of English ships that passed through here in the eighteenth century."

The man's eyebrows lifted slightly, interest kindling behind his eyes. "There aren't many," he said. "But... there are some old reports. I can show you."

He led them into a back room lined with floor-to-ceiling shelves. Bundles of papers wrapped in string were stacked alongside thick, leather-bound ledgers. A small heater rattled in the corner, barely denting the cold.

Jake set Grey's journal on a table and pulled out a chair for Isabelle. "You take the ledgers; I'll start with the loose logs."

For the next hour the only sounds were the whisper of turning pages and the ticking of the heater. The old man returned once with two chipped mugs of coffee, then left them alone.

Most of the entries were routine: ship arrivals, tonnage, cargo lists. Isabelle flipped page after page, her finger tracing faded ink. Brig *Antonia*, Portuguese registry... Schooner *Santa María*, coastal supply route... Frigate *Reina del Sur*, refitting after storm damage... Nothing about an English corsair.

"Grey wouldn't have docked under his own flag," Jake muttered. "Maybe he traded under a false name."

"Maybe," Isabelle said, still scanning. "But the Spanish were meticulous—they'd have noted any unregistered ships sighted in the Strait."

"Unless he paid them off—like with the Carmelites."

She turned another page and paused. A marginal note had been squeezed into a customs report: *A foreign ship sighted south of Cape Froward. Unidentified. English crew.*

Her pulse quickened. "Jake—look at this."

He crossed over, coffee in hand. She pointed to the notation, its ink browned with age.

He read it aloud, lips moving softly. "1719. That's right in Grey's window."

The handwriting continued below in a different pen—perhaps an officer's later note: *No further record. Presumed to have continued west.*

Isabelle let out a slow breath. "It's not proof, but it's something."

Jake smiled faintly. "We'll need a little more than that."

She copied the entry carefully into her notebook. Still, the report left them unsatisfied. Isabelle felt the itch that came when she was close to an answer but not quite touching it.

She leaned back in her chair, rolling the stiffness from her neck. Through the narrow window above the table, she could see a sliver of the town—red roofs, iron chimneys—and beyond them, on the far rise, the outline of a white chapel with a cross glinting faintly in the pale light.

She frowned. "What's that building up there?"

Jake followed her gaze. "Looks like a church. Why—you think he buried it under another church?" he added, dryly.

She chewed her lip thoughtfully. "If Grey stopped here, there would've been injuries, maybe even deaths. The Spanish kept ship logs, but the church kept souls. Baptisms, marriages, burials—those records would've outlived everything else."

He smiled faintly. "So, you're thinking less customs office, more grave-yard."

"Exactly."

She stood and closed the ledger, brushing dust from her gloves. "We've hit the edge of what the paper remembers. Time to see what the stones do."

Jake folded the oilcloth back around the journal, his grin lopsided. "And here I was hoping we'd get a day off from crawling through tombs."

"Sorry," she said, slipping her notebook into her satchel. "You can rest when we find Grey."

He laughed under his breath. "So never, then."

They thanked the archivist, who seemed pleased that anyone still cared about his brittle ledgers, and stepped back into the daylight. The cold slapped them instantly; the wind had sharpened since morning.

From the steps of the archive, the chapel was clear now—perched on the hill above town, its bell tower bright against the gray. The way the light caught it made it look almost spectral.

Isabelle nodded toward it. "Let's go."

Jake adjusted his jacket and fell into step beside her. "Lead the way, professor."

They started uphill, the wind tugging at their coats, the sound of gulls echoing faintly over the rooftops as they left the last warm breath of the archive behind.

The road wound upward through narrow lanes lined with weathered houses, their walls patched with corrugated metal and faded paint. Wind clawed at the wires overhead, carrying the sharp tang of seawater and smoke. Each step felt like walking into a colder century.

The chapel stood on the ridge above the town—small, whitewashed, its bell tower leaning slightly as if braced against the gale. A low stone wall enclosed the graveyard behind it, the gate hanging crooked on one hinge. The sign over the entrance read: *Capilla de los Navegantes — est. 1637 (Chapel of the Sailors — est. 1637)*

Jake pushed the gate open, and the hinges shrieked in protest.

The wind didn't stop at the wall; it howled through the iron crosses and the brittle weeds that grew between the graves. Dozens of markers stood crooked in the earth—some marble, some wood, most too weathered to read. The salt air had eaten away whole names, leaving behind only ghosts of letters.

"This place has seen everything," Jake murmured.

Isabelle nodded, scanning the rows. "Let's split up. Look for anything that doesn't sound Spanish—names, carvings, dates around 1719."

They moved separately among the stones. Isabelle knelt by one marker half-buried in moss, tracing her gloved fingers over the faint etching: *María Carvallo, 1821. Too late.* She moved on.

Jake followed the outer edge of the wall, where the stones were oldest. The air was raw, briny on his tongue. He crouched beside one headstone leaning under its own weight—its inscription nearly gone. He brushed away lichen with his sleeve.

Tomás Blay, natural de Inglaterra — 1719.

Below the name, faint but unmistakable, was the engraving of a serpent coiled around an anchor.

Jake stared at it, the breath catching in his throat. The same symbol that had followed wherever Grey had been. His fingers hovered just above the weathered stone, tracing the grooves without touching them.

"Isabelle," he called softly.

She looked up from across the yard, the wind carrying her hair in a dark tangle. When she saw his face, she hurried over, kneeling beside him.

He pointed to the symbol.

Her eyes widened. "One of Grey's men." She brushed her gloved hand over the name. "*Tomás Blay, natural de Inglaterra. Born in England*. I've seen his name in Grey's journal—except it was Thomas Blythe. This is the Spanish spelling."

Below the date, smaller lettering marked:

Esposo de Ana Lucía Carvallo.

And beneath that, a newer plaque embedded in the stone:

Familia Vega Carvallo — Custodios desde 1831.

Isabelle read it aloud, her breath misting in the air. "Vega Carvallo. Not Blay anymore."

Jake's gaze lingered on the serpent carving. "Names change," he said quietly. "Blood doesn't."

She nodded, tracing the letters with care. "They must've taken her family's name. The English would've faded from the records—but the story stayed." She looked up at him, eyes catching the gray light. "The plaque—*Familia Vega Carvallo*. Her descendants might still be here."

Jake nodded slowly. "Then maybe they've got more than a grave."

"We can start with the parish," Isabelle said, glancing toward the chapel. "They'd know where the family records went."

Jake followed her gaze. Through the open doors, he could see flickering candlelight. The interior was simple—wooden pews, a crucifix blackened by age, a few saints' icons watching over the silence.

As they stepped inside, the air shifted from the raw chill of the graveyard to the dim warmth of incense and wax. A single woman in a gray habit stood near the altar, arranging flowers at the foot of a statue.

"Buenas tardes," Isabelle greeted softly. The woman turned, smiling faintly, and wiped her hands on her apron.

Isabelle explained in Spanish that they were researchers tracing the history of a sailor named Tomás Blay buried outside. The nun nodded, eyes brightening with recognition.

"Ah, sí. Don Tomás. The Englishman," she said in accented English, pleased to recall him. "His family moved his remains from the old burial ground long ago. They still live near the port. The Vega family."

She disappeared briefly through a side door and returned with a leather-bound registry. The pages crackled as she turned them. Her finger stopped on a line written in looping ink: *Remains transferred to the parish cemetery by the Vega family, descendants of Tomás Blay, year 1831.*

She tore a small scrap of paper and wrote down an address. "Don Ernesto Vega," she said, handing it to Isabelle. "He keeps the family's things. Old letters, I think."

Isabelle accepted it carefully. "Muchísimas gracias, hermana."

The nun smiled. "You are welcome. He will be pleased that someone still asks about Don Tomás."

Outside, the wind picked up again, lifting the edges of Isabelle's coat. Jake glanced once more at the grave before they left the gate. The serpent carving seemed deeper now, as if the wind had revealed it.

He adjusted the oilcloth bundle under his arm. "Looks like we have a lead, detective."

Isabelle folded the note into her pocket, her eyes still on the hill of graves. "And maybe the next piece of Grey's story."

They started down toward the harbor, the cold pressing at their backs, the faint toll of the chapel bell chasing them downhill.

Ernesto Vega, late seventies, met them at the door of a modest seaside house. Nets hung drying from the porch, and the air smelled faintly of kerosene. He studied the strangers for a long moment before opening the door wider.

Inside, the walls were lined with framed photographs—fishing boats, family portraits, and one old black-and-white image of the Capilla de los Navegantes, its bell tower leaning in the wind just as it did now.

"You're looking for Don Tomás," Ernesto said at last. His voice was low, gravelly, but not unkind. "He was my great-great-great-great-grandfather."

Isabelle nodded. "We found his grave this morning. The chapel caretaker said your family has kept his records."

Ernesto's eyes softened. "Yes. They moved him there before the old cemetery washed away in a storm." He smiled faintly. "He was married in that same chapel, you know. The one on the hill. They say he helped rebuild it after a fire, years before the town even existed. My grandmother used to say he called it 'the sailors' promise.'"

Jake leaned forward slightly. "He rebuilt it himself?"

"That's the story," Ernesto said with a shrug. "The church was already old then—founded by sailors in the sixteen-hundreds, before any country claimed this place. He said it reminded him of home."

He paused, studying them for a moment before continuing. "Most who come asking about him are historians, or tourists chasing family names. But you—" His eyes drifted to the oilcloth bundle Jake carried. "You came for something else, didn't you?"

Jake hesitated, then nodded. "We're following the trail of a ship called *The Specter*. Tomás Blay sailed with her."

Ernesto's expression changed—curiosity tempered by something more cautious. "That name hasn't been spoken here in a long time." He rose slowly and walked to a small cabinet near the corner of the room. From inside, he drew out a tin chest, its hinges green with age.

"This belonged to my grandfather," he said, setting it on the table. "He was the last to keep our family's papers. He used to tell me that when the wind howled too loud, it was the sea trying to call them back."

The lid creaked open, revealing a bundle wrapped in linen. Inside was a small leather logbook, its spine cracked but intact, and a brass key, dulled by time but still gleaming faintly under the lamplight. The bow of the key was a simple loop; etched on the barrel was the serpent and anchor.

Isabelle drew in a breath. "It's the same design," she whispered.

Jake's brows furrowed as he pulled out his own key. The match was perfect—same weight, same tool marks. He turned his to the light. Where the barrel should have shown an etching like Ernesto's, the metal was almost worn smooth—but the serpent-and-anchor was still there. He had always thought the marks on his were just scratches from use. Now he could see it clearly: they were the same.

Ernesto stared at them both, the keys glinting together. "So the stories were true," he murmured. "The Captain gave each man a chest—and a key."

Jake frowned. "A chest?"

Ernesto nodded toward the logbook. "It's written there, near the end. You can look, but please—handle it gently."

Isabelle opened the cover. The pages were yellowed, the edges brittle. The handwriting slanted sharply, but the ink was still legible. She turned carefully until one passage caught her eye:

"The Captain says we sail with the tide in the morn. I hate to leave my sweet Ana. I have fallen in love with her these past few weeks while we have been

refitting the ship for the run around the end of the world. When my quest is through, I will return to her. The Captain says we are headed to the isles where the sea boils with life. We are sailing into unknown waters for many of us. If I shall not return, may God watch over my sweet Ana."

Her pulse quickened. "The isles where the sea boils with life," she whispered.

Jake looked up from the page. "So he did sail around the Horn."

Isabelle turned another few brittle pages, scanning each line until she found a later entry written in a shakier hand. She read aloud:

"March 12. Returned to Punta Arenas. I carry my share of the treasure in a small chest, as the Captain promised. I have returned to my sweet Ana, and we will start anew—far from the sea and its ghosts. May this be the last voyage I ever make."

Ernesto's gaze lingered on the page, then on Jake's key. "We've kept his memory, but not his burden," he said quietly. "Whatever he brought back, it didn't stay long. My grandmother said he came home sick from the voyage, and that when he died, there was little left but the logbook and the stories."

Jake shook his head. "No one should carry a burden that long."

The old man smiled faintly. "Perhaps. But someone always does."

Isabelle copied key passages into her notebook, then closed the logbook with care. "You've preserved something extraordinary," she said.

"It's all we have left of him," Ernesto replied. "He was buried with nothing but the sea."

Jake hesitated. "And the chest?"

Ernesto looked toward the darkened shelves. "If he ever brought it home, the sea took it back long ago."

A knock of wind rattled the windows, as if punctuating the thought.

Ernesto rewrapped the logbook and key in linen, placing them back into the chest. "These stay with us," he said firmly, not unkindly. "But I think you've found what you came for."

Jake nodded, gratitude and awe mingling in his chest. "More than we expected."

Ernesto smiled again, weary but kind. "Then go carefully. The sea keeps its own history—and she doesn't give it up easily."

⋅——◈——⋅

Outside, the wind had turned colder, slicing through the narrow streets. Isabelle held her satchel close, the copied notes from the logbook tucked safely inside.

"The isles where the sea boils with life," she murmured.

Jake adjusted the oilcloth bundle under his arm. "What are you thinking?"

"I think we need a to look at a map."

They stopped at the corner, looking back once at the house, its light flickering behind a curtain like a candle in the wind.

Isabelle's breath clouded the air. "Elias Grey's journey continued," she said.

Jake's voice was low. "And ours."

They turned toward the harbor, the sound of the surf mingling with the unending wind as they disappeared down the hill.

The café behind the inn was warm and dim, the air thick with the scent of stew and coffee. The stove pulsed in the corner, its soft hiss mixing with the low murmur of a radio playing an old bolero. The windows were fogged from the contrast of storm and heat, turning the reflections of other diners into wavering ghosts.

Jake and Isabelle stepped inside, stamping the cold from their boots. The innkeeper looked up from behind the counter and smiled as though she'd been waiting for them.

"Ah," she said, eyeing their new coats. "You found Diego's stall in the market! You look like real Patagonians now."

Jake grinned, brushing sleet from his collar. "Best advice we've had all trip."

The woman laughed and waved them toward a table near the stove. "Then you must be ready for dinner."

Within minutes she returned with two steaming bowls of stew and mugs of hot tea. The smell alone was enough to make Jake's shoulders drop.

They ate in comfortable silence at first, thawing out as the wind howled softly against the shutters. The world outside felt impossibly far away—just the two of them and the steady pulse of the stove.

After a while, Jake pushed his empty bowl aside and slipped the brass key from around his neck. It caught the candlelight, its faint etching of a serpent and anchor. He turned it over slowly in his palm.

"I can't stop thinking about this," he said quietly.

Isabelle looked up, her voice soft. "Your family key."

He nodded. "Pops used to say it was Silas's. I thought it was just another story. Something he made up to keep me interested in the old tales."

"And now?" Isabelle asked.

Jake exhaled slowly. "Now I know it wasn't."

She studied him for a moment, candlelight flickering in her eyes. "How does it feel—to know for sure you're a descendant of Silas Morgan?"

He gave a small, half-laugh. "Strange. Heavy, I guess. Like I've been chasing something my family started three hundred years ago without even realizing it."

"Maybe you were meant to find the rest of the story," she said softly.

He looked at the key again, thumb tracing the worn brass. "Pops used to say Silas settled somewhere in the Caribbean. Said that's how the Morgan's ended up in the Keys."

Isabelle leaned forward. "And the chest Grey gave him?"

Jake's gaze drifted toward the window, where snow traced crooked lines down the glass. "If it came home with him, nobody ever said. Maybe it was lost, maybe buried. Pops used to say Silas took his secrets to the sea. Guess he wasn't wrong."

"Or maybe it's still out there," Isabelle said, teasing lightly. "Waiting for you to find it."

Jake smiled faintly. "You already planning our next expedition?"

She grinned. "I just want to make sure we've got job security after this one."

He chuckled, shaking his head. "If we find Silas's chest, we're retiring."

"Deal," she said, clinking her mug gently against his.

For a while, they sat in quiet warmth, the storm outside fading to a steady whisper. Jake turned the key once more, then slipped it back around his neck, feeling its weight differently now—less an heirloom than a promise fulfilled.

"So," he said, pulling a folded map from Isabelle's satchel and spreading it between their mugs. "Where does the sea boil with life?"

They leaned over the map, their fingers tracing the western coast of

South America, moving north until they both stopped at a small cluster of islands off Ecuador.

Their eyes met.

"Really?" Jake said, incredulous.

A small smirk played across Isabelle's face. "Really."

They looked back at the map—and the name scrolled across the islands. *The Galápagos.*

Back in their small room above the café, Isabelle studied the map while Jake paced the narrow strip of floor between the bed and the window.

"So once again," he said, "we have to figure out how to get somewhere without being noticed."

Isabelle frowned. "By sea would take weeks. And we still can't risk commercial flights. We don't even have our passports."

Jake leaned back against the wall, rubbing a hand along his jaw. "So we're trapped at the end of the world."

The wind moaned through the eaves. For a moment, neither of them spoke.

Then Isabelle's gaze drifted toward the fogged window, where a faint red light blinked in the distance—the rotating beacon of the airport across the bay. Slowly, her expression changed.

"Jake," she said, thoughtful. "Punta Arenas is the hub for Antarctic logistics."

He looked up. "Meaning?"

"Flights to and from the research bases. Supply runs. Crews heading north after the season ends. Some of those planes go as far as Santiago or even Guayaquil for refueling."

Jake's grin spread as he caught up. "And they won't care who's in the back as long as we don't make trouble."

"Exactly," Isabelle said, eyes brightening. "If we can get on one of those flights, we can reach the coast—and from there, the Galápagos."

Jake let out a slow laugh. "You just saved us another few thousand miles of bad ideas."

Jake met Isabelle's eyes. "From the world's end," he said softly, "to the sea that boils with life."

Isabelle's smile was tired but sure. "Let's hope it's a one-way trip."

Dawn thinned the fog over the Strait, pale light skimming the wet tarmac. The air smelled of fuel and exhaust. Jake pulled his collar tight as they crossed the service road toward the hangars, breath fogging in the chill. The sign over the fence read *DAP Antarctic Airways*—letters half-peeled by wind.

Engines rumbled somewhere beyond the mist. A refitted Basler BT-67 sat at the edge of the tarmac, twin turboprops turning lazily, exhaust curling into the gray air. The old DC-3's skin was a patchwork of dull aluminum and fresh rivets, a machine that looked too stubborn to die.

Isabelle stopped near the fueling cart, eyes narrowing on a clipboard swinging from a hook.

"*Guayaquil, vía Santiago,*" she read.

Jake gave a low whistle. "That's north enough for me."

She smiled. "Then that's our plane."

Two ground crew moved through the fog, shoulders hunched against the cold. A man in a heavy parka—mid-forties, face worn by weather and long hours—checked a manifest beside the tail. Jake motioned toward him. "He'll trust you more than me."

Isabelle nodded and stepped forward, her voice steady and fluent.

"Perdón, señor. We're scientists returning from the south, trying to catch a ride north—Guayaquil, if possible. We can pay a little and stay out of the way."

The pilot looked up from his clipboard, studying them. "This flight's for cargo. No passengers."

"We understand," Isabelle said. "We'll help with the load. No trouble."

He hesitated, eyes flicking between their tired faces and the battered satchel at Isabelle's side. Finally, he sighed. "Always someone trying to flee the end of the world..." He waved toward the side doors. "Find a seat—don't touch anything frágil."

"Gracias," Isabelle said softly, relief threading through the word.

The crew swung open the tall cargo doors set into the fuselage just ahead of the tail. A short aluminum stairway led up into the dim interior. Jake followed Isabelle inside, ducking under the frame. The cabin smelled of oil and must. Cargo nets hung from the ribs of the fuselage, and condensation dripped from the curved ceiling. A crewman crouched near the bulkhead, securing the last of the crates stenciled *Valparaíso Transfer and Survey Equipment — Return.*

Jake brushed a hand along the riveted wall. "Feels like something out of a museum."

"A miracle it still flies," Isabelle murmured.

Outside, the pilot gave one last look down the length of the fuselage as the cargo door latched shut. Satisfied, he climbed the steps and disappeared into the cockpit. Moments later, his voice carried forward:

"We'll stop in Santiago for fuel. If the wind's kind, Guayaquil by nightfall."

Jake grinned. "Closest thing to first class we've had in weeks."

Isabelle smiled faintly. "Sure beats the bus."

The engines deepened to a steady thunder that vibrated through the floor. Through a small porthole, Jake watched the ground crew wave them forward along the taxiway.

The intercom crackled. "Hold short—tráfico en aproximación."

The Basler slowed to a stop near the runway threshold, props idling. Jake leaned to the window—and froze.

Out of the fog, a sleek black Pilatus PC-12 dropped through the haze, landing lights cutting sharp cones across the wet tarmac. It touched down in a spray of mist, the words *BLACK TIDE GLOBAL* flashing across its fuselage as it rolled past.

Jake's jaw tightened. He felt the sound of it more than heard it—a low, rising hum that seemed to vibrate through his ribs. "He's here."

Isabelle sat up beside him, eyes narrowing against the glare. "Serrano."

Jake shook his head slightly. "Luca, rather, I'd wager."

The PC-12 taxied down the line of hangars, its strobes blinking through the fog like a heartbeat. Even as it vanished into the white, the hum lingered—an echo that seemed to fill the night.

Neither of them moved. Their breath misted in the chill of the cabin, each exhale loud even over the drone of the engines, and for the first time, the distance between them and their pursuers felt measured not in miles, but in moments.

The pilot's voice returned, brisk now. "Runway clear. Listos."

The engines surged.

The Basler began its roll, heavy and certain, gathering speed until the tremor under their feet turned to weightlessness. The town fell away beneath them—rows of rooftops, the harbor, the thin silver thread of the Strait stretching toward Antarctica. The sky ahead opened wide and gray.

Jake let out a slow breath. "Goodbye, world's end—and Luca."

The engines settled into a rhythmic drone. Isabelle sat beside him, watching light spill over the horizon.

"Guayaquil," she said softly. "The gateway to the Galápagos."

He lifted a hand to the key hanging from his neck, fingers closing around it. The metal was warm from his touch, heavy with meaning.

The Basler climbed through the fog, wings flashing in the new sunlight. Below, the Strait glinted like a blade between continents.

The last edge of the world fell away beneath them, and ahead waited the sea that boiled with life.

CHAPTER THIRTY

The Hunt at the Edge

The Pilatus PC-12 broke through the cloud ceiling and touched down hard at Punta Arenas International, tires screeching on wet tarmac. Spray arced off the landing gear and vanished into the gray. Luca watched from his seat as the flaps eased up, the vibration settling into a steady hum. He'd been awake for twenty hours, though fatigue registered as something distant, buried beneath the rhythm of movement and objective.

The plane taxied past a line of idle fuel trucks and turned toward the far hangars, its propeller slicing the mist into ribbons. The runway lights strobed through the cockpit glass—green, amber, red—reflected in Luca's eyes as the aircraft slowed.

Across the airfield, on the opposite taxiway, another sound rose—a deeper, rougher growl. A DAP Basler BT-67 sat at the hold-short line, props spinning, wings slick with moisture. Its pilot waited for clearance, radio chatter crackling over the tower frequency.

For a moment, both aircraft existed within the same pocket of fog—the PC-12 rolling past, the Basler poised for takeoff. They were close enough that if the air had been clear, Luca might have seen the blurred outline of the other plane, might have even noticed the figures inside: a man and a woman in worn jackets, faces drawn but determined. Instead, the world was gray and depthless. Three engines, two directions, divided by seconds.

The Basler's lights flashed once, twice, then it lurched forward, gaining speed down the main runway. Its twin props clawed through the mist, the roar rising to a scream as it lifted into the fog, disappearing completely within seconds. Only the low thunder of its passage remained, fading toward the north.

The PC-12 turned into position at the edge of the field, water streaming down its fuselage. The co-pilot's voice came over the intercom, muffled by static. "Welcome to Punta Arenas, sir."

Luca unbuckled his seat belt and checked his watch: 06:14. He glanced toward the window but saw nothing—only the blurred reflection of his own face against the glass.

He gathered his coat and the small duffel at his feet, every motion measured. Outside, ground crew moved like ghosts in high-visibility jackets, their shouts lost in the wind. He descended the metal steps to the tarmac, boots splashing through shallow puddles, the cold biting at his skin even through the gloves.

The fog wrapped around everything—planes, hangars, horizon—erasing distance. Somewhere out there, engines still echoed faintly, growing softer with each second. Luca stood for a moment, listening, eyes narrowed toward the sound he couldn't place. Then he turned toward the road, the phone in his pocket buzzing with unread requests from Algeciras.

Behind him, the airfield faded. The fog closed like a curtain. Two paths had crossed and passed through each other—one rising, one descending—neither aware how close the other had come.

Rain hammered against the glass wall of the office, turning the lights of the port below into streaks of gold and white. Tankers moved slowly through the Strait, their outlines distorted by the storm. Each flash of lightning threw Victor Serrano's reflection back at him—doubled, fractured—one face upright, the other trembling slightly behind the glass.

He pressed a hand against the window. The glass was cold enough to burn. Beneath the cuff of his tailored sleeve, his leg trembled in a restless rhythm he couldn't stop. The muscle jumped on its own accord, an arrhythmic pulse that climbed through his thigh into his ribs. He clenched his jaw until he felt the dull ache of his teeth grinding together. The tremor continued anyway.

He turned back toward the desk. A half-dozen reports lay open across the polished surface. He tried to pick up the pen lying beside them, but it slipped from his fingers, striking the glass edge and falling to the floor.

Victor stared at it for a moment before crouching, slower than he meant to. The simple act of balance felt treacherous now, his center of gravity a moving target. When he straightened again, breath shallow, the tremor had grown worse.

The papers blurred before him. His right hand jerked once, sending a splash of water from his untouched glass across the top page. Rage hit before thought. He swept the files aside, the crash of paper and glass sharp against the rain. The tumbler rolled off the desk and shattered on the tile.

He stayed like that a moment—head down, breathing hard—until the pounding in his chest steadied. When he looked up, the reflection in the window had changed again. Lightning forked across the Strait, washing the world in white. In its glow, he saw himself doubled and shaking—one clear, one blurred by the glass.

He muttered to that reflection, almost under his breath. "Every hour," he said, "the body betrays a little more."

He opened the drawer, found the bottle of pills, and shook one into his palm. His hand trembled so badly it almost bounced free. He swallowed it dry, the pill scraping his throat, then leaned forward on the desk until the shaking eased.

Thunder rolled close. The window flexed slightly with the pressure. For a heartbeat, the whole tower seemed to breathe.

"Sir?"

It was his aide. She hesitated when she saw the wreck of the desk. "Word from Chile," she said. "Moretti's landed in Punta Arenas."

Victor didn't turn. He stared at the rain. His fingers drummed against the desktop—not consciously—just the residual tremor acting of its own will.

"Get him on the phone," he said quietly.

"Already did, sir—he's on line one."

Victor nodded once. The tremor in his leg shifted upward again, turning into a small, visible shake at his shoulder. He gripped the desk to steady it, eyes narrowing on the reflection.

He picked up the phone and jabbed at the blinking light. "No more patience," he said. The words came clipped, uneven. "They lead us to it—or we squeeze until they do. Capture them. Make them talk."

Luca's response came calm and collected. "About time."

Victor dropped the phone back on its cradle.

He exhaled slowly, control returning in measured breaths. The medication dulled the tremor, but not the rage that followed it. He pressed both hands flat on the desk, letting the pulse in his palms sync with the hum of the storm.

Across the glass, the reflection steadied—just enough to look human again. He studied it, as though searching for the man he remembered being. "Before my body completely fails me," he whispered.

Outside, lightning struck the water, illuminating the port cranes in a sheet of light. For an instant, Victor's shadow loomed across the office wall—tall, unsteady, and trembling with the same rhythm as the storm.

Wind pushed at Luca as he climbed the last spit of scrub toward the ridge. The hill fell away beneath his boots into a shallow bowl of town: roofs half-swallowed by fog, a thread of road that led like a pale vein toward the harbor, and the docks glinting faint through mist. Chimney smoke rose in thin columns; a gull screamed somewhere below and was answered by another from the piers.

The Hilux sat crooked on the shoulder, its metal skin dulled by salt and grit. The hood was propped with a length of pipe; tools lay in the lee of the fender like offerings to a stalled god. Frost rimed the windshield; a dark ring of coolant stained the ground beneath the radiator. A snapped belt lay on the gravel—cleanly torn, as if whatever gave way had done so in a single, reluctant motion.

He moved with the same economy he brought to everything: gloves on, fingers checking points and seams. The engine was cold. No recent tire marks on the soft shoulder suggested it hadn't been dragged far since it stopped; only a set of footprints led away from the driver's side into the scrub and then faded as the slope shallowed. A boot tread, measured steps—no hurry—pointing down toward the road and the town beyond.

Luca crouched and studied the prints, the way the toes pressed into the grit. He noted the flat tread pattern and the cadence. He let the detail sit in his head like a notation on a ledger. Close enough to town to walk. They'd taken shelter where people gathered—shops near the harbor, a cheap inn, wherever heat and coffee conferred temporary anonymity.

A gull wheeled and the wind tried to pry his collar open. He rose and walked the rim of the shoulder, looking down on the map of the town as if the houses and lanes were tokens on a chessboard. From here he could see the shortest route: a narrow lane that funneled into the pier road, two blocks to the hostal district, and the small square where fishermen still hawked bait. If they had wanted to disappear, that's where they would have gone.

He picked up the footprints where they became less defined—an occasional heel, a smear in the grass—then the lane itself. The town smelled of diesel and frying oil, a comfort of human commerce that made the air taste less like the empty sea. People were beginning the slow business of another day: a man sweeping a stoop, a woman hauling a crate, a child chasing a wayward hen.

Luca kept his head low. He did not hurry. He calibrated his steps to the rhythm of the place, watching doorways and faces, cataloguing the kinds of shoes he passed, the cracked patterns of the plaster. Each small observation folded into the larger calculation: which bar would offer privacy; which innkeeper would be gullible; which fisherman would trade silence for a carton of fuel or the promise of a cut.

At the corner where the lane met the main street, he paused and looked back up the slope. The Hilux sat like a dark punctuation mark against the gray. They had abandoned a vehicle and chosen human shelter over the cold of the ridge. That choice told him enough—the hunted favored warmth, routine, small comforts. They were not after spectacle; they were after an answer, and people who go looking for answers do not often plan to stay hidden once they find the scent.

He stepped around a stack of crates, pulled the collar of his jacket higher, and blended into the muted cadence of morning. The town would show him where to look. He intended to follow it all the way to the harbor and beyond—if need be, to the edges of the world.

The bell above the door jingled once as Luca stepped inside.

The air changed immediately—stew, coffee, and the faint sweetness of frying bread mixing with the smell of wet wool. Condensation streaked the front window where a small heater struggled against the chill.

A woman stood behind the counter, wiping the same spot with a damp rag. She looked up when she heard the door close and froze for half a second, eyes darting to the stranger's coat, the boots still dripping from rain.

"Señor, the kitchen isn't open yet," she said.

"I'm not hungry."

He drew a photograph from the inner pocket of his jacket and set it on the counter. The paper left a small circle of moisture. "Have you seen these two?"

Her hand hesitated over the rag. "We have many guests."

"I doubt you have many like them in a place like this."

She risked a glance down at the photo. Her eyes lingered a fraction too long before she shook her head. "No. I haven't seen them."

Luca let the silence stretch. Outside, a truck passed, tires hissing over wet cobblestone. He could hear the heater's fan clicking unevenly, the kind of sound that filled quiet rooms when people were afraid to speak. It was all the confirmation he needed.

He picked up the photo, slid a small card across the counter in its place. "If they return," he said softly, "call this number. Any time, day or night."

The woman nodded too quickly. "Of course."

He smiled—a thin, professional courtesy that never reached his eyes—then turned for the door. The bell jingled again as he stepped back into the wind.

Through the fogged window she watched him walk away until his shape dissolved into the gray street. Only then did she exhale and wipe the circle of moisture from the counter, though her hand still trembled.

The municipal archive sat near the harbor, a squat building of chipped stone and peeling blue paint that looked older than its records. The front door creaked open under the push of wind, carrying the smell of salt and old paper through the narrow hall. Inside, a single bulb buzzed above the counter where an elderly archivist sat, glasses slipping down the bridge of his nose as he catalogued water-stained ledgers.

Luca crossed the floorboards that flexed beneath his boots. The walls were lined with tall shelves, every one bowed with damp folios and curling charts. Somewhere behind them, a gull cried, its echo finding its way through the cracked windowpanes.

"Morning," Luca said.

The man looked up, cautious but polite. "We're not officially open until nine."

"I won't be long." Luca drew a folded photograph from his pocket and set it on the counter. The archivist leaned forward, blinking behind the lenses.

"Have you seen them?"

The old man hesitated. "Yes... yesterday. The woman spoke good Spanish, Columbian I would guess." He adjusted his glasses and tapped the open ledger beside him. "They were asking about eighteenth-century ships with English crews that passed through the Strait. Privateers, merchantmen—anything from that time."

Luca nodded once. "And you had records?"

"Some," the archivist said with a shrug. "Not much survived the fires, but they looked through what we had. Took notes. Very polite. The woman, especially."

Luca's eyes flicked toward the rows of bound books behind him. "Did they mention where they were headed next?"

The archivist frowned, trying to recall. "When they left, I heard them talking about the old church on the hill—the Capilla de los Navegantes." He gave a small smile. "Tourists always end up there. It's the view, I think."

Luca returned the photograph to his coat pocket. "The church," he repeated, as if testing the word for weight.

"Yes, sir. Old place. Sailors' chapel. Half the stones up there came from ship ballast."

Luca thanked him with a brief nod, turned for the door, and stepped back into the cold wind. Outside, the fog had thinned, the harbor beginning to take shape—cranes, warehouses, the outlines of ships waiting at anchor.

He paused at the edge of the steps, the chill stinging his lungs as he looked toward the gray rise of the hill in the distance. Somewhere beyond the mist, the chapel waited, its bell tower leaning into the wind.

Luca started walking.

Wind clawed at the hillside as Luca climbed, the cold biting through his coat.

The path twisted between stones and low brush, slick from the drizzle. Ahead, the Capilla de los Navegantes emerged from the fog—its white-wash weathered to gray, its small bell tower leaning into the wind. The wooden doors stood open, candlelight flickering faintly inside.

He paused at the threshold. The air within was still and warmer, heavy with the scent of wax and old incense. Through the open doors he saw the simple interior—wooden pews, a crucifix, and a handful of saints' icons.

Luca stepped inside, boots creaking on the boards. The sound echoed softly in the small nave. He moved with deliberate precision, eyes sweeping the altar, the floorboards, the walls. He touched the edge of the lectern, traced the seams where plaster met stone, checked behind the icons for anything hidden. Nothing. Only silence and the faint hiss of the wind through a cracked pane.

Turning back toward the door, he noticed the graveyard behind the chapel—rows of stones half-lost to fog and time. The ground was uneven, the grass slick with rain. He stepped out again, boots sinking slightly into the wet soil.

He moved among the headstones, reading what names he could. Most were worn smooth, the letters eroded to ghostly impressions. Then one marker caught his eye—a stone leaning under its own weight, the inscription nearly erased.

He crouched, he could tell the stone had recently been brushed by a hand trying to read the inscription: *Tomás Blay, natural de Inglaterra — 1719.*

Below the name, faint but unmistakable, was the engraving of a serpent coiled around an anchor.

Luca's breath clouded the air as he studied it. He'd seen this same emblem carved deep into the stone chamber on La Isla de Sombras. Elias Grey's mark.

He glanced lower and saw a small bronze plaque embedded in the base of the headstone, newer than the rest: *Familia Vega Carvallo — Custodios desde 1831.*

That single word—custodios—landed with weight. *Guardians. Keepers.*

He pulled his phone from his coat and snapped a photo, rain spattering the screen.

The message to Victor was short, clinical: *Grave located. Markings match Isla de Sombras. Name: Tomás Blay. Need local next of kin.*

He waited, watching the fog roll between the stones until the reply flashed across the display: *Identified: Tomás Blay. Closest living kin—Ernesto Vega. Residence near the harbor.*

Luca pocketed the phone, gave the stone one last look. The serpent's curve caught the light like something alive.

He straightened, collar snapping in the wind, and started back down the hill. Behind him, the candle inside the chapel guttered once and went out.

By the time Luca reached the harbor, the rain had turned to a steady curtain.

He followed the narrow road along the seawall until the pavement gave way to gravel and the houses thinned to weather-beaten shacks.

Fishing nets hung from porches like faded banners, dripping into puddles below. The air smelled of fish, diesel, and kerosene, undercut by the sour reek of low tide.

A single light glowed ahead through the storm.

He stopped before a small seaside house, the windows clouded with condensation, the flicker of a lantern inside shifting across the curtains. A hand-painted sign over the door read *Vega Carvallo.*

He knocked once. The wood felt soft with moisture.

After a long pause, the door opened just enough for one gray eye to appear in the gap.

The old man studied the stranger on his porch for several seconds before saying, "Yes?"

"You're Vega," Luca said, voice low and certain. Not a question.

Vega's gaze narrowed. "Depends who's asking."

"I'm looking for two travelers," Luca said. "A man and a woman. They came to you asking about the chapel."

Vega's expression barely changed. "I don't know who you mean. Now go. I'm busy."

He started to close the door, but Luca's hand came up, palm against the wood.

"Careful," Vega warned. "You're not from here."

"That's right," Luca said. Then he pushed.

The door swung inward under the force, striking the wall. Vega stumbled back a step as Luca stepped across the threshold.

"You shouldn't have come," Vega said. His voice shook—not with fear, but anger.

Luca's eyes moved over the photographs on the wall, committing each one to memory. "They were here," he said quietly. "Where did they go?"

"I told you," Vega said. "I don't know anyone like that."

Luca turned to face him fully. "You're a poor liar."

Vega's jaw set. "And you're trespassing."

Luca took one slow step forward. The floor creaked. The storm rattled the windows in their frames.

"Don't make this harder than it has to be."

Vega didn't move. "You think you're the first to come looking for him?" he said, voice low. "Others have tried. The island keeps its secrets."

That stopped Luca. "Which island?"

Vega said nothing. His eyes flicked, almost imperceptibly, toward the photograph of the chapel.

Luca saw the movement. He closed the distance in an instant, fist tightening in the old man's shirt. The lamp quivered, shadows jerking across the walls.

"Where did they go?"

The first impact was dull, the sound swallowed by thunder. Vega's breath caught. He sagged against the wall, a hand pressed to his ribs.

Still, he glared back, defiant. "You have no right," he rasped.

"Tell me," Luca said quietly, almost gentle. The knife slid from his pocket, the blade catching a shard of light just long enough for Vega to see.

Rain hammered the tin roof. Wind moaned through the eaves.

Vega's eyes dropped, the fight gone out of them. "Galápagos," he whispered.

The word hung between them—fragile, final.

Luca released him, stepping back. The old man slid down the wall until he found the chair behind him.

Luca glanced once more at the photographs—the chapel, the fishing boats, the generations of faces staring out from frames of salt-stained wood. He said nothing. He didn't have to.

Outside, the door banged against the wind as he stepped into the storm.

Rain lashed the harbor, the smell of the sea rising sharp and cold.

He walked without looking back.

The storm had broken by the time Victor returned to his desk. The rain on the windows had thinned to beads, streaking slowly down the glass. Beyond the port, the lights of Algeciras glowed like embers under low clouds, their reflections rippling across the water. The world was quiet again — too quiet.

He sat with his back straight, the tremor in his leg dulled to a faint quiver. The medication left his head clear but hollow, like the calm after a fever. A half-empty glass of water rested near the pills, untouched since the last dose.

A soft tone from his phone signaled an incoming call.

He tapped the speaker button. Luca's voice came through the encrypted line, steady as ever.

"Vega gave up the location — Galápagos. That's where they're headed. Must have just missed them."

Victor leaned forward, fingertips steepled beneath his chin. "Any collateral damage?"

"None." A pause. "Minimal."

"Good," Victor said. His voice was level again, stripped of the volatility that had ruled it hours before.

"Deploy the intercept teams. One to Ecuador for logistics, one to the islands."

"Sure."

"I'll meet you there, Luca."

The call ended with a brief click. The sound of rain filled the room again, soft against the glass. Victor exhaled through his nose and turned back to the map on the screen.

He zoomed in on the Pacific — the archipelago spreading like dark stones across the sea. A place beyond the usual reach of men, where the old routes ended.

He watched the blinking cursor mark Luca's current position.

For a long moment, he said nothing. The tremor returned faintly in his fingers, but his hand stayed steady on the desk. The reflection in the window stared back — the same man as before, but smaller now, more contained.

Behind him, the door opened softly. His secretary's voice carried in from the threshold. "Orders confirmed. Flights are preparing, sir."

Victor didn't look away from the map. "Good. Ensure all channels are dark — no chatter, no tracking."

"Yes, sir." The door clicked shut again.

He reached for the remote and killed the office lights, leaving only the glow of the map against the glass.

For the first time in hours, the tremor stopped completely.

"Enough games," he murmured.

Outside, the clouds began to break apart over the Strait. The first edge of moonlight slid through, silvering the cranes along the dock. In its reflection, Victor's silhouette leaned toward the map — still, silent, and very much alive.

The wind over the airfield carried the taste of rain and jet exhaust. Floodlights washed the tarmac in pale yellow, cutting long shadows beneath the wings of the PC-12. Mechanics moved like silhouettes through the mist, removing the last tie-downs, their voices lost under the drone of turbines winding up.

Luca crossed the apron without hurry, coat collar up against the cold. His boots splashed through puddles, each step a sharp counterpoint to the hum of the engine.

He paused at the base of the stairs, looking once toward the dark edge of the field where the ridge rose — somewhere beyond it, the road, the chapel, the harbor, the man who had given him the final word.

Galápagos.

He climbed aboard.

The cabin lights were dim, the air smelled faintly of aviation fuel and wet cloth. He set his duffel in the narrow seat beside him and buckled in as the door sealed.

From the cockpit, the co-pilot gave a quick thumbs-up. "Clear to taxi."

Luca nodded once.

Outside, the propeller spun faster, its rotation blurring into a disc of light. The plane began to roll, tires hissing on the wet runway. Rain streaked across the windows, the lights of Punta Arenas smearing into bands of gold and red behind the glass.

He rested his hand on the armrest and watched the reflection of his face ripple over the windowpane. The vibration climbed through the frame as the engine throttled up, a steady, living heartbeat.

The PC-12 accelerated, the pressure of the seatback rising against his shoulders. At the edge of the runway, the nose lifted; earth fell away.

Below, the lights of the coast dissolved into cloud.

For a long moment, there was only the sound of the engine and the faint creak of the fuselage as the plane climbed through the weather. Luca glanced at the altimeter, then toward the compass display glowing faintly in the dark.

"North," he said quietly.

His voice was barely audible above the turbines. "To the islands."

The plane banked toward the unseen horizon, swallowed by the night. The storm followed behind, closing the sky like a door.

CHAPTER THIRTY-ONE

The Map and the Margin

The Basler's wheels hit hard, skidding once before the tires caught in a screech of smoke. The cabin had grown steadily warmer over the last hour, but as the engines slowed, the real heat arrived—dense, wet, alive. Outside, Guayaquil shimmered—cranes over the river, palms in molten haze, jet fuel and wet concrete thick in the air.

"From the world's end to the equator in a day," Isabelle murmured.

Jake wiped his neck with his sleeve. "Feels like a different planet."

Up front, their pilot—Rojas—leaned through the cockpit door, grin tired but genuine. "This is as far north as I go. But if you're still chasing west..." He pointed across the tarmac to a smaller twin-engine plane gleaming white and gray, the crest of the Charles Darwin Foundation bright on its tail. "Captain Camila Ortega. She flies supplies to the islands twice a week. Tell her I sent you—and that she still owes me a generator." He tipped a hand in parting. "Good luck, mis amigos."

Heat rose in visible waves as they crossed the apron. The Basler's props slowly spun to a stop behind them, its rumble fading under the whine of cicadas and distant thunder. Ahead, a Twin Otter sat ready—short takeoff wings, twin turboprops ticking in the heat. At the far hangar, a woman in khaki flight overalls checked straps on crates marked *SANTA CRUZ / ISABELA – RESEARCH SUPPLIES*. Dark braid, mirrored lenses—someone who'd lived too many hours in the sun.

"You two lost," she called, "or just brave enough to wander out here?"

"Captain Ortega?" Isabelle asked, brows raised. "Rojas said you might be heading for the islands."

"—And that you still owe him a generator," Jake added with a grin.

Camila smiled. "Rojas still trading favors, I see."

Her gaze flicked over them—travel-stained clothes, watchful eyes. "You don't look like scientists."

"Technically, I am a scientist—marine archaeologist," Isabelle said, the corners of her mouth slightly upturned. "Isabelle." She offered a hand.

Camila accepted the handshake with pleasant surprise.

Jake looked at Isabelle with amusement, then back to Camila. "I'm not," he said, "but we can pay and help load the cargo." He added, shaking her hand. "Jake."

Camila tapped the cracked bezel of the watch at her wrist; a Saint Christopher medal flashed from around her neck. "Cash is nice. Hands are better. Help me load, and you've got two seats. We leave as soon as we're loaded."

They fell in beside her, the three of them moving through the heavy air—lift, pass, tie-down—until sweat streaked their sleeves and the rhythm steadied their nerves.

When they finished, Camila nodded toward the plane. "Good work."

Isabelle wiped her brow with her sleeve. "Been doing this long?"

"A few years. Air Force before this," Camila said. "Cargo and people. Quit when the politics started outweighing the payload. You can only fly blind so long before you start wondering what's below you." She studied them a moment longer, something like respect behind the humor. "You look like you've already flown through worse weather."

"Just a couple squalls," Jake said.

Camila slammed a panel shut; the compass on the control panel trembled, needle twitching east, west, east. "She's got some miles on her," Camila said, tapping the compass. "Old magnetics never did like this latitude."

Isabelle pressed a hand to the compass in her pocket.

Thunder rolled close. The sun slid low, turning the runway to liquid amber.

Camila finished her forms and called over her shoulder. "Still sure about going farther west?"

Isabelle nodded. "We have to."

"Then climb aboard before I change my mind."

The cabin smelled of canvas, oil, and metal. Jake dropped the few things they had beside a stack of medical kits while Camila settled into the cockpit, hands sure on the switches. Jake and Isabelle buckled into the seats directly behind the cockpit. Propellers blurred, prop wash flinging dust and heat around them.

Through the window, Rojas lifted a hand in farewell as he supervised cargo being loaded for the flight back south. The engines deepened to a steady roar, a sound Isabelle felt in her ribs before she heard it. The Twin Otter began to roll. She felt Jake's shoulder brush hers, grounding her as the wheels bumped once, then lifted. Below, the city unspooled into rivers and mangrove, the Pacific stretching out like hammered gold. For the first time in days, it felt like they weren't running from something—but toward something.

The engines hummed like a heartbeat in the dark. For a while, the lights of Guayaquil glimmered along the coast like embers in fog, then were gone. Ahead lay only sky and sea—both black, both endless. The Twin Otter cut through it in steady rhythm, the red glow of the cockpit instruments painting soft halos across the cabin walls.

Camila's voice came over the headset—low, even, touched with humor. "Settle in. Nothing but ocean between us and anything else for a while."

Both Jake and Isabelle leaned their heads back against the seats, shoulders sinking as the hum settled around them. They'd spent the day chasing horizons, and this was the first time the motion felt still.

Later, conversation drifted back like the tide.

"You've done this run often?" Isabelle asked.

"Twice a week, sometimes more," Camila said. "I move equipment, food, spare parts—whatever keeps the scientists from going feral. The Galápagos live off these runs. Out there, it's nothing but rock, heat, and whatever the sea decides to give you."

"You always fly alone?" Jake asked.

Camila nodded. "I prefer it that way. Sometimes the radio goes quiet for hours—just me, the engine, and the stars."

Isabelle glanced toward the window. The stars were bright enough to cast reflections in the glass—faint ghosts drifting across her face. "Elias Grey would've known this silence," she said without thinking. "And these stars."

Camila tilted her head. "Grey?"

Jake answered. "A sailor—the one who started this whole mess a couple of centuries ago."

Camila's mouth curved. "A good one?"

Isabelle's voice softened. "One of the best, I think."

Camila didn't press further. The hum of the engines filled the pause. Isabelle retrieved her journal from the satchel and flipped through it until she found notes from Thomas Blythe's logbook: *the sea that burns with life*. She traced it once with her thumb before closing the cover again.

"You two chasing stories," Camila asked, "or running from them?"

"Hard to tell the difference sometimes," Jake said.

The hum settled back in. Isabelle leaned forward. "When we get there—where do we even start? The Galápagos aren't small. Grey could've landed anywhere."

Jake worked his thumb along the edge of the key around his neck. "Not anywhere. The Specter was a brigantine. Laden, she'd draw about thirteen—maybe fourteen feet. He'd want at least a couple feet under the keel at low tide, so call it twenty to twenty-five feet minimum in the approach. To anchor safely, better in twenty-five to thirty-five."

Camila's eyes stayed on the instruments, but she was listening. "That already kills half the archipelago. Most of the small islets are bare lava and shoal out fast. Poor holding, too—lava plate won't bite an anchor."

"Then he'd need a pocket," Jake said. "Cliffs to break the wind, a bowl that hides the masts, sand or sand-over-lava for holding. Room to swing or set two hooks. And fresh water close enough to cask."

Isabelle nodded, the shape of it forming. "Deepwater approach, concealed anchorage, some way to provision without being seen."

Camila considered. "Santa Cruz has decent lee corners, but they're exposed to traffic. If you want places that keep secrets—Isabela. Biggest island, multiple volcanoes, inlets and lava tubes, deep embayments. Hard land, but there are coves where you can sit in thirty feet and no one at sea will see your topmasts unless they are right on top of you."

"A place to disappear," Jake said.

"Exactly what Grey needed," Isabelle murmured.

Camila's mouth tilted. "Then start there. I've got a run to the Darwin Station, but once I drop the gear, I could take you on to Isabela. Haven't had a proper adventure in a while."

An hour later, the horizon grew a shade less black—a ridge taking shape against the stars. Then another. Then five more. The Galápagos emerged as darker shadows on a dark sea, their outlines jagged under a thin wash of moonlight. Somewhere below, surf stitched a pale line along the rocks.

Camila throttled back. "Inbound to Baltra," she said. "Hold on—the wind here likes to make things interesting."

The descent was rougher than Isabelle expected. The plane dipped once, hard, then steadied as Camila's hands worked the controls with quiet precision. Runway lights appeared—thin, amber, distant—and drew closer.

They touched down with a double bounce. The engines reversed, roaring against the dark until the sound dissolved into a low, steady whine. Outside the window, the world glowed faintly under the moon—the ground black and cracked, steam catching silver where the light found it. Beyond the short strip of runway, the sea shimmered like glass, and across a narrow channel the larger island of Santa Cruz rose in silhouette, its volcanic ridges etched against the stars.

After taxiing off the runway, Camila powered down the systems and unbuckled her harness. "Welcome to Baltra," she said. "Watch your step—the ground's younger than we are."

Jake chuckled softly, rubbing his eyes. "I'll take that over ice any day."

Floodlights buzzed with moths as they worked beneath them, pale wings batting at hot glass. The world beyond the cones of light was soft and breathing—the hangar's dark bulk, the sky rinsed with moon. The air was thick with warmth and the faint sweetness of volcanic stone.

Camila signed the Baltra manifest on the tailgate of a dented pickup. "We'll cross to Santa Cruz and sleep a few hours," she said, flicking a glance at the stacked crates. "Most of this goes to the Darwin Station in the morning. After that, if the weather behaves, we can head on to Isabela."

Jake rolled the last drum into place and tightened the strap. "We'll be ready."

Camila tapped the tailgate once in satisfaction. "Good. Help me load what's headed for the Station into the Jeep. Easier to move it now than at dawn."

They worked beneath the floodlights, the air humming with moths and heat. Together they stacked crates marked *CHARLES DARWIN FOUN-DATION – RESEARCH SUPPLIES* until the Jeep's suspension groaned under the weight. The metal was warm to the touch, smelling faintly of oil and salt. When they finished, Camila latched the tailgate and brushed her hands on her flight overalls. "That'll do. We'll offload first thing, before the sun gets any ideas."

Isabelle looked up toward the ridge where haze hovered in the moonlight. Even at night the ground felt awake, the silence alive with small sounds.

They loaded into the battered Jeep, its dashboard patched with tape and sun cracks. Camila turned the key; the engine coughed to life. Camila eased them through the gate, where a sleepy guard waved without looking up from his phone.

The short road from the airstrip ended at a dim ferry slip. A flat barge waited under a single bulb, the water around it black and glassy. They rolled aboard with two other trucks, the engine idling as the ferry nosed across the narrow channel. The night was so still that Isabelle could hear the slap of the current against the hull and the faint hiss of wind through the volcanic brush.

On the far side—Santa Cruz—the road climbed through low, dark hills. The headlights carved narrow tunnels of visibility through black lava and coarse grass. Every so often the beam caught movement: crabs like shifting stones, a marine iguana soaking the last warmth from the asphalt, the sudden round flare of an owl's eyes before it lifted into the dark. Steam curled from a fissure, a thin white thread that drifted away in the wind.

Jake dozed, arms folded. Isabelle stayed awake, feeling the island—the way the air lay on her skin, the stillness with weight. The road wound down through cacti and mist until the sea's scent returned.

Puerto Ayora appeared by degrees—first a soft glow on the horizon, then low buildings, then lamps strung along a narrow street. Camila parked beside a stucco inn with a veranda and two lazy ceiling fans turning over the doorway. A generator purred somewhere out back. The night smelled of warm stone and flowers.

Inside, a clerk slid keys across the counter and stifled a yawn. Camila exchanged a few words in Spanish, then handed them a key.

"Showers are honest," she said. "Beds softer than they look." She tilted her head toward the faint hush of surf. "Go see the water first—it's worth it."

The hallway was lined with faded charts and photographs of sun-burned researchers beside turtles the size of bathtubs. Ceiling fans moved the air in patient circles. The room was small—whitewashed walls, stone floor, a bed under a net—and oddly perfect.

Jake and Isabelle dropped their things and followed the sound of surf outside.

A sand path wound through low scrub to a narrow curve of bay. The beach looked black where it met the water, glassy and fine. When Isabelle stepped into it barefoot, cool grit sifted between her toes. Waves slid up and withdrew with a hush, and as they did, the sand beneath them briefly caught fire—blue-green ghosts blooming and fading.

Isabelle laughed softly. She took another step; the halo followed. "Bio-luminescence," she said, though the word felt small.

Jake waded ankle-deep and dragged his foot in a slow arc; the water wrote light around his ankle and dissolved. "Looks like walking on sparks," he said.

Isabelle's voice was barely above the hush of waves. "Where the sea boils with life..."

The wind came off the bay warm and clean, carrying the faint sweetness of something blooming in the dunes. Frigate birds drifted as smudges against the stars.

They lingered there a while, saying little, the surf whispering at their feet. When the glow finally dimmed with the tide, they turned back toward the inn, shoes in hand.

Camila was still awake under the veranda, notebook open beside a half-empty bottle. She poured three small cups. "Nightcap," she said.

Jake took his and sat. The drink tasted dark and steady, like a door closing softly.

A low sound came beneath them—so gentle it took a breath to hear, like a giant animal turning in sleep. Cups ticked together; dust sifted from the rafter.

Camila looked up. "Volcano breathing," she said. "You learn not to count the seconds between."

No one spoke. The night pressed close and comfortable around them, full of insect songs and the whisper of the bay. Isabelle reviewed her journal. Jake's knee touched hers beneath the table and stayed there.

"Four hours," Camila said, glancing at her watch. "Then we go."

They took the quiet as permission and climbed the stairs. Isabelle rinsed her face, lay back, and watched the fan's slow spokes of shadow. The ground's subtle pulse reached even here, a breath under the mattress. She drifted with it.

When Isabelle woke, the window had gone pewter. The bay beyond had turned to metal, the surface just beginning to take light. She dressed while Jake still slept and stepped out barefoot onto the veranda.

Camila was already there, elbows on the rail, the ember of her cigarette small and stubborn. Jake joined them a minute later, hair flattened on one side, eyes clearer.

They stood together without speaking. Farther out, a frigate bird skimmed the water and turned, its wingtip tracing the sea.

Camila crushed the cigarette and flicked it into a tin. "Load in ten," she said. "We'll be over the channel before the heat has time to think about it."

The world felt newly assembled—stone waking, water brightening, air lifting from the night. Somewhere ahead, a line threaded forward, simple as a heading on a chart. They only had to follow it.

The light came thin and sharp over Santa Cruz, silvering the palms and the roofs of the harbor. The road east followed the curve of the bay, quiet except for the soft rumble of the engine and the cries of frigate birds overhead.

They reached the Charles Darwin Research Station just as the sun cleared the ridge. The compound looked more like an outpost than a laboratory—low white buildings and solar panels scattered among palms and volcanic rock, the sea glinting beyond. Scientists and technicians were already moving through the courtyard, the air filled with the sound of rolling carts and gulls.

Camila parked beside a row of fuel drums and cut the engine. "Ten minutes to unload," she said, climbing out. "Try not to start any revolutions."

Jake grinned as he swung down to the gravel. Isabelle followed, the warmth already rising off the stone. Together they unlatched the tailgate and began passing crates down, each one stenciled with the crest of the Charles Darwin Foundation—filters, sensors, field rations, and the strange necessities that kept research alive on the islands.

A young logistics officer waved them toward a corrugated warehouse where workers were already unloading the freshly delivered supplies. Among them stood Dr. Renata Solis, a marine biologist with sun-faded sleeves and a clipboard tucked under one arm.

Camila greeted her easily. "Morning, Renata. Got your filters, sensors, and whatever mystery boxes Quito sent this time."

Renata laughed. "You always arrive when the air conditioners die." Her gaze flicked to Jake and Isabelle. "New crew?"

"Guests," Camila said. "Historical fieldwork."

That earned a curious tilt of the head. "Not our usual cargo," Renata said. "Come in out of the sun. You can tell me what you're looking for."

Inside, the main office was cool and dim, its walls lined with maps and framed photographs of ships, reefs, and tortoises. A large chart of the archipelago dominated the far wall, threaded with red lines tracing research routes and old sailing paths.

Isabelle's eyes caught on the sweep of Isabela Island—long, uneven, crowned by black ridges. She stepped closer. "You keep hydrographic records here?"

Renata nodded. "Spanish copies, British surveys, whaler logs—whatever survived humidity and neglect. Why?"

"Eighteenth-century anchorages," Isabelle said. "We're following the track of an English brigantine believed to have sheltered somewhere along Isabela's west coast."

Renata's curiosity sharpened. She crossed to a drawer of rolled charts and pulled one free. "That coastline is treacherous. But there's something—here."

She unrolled the map across a steel table. The parchment was yellowed, the ink brown with age. Near the western rim of Isabela, a small crescent bay had been labeled in careful script: *Caleta del Fuego Dormido — Cove of the Sleeping Fire*. Beneath, a later hand had added: *Bajo las dos lomas — beneath the twin ridges*.

Renata tapped the margin. "That note isn't standard. Probably added by a survey officer who actually made landfall. The name's poetic for the Spanish navy—but they saw things differently back then."

Jake leaned over her shoulder, tracing the coastline with a finger. "Twin ridges," he said. "That's how Grey marked his positions—landmarks, not latitude."

"Could a ship that size anchor there?" Isabelle asked.

Renata thought for a moment. "If the bottom's sand and the swell's kind, yes. But it's a hard coast—volcanic shelves, unpredictable current. Few have reason to go, but there are reports of a spring inland." She pointed to a faint mark on the margin.

She flipped through another folder and slid out a brittle page—a page from an old whaler's log. "Anchored under twin ridges. The air turned sharp and cold, as if winter had slipped beneath the hull."

Jake frowned. "Cold?"

Renata nodded. "Strange, isn't it? That side of Isabela usually steams in the heat. No record of upwellings that far north." She hesitated, fingertips resting on the paper. "Locals say the sea forgets itself there—turns against its own temperature. Most don't like to sail that coast."

Isabelle read the line again, the words lodging in her chest. "He felt it," she said quietly. "Whatever it was."

No one spoke for a moment. Outside, a gull cried once and was gone.

Jake finally exhaled. "Twin ridges. Deep water. Sudden cold. That's our place."

Camila appeared in the doorway, wiping her hands on a rag. "We good? Because the sooner we lift, the less crosswind we'll fight."

Isabelle finished scribbling notes before slipping her notebook into her satchel. "We're good."

Renata arched a brow. "You're going out there?"

Camila answered for them. "They are. I'm the ride."

Renata smiled faintly, half in disbelief. "Then take this," she said, handing Isabelle a laminated copy of the western coastline. "If you really find something, tell me when you come back."

"If we come back," Jake said under his breath.

Ten minutes later, the last crate was signed over and stowed. Camila wiped her hands on a rag and checked her watch.

They climbed back into the Jeep and started north, the road winding through the highlands in bands of sun and shadow. Mist drifted between the cacti, thinning as they descended toward the coast. By the time they reached the ferry slip, the heat was already rising in waves off the black rock.

The crossing to Baltra was quick, the water flat and metallic under a brightening sky. On the far shore, Camila's Twin Otter waited on the apron, its fuselage shimmering in the sun. They loaded the last of their gear, double-checked the straps, and climbed aboard.

Camila settled into the cockpit, flipping switches with practiced ease. The engines coughed once, twice, then steadied into a low, even hum.

Moments later, they were airborne again, the sea unfurling below in endless blue. Camila leveled the plane at nine hundred feet, sunlight flashing off the wings.

Isabelle spread the laminated chart across her knees, watching the black shape of Isabela grow in the west, vast and volcanic.

Jake looked over, reading the faint letters. "Caleta del Fuego Dormido."

"The Cove of the Sleeping Fire," Isabelle said softly.

Camila glanced back, eyes hidden behind her aviators. "Sounds like trouble."

Jake smiled. "That usually means we're on the right track."

Ahead, the island swelled out of the horizon, its twin ridges dark against the morning sky.

CHAPTER THIRTY-TWO

The Sleeping Fire Wakes

The Twin Otter banked northwest, sunlight flashing off its wings as it climbed toward the northern end of Isabela.

"It's only about a hundred miles to Caleta del Fuego Dormido," Camila said, glancing at her airspeed. "At one-sixty knots—half an hour, give or take a headwind."

Below them, the island unrolled in black and gold—lava rivers frozen mid-flow, glass seams glinting between ridges where sparse scrub held on. The sea glittered far off to the east, but ahead the land rose in waves of dark stone.

They passed Volcán Darwin's broad shield, then Volcán Wolf rising ahead, its summit lost in cloud.

"Hard to believe anything lives up there," Isabelle said.

"The iguanas don't seem to mind," Camila replied, smiling.

They banked west. The land changed—dark rock veined with newer flows, each a line of frozen fire running toward the sea.

"There," Camila said. "Between those two ridges."

Jake followed her gesture. The twin peaks framed a narrow bay, its water dark as obsidian. Heat shimmered along the ridges.

Isabelle checked the laminated chart on her lap. "That's it. Depth fits an eighteenth-century draft—and that's where the cold-pulse reports came from."

"Then we've found our bay."

Jake eyed the terrain. "I don't see any runways down there."

"Any where's a runway if it's flat and long enough," Camila said, easing back the throttles. "That flow near the ridge looks solid. Hold on."

The engines dropped to a growl. Flaps came down in stages—fifteen, then thirty degrees—as the airspeed bled off. The fuselage rattled in the crosswind, every surface alive with vibration. The lava plain swelled beneath them, a cracked sheet of black glass glinting like ice.

Camila studied the ridge ahead. "Maybe five hundred feet of flat—should be enough."

"Should be?" Jake muttered.

"She's a Twin Otter," Camila replied. "Built for stupid."

The vertical speed indicator needle settled just below five hundred feet per minute—enough descent to keep speed without dropping hard. She eased the throttles, eyes locked on a stretch of crust without fissures. "Seventy-five knots... flaps forty."

The last segment of flaps thumped down. Drag ballooned; the nose wanted to sink. Camila trimmed nose up, balancing throttle and rudder, working the yoke through fine adjustments. The ridge lip slipped beneath them at mast height. The stall horn chirped once.

"Ten feet," she murmured.

The mains kissed the rock with a dry hiss. The tail bounced; she dropped flaps, yanked both props into beta, and shoved the levers flat. Reverse thrust erupted in a thundering roar. Dust and ash exploded around the cockpit, turning the world white-gray.

The Otter slewed left; Camila caught it with rudder and differential power. "Come on, girl." The wheels bit again, tires chattering over uneven crust.

Airspeed fell through forty. She eased out of reverse, let the props bite clean air, and feathered the brakes. The nose dipped, straightened, and the motion steadied to a rolling crawl—barely four hundred feet from touchdown.

Camila swung the aircraft in a tight arc, nose uphill toward the ridge, and let it coast to a stop.

The engines wound down, props ticking as they spun to stillness. Silence settled—thick, shimmering, and hot enough to taste of metal and dust.

Jake exhaled. "Define smooth landing."

Camila grinned, unstrapping. "Not smooth, but efficient."

Isabelle looked out the window—black rock, white glare, a faint sulfur haze. She reached for the handle. "Let's see what kind of ghosts this place holds."

The heat hit harder once they started down from the ravine. The ridge fell away into steep terraces of fractured basalt, every step a grind of grit and glassy shards. The air shimmered, thick with salt and sulfur.

"Careful," Camila called. "Unstable crust—watch for voids."

Jake tested each step. The rock drummed hollow under his boots. Isabelle followed close, one hand on the wall for balance. She slipped, sliding a few feet before catching herself. Jake reached out, steadying her.

"You okay?"

"Just a bruised ego," she said, breathless. "And maybe a bruised butt."

"Better that than a broken leg," Camila called up.

They zigzagged down to a low shelf above the water. The cove opened—black cliffs curving into a crescent, water still as oil.

Jake crouched near the tide line. Something metallic glinted—a half-buried iron ring fused into the basalt. He brushed away grit. "Found something."

Isabelle knelt beside him. "Eighteenth century, maybe earlier. Hand-forged."

A few more rings dotted the curve of the shore. "Three, maybe four," Jake said. "Big enough for mooring lines."

"Or several boats," Camila added. "Someone anchored here."

Isabelle traced the pattern—deliberate, just above high tide. "If the *Specter* made landfall, this fits."

Jake touched the nearest ring. A few pale fibers clung to it, frayed as bone. "Rope," he said softly. "What's left of it."

Heat wavered. The world shrank to glare and the faint hiss of surf.

Then the temperature broke.

The air collapsed inward with a low, breathless *thump*—a rush of cold that hit hard enough to steal balance. Dust lifted in tiny whirlwinds. The wave line flattened, then surged outward as if the sea itself had flinched.

Jake staggered, bracing against the basalt. His breath fogged white. Isabelle's hair lifted in the charged stillness; her skin prickled as if the air were pulling heat straight from it.

"What the hell—?" Camila whispered, half a shout over the gust.

Jake met Isabelle's eyes. Both remembering the same sensation—the hollow pressure, the unnatural chill.

"La Isla de Sombras," she said.

"Same thing."

She pulled her brass compass. The needle spun madly, clicking against the glass like teeth.

"Disrupted magnetic field."

Camila rubbed her arms, voice tight. "You've seen this before?"

"Not like this," Jake said. "Feels...alive."

The cold deepened until it ached in their bones, the air trembling between pulses. Then, as suddenly as it came, it released—warmth flooding back in a rolling gust that sent ash and grit streaming toward the sea. The next wave came higher, crashed harder, and hissed across the stones before receding.

Isabelle watched until her compass steadied, then slipped it away. "The land still remembers what was here."

"Let's hope it keeps that memory to itself," Camila muttered.

Jake brushed the sand from his hands. "We've got proof of an anchorage, not answers."

"Then we keep moving," Isabelle said.

The ravine between the twin ridges cut inland, a narrow gash of black stone shimmering in the heat. They followed a dry runoff channel winding like an old scar.

"If Grey anchored here, he'd send men inland for water," Isabelle said. "This is the only path that would hold a stream."

Camila's GPS flashed static, then steadied. "Let's hope we're not chasing ghosts."

"Too late for that," Jake muttered.

They climbed in silence, the air tasting of metal and dust. A faint carving caught Isabelle's eye. She brushed away ash—a crooked serpent and anchor etched into the rock.

"Grey's mark?" Jake asked.

"Almost. Whoever made this was copying, not creating."

"Bored soldiers, maybe," Camila said.

"Or men waiting," Isabelle murmured. "Idly tracing a symbol they'd only seen—hoping it meant something."

The ravine funneled tighter. A pressure, not quite sound, vibrated through the stone.

"GPS just died," Camila said.

"Compass too," Isabelle added.

"Volcanic minerals maybe," she offered, though uncertain.

The path widened to a terrace shaded by overhanging rock. A trickle of water gleamed down one wall into a shallow basin.

"Fresh water," Jake said, tasting it. "Clean enough."

"Flat ground, cover—perfect for a camp," Camila noted.

They found the traces quickly: a blackened fire ring, a rusted pot, a half-buried buckle. Jake turned up a bayonet tip.

"Military."

"Spanish," Isabelle confirmed. "Eighteenth-century marine issue." She lifted a brass button, the crown still faint. "Captain-General's marines—from Cartagena. The pursuit forces."

Jake looked around the terrace. "They followed Grey this far…"

"But why camp here?"

"High ground and a great spot for an ambush," Camila said. "Maybe they were waiting for him."

"Or never left," Isabelle murmured, pocketing the button.

The warmth began to pulse—waves of heat and cold rolling through the ravine. Isabelle's compass needle froze due north.

"Tell me that's normal," Camila said.

"I was hoping you would know."

Steam drifted from the trickle of water.

"Let's move before the ground decides otherwise."

Dust turned amber in the lowering light. Jake led the way back down the ravine until something flashed in the ash ahead—metal half-buried under rock.

"Down there," he said.

They followed the slope toward the sea. In the shadow of a collapsed lava tube, a brass-bound shape jutted from the debris.

"Chest," Jake said quietly.

The hollow reeked of sulfur and old heat. The chest was wedged at the base, brass fittings green with corrosion.

"Thin crust," Jake warned. "Could've been runoff."

"Careful," Camila said. "These flows trap air pockets."

He worked the knife into the seam. A faint tremor ran underfoot—soft, like the ground breathing. Dust sifted from the ceiling.

"Tell me that's wind," Camila said.

"Doesn't sound like it."

They worked in silence until the chest came free with a muffled pop. Jake pried the latch. Inside lay fragments—cloth long since turned to powder, a pistol rusted to its holster, a blackened rosary—and a single packet wrapped in waxed oilcloth, sealed with the royal crest of Spain.

Isabelle unwrapped it carefully. A folded letter, ink still legible in places. *"June 17th, 1719,"* she read.

"We have pursued the corsair Elias Grey to these western isles. His vessel Specter departed the anchorage on the fourth day, course set W by S ½ S toward uncharted waters.

We remain concealed by the bay, resolved to seize the pirate should he return and reclaim the treasure taken from the Crown.

—Captain Luis de Montoya, Third Company, Marines of Cartagena."

They stood in silence. Only air moved through the cracks.

"He wrote it after Grey escaped," Jake said.

"And stayed to ambush him," Isabelle answered. "An ambush that never happened."

"If the island didn't take them, time did," Camila murmured.

The tremor deepened. Pebbles rattled. Isabelle refolded the letter.

"Let's get it out. If we lose this, we lose proof."

Jake lifted the chest. "Whole thing's too fragile to split."

They climbed for daylight. The air felt charged, breaths metallic. A deep rumble rolled through the ridge; ash began to fall.

"Move!" Camila shouted.

They scrambled upward. The slope quivered, slick with dust. Jake kept the chest tight, Isabelle close behind. At the top, the tremor eased—but below, the hollow split open, steam curling from the new fissure.

They ran.

The light had gone copper-gray. The air trembled with each distant pulse. Ahead, the Twin Otter waited—a white shape wavering in heat.

The ridge bucked once, hard enough to jolt teeth. Steam hissed from cracks.

"Go!" Jake grabbed Isabelle's arm.

They sprinted across the lava flat, heat rolling up through their boots. Cracks raced beside them, snapping like glass.

"The field's coming apart!" Camila yelled.

The chest slammed against Jake's leg. Isabelle's compass banged her hip.

The ground dropped, held, then fractured again. Steam jetted across their path. Camila veered right; they followed, skidding.

The plane loomed closer—paint blistering on the wing.

They reached it as another crack split the ridge with a sound like tearing fabric. Jake threw the chest inside. Isabelle followed, one hand clamped on her satchel.

Camila vaulted into the cockpit, slid into her seat, breath short. She'd flown through storms—but never an island coming apart beneath her. "Strap in."

Jake slammed the door. The frame shook. He cinched the harness. Isabelle was already buckled, ash streaked through her hair. She nodded once. He touched the brass key at his chest and faced forward.

Camila's hands moved without hesitation—battery, fuel, boost, starters.

The first engine coughed once, then choked on a lungful of dust. Warning lights blinked amber.

"Come on," she muttered, cycling the boost pumps again. The second starter whined, slow at first, then caught a rhythm. Both turbines spooled, one lagging behind.

Jake felt the silence between them stretch thin.

Another cough—then a rising snarl as the prop discs blurred to gray, dust whipping away from the blades.

Camila exhaled once, hard. "That's better. Hold on."

The Otter lurched over uneven rock. Ahead, the flat stretched barely two hundred yards before breaking apart again.

A fissure leapt across their path. Camila didn't lift. She held the nose low, power steady, wheels hammering over ridges. The tires slapped, skidded, bit again.

"Come on," she muttered, eyes flicking between torque gauges and the horizon line shaking through the windshield.

A vent exploded to their right, steam hammering the glass in a whiteout flash. The cockpit filled with sulfur and heat. Camila ducked her chin, hand light on the yoke. "Can't see—trust the feel."

They punched out of the steam, wings rocking. The airspeed needle jittered. "Sixty-five... sixty-eight... good enough."

Another fracture raced them from the left, splitting the ground in a jagged Y that angled toward their nose.

"Fissure ahead!" Jake shouted.

"I see it!"

Camila shoved the props full forward, throttles to the stops. The engines howled, torque needles redlined. The vibration deepened, rattling through their bones.

"Come on, girl. Fly for me."

The gap ahead glowed red-orange, widening by the heartbeat. Camila eased back pressure, just enough pitch to lighten the nosewheel. The stall horn chirped.

"Now!" Jake shouted.

Camila gave it everything—props screaming in full power climb, yoke back against her palm. The Otter surged. Wheels lifted, touched once, then lifted again. For a heartbeat they skimmed nothing but air and heat—then the wings bit, the VSI came alive, and they were climbing.

The lava field fell away in slow motion. Dust geysered into the sky. A line of vents along the ridge flared in stuttering bursts of white fire. The cove below boiled, its surface alive with light.

Jake exhaled hard. Isabelle stared through the streaked glass—moorings flashing once, then vanishing under roiling water. A seam along the inner bay blew open and collapsed.

Camila held a shallow climb, trimming against the dirty air clawing at the wings. The radio hissed static, then silence.

A tremor shivered through the air itself. Ash laced the windshield. Blue sparks danced along the windows' edges.

No one spoke.

The island shrank beneath them. Plumes rose in dark columns, the sea shifting from green to black to molten copper. For a heartbeat a pale glow moved under the water—then guttered out.

Camila eased the climb. The engines steadied; the ash thinned. The air lost its metallic taste and became only air again.

Behind them the ridge slumped in a slow wave, the plume leaning west before rising straight. The sound followed for a time—a hollow roar fading into the slipstream.

Jake let his hand fall from the seatback. Isabelle still watched the shrinking shore, the oilcloth packet tight under her arm.

Camila's breathing slowed. Warning lights steadied then blinked out. The needles chose their place and held.

They leveled just below the worst of the plume. Cool light filled the cabin. Nobody said *we made it.* That would have been tempting the island to hear them.

The Otter banked toward open water. Below, the volcanic scar burned, then dimmed to a red memory. The ash column stretched upward, fraying into the wind.

Jake looked down one last time—the ridge a dark line, the cove a blur inside smoke. He found the key at his chest without realizing it, thumb pressed to the worn brass.

Isabelle closed her eyes. The compass had stopped spinning. She let it rest.

The plane held its line. Noise settled into something almost ordinary. The tremor in their bones became memory.

The sky ahead opened—less ash, more light. The sea caught the copper of the sun and stretched it flat, a path without promise beyond distance.

Behind them, the plume blossomed once more and folded into the island's shape, a silhouette against a bruised horizon. Heat haze turned it to a mirage, then to nothing.

The earth had split open behind them, and the sleeping fire woke.

CHAPTER THIRTY-THREE

Where the Sea Turns to Glass

The world steadied by degrees. The Twin Otter broke through the upper haze, engines droning in weary harmony as the island spread beneath them—black lava flats giving way to pale scrub and the shimmer of tin roofs near the coast. Far to the west, Isabela still smoldered, a faint gray column drifting across the horizon like smoke from a dying fire.

Camila eased the throttles back. "Inbound to Santa Cruz," she said, voice rough but steady. "Let's hope the runway's still where we left it."

Jake leaned forward, forearm braced on his knee, eyes narrowed against the glare. From this height the airfield looked like a strip of dull metal laid across dark earth. Beyond it, the sea caught the same muted light—a pane of glass stretching to the horizon.

The wheels kissed down once, twice. The tires squealed on the cracked tarmac and the plane bounded, then settled, dust rising in soft gray curls behind them. Camila reversed thrust; the engines howled, then fell away to a deep, shuddering silence. For a moment, all three just sat there, breathing the stillness.

Outside, the light was thick with haze. A faint ash film clung to the wings and fuselage, carried here on the upper winds from Isabela. The air smelled of salt and dry stone, touched with the faint sweetness of volcanic dust. Heat shimmered off the runway, but the island itself was calm—the kind of quiet that comes after distance, not disaster.

Camila pulled off her headset and rolled her shoulders. "Not bad for flying through a volcano's tantrum." She managed a tired grin. "And you didn't even scream once."

Jake smirked. "Came close."

Isabelle looked west through the cockpit glass. Even from here, the plume from Isabela was visible—just a gray pillar leaning seaward, thinning into high cloud. "It's still burning," she said softly.

"Burning itself out," Camila replied. "They always do."

They climbed out, the heat of the runway pressing through the soles of their boots. The air carried a faint static hum from the generators near the hangar. Every surface seemed dusted with silver—traces of ash that glittered when the sun hit just right. Jake brushed some from his sleeve; it smeared like graphite.

Camila unlatched the cargo door and handed down their satchels and the small officer's chest wrapped in canvas—the one they'd recovered from Isabela. The air smelled faintly of jet fuel and dust.

"Well," she said, tucking a stray lock of hair behind her ear, "this is where I leave you two."

Jake gave a nod. "You're heading back tonight?"

"Refuel here, then Guayaquil before sunrise," she said. "Supplies won't wait, and neither do volcanoes."

She hesitated a beat, then held out a worn business card, one corner bent, the edge smudged with ash.

"If you ever need a pilot again—or someone who owes you a drink—call."

Jake took it, sliding it into his shirt pocket. "We might hold you to both."

Camila smiled, the weariness softening from her face. "Try not to get yourselves killed before I get the chance."

She gave Isabelle a brief, warm nod. "You were good company. For a scientist and a salvage diver."

Isabelle smiled. "And you were good luck. For pilots."

Camila laughed under her breath and turned back to the plane. "Let's not test which of us needs the other more."

They stepped clear as she climbed aboard. A moment later the turbines spooled up again, rising from a low whine to a steady hum. The propwash lifted a swirl of ash around their legs as the Otter rolled slowly toward the fuel station at the far end of the strip, its silhouette fading into the gold haze.

When the engines' drone finally softened into distance, the quiet returned—the wind over stone, the faint hiss of the surf somewhere beyond the ridge. Jake exhaled, tension easing from his shoulders.

"So," he said softly, "back where we started."

"Not quite," Isabelle answered. She brushed a streak of ash from her sleeve and looked toward the western horizon, where Isabela's plume still bled into cloud. "The ground's the same, but the air's different."

They stood together as the last light bled from the sky, the heat fading, the sea turning to glass.

Evening settled over Puerto Ayora like gauze. Lanterns glowed along the inn's veranda, their reflections trembling across the bay. The air stayed warm but easy on the skin, scented with fried fish and flowers from the dunes. A radio murmured through static—an island love song older than the town.

Jake and Isabelle sat at a rough-cut table by the railing. The same innkeeper as before set down two plates of grilled parrotfish and a pair of sweating bottles.

"On the house," he said, eyeing the gray dust on their boots. "Looks like you've been close to something exciting."

Jake managed a tired grin. "A little too close. We appreciate this."

When he left, the quiet wrapped back around them.

The food tasted of lime and smoke; the beer was sharp and cold. The sky slid from copper to indigo, the bay turning mirror-black, wharf lamps doubling themselves on the water.

Isabelle exhaled. "I'd forgotten what silence sounds like."

Jake nodded toward the horizon. "I think my ears are still ringing."

"I think we all got our bell rung a little," Isabelle said, smiling.

Jake smiled back, twisting a finger in his ear. "Yeah. I think you're right."

She reached into her satchel and drew out the Pacific chart Camila left, along with Captain Montoya's oil-stained note. She flattened both, pinning the corners with forks and her beer.

Montoya's hand had faded to sepia, but the key line remained: *W by S ½ S.*

"West by south, half south—about ten degrees off due west," Isabelle said. "Old Spanish notation. Precise to a quarter point."

She set her pencil at the archipelago's edge. "From here..." The lead moved across the blue. "...that heading runs straight into the open Pacific."

Jake leaned closer, watching the graphite stretch until it met a faint scatter of islands. Candlelight trembled in his pupils.

"There," he said. "The Marquesas."

"Somewhere in that chain," she answered. "That's where he went."

"Grey sailed farther west than anyone thought," Jake said.

"And whatever he carried," Isabelle said, "he meant for it to disappear there."

They let it sit. Outside the rail, the bay lapped softly at the rocks.

Jake turned his bottle. "If Montoya's right, that's almost two thousand miles. A long run for an eighteenth-century brig."

"Grey's *Specter* wasn't ordinary," Isabelle said. "He chased distance the way most men chase gold."

She glanced at her father's compass. The needle held steady—its first certainty since Isabela. "For the first time, it's pointing somewhere that makes sense."

Jake's smile was thin. "Maybe this will be the last stop."

A faint shift in the air pressed against Isabelle's skin; the candle bent, righted, bent again. From the docks came rigging, a dog's bark, a far motor. Peace felt fragile—too clean after everything.

Isabelle smoothed the chart as if afraid to crease the new path. "Tomorrow we can check the archives—the harbor logs. See if anyone wrote about Grey or—"

"Tomorrow," Jake said. He leaned back, the chair creaking. "We rest. The ocean's not going anywhere."

She smiled, but it didn't reach her eyes. Beyond the patio, the sea had gone perfectly still—so dark it seemed to absorb the stars. Silence stretched between them.

Almost absently, Isabelle said, "The sea turned to glass."

Jake looked over. "What?"

"Old phrase. When the wind dies—when everything goes too calm before a storm."

He made a noncommittal sound. The candle guttered, its flame wavering.

The waiter returned and cleared the plates without breaking the hush. When he left, even his footsteps faded into the fan's steady hum.

"Maybe you're right," Jake said, stretching. "Or maybe it's just a calm night."

It came out half-hearted. The calm felt too complete; every sound was sharp against it.

Isabelle stared toward the bay. The lights from town breaking into long, trembling ribbons. She watched—until the reflections changed. A shadow slid where nothing moved.

Jake saw it too. He sat forward, eyes narrowing at the dark window beside them. For a breath he saw their own reflections—the candle, the map, Isabelle's pale profile—and behind them, another figure. Motionless. Watching.

"Don't move," he said.

"Jake—"

He didn't answer. Then the figure stepped out of the shadows.

Luca.

He moved with measured ease, every motion chosen. The gold light caught his eyes and made them gleam. His smile was slow, the smile of a man who knew the chase was over.

"You've come a long way," he said softly.

Jake's hand went for the satchel, but Luca's was faster. A nod—almost nothing—and from the patio's edges, Mateo and Javier appeared. One blocked the stairs to the street, another the open rail. Behind Jake, a third shadow sealed their exit.

"They found us," Isabelle said, low.

"Found you?" Luca's mouth tilted. "No. I never lost you."

He studied the chart—the penciled arc reaching west. One finger traced the line. "There's a rhythm to it," he said. "First you run fast. Then you think too much. Then you start believing you've escaped." His eyes lifted to Jake's. "That's when I like to catch them."

Jake stayed still. Mateo and Javier waited, the candlelight glinting off the steel at their hips.

"You've led me halfway across the world," Luca went on, voice calm, almost admiring. "Most men die running long before it gets interesting." He smiled, almost genuine. "But you two—you make it worth the chase."

He gestured. "Let's go. The night's wasting, and I'd rather not deliver you in pieces."

Neither of them moved. Luca's patience cooled. "Don't mistake mercy for hesitation."

Jake heard Victor's echo in the word—*Mercy*—the same idea turned by a different hand. He rose slowly. Isabelle followed, chin high.

"Good," Luca said, stepping back with easy confidence. "You know how to move when you're beaten. I respect that."

They were guided through the archway and down the narrow street to a waiting SUV.

Luca opened the rear door with mock courtesy. "After you."

They climbed in. The doors shut with a heavy, final sound. As the vehicle pulled away, Luca leaned back, watching them with half-lidded eyes—the quiet of a hunter at the end of a run.

"You have no idea," he said, almost to himself, "how long I've wanted to feel the world stop like this." He turned his gaze to them. "We could've worked together—been easier—but you had to run." The gleam returned to his eyes. "That's okay. I enjoy the hunt."

Through the windshield, the ferry's deck lights shimmered over black water as they rolled aboard. The channel was calm, the surface glassy enough to reflect the sky's thin stars. Engines rumbled below, steady and low, carrying them across the narrow stretch toward Baltra.

On the far shore, amber lights marked the airfield—thin lines glowing in the heat that still clung to the tarmac. As they neared, a black private jet took shape beneath the floodlights, engines idling, heat rippling into the night.

Jake met Isabelle's eyes across the seat—fear contained, understanding clear.

Somewhere beyond the darkness, the ocean stretched west toward the bearing they'd traced on the map, but their world had already narrowed to the edge of Luca's smile.

CHAPTER THIRTY-FOUR

The Price of Mercy

The ferry ramp clanged against the pier, jolting the SUV forward. Mateo eased them up the incline, headlights cutting through haze and heat. Jet fuel carried on the wind—a sharp, metallic scent that thickened as the airfield came into view.

Ahead, floodlights burned through the night, throwing white arcs across the tarmac. A sleek black **Falcon jet** waited beneath them, engines murmuring like something alive. Heat shimmered around its wings, blurring the guards that moved in its glow—dark figures in uniform, rifles slung low.

Inside the SUV, no one spoke. The air was dense with sweat, with the kind of silence that belongs to endings. Isabelle's wrists throbbed against the plastic ties; Jake flexed his fingers, testing the restraint until Luca's voice—quiet, almost bored—cut the motion short.

"Don't," he said. The knife lay across his thigh, catching the strobe of passing light.

The SUV slowed near the floodlit gate. The guards waved them through without question. Gravel hissed beneath the tires as they rolled toward the waiting jet.

From the back seat, Jake saw it all unfold—the line of armed men, the dark figure at the top of the stairs, the plane gleaming like obsidian under the lamps. His stomach turned—not at the sight of power, but of inevitability.

Luca looked ahead, expression unreadable. "End of the road."

Mateo stopped beside the jet. Doors opened in unison; hot air rushed in. "Out," Luca said.

Javier pulled Jake from one side; Mateo pulled Isabelle from the other. Plastic ties bit deeper as they shoved him forward. Isabelle stumbled when her boots met the gravel, but straightened before anyone could touch her again.

A row of armed men waited near the wing, motionless. Beyond them, the black jet gleamed under the lights. Every line of it was designed to dominate, to project control. Jake felt it instinctively—the same way he'd once felt the current change before a squall.

Then movement caught his eye at the top of the stairs.

A figure stepped into view—tall, thin, the cane almost elegant in his right hand. The linen jacket, the silver at his temples, the faint tilt of the head—unmistakable. Even here, framed by floodlight and jet exhaust, Victor Serrano carried the same quiet authority he'd worn that night in Key West.

"Mr. Morgan, Ms. Alvarez," Victor called down, voice smooth and steady, touched by amusement. "So nice to see you both."

Jake stared up at him, the memory of that night flashing quick and sharp—Victor's handshake, the calm eyes as he bid, the subtle chill that had followed when he smiled.

"Wish I could say the same," Jake said, voice roughened by exhaustion.

Victor's smile deepened. He took one careful step down, the cane tapping softly against metal. The sound echoed—precise, deliberate. At the auction he'd been sure-footed, graceful; now each motion seemed calculated, each breath rationed.

"I hope Luca wasn't too rough with you," Victor said. "You two have made yourselves very valuable to me."

"I'd like to file a complaint," Jake muttered, a crooked grin flickering across his face.

Victor gave a small chuckle, though no amusement reached his eyes. "Come," he said, turning toward the cabin. "We've all traveled far enough to earn some air-conditioning—and honesty."

He climbed the remaining steps, the cane striking each tread with measured rhythm.

The guards moved at once, ushering Jake and Isabelle forward.

Cool, filtered air washed over them as they stepped inside. The door sealed with a muted thud, cutting off the roar outside. The quiet that followed was almost surgical.

The cabin was sleek and dim—wood paneling polished to a deep shine, soft leather seats arranged in perfect symmetry. Everything gleamed under low amber light, like a boardroom built for judgment.

Victor stood near the forward bulkhead, the cane resting lightly in his hand. Luca remained by the door, motionless—a shadow with a heartbeat. Mateo and Javier took positions near the aisle.

"Please," Victor said, gesturing toward the seats opposite his. "Sit. You must be exhausted."

Neither Jake nor Isabelle moved.

"I'll stand," Jake said.

With a flick of Victor's gaze, Javier and Mateo shoved them into the seats opposite him.

"There, that's better," Victor said. He adjusted his cuff, voice composed. "There's no reason we can't be civil."

Victor eased himself down with care. The motion looked small, but Jake caught the strain—the brief wince before Victor smoothed it away. He folded his hands over the cane.

"I imagine you have questions," he said, tone almost conversational. "Most of them unpleasant. I'm sure."

"You could start with why," Isabelle said.

"Why?" Victor echoed, smiling faintly. "Ms. Alvarez—you, more than anyone, should understand."

She only lifted a shoulder. "Enlighten me."

Victor's smile thinned. "Don't tell me you've come all this way and don't know what Grey had taken."

Silence.

"Within the treasure Grey stole from *La Fortuna*," Victor continued, "was an idol crafted by the Muisca. The King of Spain wanted it desperately—because he was dying. His alchemists believed the idol, the one they called *Siecaza,* had the power to heal and extend his life."

He let the words settle.

Isabelle spoke, voice steady. "Grey didn't hide *Siecaza* to protect it. He hid it to protect us."

Victor regarded her a moment. "That's what scholars say when they find something they don't understand—or fear."

"It's not fear," she said. "It's restraint—something I'm sure you've never believed in."

"On the contrary," Victor murmured, "I'm exercising great restraint at this very moment."

A flash of violence crossed his eyes. "Do you know what Huntington's disease does, Ms. Alvarez? Have you ever watched someone dissolve from it? My father did. Brilliant man. Built empires. In the end he couldn't hold a spoon. It took ten years to finish him—ten years of mercy killing him an inch at a time."

His voice stayed calm, almost clinical, but the tremor beneath it was audible—the rhythm of anger turned inward.

"And now," Victor went on, "it eats away at me."

Isabelle's composure faltered. "You're dying."

"We're all dying," he said softly. "I'm just ahead of schedule."

He lifted one hand from the cane. The tremor showed plainly before he closed his fist.

Jake exhaled sharply. "You think some ancient trinket's going to cure a genetic disease?"

Victor's eyes slid toward him. "Your cynicism is your greatest limitation, Mr. Morgan. Faith built empires from less."

Isabelle leaned forward. "I've read Grey's journal. *Siecaza* isn't a healing artifact. He understood its danger—and its cost. He kept it out of reach to protect people. His sigil means balance, mercy, consequence. *Siecaza* changes those who touch it, and not for the better."

"And yet he touched it," Victor said softly. "And he lived to write about it."

"Did he really live, though?" Isabelle shot back. "It was driving him mad. The only thing that kept him going was his will to do the right thing."

Silence. The hum of the cabin systems filled it—a mechanical heartbeat.

Victor studied her, something like admiration in his expression. "You really do believe him," he said. "That makes you dangerous—and valuable."

He turned to Jake. "And you—your lineage alone makes you essential. Silas Morgan's bloodline, isn't it? A convenient key to a very old lock."

Jake met his gaze, unflinching. "You've been reading too many myths."

"Myths," Victor said, "are just facts waiting for proof."

He rose with visible effort, the cane catching the light as he steadied himself. "The King wanted *Siecaza* for salvation. Grey stole that from him. He won't steal it from me."

He looked between them. "You've followed Grey's trail farther than anyone alive. You know my ancestor was the man ordered to hunt him down? When he failed, our family legacy shattered."

"Don Rodrigo Serrano..." Jake said, almost mocking.

Victor's eyes lit briefly. "Exactly. You've heard of him."

"We found one of his letters asking for reinforcements," Jake replied. "Seemed like a real piece of work."

Victor stared a moment before regaining composure. "Tell me where *Siecaza* is. Where did Grey hide it?"

Neither answered.

The silence grew heavy. Outside, the wind scraped over the tarmac. The jet's cabin lights dimmed fractionally.

Victor's expression didn't change, but the air shifted—pressure before a storm. He exhaled once through his nose and spoke gently. "You misunderstand me. This isn't an interrogation. It's a partnership."

He looked to Luca. "But partnerships work best when everyone remembers what's at stake."

Luca moved without sound. The knife was already in his hand, its edge catching the light as he stepped beside Isabelle's chair. His other hand tangled in her hair, forcing her chin up. The blade whispered against her skin—barely contact, but enough to draw a single red line.

Jake surged forward; Mateo's arm barred his chest.

"You've seen what I can do," Luca murmured, voice almost kind. "Don't make me show her."

Victor's tone stayed even. "You've seen the relic's trail, Mr. Morgan. Every map, every cipher. You know where Grey went next."

Jake clenched his fists. "Even if I did, you'd never—"

Luca pressed closer. Isabelle drew a sharp breath.

"Jake," she said quietly, eyes full of defiance. "Don't."

He looked at her—the calm in her face, the unshakable will despite the thin line of blood at her throat. Something broke.

"I'm not making the same mistake again, Izzy." His voice cracked. "You're more important than the treasure—or the relic."

Isabelle met his gaze. She wanted to tell him he was wrong—but knew if it were reversed, she'd do the same.

"The Marquesas," Jake said. His voice was hoarse, barely above a whisper. "Grey hid it in the Marquesas."

Victor stopped. Silence. Then softly: "There it is."

He turned toward the cockpit. "Captain, draw up a flight plan for the Marquesas. We leave before dawn."

Luca withdrew the knife, wiping it clean on a folded cloth. Isabelle's breath trembled; her hand rose to her throat, pressing against the cut.

Victor adjusted his cufflinks, composure restored. "You've proven remarkably resourceful," he said. "You'll come with us, of course. Far too valuable to leave behind."

He nodded to Mateo and Javier. "See that they're comfortable. I expect their full cooperation."

Jake glared. "Comfortable isn't the word I'd use."

Victor's smile was almost sympathetic. "Perspective, Mr. Morgan. Everything depends on it."

He lowered himself slowly, cane tapping once against the carpet. "You may yet thank me," he said quietly. "Before the end."

The guards moved quickly—procedure, not cruelty. Mateo and Javier guided Jake and Isabelle through the narrow corridor at the rear. The hum of the cabin deepened as they passed the galley and a closed lavatory door. The air smelled faintly of jet fuel and citrus polish.

At the rear, a small compartment waited—two narrow bunks, bolted lockers, no windows. A pair of cuffs hung from the bulkhead.

"Get some rest," Mateo said, voice flat. "You're going to need it."

The door shut with a hydraulic hiss and the soft thud of a lock. The sound was final.

Inside, the air was close and stale. Isabelle sat on the lower bunk, wrists raw. Jake leaned against the wall, elbows on his knees, eyes on the floor.

Silence pressed down.

Finally Isabelle spoke. "You shouldn't have done that."

"Didn't seem like we had many options," Jake said dully.

"There's always a choice."

"Not when it's your throat under the knife."

Her breath hitched, half anger, half grief. "You think that makes it easier? Watching you give up everything we've fought for?"

"I'd give up a hell of a lot more before I watched him hurt you," Jake said.

She stared, trying to hold on to anger, but it thinned. She saw the shame in his face—the exhaustion, the helplessness mirroring her own.

After a moment she reached across the narrow space and laid a hand on his arm. The gesture was small but steadying.

"You shouldn't have done it," she said again, softer. "But I understand why."

Jake nodded once, unable to meet her eyes. "Doesn't mean it was right."

"No," she said. "But it was human."

Silence followed—the kind that holds instead of punishes.

Jake leaned back, staring at the ceiling. "He's not going to stop. Whatever he thinks *Siecaza* is, it's already poisoned him."

"Then we find a way to stop him," she said quietly.

He turned his head. "You really think we can?"

"Grey did."

Jake's mouth twitched—not quite a smile. "And look how that ended."

Isabelle met his eyes. "It's not over yet."

At the front of the plane, Victor sat alone. The others had dispersed—Luca to the rear, Mateo and Javier outside for a smoke in the floodlight haze.

Only the hum of the auxiliary systems filled the space.

Victor stared out the oval window, the floodlights reflected in the glass like twin suns. Heat still rose off the volcanic ground.

He rested the cane across his lap and pressed his fingertips to his neck. The tremor was stronger now—small, irregular spasms rippling through his hand. He watched them dispassionately, as though they belonged to someone else.

"The fire sleeps only so long," he murmured.

Outside, movement began. Mateo and Javier climbed the stairs and sealed the hatch. A heartbeat later, the hum deepened to a steady vibration.

Cockpit lights glowed green. A faint whine built under the floor—soft at first, then rising into a low, resonant growl.

The Falcon's engines came alive, their sound rolling across the airfield like distant thunder. Heat shimmered behind the exhaust cones, blurring the floodlights.

Victor watched the reflections tremble on the glass. The corner of his mouth curved—not quite a smile, not quite control.

The tremor in his hand steadied for a moment—as if balance itself had paused to watch.

Beyond the windows, the night seemed to pull back, as though the darkness were taking flight.

CHAPTER THIRTY-FIVE

The Black Wing

The Falcon rode a seam of air thirty thousand feet above the Pacific, its engines a low, constant murmur that vibrated through bone. Outside, there was only darkness—the kind that erased the horizon entirely. Every few minutes, a faint tremor passed through the fuselage as crosswinds brushed the wings, then steadied again.

Inside, the cabin glowed in muted amber. The air smelled faintly of ozone and polished wood. Papers, maps, and tablets littered the fold-out table between Victor and his captives. A decanter of water sat untouched, beads of condensation running down its sides and vanishing into the grain.

Victor leaned forward, elbows on the table, the cane propped within easy reach. His jacket was off, sleeves rolled to his forearms, the tremor in his right hand barely suppressed as he scrolled through a set of documents.

Luca stood near the galley bulkhead, silent and watchful. Mateo and Javier had retreated to the rear cabin to rest, leaving the four of them in an uneasy quiet broken only by the hum of the engines.

Jake sat opposite Victor, posture rigid, arms free but useless—nowhere to go, nothing to grip but the edge of the table. He'd stopped counting the hours since they'd left the Galápagos; time dissolved somewhere over the dark. Isabelle sat beside him, hands folded neatly in her lap, eyes fixed on the digital map projected on the far wall. It showed the Pacific as a single blue void stretching west, a slow pulse marking their trajectory.

Victor finally looked up from the tablet.

"Do you know what fascinates me about the Pacific, Mr. Morgan?"

"The water?" Jake replied smartly.

Victor didn't react, eyes steady. "It's the closest thing to eternity we have left. No borders, no kingdoms—just depth. Even in the age of satellites, there are places no one has seen. I find that comforting."

"Comforting?" Jake said, the edge in his voice sharpening the air between them.

Victor smiled faintly, as if expecting that. "What fascinates me is what lies beneath it—and how completely it hides its dead. Grey understood that kind of solitude better than either of us."

He tapped the table once, pulling up a grid of island chains—dots scattered across an infinite blue. "The Marquesas. Six hundred miles of rock and memory. Somewhere in that maze, Grey disappeared. So tell me, Ms. Alvarez—if you were a man like him, where would you hide what the world should never find?"

Isabelle's eyes flicked to Jake, reluctant, but Victor's stare left no room to refuse. She leaned forward, the faint glow tracing her features. "Somewhere unreachable," she said. "Somewhere the current itself would keep strangers away."

He reached for a leather folder beside the tablet. The motion was smooth, almost casual, but the tremor in his hand betrayed the effort. "I want you both to see something. It's the last voice to ever speak of Grey's trail."

He opened the folder, revealing a single laminated page—an old Spanish letter sealed with a cracked royal insignia.
Victor slid it toward Isabelle. The wax had bled into the paper over centuries, the insignia barely visible beneath the sheen of lamination.

"This," he said softly, "is the final record of the expedition sent to reclaim what Grey stole."

Isabelle's fingers hovered over the page but didn't touch it. The ink was brown with age, written in a steady, formal hand that faltered near the end.
January 8, 1721
The island rises from the sea like iron itself. Its cliffs are black and smell of smoke. Twin ridges cleave the sky, and the western surf roars as if the world ends there. Our compasses will not hold north. The men whisper that the fire beneath us still sleeps, though we feel its breath through the hull. I have named this place Terra del Espíritu, for it feels not of this world.

Victor leaned back. "Written by one of the King's officers. A survivor—or at least, he was when he penned this. The letter was found decades later in Cádiz, among estate records of the Serrano line."

He gestured toward the wall display. At his command, the central monitor lit with a grid of volcanic islands. "For years, I believed the island he described lay off the South American coast—*Terra del Espíritu*, as he called it. But that phrase... it might have meant something else entirely."

Isabelle reread the text, then looked up. "Spirit lands. It could have been a sailor's term for the far reaches—unmapped territory. The Pacific."

Victor's eyes glinted. "Go on."

"The twin ridges, the magnetic stone, the western surf—they fit the Marquesas more than anywhere near the mainland," she said. "If you overlay colonial wind routes, a pursuit leaving Panama or Lima could've drifted that far."

He nodded once, pleased, and activated another overlay—geologic charts, magnetic anomalies, old Jesuit surveys stitched to modern satellite scans. The cabin's amber light dimmed as data filled the walls.

Jake watched in silence. He couldn't follow the coordinates, but the shapes spoke their own language—sheer cliffs, deep inlets, violent surf. He recognized the kind of place a man like Grey would choose: where the sea itself guarded secrets. Somewhere Pops might've called *a place the ocean keeps for itself.*

One by one, Isabelle and Victor dismissed the wrong islands—Nuku Hiva, Hiva Oa, Tahuata—each too inhabited, too open. At last, the image stabilized: a dark, oblong island ringed by cliffs and surf.

"Eiao," Isabelle murmured. "Uninhabited. Basaltic ridges, twin plateaus, magnetic interference recorded since the French mapping in the 1800s."

Victor stared at the display as if seeing a ghost. "The island the Crown could never reach."

Jake frowned. "What do you mean?"

Victor's gaze didn't leave the screen. "That letter was the last thing they ever sent. Four ships reached that island in early 1721... and were never heard from again."

The engines' low hum filled the silence that followed. Even Luca turned slightly from the galley, eyes narrowing.

"Four ships," Isabelle repeated. "Gone?"

"Vanished," Victor said. "No wreckage, no survivors, no return." He smiled faintly, touched with awe rather than fear. "Perhaps they found what they sought. Perhaps it found them."

No one spoke. The data feeds flickered like static ghosts across the walls, as if the past itself were still transmitting.

The Falcon pressed on through the dark, a thin black hum cutting the miles between past and present. The projection of Eiao hovered in pale blue light—two ridges, black cliffs, and the word *uninhabited* blinking faintly in the corner.

Victor closed the display with a flick of his trembling hand. The effort seemed to drain him. He reached for the decanter, poured water into a glass, and steadied it against the ripple in his fingers. From his pocket, he shook a small pill into his palm and swallowed it with the water, the motion deliberate, practiced. The cane rested across his lap—his lifeline to gravity.

"Four ships," he murmured, mostly to himself. "An entire fleet erased—and not a word survives outside that letter. Do you understand what that means? History itself tried to bury them."

Isabelle's eyes softened despite herself. "Or warn us."

He looked up sharply. "Warnings are for men afraid of consequence. I've spent my life correcting those who were."

Jake studied him—authority thinning into exhaustion. The man who once commanded rooms with a whisper now fought to control his own body. The tremor crept from his hand to his jaw, a brief spasm he masked by lifting the glass again.

A sudden thud rolled through the fuselage. The Falcon dipped, then steadied. Turbulence. The lights flickered once, holding steady.

Victor exhaled, grip tightening on the cane. "Find some calm sky."

From the cockpit, a pilot's voice crackled back, calm and efficient: "Adjusting course. Crosswind over the equatorial stream."

Luca didn't move. He stayed where he was, the knife clipped to his belt catching a glint of light. His gaze stayed fixed on Victor—not in concern, but in appraisal. Predators didn't intervene when another stumbled; they waited to see if he could stand again. His fingers brushed the knife's hilt, almost absently.

Victor caught the look and held it. Something cold passed between them—an understanding stripped of loyalty.

"I don't need your concern," Victor said, voice rough.

"Wasn't offering any," Luca replied.

Silence edged the air.

Isabelle broke it—not out of sympathy, but clarity. "You keep calling it destiny," she said. "But what you're describing looks a lot like desperation."

Victor turned his head toward her, fury cooling to ice. "You mistake weakness for mortality, Ms. Alvarez. I'm merely outpacing it."

She met his gaze. "No. You're accelerating it."

For a heartbeat, only the hum of the engines answered. Victor's jaw flexed, pulse twitching at his temple. Then he turned away, forcing composure.

"Send orders to Algeciras," he said. "I want satellite sweeps of Eiao—topographic and coastal. Cross-reference volcanic fissures, uncharted inlets."

Luca stayed in the shadows, his gaze moving from Victor's trembling hand to Jake and Isabelle. Two survivors. Two keys. For the first time, he wondered if the future might not belong to Victor—but to whoever had the nerve to take it.

The air in the cabin felt thinner, as if even the pressure sensed the shift in power.

Outside, the first gray hint of dawn brushed the horizon—an indistinct seam between ocean and sky. The Falcon's engines droned in their endless rhythm, the sound too steady to trust.

Victor stood by the forward display, one hand braced on the seatback for balance. The tremor in his fingers hadn't subsided, but he no longer seemed to care. Eiao rotated slowly in holographic relief before him: twin ridges, fractured cliffs, a jagged western bay where waves struck white against basalt. "There," he said. "The island that swallowed a fleet."

He looked toward the cockpit. "Plot a descent corridor for Eiao. We'll begin aerial passes at first light."

A soft vibration shifted through the floor as the Falcon began a gradual turn.

Jake and Isabelle exchanged a look—small, almost imperceptible. Neither needed to speak; they both knew the pattern of Victor's victories. Each was a narrowing corridor leading closer to collapse.

Isabelle studied the island's rotation. "It fits the letter," she said. "But if Grey reached it, he wouldn't have stayed long. He never lingered where the tide could betray him."

Victor smiled faintly. "You sound as though you knew him."

"I've read enough to understand him," she replied. "He believed Siecaza turned on anyone who tried to claim it."

"And yet he still carried it." Victor's smile deepened. "Faith and greed have always been excellent traveling companions."

Jake leaned back, arms folded. "If you're right, maybe he tossed it overboard halfway across the Pacific."

Victor let a half-chuckle escape. "I think he kept it for himself," he said simply. "My ancestor failed to finish what he began. I intend to correct that."

The words hung—half confession, half prophecy.

Isabelle forced her gaze back to the display. The Spaniards hadn't vanished because of storms or error. Every description—the tremors, the fire beneath the sea, the silence that followed—read like consequence.

If Grey reached that island, he hadn't just hidden something there.

He'd ended something.

She said nothing.

Jake's voice was quiet. "Eiao might be where the Spaniards died, but that doesn't mean it's where Grey stopped."

Victor glanced at him, amused. "Then it seems we'll find out soon enough."

Across the cabin, Luca shifted his weight, silent as ever. Three versions of obsession orbiting the same prize: Victor's faith, Isabelle's reason, Jake's defiance. Luca needed only to be the one left standing.

The Falcon banked west. Faint light edged through the windows, tracing thin gold lines across the cabin.

Victor steadied himself on the armrest. "We're close," he said quietly. "Three centuries chasing ghosts—and it ends soon."

Isabelle's eyes flicked toward Jake. "If it ends," she whispered.

He met her look and gave the smallest nod. It was enough.

Hours later, morning light spread across the Pacific like spilled metal. The Falcon's nose tilted downward through thinning cloud, and the endless sea gave way to shadow.

Jake pressed a hand against the window, squinting through the glare. "There," he said quietly.

A jagged smudge broke the surface below—a shard of land wreathed in haze, black cliffs stabbing from the water. The twin ridges rose like ribs of a buried creature, their flanks streaked with pale seams where the rock had torn and cooled. Even from thirty thousand feet, the island looked wrong—magnetic, alive.

Isabelle leaned closer. "Eiao."

Victor stirred, head lifting. He had been silent for most of the morning, lost somewhere between exhaustion and focus. At Isabelle's words, his eyes fixed on the growing shape below.

"Magnificent," he whispered.

The Falcon banked, sunlight flashing across the glass. The ocean foamed around the cliffs, white breakers gnawing at basalt shelves. Further inland, the ridges cleaved toward a central valley drowned in mist. Heat shimmered faintly off the rock—too much for the hour, as if the ground remembered something it shouldn't.

Isabelle leaned over the Falcon's sensor console, the magnetometer display flickering beside thermal imaging feeds. "No vegetation above the low plateau. Magnetic distortion across the western ridge. Readings spike every few seconds."

Victor's smile returned. "The relic's echo."

Jake's voice was low. "Or what it left behind—like on Isabela."

They dropped lower, following the coastline. The cliffs loomed now—basalt walls black as obsidian, pocked with cavities that caught the sunlight in flashes of metal. Isabelle frowned. "Wait—what is that?"

The Falcon passed over the western ridge, and the light struck something impossible.

Embedded in the cliffs, half-buried in stone, were the remnants of ships—timbers fused into rock, gunports twisted mid-burst, cannon barrels jutting like broken bones. Farther along, a section of hull hung out from the cliff face, petrified, its ribs tangled with anchors and chain.

Jake stared in disbelief. "What the hell —."

Isabelle breathed. "The stone's fused around it—melted."

The plane turned eastward. More wreckage came into view: fragments of masts and hulls scattered along the ridges as though thrown there by a giant's hand. The entire western face of the island was a graveyard—wood, metal, and human ruin crushed into the rock and preserved by time.

Victor rose from his seat, gripping the backrest for balance. His voice was quiet but fervent. "You're looking at history's erasure. Four ships—gone without a trace—because one man commanded the power of gods."

"Grey did this," Isabelle whispered. "He used Siecaza."

Victor's reflection shimmered in the glass, eyes fixed on the scarred cliffs. "A weapon of balance, wasn't that what you called it? Then perhaps balance demanded consequence."

Jake studied the wreckage, the sea still frothing beneath it as if something unseen stirred there. "If that's true, maybe he knew what was coming. Maybe he sent his crew away first. At least one of them made it home."

Isabelle's brow furrowed. "The sailor who returned to Punta Arenas." Her voice softened. "He must have watched this from the water."

Victor turned, eyes alight. "Then he saw a miracle."

Jake's reply came quiet and cold. "He saw a massacre."

Silence filled the cabin, broken only by the engines' low whine.

The Falcon circled wider. Smoke-colored mist clung to the valley, drifting between fissures that glowed faintly with trapped heat. Isabelle's monitor pinged once—a spike in thermal imaging, then another. The valley floor burned hotter than open lava.

Victor leaned closer to the glass, almost reverent. "The fire sleeps," he said. "Waiting for the hand that woke it to return."

Luca watched his reflection. "And when it does?" he asked quietly.

Victor didn't answer. His eyes never left the island.

Jake and Isabelle exchanged a look—both knowing what neither dared to say aloud.

The Falcon banked again, sunlight cutting across the cabin in narrow gold slants. The island filled the windows—black stone and broken memory rising from the sea. The hum of the engines deepened, and the water below shimmered with fragments of light.

The Falcon's shadow skimmed across the waves, small and dark against the burning surface.

Victor stayed at the window until the island slipped behind the wing. Even as the Falcon climbed, the image lingered—cliffs glinting with iron and ruin, the sea breaking white against their base like foam over a scar.

"Set course for Nuku Hiva," he said at last. "We'll need a closer look."

The pilot acknowledged, banking east. The engines lifted in pitch; the horizon tilted. Eiao fell away beneath them, shrinking into haze, but no one looked away.

Jake sat back, jaw tight, watching the reflection fade. Isabelle followed it until only the shimmer of heat remained.

Behind them, Victor's cane tapped once against the floor. "Have a helicopter waiting for us at the airport," he said softly.

Outside, the Pacific stretched unbroken, the Falcon's shadow vanishing into its own reflection.

The hunt had reached its final shore.

CHAPTER THIRTY-SIX

The Island That Remembers Fire

The rotor wash tore at the sea. Spray burst upward in silver sheets as the helicopter skimmed the surface, climbing sharply toward the dark cliffs ahead. Wind hammered the fuselage, driving salt through the seams until the air itself tasted of iron.

The helicopter—an Airbus H225 Super Puma—had been waiting at Nuku Hiva, a Black Tide Global charter diverted overnight from Tahiti, its matte-black skin still streaked with salt.

Jake braced against the vibration, one hand gripping the overhead bar, the other steadying Isabelle beside him. Through the forward glass, the island loomed—black and jagged, rising from the ocean like a shard of cooled metal. Twin ridges flanked a valley drowned in mist, their edges catching the morning sun in fleeting, molten flashes.

Even from this height, it didn't look alive—only burned.

Victor sat forward in the jump seat behind the pilot, both hands on his cane. The wind off the rotors whipped his hair and jacket, but he didn't blink. His eyes stayed fixed on the ridges, on the scars cut through the stone.

"Three centuries," he murmured. "And the island still breathes."

"Breathes," Isabelle said quietly, "or bleeds."

The words were swallowed by the noise, but Jake heard them. So did Luca.

Luca sat opposite, helmet on, rifle slung across his chest, every motion economical. He didn't look at Victor or Isabelle—just at the cliffs, calculating range, angles, risk.

The pilot's voice crackled through the headset. "Approaching the eastern plateau. Limited clearance—surface looks unstable."

Victor didn't hesitate. "Put us down."

The helicopter banked hard. The horizon tilted—ocean and sky trading places. Sunlight flared off the water, then vanished as the cliffs rose up to meet them. Jake caught a glimpse of fused wrecks below—iron ribs and gunports half-buried in stone, like fossils trapped mid-death.

Wheels kissed rock, bounced, held. The roar collapsed to a low, trembling hum.

Jake stepped out first, boots crunching against black glass. Heat radiated faintly through the soles—subtle but alive, like an exhale from the earth.

Isabelle followed, shielding her face from grit. The air shimmered off the basalt, distorting the horizon. She crouched, running her fingers over the surface—cooled slag mixed with ash. When she lifted her hand, faint smudges streaked her skin like soot.

Victor descended last, careful but unassisted. The cane struck stone with a hollow ring. He inhaled deeply and smiled.
"Grey's altar," he said.

Jake scanned the horizon, jaw tight. "Where a sacrifice took place, by the looks of it."

No one argued. The wind carried the echo away.

Without the rotor wash, the island's breath rose—dry, metallic, faintly sulfurous. Every inhale tasted like stone.

The plateau stretched in uneven slabs, black glass fractured into plates the size of doors. Fine ash whispered underfoot. Beyond the landing site, the ground fell away toward the sea—a jagged drop of several hundred feet. Below, waves broke white against the cliffs, vanishing in spray before the sound reached them.

Luca swept the perimeter, rifle steady. Mateo and Javier hauled packs; two more guards carried a crate, its stenciled markings half-erased by salt.

Jake's gaze tracked the horizon. He'd seen volcanic rock before—on dives, in fault zones, on seafloors torn apart by heat—but never anything like this. Some sections glittered like powdered glass. Others rippled under the sun, frozen waves of stone. "Feels like walking on a forge," he muttered. He exhaled through his nose, half a laugh. "I was hoping we were done with volcanic islands."

Isabelle brushed ash from a smooth patch. "Look at the layering," she said. "It's not lava flow. The surface vitrified in place—instantaneous heat. Strong enough to melt basalt."

Jake frowned. "If not lava, then what—lightning?"

She shook her head. "Not like this."

Victor stepped closer, cane clicking faintly. "Grey left his mark even here," he said. "You can feel it—the island remembers him."

Jake looked over. "Or remembers what he did."

Victor didn't respond. His gaze had locked downslope, toward a ridge where the black rock met the sea. Even from here, something caught the light—long, angular, metallic.

"Luca," he called. "Down there. Take us closer."

The descent twisted along the ridge, a precarious path carved by erosion and time. Each step dislodged shards that skittered into the void. The wind came harder, carrying the tang of salt and decay.

The shape resolved—an iron cannon, half-fused into the cliffside. The barrel jutted over the water, its mouth filled with solidified slag. Around it, timbers protruded from the stone like ribs, twisted and fossilized mid-scream.

Isabelle stopped short. "Ship remnants," she said.

Jake moved beside her. He'd seen wrecks swallowed by coral—never by stone.

More wreckage emerged as they moved—planks, gunports, fittings—each swallowed and warped by rock.

Luca ran a gloved hand along the cannon, tapped it with his knife. The metal rang dull, encased. "Poor bastards," he muttered. "Cooked where they stood."

Victor's eyes gleamed. "The fire that swallowed the fleet."

Isabelle turned on him. "You're looking at people's deaths."

Victor's expression tightened. "I know. My family among them." He paused, eyes on the stone. "Fire remembers what mercy forgets."

Jake crouched beside the embedded hull, fingers brushing where molten rock had sealed wood and iron together. The surface still radiated faint warmth. He pulled his hand back. "Still warm."

Isabelle's scanner pulsed with erratic thermal spikes. "Temperature variance," she murmured. "There's a pulse to it."

Victor leaned closer, reverent. "It's still alive," he murmured.

Jake looked up sharply. "Alive, or remembering?"

Victor's eyes traced the fused cannon. "The line between the two is thinner than you think."

For a moment, no one spoke. Then the ground shivered once—a subtle vibration through boots and bone.

Luca lifted his head. "You feel that?"

Jake nodded. "Yeah."

Victor smiled faintly. "Good. Then we're standing in the right place."

They followed the ridge inland, climbing uneven terraces cut by old fissures. The air grew thicker, the scent of salt fading to hot iron.

After a few hundred yards, Isabelle slowed. "Wait."

She brushed ash from a cluster of dark shapes. Chisel marks emerged—short, double-cut strokes forming clean right angles.

Jake knelt beside her. A square-cut block glinted under the sun.

"These aren't Spanish," Isabelle murmured. "Grey's crew?"

Jake looked around; patterns revealed themselves—low mounds, flat stones like fallen walls. "They built here?"

"They must've," Isabelle said. "Leveled sections, carved channels. This wasn't a campsite. It was a settlement."

Victor watched, awe flickering beneath control. "So he stayed. Long enough to prepare."

"Prepare for what?" Jake asked.

Victor smiled faintly. "For transcendence."

The ridge narrowed, then opened into a broad shelf of fractured stone. Circular depressions pocked the surface. Isabelle traced one with her boot. "Post holes," she said. "Supports. He wasn't hiding—he built something."

"A temple," Victor breathed.

Jake exhaled. "You mean a fortress. Something to keep everyone else out."

"Or to keep something in," Isabelle said.

Jake studied the terraces. Arcs and triangles curved inward—the same nesting geometry they'd traced in Rio, only scaled to landscape. "Isabelle," he said, "these shapes—do they look familiar?"

Her eyes widened. "They match the Rio labyrinth. Scaled up."

Victor's smile deepened. "Then he sealed Siecaza at the heart of it. The labyrinth itself was the tomb."

Wind hissed, swirling ash between them. The pulse beneath their feet strengthened—a low, patient vibration.

"He knew the island wasn't stable," Isabelle said. "He must've understood what it could do."

"Or what he could do with it," Victor replied.

"You're walking a different path than he did."

"Then perhaps I'll finish it."

Jake looked toward the valley below—dark glass and sand. "If it doesn't finish you first."

They stood in rising heat, surrounded by ghost foundations and faint geometry.

Far up the ridge, the helicopter crouched on the plateau, heat rippling around it, blurring its edges as if the island were trying to erase the intruder.

The only sound was wind through fissures—a low, steady breath from below.

The ridge fell away in a steep black funnel, the air thick with minerals. Isabelle's boots scraped glassy rock, sending fragments spinning—but they didn't fall. The shards drifted, hung, then rose slowly through the haze.

Jake stopped short. "Please tell me that's not just me."

Isabelle stared. "It's not wind. The gravity field's shifting."

Victor's eyes gleamed. "Not failing—changing."

They descended into the basin, boots crunching on fused stone that pulsed faintly with trapped heat. The air grew dense, humming with a low frequency they could feel in their bones. Then, as the slope leveled, the world opened.

The valley floor was a frozen storm.

Rocks—some pebbles, others wagon-sized—floated motionless in midair, suspended at odd heights, undersides smooth and glassy from ancient heat. A few turned imperceptibly, like slow planets in invisible orbits. Vines spilled down from them in tangled draperies, stretching toward the ground but never touching. Even the moss had adapted, its threads swaying in nonexistent wind.

Silence had texture here.

Jake stepped forward, awed despite himself. A boulder drifted three feet above the ground beside him, a fern trailing from its underside. He reached out and pushed—it slid away in perfect silence, gliding several yards before stopping as if the air itself had substance.

Isabelle watched her compass spin wildly. "The gravitational field's fractured," she said. "Whatever Grey did—it left a scar."

Victor moved past them, cane tapping stone that rang faintly like metal. "He didn't destroy the Spanish fleet," he said softly. "He erased its weight."

They followed him toward the center of the valley. Heat shimmered visibly, the air bending around a half-buried shape. Every step felt uncertain—some heavier, some lighter.

"Careful," Isabelle warned. "The field's unstable—mass could drop out at any—"

Her words cut off.

Before them stood a wall.

Fifteen feet high, twice as wide, its surface black and glossy—the color of cooled lava seen through water. Around it, the stone had melted and run, frozen mid-flow in ripples that caught the dying light. At its center, beneath a glaze of fused rock, a serpent coiled around an anchor, metal veins warped and iridescent.

Victor stepped forward, his reflection warping across the glass. "The seal," he whispered. "He poured the island's fire over it."

Jake crouched near the base. Pebbles floated inches above his boots.

"Grey's sigil—balance, mercy, consequence. He closed the labyrinth behind it." Isabelle said quietly.

Victor pressed his palm against the seal. The surface was warm, pulsing faintly—alive. "Three centuries," he said, "and it still hums."

The ground trembled once, a deep thud rolling through their chests. Dust drifted upward in thin columns that refused to fall.

Luca stepped back, hand on his weapon. "We should move. The place is—wrong."

Victor didn't answer. His gaze stayed on the sigil, the tremor in his fingers barely visible. "Tomorrow," he said at last. "We bring the equipment down and open it."

"You open that," Isabelle said, voice hard, "you'll unleash whatever he tried to contain."

"Containment is the refuge of the fearful," Victor murmured. *Ergo, cages are choices.*

Jake looked around—the suspended stones, the faint hum. "Fear might've kept this place alive."

"Then let's see what courage buys."

He tapped his cane once. The sound rang clear and unnatural, echoing through the hanging stones. Several quivered, rotating before settling again.

They began the climb back up the ridge. The last light bled through the haze, glinting off floating debris. Isabelle looked back once. The serpent and anchor shimmered in the gloom, the air around it rippling faintly, as though it drew breath.

Behind them, the valley waited—silent, suspended, impossible.

They made camp high on the ridge, heat rising from below. The helicopter crouched upslope like a black insect, rotors tied down, metal skin breathing faintly in the wind. Beyond it, the world fell away into haze—no view of the valley floor.

Victor sat near the lantern, cane across his knees, his men working quietly. Every so often a low pulse rolled through the ground—subtle, rhythmic, like the slow beat of something buried alive.

Luca patrolled the perimeter, rifle slung, gaze slicing through the dark.

Jake and Isabelle were kept near the supply crates. Their wrists were free now, but two guards watched from a few yards away. The men looked tired—days of heat and silence dulling their edges—but Luca's movements were constant.

Jake leaned close. "He's never going to quit pacing."

"He doesn't have to," Isabelle whispered. "He just has to look the right way once."

"You see something?"

"When we came up earlier," she said, "I saw a drainage cut west of here. Old creek bed—narrow, steep, but it wraps the ridge. If it runs true, it might drop behind the basin wall."

Jake frowned. "You think it connects to the valley?"

"I think Grey would've built a second entrance. He never trusted a single way out—and we're lucky he didn't."

Jake studied the shadows. "Then we just have to get past him."

"Luca?" Isabelle asked.

Jake's mouth twitched. "Yeah. Him."

Across the camp, Victor called to his men. "Two-hour watches. We start at dawn."

He rose unsteadily and disappeared into his tent. The guards shifted; one stoked the stove while the other checked cables near the gear crates. Luca kept his circuit, a clock hand through light and shadow.

Jake's eyes drifted toward the helicopter and the stacked fuel drums. One still had a refueling hose draped across its lid, rocking faintly in the breeze. He watched it a long moment, the faint slosh of liquid whispering against metal.

Isabelle noticed. "Whatever you're thinking," she murmured, "don't."

He grinned quietly. "Too late."

When Luca's next circuit carried him toward the far edge of camp, Jake crouched low behind the crates. He pulled a multitool from his boot, loosened a clamp, and let a thin stream of fuel trickle down the drum's side. He eased the nearby lantern closer—just enough for the fumes to find it.

"Jake," Isabelle whispered sharply. "You'll—"

The flare went off with a soft *whoosh—just vapor catching,* bright and brief. One of the guards swore, stumbling backward. "Fire!"

Luca spun, sprinting toward the drums. "Sand! Blankets—move!"

Jake grabbed Isabelle's hand. "Now."

They slipped into the dark as the camp erupted. The flare's pulse lit the helicopter's fuselage, masking their shapes as they darted beneath its tail and toward the shadowed western slope.

The cut was right where Isabelle remembered—narrow, steep, half-choked with gravel and glassy shards. Heat shimmered across it like invisible water.

Jake crouched at the edge, peering down. "You sure about this?"

"No," Isabelle said. "But it's the only path that doesn't go through him."

They began their descent, boots scraping, stones sliding silently into the dark. Above, Luca barked orders, silhouette stark against the light. Smoke curled through camp; the flare guttered out.

Luca turned, scanning the shadows—and froze. The space where Jake and Isabelle had been was empty. His eyes swept the slope, the crates, the dark beyond. Then he moved, fast, rifle low.

Halfway down the ravine, Jake glanced back and saw him framed against the lantern glow, motionless but listening. For a second, the island held its breath.

Isabelle touched his sleeve, counting the hum. "On the next low—step *now.*" They dropped in sync as the pull eased, vanishing beneath the ridge lip.

A gust tore across the slope, scattering dust. The glassy scree took no prints; what little gravel had shifted left nothing to read. Luca vanished into the haze.

"Go," Isabelle whispered.

They descended lower, the hum deepening until they could feel it in their bones. The ridge curved inward, hiding them completely. Ahead, a faint red glow seeped through the haze—light reflecting off glass far below.

By the time they reached the base, the world above was silent. The air pressed close, heavy with heat and the slow pulse of the earth.

Jake exhaled, breath trembling. "I think we made it."

Isabelle looked toward the valley, where the glow flickered faintly like breath beneath skin. "No," she said softly. "We just found where it starts."

CHAPTER THIRTY-SEVEN

The Heart of the Labyrinth

The world narrowed to heat and darkness. Jake kept one hand on the wall, the other clasped around Isabelle's. He hadn't let go since the camp. The dry creek bed twisted steeply downhill, the walls closing until they were barely two feet apart. The air smelled of stone and old fire—each breath thick with dust that clung to his tongue like ash.

Isabelle's light flickered across glassy rock, its beam cutting thin paths through the dark. The surface shimmered where the heat warped it—black basalt glazed to near transparency. Their footsteps made no sound, just a faint crunch the air swallowed before it could echo.

"Easy," Jake murmured as the ground sloped away again.

"I'm fine," Isabelle said, voice low but even. "Just feels like the ground's moving."

"It is," Jake replied.

They reached a bend where the chute widened into a hollow. The air shimmered, distorting the light into ribbons. Dust hung suspended instead of falling, each grain drifting in slow, lazy arcs. A pebble rolled off the ledge near Jake's boot, dropped three feet—and hung there, spinning before settling against the opposite wall.

Isabelle froze. "Did you see that?"

"Hard to miss."

She stepped forward, watching as her hair lifted slightly, tugged by something unseen. The beam of her light trembled across the walls, revealing faint carvings etched into the glass—spiraling grooves that glimmered like metal veins when the light touched them.

"Jake," she whispered. "They're conducting heat—or something close to it."

He crouched beside one of the spirals, running a gloved hand along the groove. It was warm, almost vibrating. "Grey's crew?"

"I," Isabelle said. "But look at the flow. These lines converge—they're channeling energy."

Then the hum began. Faint at first, like distant thunder trapped underground, then rising into a low tone that pressed through their chests. Isabelle's flashlight spasmed once before steadying again.

Jake glanced around. "That coming from below?"

She turned slowly, the light sweeping the floor—and stopped.

The rock beneath their feet wasn't uniform. A subtle seam crossed it, barely perceptible until the dust began to shift. Each grain slid sideways, drawn toward a faint line of blue light leaking through the crack. The sound deepened as the glow pulsed—once, twice—then steadied, like the heartbeat of the island itself.

"Jake..." Isabelle's voice barely carried. "That's not a fissure."

Jake knelt, brushing away a layer of ash. The blue line widened, revealing the edge of a circular pattern—carved metal embedded in fused glass. Sigils traced its rim: a serpent's tail, the curve of an anchor.

He exhaled slowly. "It's a hatch."

The hum receded, leaving only silence and the faint ticking of cooling stone.

Isabelle crouched beside him, tracing the outline with her fingertips. "Grey didn't just seal it. He buried it alive."

Jake looked from the glowing seam to her. "You think it's reacting to us?"

She hesitated. "No. I think it's watching us."

The faint light pulsed again—slow, deliberate, like breath beneath glass.

Jake tightened his grip on her hand. "Then we're close."

The ridge above the basin still glowed from the dying flare. Smoke drifted low across the camp, mixing with sulfur rising from the rock. The others had gone quiet, worn thin by exhaustion and dread. Only the rhythmic hum of the island broke the stillness—steady, deep, alive beneath their feet.

Luca stood at the edge of the drainage cut, helmet off, eyes fixed on the black ravine below. The air moved differently there, rising in uneven gusts that carried heat and vibration. Two sets of footprints led to the drop—sharp, deliberate. Then nothing.

Mateo approached from behind, voice careful. "Victor said to hold until morning. He wants the team rested before—"

"I don't take orders from a dying man," Luca said.

The words came flat, almost casual, but they hit like a gunshot in the quiet. Mateo hesitated, jaw tightening, then backed away without another word.

Luca adjusted the strap of his rifle, crouched, and began his descent.

The ravine swallowed him whole. Heat pressed close, wrapping him in its slow, pulsing rhythm. The rock walls on either side were slick and glassy, reflecting faint light that seemed to come from nowhere. Every few steps, the vibration deepened—crawling up through his boots and into his bones.

He paused halfway down. Dust hung suspended, drifting like ash underwater. When he reached out, the particles slid toward his fingers, pulled by static. Gravity felt wrong here—every motion took a fraction longer to end than it should have.

"They came this way," he murmured.

He kept moving. The tunnel narrowed, then widened again, curving gently left. The glow ahead strengthened—pale blue bleeding through seams in the rock like veins under skin.

He cut his lamp, letting the light guide him.

The air shimmered at the hollow's edge. Luca stepped through—and froze.

The floor ahead had been cleared, ash brushed aside, the glassy surface beneath polished by recent movement. A circular pattern gleamed under the haze: black stone veined with metal, faintly luminous. At its center, a serpent wound around an anchor.

Luca crouched, fingertips brushing the sigil. The metal hummed—not warm, not cold—alive. He could feel the current through his gloves.

"They another way in," he said quietly.

Two sets of tracks led straight to the sigil—then a smear, a drag mark. The faint blue glow brightened along the seam.

Pressure shifted. A heavy exhale rolled through the cavern, and the seam widened half an inch.

He stepped back, eyes narrowing. The light pulsed once, then settled.

For a long moment he stood there, caught between instinct and curiosity. Then he looked up toward the ridge—the faint silhouette of the camp against the sky. Victor's shape was nowhere to be seen.

Luca's mouth curved—not a smile, but close. "I'm done waiting on him."

He tightened his grip on the rifle, placed one hand against the glowing sigil, and slipped through the widening seam into the dark below.

The world reassembled in silence. Jake landed hard on his shoulder and slid several feet before stopping against smooth stone. For a moment he thought the floor had tilted—but then realized it wasn't the floor that moved. It was him.

Gravity here came in pulses, shifting direction like a breath that forgot which way was up.

"Isabelle?"

"Here." Her voice came from somewhere above—or below. A soft beam of light found him. She stood—or floated—on a plane that intersected his at a diagonal, her boots touching glass that glowed faintly from within.

Jake pushed himself up. The surface felt slick, faintly warm. The chamber was vast but disorienting—no corners, no fixed up or down. The walls curved away in mirrored arcs that bent the light into spirals. Every reflection shimmered like trapped lightning.

They were inside the island's heart.

"Grey built this?" Jake asked. His voice echoed, doubled back, then returned half a second late, pitched lower.

"Not built," Isabelle said softly. "Shaped. Melted. Folded the stone on itself—with Siecaza."

She reached toward one of the walls. Her fingers met resistance an inch before touching—like glass under tension. Tiny motes of dust trembled between them.

"This isn't stone anymore," she murmured. "It's vitrified basalt—charged somehow. Every surface is holding current."

The hum they'd heard above was louder here, steadier, almost harmonic. It vibrated in their bones. When Isabelle spoke again, her words rippled through it.

"This whole structure's alive."

Jake tested his footing, one hand against the nearest surface. "Feels wrong—like it's deciding whether to hold us or spit us out."

He took a cautious step forward, and the ground drifted sideways beneath him. Pebbles lifted, floated past his knees, then settled again. Isabelle caught his arm, steadying him.

"You okay?"

"Nothing about this is okay," he said, managing half a smile.

She gave a faint, nervous laugh and kept her hand on his sleeve as they moved deeper—or what felt like deeper. The walls flowed in slow arcs, etched with faint lines that caught the light: not writing, not quite symbols, but geometry turned ritual.

Isabelle paused beside one marking, tracing it with her beam. "These are harmonic ratios," she murmured. "Frequencies. He wasn't building a vault—he was building containment."

"How would he even know how to do that?" Jake asked.

"He wrote that it was *messing with his mind*," she said quietly. "Maybe it showed him things too."

He looked up. The passage ahead seemed to breathe, dust rising and falling in rhythm with the hum beneath their feet.

Then something clicked—metallic, echoing from far behind. Jake spun, lamp raised, but the light bent around the curve and vanished.

"Movement," he said.

Isabelle's jaw tightened. "Luca."

The hum deepened, and for a heartbeat the air between them shimmered, heavy enough to make the world stutter. Jake grabbed Isabelle's wrist to steady her.

"Then we don't have time to look back," he said.

She nodded once, pale in the light, then led the way forward—toward the pulse at the labyrinth's center.

Behind them, faint but growing clearer, came the echo of footsteps.

The corridors shuddered like something breathing beneath the rock. Jake led the way down the narrow passage, the beam of his flashlight trembling against glass that rippled faintly, as though it were remembering how to move. Isabelle followed close, one hand tracing etched markings—spirals, serpents, anchors—patterns too deliberate to be decoration.

The air pressed against Jake's lungs. The hum that had started as vibration now pulsed audibly—a low, resonant tone rising and falling with his heartbeat.

Behind them, faint but unmistakable, came another set of steps.

Jake stopped. "That's not the wind."

Luca's voice drifted through the corridor, distorted by the stone. "Ready or not—here I come."

Jake's grip tightened on the flashlight. "He's on us."

Isabelle glanced back. "Keep moving. The labyrinth's shifting—we can't stay in one place."

They pressed deeper. Light bent and scattered off the glass until the walls seemed to close like water. The passage forked ahead—two tunnels, each pulsing with the same faint internal glow.

"Left or right?" Jake asked.

Isabelle scanned both, then shook her head. "Doesn't matter. He's too close—just move."

Jake caught her wrist as she started to step away. "No. Stay with me."

The hum spiked.

A shockwave rolled through the floor, throwing them apart. The air twisted—the space between the two corridors shimmering like heat haze. Isabelle reached for Jake, fingers inches from his—but the air solidified between them like cooling glass.

"Jake!" she shouted, striking the barrier.

He hit the same wall from his side, the glow flaring where their hands met. "Don't move! I'll—"

The tone rose to a deafening pitch, and the barrier flashed white. When the light faded, they were gone from each other's sight.

Jake was alone in a sloping tunnel, walls narrowing, the hum beating in his chest like a second heart.

He exhaled once, steadying his breath. "Hang on, Izzy," he murmured. "I'm coming."

He started down the left-hand path, light cutting through the blue haze.

On the other side, Isabelle stumbled backward, disoriented. The passage she'd come through was gone—sealed behind a seamless wall of glass. The air buzzed with static. Her compass spun once, then froze—its needle fixed down the tunnel.

"Jake?" she called.

Only her own echo answered—warped, fading into the hum.

She steadied herself with one hand on the wall. The glass was warm—almost alive. "Not a maze," she whispered. "A mechanism."

She turned, tracing the etchings down the corridor. Serpents wound into anchors, their tails vanishing deeper into the dark—a map, if she could read it. She started walking, her light carving a thin golden thread through the blue.

Outside the labyrinth, dawn bled slowly across the ridges. Victor Serrano stood at the valley floor before the sealed wall, his cane planted in the ash. The serpent-and-anchor sigil gleamed faintly in the dim light. Around him, his men worked in organized chaos—unloading crates, rigging lamps, setting up tripods of scanners and thermic lances.

"Start cutting. I want that open within the hour," he ordered.

The thermic lance roared to life. Its white flame gouged into the black stone, molten rock spattering like rain. The serpent's carved coils glowed orange where the heat kissed them.

Victor stepped closer, the light dancing across his face. "Grey sealed his secret in fire," he said softly. "We'll answer it in kind."

Far behind him, the wind shifted—carrying up from the depths a low vibration that trembled through the valley floor. The men hesitated. Even the cutting torch flickered, its beam wavering.

Victor smiled faintly. "Do you feel that?"

Mateo frowned. "Sir?"

"The hum," Victor said. "It's waking."

The lance cut deeper, its light flickering against the black wall like lightning trapped in stone.

The serpent's eyes began to glow—first red, then white—as if the heat were waking something beneath. A pulse rippled outward through the rock, too low for sound but heavy enough to rattle crates and tremble in the men's chests.

Far below, deep in the buried maze, that same vibration rolled through the corridors—first a whisper, then a heartbeat. The labyrinth shuddered and exhaled, the light inside shifting from blue to gold.

Deep inside, the sound built in waves. The tunnels no longer felt static—they breathed. The walls dilated, the light brightened, and the vibration took on rhythm.

Luca descended slowly, rifle slung across his back, knife loose in his hand. His headlamp barely cut through the haze. He reached the fork where the others had vanished, studied the tracks, then the shimmer in the air. For a moment he stood motionless, listening. The hum rolled through the corridor like a voice underwater.

He tilted his head, letting the sound fill the silence. Something in it felt aware—testing him. Measuring. He smiled faintly.

Then he slung the rifle forward and chose the right-hand path, stepping into the dark.

The hum swallowed him whole.

The labyrinth was breathing. Jake felt it in his ribs—every pulse rolling through the glass like a second heartbeat. His flashlight beam quivered against the walls, bending as though the air itself had weight. Somewhere ahead, the tunnel widened, and a faint glow shimmered across the floor like light beneath deep water.

He slowed, crouched, and ran his fingers along the surface. It was warm. The pulse beneath it matched the rhythm of his chest. Then, deep within the translucent stone, something moved.

A shadow took form below—blurry, indistinct. A shape. For a heartbeat it looked human.

Jake leaned closer. The figure resolved into the outline of a man drifting just beneath the surface like a reflection caught in liquid glass. He couldn't see the face—only the pale blur of eyes opening in the dark.

He stumbled back, light flaring across the floor. The image vanished.

His breath fogged the air. "It's not real," he whispered. "You're losing it Jake."

But then a voice answered—quiet, close, impossible.

"Are you sure?"

Jake turned sharply. The corridor was empty. The voice came again, low and familiar.

"Still running, Jacob."

His stomach clenched. He knew that voice. "Dad?"

"Still diving into holes you can't climb out of."

Jake's hand tightened on the flashlight. "You're not real."

The voice shifted, now behind him, threaded through the hum. "You left me when I needed you, Jacob."

He turned in a slow circle. The walls rippled with reflected light, faces half-formed in the glass. He saw the outline of *The Wayfinder's* hull, Isabelle's silhouette at the bow—then both dissolved into haze.

He pressed a hand to the wall. It throbbed beneath his palm, like skin over a pulse. "It's not you," he muttered. "It's the island."

The hum deepened, matching his heartbeat.

Then the whisper came again, softer.

"Mercy always costs more than you think."

Jake closed his eyes, forcing his breath steady. When he opened them, the corridor ahead was clear again—empty, waiting. He started walking.

Across the labyrinth, Isabelle stumbled against the curve of the wall. Her light flickered, then went out entirely. For a moment she stood in total blackness.

The hum surrounded her—soft, layered, like a choir breathing in unison. Then a faint glow bled from the floor, blue at first, then gold. The walls shimmered and shifted until she saw movement ahead.

A figure stepped out of the haze—Jake. He was bathed in warm light, eyes soft, voice calm.

"There you are," he said. "I thought I'd lost you."

Relief broke through her chest. "Jake—thank God. The tunnels—"

"You left me," he said quietly.

"What?"

"You always do."

She took a step back. "That's not—"

"You think you understand me?" His voice changed—lower, distant. The light behind him pulsed, the edges of his body blurring. "Running away while everyone else pays the price?"

Her throat tightened. "Jake, stop it."

But the figure kept walking forward, his face shadowed. When he lifted his head again, the eyes that met hers weren't Jake's. They were her mother's—dark, sad, familiar.

"You could have saved her," the voice said. "But you hid behind faith. Behind rules. You called it restraint."

Isabelle's breath caught. "You're not real."

The voice softened. "Neither is mercy."

The glow dimmed. The figure dissolved back into haze, leaving her alone in the blue dark. She pressed her hand to the wall, feeling the warmth pulsing through it—steady, alive.

Elsewhere in the labyrinth, Luca moved like a shadow given shape.

He kept low, knife in hand, the hum pressing against the inside of his skull. The air here was heavier—electric, saturated with memory. His headlamp sliced through dust that wasn't dust at all, but fine motes of glass suspended in air.

He paused, listening. Something moved ahead—slow, dragging, deliberate. But when he advanced, he found nothing but his own echo returning late, warped and doubled.

He smirked. "Not the first hole I've hunted through."

The hum deepened. Then—clear as if whispered in his ear—came a child's voice.

"Luca..."

His smile faltered. *No.*

A second voice followed—his mother's—soft, breathless, terrified.

"Stay down. Don't move."

The corridor ahead shimmered, and the light bent until the glass reflected fire. A narrow room took shape inside the wall—wooden floorboards, a bed draped in white. Shadows moved beyond the doorway, flickering with muzzle flashes.

He saw it again—the boots, the shouting, his father falling. His mother turned toward the bed, eyes wide, hands lifted. Then came the flash, the sound like air tearing apart, and she dropped out of sight.

The reflection trembled. The bodies froze mid-motion, then turned their faces toward him. Their eyes were glassy, filled with that same blue light.

"You watched," his mother whispered. "And you lived."

Luca's breath came shallow. "You're not real."

His father's voice joined hers, overlapping. "You never stopped hiding."

He backed away, knife raised, the reflection following him like water.

"Mercy," they said together, voices hollow. "Balance. Consequence."

The light pulsed once, the image shattering into bright shards that scattered across the glass. Each fragment caught his reflection—blood-spattered, wide-eyed, older.

Luca kept walking, deeper into the dark. Behind him, the hum followed—low, rhythmic, almost like breathing.

The pull came from everywhere at once—down, forward, inward. Jake staggered as the floor tilted beneath him, the red glow surging through the walls in waves. Loose stones lifted, hanging weightless for a breath before falling again. The hum thickened until it pressed against his ribs.

"Isabelle!" he shouted into the dark.

His voice bounced through a dozen passages at once, echoing back in tones he didn't recognize—his own words twisted by the labyrinth.

Then, faint but clear: "Jake!"

He turned toward it and ran.

The passage bent and reformed around him, seams of molten light tracing the stone. The hum grew sharper, almost melodic, a vibration that carried direction more than sound. He broke through a final wall of heat—and she was there.

Isabelle stumbled out of a crossing tunnel, hair plastered to her face, eyes wide in the glow. For a heartbeat they only stared—disbelieving. Then Jake closed the distance between them.

She reached for him at the same instant. Their collision knocked the breath from both, arms locked tight as the world tilted and steadied. For the first time in days, there was something human to hold.

"I thought—" she began.

"Me too," he said, half a laugh, half a tremor.

They held on a moment longer before she drew back, eyes bright in the glow.

"It's leading us somewhere," she whispered. "I can feel it."

The floor trembled again. Dust lifted and hung between them, caught between gravity and the pulse. Ahead, the tunnel widened into a low chamber breathing heat and metal.

They stepped through together.

The chamber was round, smooth as poured glass, its walls threaded with veins of gold that pulsed in time with the island's heartbeat. At the far end stood a single black wall—seamless, fused—marked only by the faint outline of a serpent and anchor at its center.

Beneath it sat a man.

He was slumped against the stone, one hand pressed to the sigil, the other clutching a leather bound journal to his chest. His hair was pale, his clothes stiff with age, yet the skin beneath was whole—untouched by decay, as if time itself had paused to keep watch.

Isabelle's breath caught. "Jake..."

He knelt beside the body. The air around it was warm and alive, humming faintly—as though the man still drew breath.

"Elias Grey," he said.

Isabelle lowered herself beside him. "He died sealing it," she whispered. "And the island never let him go—never even let him decay."

The light along the walls pulsed once—slow, deliberate—like a single heartbeat echoing through stone. Dust lifted in thin spirals, refusing to fall. The hum settled to a tone that lived between sound and silence.

Jake looked up at the wall—the serpent's coils glimmering faintly in the red-gold light. "This is it," he said. "The vault."

Isabelle nodded, voice barely breath. "The end of his trail."

Above them, thunder rippled through the island—the echo of Victor forcing open what should have stayed closed.

Jake and Isabelle stayed where they were, caught between the living and the lost, the hum of Siecaza trembling through the floor beneath their hands.

Then, from deep within the vault, something answered.

CHAPTER THIRTY-EIGHT

The Heart Awakens

T he air in the antechamber felt thin, stretched between heat and silence. Dust hung in the amber glow bleeding from the serpent-and-anchor sigil. The hum beneath the floor had steadied into something almost human—the slow pulse of a world remembering how to breathe.

Jake crouched beside the body, prying loose the journal clutched in Grey's arms. The small leather journal was scorched at the corners, its clasp fused by heat. When he forced it open, the scent of salt and ash bled into the air—like the ghost of a fire long since drowned.

Isabelle knelt beside him, her light steady in the gloom. The pages were thin and brittle, some half-melted together. Jake turned them carefully, the script growing looser as it neared the end. The early pages bore the hand of a captain—calm, deliberate. The final entries were those of a man preparing to die.

He began to read, voice low.

The sea grows restless. The fleet lies beyond the western shoal—four ships under the Crown, guns enough to erase us all. I have dismissed the crew of the Specter. Each man sails with his share and a key, that they may live as free men rather than ghosts. I will remain. The relic calls for balance, and it will answer to none but consequence. If the Spaniards reach this shore, they will find only fire. When dawn breaks, I will climb to the ridge above the bay. The relic will speak for the last time.

Jake turned the page. The next bore a smear of blood and a few scattered lines—the last words Grey would ever write.

It is done. The fleet is ash. The sea will remember. I have sealed the relic with my own blood. I know now its power was never meant for one man to bear; it has claimed the last of my strength. Let the world remember me not as a thief, but as a man who defied an empire. *Some treasure is not meant to be fou...*

The final stroke trailed off mid-word, as if the pen had fallen from his hand.

Silence followed—dense, reverent. Even the low vibration beneath the floor seemed to pause.

Jake exhaled slowly. "He sealed it," he said. "With his own blood."

Isabelle's gaze followed his to the wall, where Grey's blackened hand still rested against the serpent's coils. The faint shimmer of dried blood caught the amber light—too bright, too alive for centuries gone.

"Jake," she whispered. "His hand's still on the seal."

He crouched beside her, fingers brushing the surface near Grey's wrist. The stone was warm, faintly slick beneath his glove.

"He said he sealed it with his own blood," Isabelle murmured. "What if that wasn't a metaphor?"

Jake looked from the journal to the wall, the bass note underfoot deepening. "You think—"

"It's the key," she said. "His blood. That's what's holding it shut."

The sound around them shifted—no longer a hum, but a slow pulse rolling outward from the sigil like a heartbeat. Dust lifted from the floor and hung motionless in the air.

Jake stared at the mark, his voice barely above a whisper. "Maybe it's safer in there—sealed away."

"We heard Victor break through the outer wall," Isabelle replied. "He'll do the same to this one."

Jake nodded slowly. "So we take it before he can."

Isabelle met his eyes. "It's the only way."

Together, they eased Grey's body away from the wall. As they laid him flat, something slipped from his coat pocket and rolled across the floor—a gold coin, dulled by centuries but still catching the light. The serpent-and-anchor sigil was faintly pressed into one side.

Jake picked it up, turning it in his palm. "His one piece of the treasure," he said quietly. "The rest he gave away."

"Maybe because he knew what it really cost," Isabelle said.

He nodded once, pocketed the coin, and drew his dive knife. The blade caught the light, trembling slightly in his hand.

"Jake," Isabelle said softly. "If we open it, there's no taking it back."

He looked at her. "Like you said — there's no taking it back if Victor opens it either."

He crouched beside Grey again, the knife hovering a moment above the blackened wrist. "Guess it's up to us to finish what they started."

He drew the blade across the vein. The skin parted like cooled resin, and from the cut welled a single bead of blood—dark red, impossibly fresh.

Jake slid his finger through it, then walked to the wall and pressed the blood onto the sigil.

The chamber reacted at once.

The serpent's coils blazed gold, heat radiating outward in a slow, expanding ring. The vibration deepened into a steady force that filled the air and bone alike. The wall seemed to breathe. Dust suspended in the pulse.

Isabelle shielded her face, shouting over the rising sound. "Jake—what's happening?"

He pulled her behind him, eyes locked on the wall. "I gave it something it remembered."

The gold veins brightened, converging on the serpent's heart. The air drew inward—a deep inhale—and the sigil split open down the center.

Light spilled out—white, gold, then red, like a wound bleeding brilliance. The heat wasn't burning but immense, the air itself rippling around it. From the depths came a low, resonant tone that filled their heads.

The sound grew into vibration, through their chests, through the floor, through the world.

Isabelle's voice trembled. "It's opening."

Jake stared into the widening glow, the dive knife still slick with Grey's blood. "Then let's be ready."

The serpent's coils uncurled, and the vault began to breathe.

The light faded slowly, reluctant to reveal what waited beyond.

When the last of the glow steadied, Jake and Isabelle stood at the threshold of a vast circular chamber. The walls were black as glass, veined with molten gold that pulsed faintly—a heartbeat made visible through stone.

Jake stepped inside first. The air was cold and dense, pressing against his skin like water. His footsteps seemed swallowed before they could reach the walls, yet every breath came back to him, magnified—as if the space chose which sounds to keep.

In the center of the chamber stood a pedestal of fused basalt, its surface reflecting faint amber light. Resting on it, untouched by time, was the thing they'd crossed half the world to find.

Siecaza.

The relic was smaller than they imagined—a near-perfect sphere of black obsidian, no larger than a grapefruit. Yet even in the half-light, it commanded the room. Its surface was impossibly smooth and flawless, but reflections warped across it. The air near it shimmered faintly, charged with static and heat.

Isabelle stepped closer, transfixed. "It's... beautiful," she whispered.

Jake didn't answer. He was watching how the light behaved—bending and splitting at strange angles around the orb. It wasn't reflection. It was distortion.

She crouched, shining her lamp over the surface. Inlays of gold traced across the obsidian in spiraling lines, each one perfectly symmetrical, radiating from a single central point. Between them ran serpentine patterns, coiled into triangular lattices that intersected like seals rather than ornament. Along the outer ring, tiny emeralds glimmered at precise intervals, catching her light and scattering it into green sparks across the gold.

"Jake," Isabelle breathed, "look at the geometry. The ratios—they're harmonic. Perfect."

He crouched beside her, brow furrowed. "Who crafted this?"

"The Muisca people," she murmured. "It's not just a relic—it's an equation in physical form."

Her fingertips hovered an inch from the surface. "It's cold... but I can feel it humming."

Jake reached out and held her wrist. "Maybe don't touch it."

She looked up, meeting his eyes, then back to the orb. "The Muisca legends said Siecaza was forged by the gods—the balance between mercy and consequence."

"Mercy?" Jake echoed.

She nodded faintly. "Bochica and Chibchacum—creation and punishment, harmony and storm. When the balance broke, they forged Siecaza to restore it. A vessel for both forces—light and shadow, restraint and release."

She stepped back, voice soft but reverent. "Grey must've eventually realized that. He didn't lock it away out of greed—he locked it away because he understood what it could do."

Jake studied the orb, the reflections of the gold spirals dancing across his eyes. "Then he died making sure no one ever used it again."

A tremor rippled through the chamber—subtle, rhythmic, like a slow inhale from deep within the island. Dust drifted upward in thin, floating streams.

Isabelle looked toward the ceiling. "It's reacting again."

Jake's jaw tightened. "That'll be Victor."

She turned back to him, alarm in her voice. "If he gets this—"

"He won't," Jake said, steady now. "Not while we're breathing."

The pressure beneath them deepened, the gold running through the walls brightening—from faint amber to molten white. The serpent-and-anchor sigil above the door pulsed once, as if recognizing what lay within.

Jake and Isabelle stood shoulder to shoulder before the pedestal, staring into the heart of Siecaza.

For a long, suspended moment, nothing moved—only the island's heartbeat, slow and inexorable.

Then, from somewhere above, a dull concussion rolled through the rock—the sound of something forcing its way in.

Jake looked up. "He's here."

Isabelle's hand tightened around his sleeve. "Then this is where it ends."

The chamber answered—low, alive, aware.

Far above, the valley floor trembled.

Victor Serrano stood before the black wall at the base of the ridge, his cane planted in the ash, breath ragged from the climb. The carved serpent-and-anchor sigil glowed faintly through the dust—a pulse in time with the deep vibration rising from below. Around him, his men worked under the glare of floodlights: Mateo directing the thermic lance, Javier feeding cables from the generator, others bracing the unstable glass.

The heat from the stone was unnatural. Even the air near the wall shimmered as though a fire burned just beyond it.

Mateo's voice cracked over the rumble. "Sir, the last core reading's off the scale—pressure, heat, radiation, everything. If we cut deeper, this whole section could—"

"Do it," Victor said.

He didn't raise his voice, but the tone carried finality. Mateo hesitated only a moment before nodding and motioning to Javier.

The cutter screamed back to life. White fire bit into the black wall, sparks bursting outward and dying midair. The serpent's carved coils glowed brighter, red veins pulsing across the stone.

Victor leaned heavily on his cane, eyes wide in the reflection. Sweat gleamed along his temple; his tremor was worse now, running through his hand even as he tried to steady it.

The lance hissed deeper. The wall softened, folding inward like molten glass. The glow intensified, and a gust of hot air rolled across the valley floor, scattering ash.

Mateo flinched. "Sir, we've hit a cavity!"

Victor stepped forward, ignoring the heat. "Then open it."

The glass gave way with a sound like stone breaking underwater. A fissure spread across the sigil, light bleeding through the cracks—gold, then white, then a deep, impossible red.

The ground shook, tools skittering. The men stumbled, bracing against the blast.

"Pull back!" Javier shouted, but Victor didn't move.

He stared into the widening fissure, eyes fever-bright. "Do you feel that? He failed because he was afraid," he said, voice rising over the roar. "Fear kept him weak. I—" he pressed a trembling hand against the heat, "—I have the courage to wield what he couldn't."

The wall split open.

A flood of light poured from the crack, flattening the shadows. The wind that followed wasn't air but pressure—a rush drawn upward from the labyrinth below. The valley seemed to exhale.

Mateo threw an arm over his face. "Sir, we have to move—"

Victor ignored him. He took a step closer, heat rippling around him, eyes locked on the breach. "It's real," he whispered. "It's all real."

Behind him, the tremor built to a low roar. One of the generators blew, fire spilling from its vents. Javier dragged two men toward the ridge, coughing, as Victor stood transfixed in the storm of light.

———————— ◈ ————————

Far below, in the labyrinth's twisting corridors, Luca stopped.

He'd felt tremors before—explosions, quakes, bombardments—but this was different. The vibration wasn't shaking the ground; it was inside him.

The air pulsed in time with his heartbeat.

He switched off his headlamp, crouched, and listened. The thrum rolled through the glass walls like a living thing. Then another sound—faint, distant, human.

Voices.

He adjusted his grip on the rifle and kept moving, following the heat and the faint red light bleeding through the rock. The passage sloped downward, tighter now, the air hot and metallic. Somewhere ahead, movement flickered—bright and unnatural.

At the edge of the final corridor, he saw it: an open archway and, beyond it, a chamber awash in gold. Light ran in veins through black stone, all of it converging toward the center.

Luca's lips parted. "Well, I'll be damned."

Two figures stood near the center—Jake and Isabelle—before something small and dark on a pedestal. Between them and the far wall, the air shimmered like heat off a road.

He lifted the rifle halfway, then paused. For once, he didn't know which side he was on.

Back above, the fissure widened into a breach. Air screamed through, pulling dust and debris into a vortex of light. Victor dropped his cane and stepped into the glow.

Mateo reached for him, shouting, but the words vanished in the roar. Javier hauled Mateo back as the breach avalanched.

The light swallowed Victor whole.

The heat hit first—a wave that pressed from every direction, humid and metallic.

Jake turned toward the tunnel as the sound reached them: a low roar, followed by the hiss of shifting stone. The light overhead flared red, then white, before dimming again to gold.

"Someone's coming," Isabelle said.

A second later, the echo of boots confirmed it.

From the haze of the passage, Victor Serrano emerged—cane gone, shirt clinging to his frame with sweat, eyes wild and shining. Behind him came Mateo and Javier, both half-blind in the glare, weapons drawn but useless in the disorienting light.

Luca slipped through the shadows a few steps behind, unseen.

Victor stopped when he saw the pedestal. For a long moment, he said nothing—only stared at the relic as though he'd found an altar instead of a weapon.

"Centuries," he breathed. "My family bled itself chasing this." His gaze shifted to Jake and Isabelle, voice trembling with a manic kind of joy. "Grey thought he could bury redemption. But I've found it."

Jake took a step forward, fists tight at his sides. "You don't know what it'll do."

Victor's smile flickered. "I know what it's meant to do."

"You know what it takes," Jake said. "It doesn't give without taking something back."

"I've spent my life watching things get taken from me," Victor snapped. "My body, my name, my future. That debt is paid."

Isabelle's voice cut through the heat. "Victor, listen to me. That isn't medicine—it's balance. It doesn't heal without consequence."

His eyes narrowed. "You've studied myths. I built an empire. I'll decide what's real."

Jake stepped closer. "If you touch it, you'll damn everyone in this room."

Victor's jaw set. A whisper escaped him—almost a prayer. "Please."

He reached out.

The instant his fingers brushed the obsidian, the relic moved.

Not a mechanical shift—something living and responsive.

The inlays of gold flared white-hot, lines running outward like molten veins. A sound tore through the chamber—part thunder, part breath. Air compressed; grit lifted in a circular burst, suspended as if gravity had forgotten itself.

Victor staggered, gasping as the light climbed his arms in serpentine bands, winding toward his chest. The veins in his neck bulged; his back arched. For an instant, his eyes rolled white. Then, slowly, the tension drained from him. He exhaled—one ragged, shuddering breath—and straightened.

The tremor in his hands was gone. His posture firmed. Color came back to his skin.

"It's working," he whispered, then louder, elated, "It's working!"

The orb's glow steadied, a living pulse that synchronized with his own. The chamber's resonance deepened, walls vibrating like struck glass.

Isabelle edged forward, shouting over the deepening thrum. "Victor, it's feeding on you! You can't control it—"

"I can!" he roared. "It obeys me!"

Light from Siecaza crawled up the walls like a living heartbeat. The floor shivered.

Mateo reached toward him. "Sir—"

The word died in a burst of light. Mateo crumpled, veins flaring gold before going dark. Javier recoiled, choking, and stumbled back toward the archway, half-blinded.

"Victor! Stop—" Jake began.

The moment broke differently.

From the shadows, Luca moved.

"So much for mercy." The knife flashed. "See if it saves you from this."

The blade struck deep beneath Victor's ribs.

Victor gasped, the sound sharp and wet.

Luca leaned close, voice cold. "Let's see if it heals that old man."

He ripped the knife free.

Victor staggered, blood spilling dark and fast.

Siecaza pulsed brighter, gold veins flaring white-hot as though reacting to the damage.

The ground split. The force in the room pressed down, rattling bone. Stone cracked, molten light bleeding from every seam. The walls seemed to writhe.

Jake staggered, shouting over the roar. "What did you *do*, Luca?!"

"Jake!" Isabelle shouted. "It's trying to heal him—it's taking energy from the island!"

Victor fell to his knees, hands still clutching the relic. "You see?" he gasped, half laughing. "It's giving it back—it's giving me everything!"

"No—it's taking everything!" Jake lunged.

Luca slammed Victor away from the relic. Siecaza rolled, spun once, and hovered—light rippling from its core.

Jake caught it bare-handed.

The effect was instantaneous.

Power hit him like lightning. His whole body locked, the shock ripping through muscle and bone, veins burning gold under his skin. The weight of it was aware, pushing back.

"Jake!" Isabelle screamed.

He couldn't breathe. "It—won't—stop—"

For a heartbeat she froze, horror in her eyes as the light climbed his arms. Then she moved—no hesitation left. She lunged forward and caught his hands around the relic.

The instant her skin touched his, the current leapt between them—an unbearable torrent, like holding the heart of a star.

The world vanished.

Light consumed everything—then reshaped it.

They stood not in stone and heat but beneath a sky split between gold and storm. One half blazed with sunlight, the other boiled with thunderclouds, the horizon torn in two.

Before them towered two vast figures wrought of the same opposing light:

Bochica, the radiant bringer of order, carved in gold and air; Chibchacum, his shadow, the storm that punished mankind.

Between them hovered Siecaza—no longer an orb but a living heart of obsidian and flame, pulsing with both radiance and flood. Each beat sent ripples through the sky—creation and destruction woven together.

Jake reached for Isabelle. Their fingers met, and the figures turned. The gods did not speak, but their intent thundered through the void: *Balance must be restored.*

Bochica's hand opened in mercy. Chibchacum's clenched in consequence. And from the space between their palms, light bled through the world.

Jake felt himself dissolving—flood and fire and heartbeat all at once.

Isabelle's voice came through the light, faint but certain: "It's showing us what it is—what it was made for."

He gritted his teeth. "Then we finish it the same way—together."

The vision fractured—light collapsing inward as reality roared back.

"Together," he forced out.

Isabelle met his eyes, ragged. "Turn it's power inward."

They pushed back against the current surging up their arms, every muscle straining as if they were trying to hold back a tide made of light.

The air convulsed. Their bodies arced with light, every nerve a wire, every breath a fire. Between their hands, Siecaza writhed, the gold inlays glowing molten white as fissures spidered across the obsidian.

Hairline cracks—tiny veins spreading like frost over glass. The relic shuddered, emitting a low, keening tone that seemed to echo from everywhere at once.

Jake's voice tore through the roar. "A little more!"

The cracks deepened, gold lines splitting wider until a fragment sheared away—revealing a pulsing meteorite core, dark metal shot through with threads of glowing red. The light inside beat like a living heart, each pulse stronger than the last.

The chamber bucked. Every surface glowed; every sound became one sound—the roar of a dying world.

The meteorite's pulse accelerated, erratic now, fighting the pressure. Then its light faltered.

The core fractured—once, twice—then split completely down the center, spewing radiant energy in every direction.

Jake and Isabelle screamed, the force slamming through them as the relic collapsed inward, its mass folding to a single blinding point.

Silence so deep it erased every other sound—

—and Siecaza exploded.

Light swallowed the chamber, washing over stone and flesh alike.

Every gold vein, every glyph, every carving detonated outward in concentric waves of pure energy.

Jake threw himself over Isabelle, the blast ripping the air from his lungs.

Then nothing—

no heat,

no gravity—

only the falling silence of a world being unmade.

The light went out.

Silence.

Not the kind born of peace, but of absence—the kind that comes after something vast has stopped existing.

Dust drifted through the darkness in slow spirals. The air no longer pulsed. The thrum was gone.

Jake stirred first. Every muscle screamed. Afterimages—red, white, gold—swam. His ears rang like a struck bell. He tried to move, but the pain was molten, deep in the bone.

He tasted blood. Rock dust. The world.

For a moment, he didn't know where he was. Then the smell hit him—scorched stone, ozone, salt. The labyrinth. Or what was left of it.

A soft sound cut through the quiet—a faint, broken breath.

"...Izzy?"

He rolled onto his side, dragging himself across the shattered floor. The heat had vanished; the stone beneath his palms was cool now, no longer alive, no longer breathing.

She lay ten feet away, half-buried under a sheet of debris. Her face was streaked with soot, her hair tangled with ash and gold dust. For a terrifying moment, she didn't move.

Jake crawled to her, hands shaking as he brushed the stone off her shoulder. "Izzy... come on... hey."

No response.

He cupped the back of her neck, pulling her upright, her head falling limply against his chest. "You're okay," he said, voice cracking. "You're okay, you hear me?"

Nothing. No sound.

He pressed his ear to her chest—only silence and the faint rasp of settling stone. His breath hitched. "Come on..." He shook her gently, smearing ash from her cheek with his thumb. "Don't do this. Not now."

Still nothing.

He tried again, his words unraveling into panic. "You can't—you don't get to quit, Isabelle. Not after all this. Not after everything."

His voice echoed through the dead chamber, small and raw. He brushed the hair from her face, fingers trembling, and pressed his forehead to hers. "Please... please, Izzy. Breathe."

For a long moment, the world refused to move. Dust floated. Air hung still. His tears streaked the ash on her skin.

Then—

A tremor under his hand. The faintest pull of breath.

She coughed, sharp and shallow, the sound breaking the silence like a spark.

Jake froze, eyes wide, then a choked laugh escaped him—half relief, half disbelief. "There you are," he whispered. "There you are."

Her lashes fluttered; she blinked up at him, dazed. "Jake..."

He exhaled hard, air shaking out of him in a ragged laugh. He pulled her tight, arms locking around her. "You look terrible."

Her voice was a whisper against his neck. "You look worse."

He laughed—raw, broken—and cupped her face, brushing his thumb along her cheek. "You have no idea how close I came to losing it."

"You didn't," she said softly. "You found me."

Their eyes met—close enough that the fractured walls painted gold across their faces. For the first time, there was no distance left to bridge.

Jake's hand slid to the back of her head, pulling her gently forward. She leaned in the same heartbeat. The kiss was slow, trembling—salt and ash between them—desperate, grateful, alive.

When they broke apart, the chamber was utterly still.

Jake pressed his forehead to hers. "We made it."

Isabelle's hand stayed against his chest, feeling his heart hammer under his torn shirt. "For now," she murmured.

He smiled faintly. "For now's enough."

They stayed that way a moment—two survivors in the ruins of something that was never meant for them. Then Jake looked up. The gold veins that once pulsed through the walls had gone dark. Gravity had returned. The air was steady again.

"It's over," he said quietly.

They both turned toward the crater at the chamber's center. The ground there was still smoking—black glass melted into a shallow depression where Siecaza had once rested. Shards of obsidian lay scattered like shattered stars, each one reflecting faint threads of dying light.

Isabelle moved closer, crouching beside the largest fragment. Inside the black glass, something pulsed faintly—a dull ember, the last remnant of Siecaza's core.

She brushed away ash, revealing a piece no bigger than her palm: rough, metallic, veined with gold. It glowed from within, as if something still alive were testing the cooling shell.

Jake crouched beside her. "Is that what's left of it?"

She nodded, eyes wide. "It's not obsidian. It's... meteoritic iron. The heart that fell from the sky. This is what the Muisca called Siecaza—a vessel forged to bind creation and destruction. But now it's just... a stone."

Jake rested a hand on her shoulder.

They watched the fragment fade, the glow flickering like a dying heartbeat—then, with a soft crack, the light went out.

For a second, silence.

Then the world shifted.

A deep groan rolled through the chamber, followed by a violent lurch that nearly threw them off their feet. Cracks spiderwebbed up the walls. Pebbles skittered; dust rained in thick sheets.

Jake grabbed Isabelle's arm. "Move!"

They ran.

The floor split behind them, slabs shearing away into the smoking pit. Heat and sound chased them up the corridor—a rolling roar that felt alive, furious.

"Keep going!" Jake shouted.

Isabelle stumbled once, catching herself against the wall. "The whole thing's collapsing!"

"Yeah, I noticed!"

They sprinted through the narrowing passage, ducking as shards rained from the ceiling. A beam of pale daylight flickered ahead—small, impossibly far. The tunnel groaned—a deafening crack running its length.

Jake shoved Isabelle forward. "Go! Don't stop!"

The final shockwave hit like surf breaking stone. Jake felt the pressure on his back—the breath of the collapsing labyrinth—and dove through the opening as the ceiling gave way.

They tumbled into open air and hit the slope hard, rolling through ash and gravel. A blast of heat followed them out, then subsided in a rush of dust and quiet.

For a long moment neither moved. Then Isabelle pushed herself up on shaking arms, coughing. Jake lay a few feet away, chest heaving.

The ridge above them steamed where the tunnel had been. What remained of the entrance was now a jagged scar.

Jake turned toward her, voice hoarse. "You good?"

She nodded weakly, wiping grit from her face. "I think... we outran it."

He gave a breathless laugh. "For once."

They sat together, watching smoke lift from the heap of rock. The island groaned once more, then went still—its heartbeat finally silent.

Jake leaned back, staring at the brightening sky. "Is it over now?"

Isabelle looked at him, her expression soft beneath the soot. "I hope so."

He smiled faintly and reached for her hand. "Then let's make it count."

They rose unsteadily, ash clinging to their clothes, and started toward the ridge—toward the waiting light of dawn.

The climb felt endless.

Every muscle burned, every breath tasted of ash and salt. The trail that had once wound gently up the slope was now fractured and half-collapsed, the ground still faintly warm beneath their boots. The hum that had haunted the island was gone, but the silence it left pressed just as heavy.

When they finally crested the ridge, dawn broke in thin gold over the shattered valley.

The helicopter sat where they'd staged it earlier, coated in gray dust, rotors still. Smoke rose in soft columns from the basin, carrying the last of the labyrinth's heat into the pale morning sky.

Jake slowed, catching Isabelle's arm. "Wait."

Someone sat near the landing pad, elbows on his knees, rifle across his lap.

Luca.

He turned at the sound of their boots, squinting against the light. His face was streaked with soot, a fresh cut along his jaw, but his grin still carried that feral edge.

"Well," he said. "You two look like hell."

Jake gave a dry chuckle. "You should see the other guys."

"I did," Luca said flatly. "They're not getting back up." He flicked a glance valley-ward.

Isabelle's gaze drifted to the haze below. "No one is."

Luca nodded, jaw flexing. "Then it's over."

"For good this time," Jake said.

A faint movement caught Isabelle's eye—a figure inside the cockpit. The pilot, face pale beneath his flight vest, had stayed. He stepped out when he saw them approach, relief visible even through exhaustion.

Jake raised a brow. "He waited?"

Luca shrugged. "Told him if he left, I'd hunt him down and shoot him." He clapped the pilot's shoulder. "Wheels up."

The pilot nodded quickly, hurrying to the controls.

Luca looked back at Jake. "So, what now? After all this—no gold, no glory, not even a cursed idol to sell."

Jake reached into his pocket and pulled out Grey's gold coin, dull with age but still glinting faintly. He weighed it, then flipped it through the air.

"Here," Jake said. "Take what's left of the treasure. I don't need it."

Luca caught it easily. His thumb found the faint serpent-and-anchor pressed into the face, the echo of everything below. "And what've you got instead?"

Jake's eyes found Isabelle.

He slipped an arm around her waist, pulling her close, a faint smile breaking through the soot and exhaustion. "Everything I need."

Before she could answer, he kissed her—slow, certain, the kind that made the rest of the world fade to quiet.

When they finally broke apart, Isabelle rested her forehead against his chest, breathless but smiling.

She looked up, her voice a whisper. "We're still going after Silas Morgan's chest, right?"

Jake grinned, thumb brushing her cheek. "Damn right we are."

Behind them, Luca gave a low, humorless laugh and pocketed the coin. "Guess that makes me the only one who didn't get what he came for."

"You got out alive," Jake called over the rising whine. "That's worth something."

Luca half-smiled. "Yeah. So much for mercy."

The rotors roared to life. Jake and Isabelle climbed aboard, the wind whipping through their hair, scattering ash into the dawn. The pilot lifted the helicopter smoothly off the ridge, banking south toward the horizon.

Below, Eiao smoldered in silence—its labyrinth sealed forever, its heart extinguished. Near the collapsed breach, a dark shape lay half-buried where the floor had given way; the last of the glow guttered from its veins and went out.

Jake reached for Isabelle's hand as the island fell away behind them. Their fingers locked, steady in the rising light.

Above them, the sky turned gold, and even through the thunder of the rotors, the world seemed finally at peace.

Epilogue

The Caribbean morning shimmered like a dream half-remembered.

Sunlight turned the water to glass, each wave a lens bending the world beneath. The air smelled of salt and warm rope; the slow thrum of cicadas drifted from the green ridge of the island beyond the bay.

Jake surfaced beside the trawler, mask streaked with salt, regulator dangling from his mouth. He spat it out and laughed—a sound carried by the easy roll of the tide.

"You're not gonna believe this," he called.

From the deck, Isabelle leaned over the rail, one hand shading her eyes. She was barefoot, sun-browned, a loose white shirt knotted at her waist, her hair still damp from the morning swim. The lines of exhaustion that had haunted her since the Galápagos were gone; even her voice sounded lighter when she said, "You've been saying that for three dives now."

"This time I mean it."

He hauled a small, coral-crusted object out of the water—roughly the size and shape of a chest, its corners banded in what might once have been brass. Sunlight glinted off it as he set it on the ladder step.

Isabelle leaned over. "Jake... that looks like a breadbox."

"Or," he countered, climbing up dripping and grinning, "a chest that's been down here since the eighteenth century."

She crossed her arms, amused. "A very small chest."

He set it on the deck between them with a wet thud. "Size doesn't matter. It's the craftsmanship."

Isabelle crouched, brushing away silt and bits of coral. A crab scuttled free. Beneath the crust, there was no mark, no emblem—just warped metal and wood eaten to sponge. She shot him a look. "Craftsmanship, huh?"

Jake shrugged, still grinning. "Okay, so maybe not the chest."

"Or any chest."

"Still closer than yesterday."

She smiled despite herself. "You're impossible."

"Yeah, maybe," he said, reaching for a towel.

The wind shifted, carrying the faint scent of rain from somewhere far off. Isabelle straightened, her eyes following the horizon—endless blue meeting endless blue.

"Maybe the sea just likes keeping its secrets."

Jake leaned against the rail beside her, gaze steady on the water. "Then we'll just have to keep asking."

The trawler rocked gently in the current, sunlight flashing off the ripples like gold coins scattered across the surface.

For a moment neither spoke. There was no hum, no trembling earth, only the sea—and the quiet promise that something still waited below.

Later, the trawler drifted on idle current. The dive gear was stowed, the deck rinsed clean. Jake sat aft, a mug of coffee cooling in his hands, watching the sunlight ripple through the wake. Isabelle moved quietly nearby, sketching the coastline into her notebook—soft pencil lines tracing reefs and ridges as if to memorize them before they vanished again beneath the tide.

Neither had spoken about the island since leaving it. The subject hung between them, unneeded but always present.

Isabelle had started curating an exhibit about Elias Grey—a way, she said, to tell the story without the curse that followed it. Letters, sketches, fragments salvaged from the wrecks—they were piecing together a truth that could finally rest in the open.

The sun climbed high and began its slow descent, painting the deck in gold and shadow. Time moved differently out here—measured not by hours, but by light and tide.

"You ever think about it?" Jake asked finally.

Isabelle didn't look up. "Every day."

He nodded slowly. "Feels wrong calling it a win. We lived. But..."

"But we destroyed something sacred," she finished. She set the pencil down, eyes distant on the water. "Maybe that was mercy too. Letting it go before it could hurt anyone else."

Jake watched her in the reflection of the waves. "You said once that Siecaza was balance—mercy and consequence. Maybe that's all it wanted.

To be balanced again."

A faint smile ghosted across her lips. "Then it chose well."

The wind shifted. A pelican dove, splashing somewhere beyond the bow. Isabelle closed her notebook and leaned back against the rail beside him. For a long time, they just listened to the rhythm of the sea against the hull.

Jake broke the silence first. "You ever wonder if Grey and Silas knew it'd end like this? All that blood and gold, just to find out the real treasure was... what, perspective?"

Isabelle smirked. "If you start talking about destiny, I'm jumping overboard."

He chuckled, then sobered. "Guess I just wish I could've told them it wasn't all for nothing."

"You did," she said softly. "Every time you kept going."

He looked at her then, really looked—at the sun on her hair, the faint smile that didn't need words. "We're really doing this, huh?"

"What, sailing around the Caribbean chasing ghosts?"

He shrugged. "Guess it beats drowning."

Isabelle laughed under her breath, tilting her head against his shoulder. "For the record," she murmured, "I like this version of us."

Jake smiled into her hair. "Me too."

For a long while, there was only the sea—the steady roll, the slow hiss of waves against the hull, the heartbeat of something vast and forgiving.

Then Isabelle said, half a whisper, "We're still going after the chest, right?"

Jake glanced down at her, a grin cutting through the quiet. "Damn right we are."

Their laughter carried out over the open water, fading into the wind.

The sea burned copper and gold, the last light spilling across the waves like molten glass.

Jake leaned on the rail of the trawler, the horizon dissolving into dusk. Behind him, the slow rhythm of the engines faded to a heartbeat's thrum.

"It's strange," he said quietly. "After everything we've lost... it still feels like it gave something back."

Isabelle stepped beside him, her hair caught by the wind, the glow of the dying sun brushing her cheek. "Maybe it never took anything," she said. "Maybe it was just reminding us what was worth keeping."

He looked at her for a long moment—the calm in her eyes, the salt and sun that had become part of her. "Yeah," he murmured. "Maybe it was."

The tide rocked the trawler, soft and steady. Far below, the water caught the last shimmer of light, as though the sea itself were swallowing a secret it meant to guard forever.

Grey's words drifted through Jake's thoughts, faint as a tide pulling back to sea: *Some treasure is not meant to be found.*

He glanced once more at the horizon and let the memory go. "Maybe not," he said. "But some things are meant to be remembered."

Isabelle slipped her hand into his, quiet as the wind. "Then we remember."

Night gathered over the water, slow and certain.

The sea breathed once—deep, endless—and the story of *The Corsair's Shadow* sank back into legend.